THE
12 PINS

PETER HODGKINSON

Paperback ISBN: 978-1-7391237-3-4
Ebook ISBN: 978-1-7391237-2-7

Cover design by BespokeBookCovers.com

For Ann

CONTENTS

1

CONNEMARA, IRELAND, 1947

'It'll go! Don't worry yourself. We'll be away soon enough', the wiry bus conductor in an oversize uniform tried to reassure her. He could sense her agitation as he issued and validated her ticket. The bus hadn't left on time but none of the other passengers appeared to either notice or mind. Dismissively wiping away a long strand of cigarette ash that had fallen onto his lapel, he punched her ticket and exhaled a cloud of smoke before continuing his tour of inspection.

It had taken ten years for Grace to make what she was calling her 'pilgrimage' to Connemara. Coming to Ireland was to be her way of starting the process of reconciliation with what had happened in Spain in 1937. However, this was not to be the usual journey of expiation, as she had no plans to return to London or indeed to go anywhere else. Her sole intent was to lift the veil of guilt that had hung over her for the past decade. Throughout her hibernation in wartime London she had been unable to reconstruct whatever meaning lay behind the impossibly brief and ultimately tragic encounter that had come to take command of her life.

And it was only now, sitting on this overdue bus in Galway that she felt enervated by the thought that a resolution was possibly within her reach. With a much-changed and chastened persona, including adopting her now apposite middle-name, she was ready at last to write her Spanish novel.

Eventually, and long after the prescribed time but seemingly well-within that of the local sensibilities, the bus began to move and as it did so the first rain of the day matched its measure. Grace thought the slow, grinding, belaboured forward movement of the vehicle was entirely misplaced as, in many ways, she was heading into the past. She also knew that the only thing one could do on such a journey was to think. The real art was to take oneself out of any notion of linear clock time by collapsing all sense of the past, present and indeed possible futures. If her story was to be told, she needed to both revisit the past and stay in the present. However, her chances of achieving such a temporal outer-worldliness were doomed to fail as the state of Galway's roads were to provide too many regular and rude reminders of the uncomfortable reality of the present.

The bus was completely full and having twice taken the same journey before the war Grace knew something of the ways-of-the-world thereabouts. She remembered to get a seat by a window, but not for the views as the rain and mist would see to that. A window seat was essential for the bodily support it offered during the many attempts she would make to doze off through the long journey ahead. Except for young children and those who might be recovering from a tour of Galway's many public houses, real sleep was nigh on impossible. She reminded herself that she was not to read a newspaper, as this invariably initiated uninvited conversation. She also knew that she should avoid catching the eye of unaccompanied male travellers and, if this rule was breached, she needed to look as if in mourning. With women travellers she was to do the exact opposite; they loved the conversations about death, death notices, funerals and funeral rites, the blessings, the congregation, the wake, the priests and so on. In which case she needed to look excessively happy, even demented or 'quare' as the locals would say.

Leaving Galway did not take long since most of the population were still in their beds at such an ungodly hour. There was little or no traffic and the roads were all but deserted, save for those early worms, the bakers' vans, horse-drawn milk floats and be-sooted coal lorries. As a result, the main town was soon left behind and the houses began to gradually disappear behind low and then higher stone walls, manicured and then wild hedgerows, and finally fields, trees and dense woods. This gradation of the scenery signalled both an escape from the urban and the beckoning embrace of the untamed hinterland beyond. Like a mechanical marathon runner, the bus found its singular pace in a slow steady jog. Grace was especially taken by the fact that the vehicle was a Leyland Titan and had newly painted livery of Coras Iompair Eireann - the CIE - with its widely ridiculed 'flying snail' logo. She thought it did indeed resemble a snail with wings and, as it transpired, this was to be an entirely accurate representation of travelling with this company. Despite its new coat there was nothing about the Titan that said 'today' or 'modern' or 'the latest'. The vintage Leyland was both symbolic and symptomatic of the British legacy to Ireland. It was a ramshackle beast that bore all the hallmarks of a troubled history. And in a strange invocation it also reminded her of the then Taoiseach, Eamon De Valera, especially with its large, proboscis shaped bonnet and prominent headlights. Although a shadow of the vehicle it once was, and preserved no doubt by some form of bus-cannibalism, it appeared to be ever-popular, or at least in demand. 'Just like 'Dev', Grace thought.

After slowing down on the main road some thirty minutes from Galway town, the bus slowed yet again. It appeared that nature had not only met but also confounded the maintenance department of Galway County Council, with the result that the pitted tarmacadam required the driver to stop and ponder the potential traps that lay beneath the many large puddles that strew the road. All these slowings and stoppings only served to frustrate Grace's attempt to think about the past.

There was an odd solemnity about her fellow passengers and hardly a word was being exchanged. Most simply sat and stared at the back of the seat in front of them. As they sat bolt upright with eyes wide open but all the while staring into nothingness and beyond, they had a scruffy, statuesque, scarecrow quality about them. The men were particularly blank and Trappist in their manner. Apart from their mostly tweed flat caps, which were obligatory it appeared, Grace thought there was something terribly un-Irish about them. Talkative, jovial and intensely interested in hearing and then re-telling anyone and everyone's story, was what she could recall of pre-war Irish folk. It took her some time to realise that conversations were in fact already in full-swing. The men were conversing with eye and facial gestures that changed in time with the staccato rhythm of the bus's movements. It had the tempo of a stilted round table discussion. A pained expression was invariably followed by a nod and then their eyes went searching for either the net luggage rack or the roof of the bus. This was reciprocated by a shake of the head or contortion of the whole face and this was obviously a challenge to the truth of what had not just been said. A dialogue of sorts was definitely ongoing, albeit without a single word being exchanged. It soon became obvious to Grace that the topic of the unspoken conversation was indeed the bus driver's competence or rather lack of it. Each of his haltings and ponderings on the state of the road instigated a flurry of nods and eye juggling amongst the men on board. The occasional 'ah' or 'oh' or simply a 'tuh' would also involuntarily escape their silence like farts.

As the bus meandered its way into the countryside and prompted by the appearance and manner of the men on the bus, memories of her father began to occupy Grace. She could feel herself going back to her formative years.

———

MARY GRACE MAUDE DEBEN had been born into what she herself described as 'stretched' circumstances. She was the only child of a Post-Office worker who had migrated from Ireland at the turn of the century and a mother who for most of her childhood she remembered as being sick with tuberculosis. Her South London upbringing was unexceptional, save for the intensity of her father's auto-didacticism and his commitment to books and reading. As an Irishman who had abandoned the faith, he had found both his soul and solace in political tracts. His socialist convictions permeated virtually all the literature he made available to his daughter and as a result she had grown up with Fabian rather than derring-do or traditional romantic heroes and heroines. Apart from her bone structure and colouring, it was difficult to identify any such lasting imprint of her sickly mother. Either through diligent family planning, abstinence or incapacity, or for all these reasons, she was destined to be an only child. And, in many respects, she had a lonely childhood; one that left her on the perimeter of many a crowd. Yet, in this she often gave thanks and only rarely wished it to be otherwise. For above all else, she had no time or desire to share her precious books with anyone. Having spent most of her childhood reading, she had acquired a vocabulary beyond her years, albeit one that was peppered with the latest Leftist terminology, and it was this that was to stand her in good stead.

After leaving school she had undertaken typing and secretarial classes paid for by her father's prodigious overtime. As a result she quickly secured a position in a small advertising agency in Kennington. She could already write with an authority and fluency that belied her years and the quality of her letter of application was the difference between herself and all the other applicants. Responsibility and promotion very soon fell upon her diminutive shoulders and she was made Chief Copywriter in the agency at just twenty years of age. This was something which was previously unheard of in the trade, least of all for a woman. And it was not long before the owner of the business, Walter Porteus, took a more personal interest in the youthful Mary Deben. By her own admission, she was by no means a good-looker or unattractive. 'Petite' was the description that was frequently appended to her, nearly always accompanied by the rider 'but severe'. The severity characteristic appears to have been a conflation of her mind and body and was usually invoked by jealous others, mostly men. No-one would have described her as humorous but neither was she dour. However, she neither danced nor sang. In fact, it was often said that her most distinctive feature was the size and penetrating brightness of her eyes which appeared to glisten in almost any light.

———

FORTY-FIVE MINUTES into the journey and a fog descended, only it was inside the bus. Grace smelt and then looked behind to see the dense miasma of a tobacco cloud that was enveloping the aisle and heading in her direction. Sweet Afton or some such national treasure was being imbibed, exhaled and then re-imbibed by strangers, neighbours and children alike. Whilst she had no real objection to the 'fags', Grace was suddenly conscious of this particular pall of smoke being unusually thick and clinging. Whilst a waft of a bonfire in the distance distributes a certain comfort and often aids a reminiscence, standing too close to a sudden effusion of smoke smarts the eyes and the lungs are left gasping and burnt. Grace was far too close to this bonfire. She began to catch her breath and coughed as the smokers' cloud made its way in, up and over her. She also realised that it had nowhere else to go. The less than deft meanderings and regular haltings of the bus meant that the air was stationery for the most part. Yet no-one said anything and no-one seemed to mind. Burning Sweet Afton hung low, like incense over a gathered congregation. Grace's attempt to open one of Titan's windows was thwarted by its obvious underuse and antiquity. Even if it had been operable, she would no doubt have been told to close it 'for the rain and awful wind'.

Titan the bus, she thought, had the ability to reduce time to a series of 'nows,' much as her life with Walter had been. Walter Porteus was 17 years her senior. An amiable and hard-working man, it was often said of him that he was 'someone who could always be trusted', a candle in the age of electricity. He was also quite exceptional for his time and certainly his profession. He saw in Mary a talent that was independent of her gender and had given her the opportunity that most other women, irrespective of age, were being denied elsewhere. Walter was also more than enamoured by Mary as a skilled copywriter. Consequently she, along with his business, flourished and profited. In turn, she was more than grateful for his benevolence and the opportunity he had given her. Yet, all the while, she remained naively unaware of his growing attraction to her as a woman. Inevitably, they started spending more time together as the demands of the job took them on business trips in and around the capital. Suppers and theatre outings followed, as did their discovery of a number of mutual interests in literature and the arts. The older man was a comfort to her and, despite his maturity and ownership of the agency, she began to feel his equal. For Walter's part, his protégé had become a woman and so it was that, after a very brief engagement, and despite Mary's mother having died just two days previous, they were married. No doubt the women on the bus would have plenty to say in that regard.

Grace looked around the bus and thought that the women passengers were only a little more animated than the menfolk. They too appeared to have the rather mysterious ability of being able to converse without moving their lips, making eye contact or acknowledging anything was being communicated at all. And they were no less traditional in their uniform of tweed shawls in various hues of brown. They looked if not out of place then out of time. The Titan could have stopped in any era in the past forty years and the women could have boarded without any comment as to their dress or manner. The only life amongst them were two little girls who were sharing a seat. They were very much alive to the present and perhaps the future as they scrapped incessantly. Grace thought they might be practicing raising the mute souls of their future men-folk.

———

UNFORTUNATELY FOR WALTER, Mary had harboured ambitions beyond finding and furnishing the comfortable middle-class suburban home they established in Clapham. She had already indicated that she thought children were out of the question: she was 'too young and he was too old'. In any case, how could they maintain the agency? As a result their sex life went from being a dialogue to the occasional stuttering conversation and then, towards the end, a loud silence. For Mary, becoming a mother was always going to be as much a professional as a personal decision and, at first, Walter seemed resigned to this being a condition of their relationship. However, slowly and over time, it became the subject that either opened or closed their increasing number of disagreements, which then gradually matured into full-blown arguments. Both became unhappy at home and frustrated and unproductive in the office. She also became increasingly agitated by the vacuous nature of the advertising industry in general. Trying to sell people things they didn't need or even want was about as pointless a waste of her time and talent as she could imagine. In revenge, she began to write a bitter novel about the advertising industry.

Ironically, her immediate success as a novelist came about as a result of Walter's intervention. He knew some people in publishing and managed to put her in touch with Frederick Jorrow. Although Jorrow didn't like the novel, he thought his readership would, '*It captured the mood of the hour,*' he told her in his fully pretentious publisher mode. Mary didn't really understand or mind what he said, all that mattered was that her first novel was about to be published. Whilst both critically and financially the book can only be described as a minor success, Jorrow contracted her to write another and then another. As with Walter, she was oblivious to Jorrow's infatuation. Before long she had quit Walter's agency and turned to full-time writing and it was not long after that she also quit Walter as her husband. They - she more than he - had slowly drifted apart and both realised that they were pushing on opposite sides of the same door in terms of their respective visions of the future. There was to be no way back for them as a married couple. Neither was acrimonious about the decision and in the modern way they remained 'very close friends'. However, their attempt at getting a divorce was to be a somewhat messy and protracted affair. If Mary, as a woman, was to cite Walter, she had to have evidence of not only his adultery but also proof of either incest, sodomy or violence on his part. Walter, in his characteristically decent and honourable way, could not and would not bring himself to supply such evidence, even if it was to be entirely fabricated. In any case, he also knew that he would be unable to brave the necessary deceit in a court of law. As a man, on the other hand, he could cite Mary on the grounds of adultery alone; but this was often a lot more damaging for the woman's reputation. Neither party were keen to pursue these paths. Fortunately, there was to be an imminent change in the divorce law, one that suggested they should wait for the new Act and then use the far less prurient ground of desertion as the basis of their separation. Far from deserting Walter, Mary felt that she was liberating him. As friends they carried on seeing each other occasionally; up until he eventually sold the agency, or rather it was taken over and he was bought out by an American 'Inc.'. Walter then moved to Bedford to be near to his ailing elder sister and Mary received reports that he was 'very happy' in his new and comfortable life.

———

GRACE SPOTTED the obvious exception in the bus' roster. A young cleric was sat across the aisle and he looked no more than a boy straight from the seminary. His blond hair rioted despite the generous portion of Brylcreem that had obviously been applied to hide its true, wild nature. His cheeks were populated with youthful acne and he cast only furtive glances at his bus-fellows, no doubt hoping that they wouldn't notice he was a man of the cloth - which of course his boyish looks suggested he was some way from being. Despite her own rules-of-the-bus, Grace caught his eye and smiled. She couldn't help herself. Everything about him suggested he was Daniel about to be thrown into the lion's den.

———

AFTER HER SEPARATION FROM WALTER, Mary had continued to develop as a writer and extended her range to cover travel and current affairs. In all this she never seemed to have a problem getting Jorrow or his kind to publish her extraordinary output. Most of the work was well-received and due to it 'touching a contemporary nerve' it was often the plat-de-jour of conversation at dinner tables in and around London's progressive circles. Success did indeed breed success and she began to get more widely noticed. After trips to Burma, China, India and Samarkand, she often retreated to the country or, as of late, to Ireland to write and recover from her travels. It was her father's family connections that had initially drawn her to the country of his birth. However, on discovery of their complete indifference to progressive politics and their one paced lives in general, avoidance of all family became her preferred tactic. Then, like now, she headed straight for the wilderness that is Connemara.

Mary benefitted from the sale of the agency and was able to concentrate on her writing career. At least, that was the case up until her father required her care. Moving back in with her father turned out to be every inch the personal and professional regressive step she thought it would be. Her whole life stopped, like a broken reel in a moving picture. He had gone into a spiral of physical and spiritual decline after her mother had died and she now felt under an intense obligation to look after him. He, she, they both had no one else to turn to. Whilst he had taken to the bottle and was just about able to hold down his job, he was seldom in any state to strike up a half-decent conversation or attend to the household chores. She also had to remind him to change his underwear. More significant perhaps, he had also ceased his beloved reading. His moroseness was also deepened by what he saw as the 'traitors' who were now in charge in Ireland; the traitors to the Labour movement in Britain and above all the traitors to the Communist cause in the Soviet Union. Then, at work one day, he collapsed and died on the spot. Apocryphally, this had happened after a bitter and vigorous argument with a group of his workmates about the need for the immediate 'common ownership of the means of production'. Mary had little doubt that it was indeed his politics rather than the drink that was the most likely cause of his premature death. One shouldn't celebrate one's father's passing, but she was thankful for the respite and the fact that her life could be resumed, albeit as an orphan.

———

BEYOND MOYCULLEN and heading out towards Oughterard, Grace had a chance at last to ponder her immediate and pressing plans for the present and the future. She had been forewarned that the cottage she was about to rent was going to be in need of some attention. It had lain empty for most of the war - or the 'Emergency' as it was known in these parts - and now for some unknown reason a period beyond that. There would certainly be work to be done on making it habitable, let alone comfortable. She also knew that the 'getting around' needed to be attended to. Her first thoughts had been on a bicycle and then in a complete flight of fantasy, a horse and cart. Even a motorcycle had made a fleeting visit to the list of transport possibilities. All of these were eventually and quite rightly dismissed as inappropriate or simply daft. The disrepair of the roads around Connemara and the reliability of the wet weather made a mockery of any means of transport that left anyone or anything open to the ever-present rain. Despite her misgivings about driving, as well as her lack of both experience and skill, Grace was nevertheless reconciled to the need to be 'motorised'. She was therefore intent on putting to good use the instruction in driving motor-vans which she had undertaken in the WVS during the last months of the war. That she had not had much of an opportunity, in fact none at all, to employ her skills, only made for a steely determination to recoup the investment in terror and pain she put herself through on that course; not to mention that she had also inflicted on the poor instructors, passengers and bystanders who had witnessed her attempt to become 'motorised'. Getting a motor-van would be her priority.

As the bus pulled into Moyst's garage in Oughterard, she couldn't wait to breathe some fresh air. The cloying tobacco smoke and the fetid atmosphere of the damp bus had tested her constitution to the limit. Almost immediately after Titan's door was opened the by now not-so-Sweet Afton was replaced by the unmistakeable aroma of a turf fire. It took only one intake of that unique and distinctive scent for Grace to locate herself in the West of Ireland and Connemara. Her head and heart were lifted by a strange sense of both homecoming and familiarity. She could already feel something of the place enter her and this immediately made her more comfortable in both body and soul. It was as if she had divested herself of at least some of the troubles she carried with her from the East and was now energised to address things anew, or at least differently, here in the West. She was at a crossroads.

Oughterard had all the feel and appearance of a frontier town. It was the last concentration of habitation before Connemara proper. Its few pubs and tightly packed shops of every kind all cried out for the customers to stock up before proceeding into the hidden perils and vastness of the wild country ahead. The fact that the hinterland was a mere twenty miles across or even less, and that the busy main town of Clifden awaited on the other side, was not to be taken for granted according to the town's canny publicans and retailers. The unknowns of Connemara were lying in wait for the unstocked traveller and it was 'best buy now before it's too late' they all profitably advised. Every trader proclaimed that this was the last stop-and-shop before the bogs and the mountains. Although this was not entirely true, those who followed the good shop-keepers' advice scuttled around and filled their bags with the essentials that were thought to be unavailable hereon in. For her part, Grace could not think what these essentials might be. Nevertheless she relented and purchased a few Everton mints for the journey rather than for survival. As she left the little newsagent shop with her paper bag of treats still in hand, the young cleric shuffled past her with his head down. Grace couldn't help but entertain the amusing thought that perhaps he too was going to buy some sweets with his pocket-money. 'Sweet boy, a bit like Tom', she thought.

Leaving Oughterard the bus climbed, groaned and splashed its way up and down the hills leading into Maam Cross where a few of the passengers decanted at the only building of any note, 'the Hotel'. At last a vista of the Connemara landscape opened up and the lochs, which seemed to be taking it in turns to appear on either side of the road, threatened to overspill onto the carriageway. The rain continued to fall and the opaque greyness of the cloud cover was playing the game of hiding the peaks that lay beyond. The Twelve Pins, the mountains that are the very essence of the place, appeared as if a Christmas present with wrapping paper clouds just waiting to be opened. The whole canvas of opaque, grey cotton-wool above the road and the brown swirls of loch water below reminded Grace of an enormous jug of dirty, frothy beer. The dreariness of the sodden landscape and unrelenting wetness on all sides was not what she had hoped for. On the other hand, she also felt that the reality of Connemara's climate is best confronted from the very start. This was what it was to be like most of the time and she needed to accommodate herself to it. There was little or no point in thinking that blue skies were to be the order of the day in this part of the world.

The next stop on route was Letterfrack, which was also destined to be Grace's nearest village and settlement. Again, a couple of passengers including the boy-priest alighted. He smiled a rather rueful smile as he caught Grace's eye, or was it a cry for help? She sensed that this was probably not a destination he had sought out for himself as there appeared to be little or nothing that warranted him getting off the bus. That is, until the bus left the village and the Industrial School came into view. Grace could now see that it totally dominated the village. The scale of the institution was totally out of keeping with its surroundings and in the remoteness of this most natural of landscapes the huge brick edifice appeared not just incongruous but almost violently obscene. The young cleric had certainly been drawn to this place by forces that were beyond his control and she immediately felt very sorry for him.

———

BY THE STANDARDS of her own time or indeed those of any other, Mary Grace Maude Deben, or M.G.M. Deben 'the writer' as she was known, was no ordinary woman. She was the only bee in her hive: queen, worker and drone. She was also an ideological lodestone and had campaigned for all manner of progressive causes. The A-Z of the radical 'isms' of her age -Anarchism, Communism, Feminism, Humanism, Socialism and Syndicalism - had all been tried and tested and all found wanting. As a result, she had become a veritable assemblage of principles, nostrums and ideas; a radical bricoleur in an age of increasing political orthodoxy.

Yet, in recent years, her embrace of new ideas had lain dormant. Something inside her had died.

Before the war, and when not being described as 'feisty' or simply 'feminist', she was often referred to as 'doughty'. It was a word which riled her more than any other, even when it was intended as a compliment. It was one of her ugly words, those that sounded and were often taken to be something they were not. Now, along with love and peace, it had become one of her proscribed words - those which she was consciously trying to erase from her vocabulary. Doughty certainly bore no resemblance or association to its similar sounding cousin 'doubt' with regard to M.G.M. Deben; she had had few doubts about anything other than her personal worth. Whenever she considered her own achievements, the bottle always appeared to be half-empty. A well-meaning critic had once made the mistake of describing her work as always 'informed and informative'; characteristically, she chose to interpret this as suggesting it was akin to a railway timetable. Needless to say she never spoke to the offender or wrote for that newspaper again. Never one to fear or flee from controversy, or a good cause, she expected nothing less of others and once upon a time, before Spain, that had been her way. Doughty did indeed best describe her.

———

Grace could never be a local, a fleeting visitor, or even just a tourist; she was always the stranger and had lived much her life as such. She was both an insider and outsider; someone who always tried to be part of and at the same time different from those she encountered. Strangers seek acceptance and yet always have to deny it. And so it had been with Grace. Above all else, the stranger is never at home and this had always been both her gift and her burden, yet it was also one she had used to the full in her career as a successful author. As a creature with a hard shell and a soft underbelly, she had developed an ability to protect herself by withdrawing into her protective shell whenever she felt threatened by the possibility of belonging. This had once been her forte and it was only now, ten years after her carapace had been fractured by her experience in Spain, that it was being rebuilt. This journey was to be the first real test of her new sense of self.

As they arrived in Clifden the rain appeared to relent or at least was demoted to a mere mist. The town was even darker than the clouds and its Protestant rectangularity made the walls of the buildings appear as if they were blank, grey pages of an unwritten book. There was nothing to fix one's eyes on apart from the monotony of the place. People huddled, scuttled and generally sought shelter from the drabness of its streets. She now knew that it was possible to dislike a town on first appearances and Clifden appeared solid evidence of this fact. It was a border town and one that, like all such entities, was profoundly functional. It represented the 'other side'; it was after Connemara and Grace couldn't wait to leave.

2

KEELY'S COTTAGE

As previously arranged, Grace was met off the bus by John Fahey a local garage owner. John was late middle-aged by appearance and dressed somewhere between church and workshop. He wore an open neck shirt and a tie that was ready to be hoisted should the occasion require it. He was waiting to take Grace to the cottage in his van. After collecting some provisions, they set off back along the road that the bus had just travelled. About two miles from Clifden they took a side road that took them over the high bog and back towards Letterfrack. The conversation, such as it was, was all about the bus journey and the unchanging weather. No-one would describe John Fahey as a great conversationalist.

John stopped the van at a crossroads and enquired as to the need to go to the village itself. Grace had no thoughts of doing this and asked that he continue to the cottage. They soon came across a gate leading down a boreen, a small grassed over lane, and John indicated that she should open it whilst he drove the van through to the other side. Half a mile further on there was a second gate and they repeated the exercise. Suddenly, as they rounded a small hill that had been denying all views on the left hand side of the road, the whole sweep of a bay appeared. The sea was chopping along either side of the inlet and the waves were trying to dismount and clamber up the rocks. Grace thought it a most beautiful sight. At the same moment, a small white cottage could be seen at the water's edge. This was her new home, Keely's cottage. John stopped the van outside the front door and she rushed to inspect her new Connemara home. There was a key in the door, which had been left unlocked in any case. Entering the cottage she was struck by its fusty, stagnant and altogether hoary smell. Animals could have been kept in here, she thought. Despite the rain which had started to return in earnest, she left the front door ajar and then opened all the windows as wide as they could possibly go.

'You'll need a fire. I'll get it going for ye', John said and then went to the store shed that adjoined the back of the cottage.

Grace came across the view from the main room. She smiled as the whole bay and the distant hills could be seen from the window. The dark clouds and the rain could not hide what was a panorama that encapsulated everything she loved about Connemara. It was indeed 'mythical', 'magical', 'majestic', 'misty and moist'; it was also 'captivating', 'crazed', 'forgotten and far-flung'. She had read and had even written some of these epitaphs herself. Now this was to be hers, every morning, and every afternoon and evening. Any question of whether the cottage was habitable had already receded without trace and she was determined to stay come what may.

'There's tinder and turf. I put some there the other day

now. Let's see how it goes,' John said and lit the fire in the kitchen-living room.

There were two very small bedrooms, one at either end of the kitchen-living room, and that was the sum total of her accommodation. It was however dry and the walls were thick. Outside, there was the turf store and a toilet.

Smoke soon escaped the chimney flue and began to fill the room. John closed the front door and the fire started to behave itself.

'I've found a kettle. Would you like some tea John?'

'I would. I'll get some fresh water.'

Whilst he was away, Grace re-inspected the cottage and thought it was deplete of any welcoming aspects. It needed to be taken out of its hibernation and she knew she would have to start from scratch to make it her 'home'.

When John returned she watched as he tried to encourage the fire, 'It was very kind of you to bring me out here,' she said.

'Not at all. How else would you have got here?'

'It's much further from Clifden than I thought.'

'Aye, it's a journey alright. But you have the village here, down the road there. That's not far,' he suggested.

'I was thinking—' Grace paused and waited for John to look up from stirring the fire, 'I was thinking I might purchase a motor-van.'

'A motor van?' he looked rather surprised and a little amused.

'For yourself?'

'Yes, I thought it would be best.'

'Can you drive a motor van?'

'I can.'

'In these parts?'

'I'm sure I'll be able,' she responded, albeit rather unconvincingly.

'Are you sure now?' John's reply also came with a good dose of scepticism.

'Yes and I was hoping you'd find me one. A decent one, suitable for driving... in these parts.'

'I can, easy enough, if that's what you want. Mind you, they don't come for nothing 'round here. And it wouldn't be the best or a new one you'd be after?'

'No. A used one will do, as long as it's reliable.'

'Of course, I'd make it that,' he offered.

'So you'll look out for me? Obviously I'd need it fairly soon. As soon as possible in fact.'

'That won't be a problem, if you have the money now.'

'I have.'

John Fahey left Grace with a decent fire and instructions on the daily routines that she needed to know about. The water spring and the toilet seemed to be his major concerns. The post and the turf delivery were also outlined. The thought of 'Miss Grace', an upper-class English lady, choosing to live a Spartan existence in such a remote spot was quite beyond his comprehension. He seemed reluctant to leave her and promised to call in the next day on his way to a newly invented nearby customer. His generous spirit and concern to make sure that she had all she needed stood out for Grace. These were the hallmarks of the sort of people she longed to know and live amongst.

That first night in the cottage was long and she slept fitfully despite the tiring journey and the excitement of the new adventure. Her bed was but a board and a half-sprung mattress and she had underestimated the number of covers required to keep warm. The fact that it was so quiet, apart from the wind and rain, did not compensate for her general discomfort. The little sleep she garnered was interspersed with rude awakenings that were reminders of where she was. Nothing, it seemed, was entirely real. It had all been so different during the war.

———

LIVING in wartime London had been a welcome distraction. Spain had all but paralysed her ability to write seriously and a few pieces for the newspapers and journals on marginal, frippery-issues was all that she had managed. Although able to live off her past earnings, she found that for her sanity she needed to write. As M.G.M.Deben, she had had the knack of getting published and by her 30th birthday she had already written over a dozen novels, numerous travel books on exotic and far-flung places, and countless articles on current affairs for both the newspapers and the weekly journals. However, it might also be said that her successes were more pointillist than broad stroke. That is, each composition on her literary canvas was in itself rather insignificant, but taken altogether they had an emergent quality.

She spent the majority of her time during the war depressed by the fact that the destruction and suffering was largely a consequence of the so-called democracies not having stood up to the Fascists in Spain in 1936. She did not hold this notion with much conviction however and recognised that it was simply a rationale for the moments of intense anger that listening to the wartime BBC news broadcasts invariably provoked. As an explanation of the war, she knew it was far too simplistic. Indeed, nothing in her contemporary situation was as clear-cut as it had once been, especially after the defeat of fascism everywhere in Europe - with the terrible exception of the crucible, Spain. Life itself was becoming more complex and the models of the world that she had previously relied upon were being overtaken or destroyed by new political realities, which were themselves becoming increasingly unreal. Now, there was very little about post-war life that made much sense. During the Blitz her nightly flight to the safety of Camden Underground station had become indicative of the gap evolving between the real and unreal. It felt like a descent into Hades. There was a falsity about the whole experience and at the same time a monstrous, sensual reality. The notional equality, the cracked bonhomie and the stereotypical pluckiness of those Londoners who were claustrophobically and often chaotically crammed into the bowels of the capital was both effective day time propaganda and unbearable night time misery. For Grace, it was only the stench of the refugees at the time of the morning evacuation that captured the essence of the experience. And after two particularly distressing nights of enduring the shelter of the Underground, she vowed never to return to the subterranean refuge. Typically, she decided that she would rather take her chance above ground.

Thus it was a strange and disquieting realisation on her part that the socialist principles that had been instilled at birth did not extend to spending nights with the masses in the London Underground. She did not feel there was either equality or a democratic spirit in their huddles and whatever communalism was being practiced was simply the exercise of individual self-interest and a primal instinct to survive. She also came to believe that German threat from above was matched only by the extraordinary amount of petty thieving that the bombing promoted in the stations below. London's outcasts and pickpockets had never had it so good. The real power in the land was certainly not represented in the sanctuary of the Tube stations. The nearest they ever came was in the shape of their proxies, the upper middle-class who, often dressed in their evening attire, had been caught unprepared by a raid. The mainstays of the Underground occupation were the poor, working-class people, who had in many cases been bombed out of their already wretched slums. Grace got the distinct impression that for some the Underground may have been a step up the ladder in terms of home comforts.

As the war 'progressed', her depression deepened and she seriously contemplated committing suicide. No-one, she thought, need know her intentions. Not for her the gas oven, the tablets or a rope. Instead, she adopted a fatalist approach and resigned herself to the possibility of a German bomb having her name on it. She stopped being scared of the nightly bombing on April Fools' Day, the 1st of April 1941. On 'Bombers' Moon' nights, when the full moon shone, she dispensed with the cellar and stayed in her kitchen where she made herself a cup of tea and listened out for the bomb that might be heading her way. On other occasions she went into the garden and panned the sky, only to be stood up by the Nazi Grim Reaper. By the time the Luftwaffe switched to moonless nights as their preferred option, she had given up on what proved to be their exaggerated technical competence and accuracy. It appeared that Hitler's drones could not hurt her, either that or they simply wished to extend her suffering as long as possible? And it was then that she decided to adopt her middle name, Grace. Why she had been given that superfluous name was never made clear - her mother's name was Mary Edith and, as far as she knew, Grace was never associated with her father or any of his known relatives. Indeed, growing up with an insignificant, random middle name was one of the things that had propelled her into telling herself stories. She could fantasise as to the nature of Grace, the alter ego who was later to become a central character in nearly all of her novels.

Grace recognised that her fatalism was guilt by another name. Seeking death, by actively and consciously failing to avoid or prevent it, was yet another attempt to assuage what had happened in Spain. She even rationalised her action by thinking that all early deaths were 'the easy ones'. She imagined her death as instant, dignified and even a little brave. However, this acceptance was only made possible by convincing herself that, if her bomb did arrive, she would have not have had to endure the wait, the attention to minute detail of an incurable medical condition, the conversations of the doctors just out of earshot in a hospital ward and the slow dimming of the light of life. She would be saved from a 'hard death', the long drawn out suffering of ageing; a fate that she was convinced would be her own. Gradually, when the Blitz ended and the bombing became less frequent, a sense of equilibrium returned and the shallowing of her life was counter-balanced by the need to furnish and make sense of what had happened in Spain. She knew that, as a writer, she had to write her Spanish novel.

———

IN THE MORNING the rain continued to fall and a mist had come down over the bay. The tide was in and a penetrating, damp greyness once again surrounded the cottage on all sides. Grace struggled to get the fire going but eventually managed to bring it to life. Her first real toilet experience had not been half as bad as she had imagined. Whilst the smell and the general discomfort of the station were unlike anything she was used to, she did not baulk at using 'the facility', as John had called it. Her experiences abroad had also stood her in good stead. The wind had risen and blew the rain straight under the kitchen door. The fire was also temperamental and Grace had let it peter out. Yet, for all that, she smiled and congratulated herself for being so bold to have made the decision to come to Connemara.

———

MIDWAY through the next morning John Fahey duly arrived with fresh bread and milk. They shared a cup of tea and spoke again of the motor-van possibilities. Grace thought that he was still unconvinced about her driving 'in these parts'. Rumour had it that there were very few, if any, women drivers west of Galway town and none at all in Connemara. For himself, he had never actually seen a woman driver other than those in the *Pathe* newsreels at the cinema in Clifden. This was all taken to be evidence of Grace's folly in wanting to drive. They went to the spring together and collected enough water for the day. The walk took them out the first gate, along the boreen and through a small gap in a dry stone wall. The well was built in a tradi-tional manner with a round bell tower effect, a bucket and a substantial winder handle. Grace had trouble lifting the bucket when it was full but with John's help it was accom-plished. She thought that she would need to get stronger if this was to be her daily routine. After taking the water back to the cottage, John left with an invitation to see a motor van he already had in his garage.

Grace spent most of the rest of the day cleaning the cottage before unpacking the few things she had managed to bring with her. The bulk of her belongings, including her books and typewriter, were still some days away in Dublin waiting to be shipped to the West. It was not until dusk that the cottage began to look and feel like some sort of home. The fire was now completely under control and the heat had despatched the remaining mustiness. The kettle had been well-employed and the only relatively comfortable chair by the hearth, the one which sagged the least, was inviting after all her domestic exertions. She could, at last, sit and think about things other than the immediate practicalities. Almost immediately Tom came to mind and she imagined him in this environment. The sights and smells would have been as familiar as they were to John Fahey and his family. Indeed, she imagined him being raised in just such a place and in just such a family. She thought he would have been very much at home in Keely's cottage. She began to make plans to start the book.

3

KITTY

KITTY WALSH WAS THE SAME AGE OR THEREABOUTS AS GRACE, only she did not wear it nearly as well. If the truth be told, this is hardly surprising as she had had a much more demanding life than her new neighbour. Growing up in Connemara had taken its toll and she was quite scarred by her experiences. She was now living alone on the farm that was above and adjoining Keely's cottage and was Grace's nearest and only direct neighbour. They also shared a common spring and that is where they met one morning. Kitty was a local girl who had, with her younger sister, been taken away 'for the best' when she was nine years of age. When she was finally better they let her return home, but only on the condition that she got married and quickly. She duly but most reluctantly complied. Her spouse, Patsy Walsh, was a local farmer who was twenty years her senior and a good deal further down life's road. Their marriage had all the hallmarks of having been made in the local Rectory and Convent.

Patsy Walsh turned out to be no catch and it was evident to everyone bar himself why his bachelorhood had been overly extended. Like most isolated and forgotten sheep farmers, he drank too much and too often. However, unlike most of the other local farmers, he was also pathologically lazy and a champion at being unproductive. The farm had no present and certainly no future whilst he continued its stewardship. Their marriage was never consummated due to Kitty's sudden and unexplained onset of 'feminine problems' and it was, in any case, to last but a few long months. One cold and foggy morning Patsy was found frozen stiff on side of the Clifden road. He had been hit by something or someone; no-one actually knows and his death remains unexplained. They say that you make your own luck and it appeared that Kitty's had finally changed. On Patsy's death it transpired that the farm had survived only because he had sold Keely's cottage to John Fahey a few years previous and had been drinking the proceeds ever since.

Kitty was soon to have another rare piece of good fortune bestowed upon her. On clearing out and fumigating the farmhouse after Patsy's interment, she discovered the residue of the sale of the cottage in a little wooden box hidden amongst his detritus. She had nearly thrown the box straight onto the bonfire with all his other contaminated belongings, only a premonition or simply inquisitiveness got the better of her and she opened it. The amount of cash was by no means great and even by local standards it was hardly a fortune. Patsy had made sure of that. It was however enough to make up the difference between what she could earn from the farm - almost nothing - and continuing to be able to survive there. All manner of local suitors at Patsy's wake had reliably informed her that the farmland was quite productive for the area, if it was 'worked correctly'. This was the code by which they proposed. Kitty had already made up her mind to do just that, to work it correctly, only for and by herself. Whilst she was away being made better, she had learned to farm sheep, keep horses and had become competent in numerous other tasks related to regular farm work. She had also learned to read properly and could look after herself in most other respects. Patsy's hidden legacy therefore enabled her to bridge the gap between the squalid condition of the farm she inherited and getting it somewhere near to being sustainable. She was still working on the latter and had for some years now also been employed in the village as a domestic and farm hand at the Industrial School in Letterfrack. She had no problem with hard work; it paid for her self-imposed privacy and, more important, her hard-won autonomy. She was never going to take orders from anyone ever again if she could help it. That was the full extent of her ambition and in this she had a lot in common with her new neighbour Grace.

———

KITTY ARRIVED at the spring without a sound and realised that she could well scare Grace if she did not announce herself,

'Fine day?' she said by way of introducing herself at the well.

'Dry for once.' Grace responded.

'Kitty Walsh. I'm up in the farm there. We're neighbours now I hear?'

She then made a very soft whistling sound and two Border collies came rushing from behind a dry stone wall. The dogs approached and squatted down at her feet. One of the dogs was quite elderly looking and the other was bright and puppyish. Both had long, matted hair and were very slight, even thin, specimens. Anyone could see that they were very much working dogs rather than pets. All Kitty did was look at them and they appeared to know what was expected. They were obviously eager to inspect Grace but remained under orders at a distance.

'Yes, John Fahey told me to expect to meet you. I'm Grace. Grace Deben. Fine dogs.'

'Not so fine if you know them,' Kitty replied, as she pretended to kick the elderly one. 'That's a pretty name, Grace. You're English?'

'Yes, well, my father was Irish and my mother was English.'

'Where was he from? Around here?'

'No, Clare. Ennis way.'

'Are ye here long?' Kitty inquired. Grace had not really thought about how she might answer that question and in any case how long is long?'

'I don't know. I think I might.'

Kitty brought her water can up to the well and Grace felt intimidated by the ease by which she lowered the bucket and raised it with one arm turning the winder. The transfer of the fresh water to the jerry can was similarly natural and without any sense of exertion. She was strong and sturdy in every move and Grace was soon in awe of her raw power.

'Make sure you lock your doors now,' Kitty unilaterally changed the subject and looked at Grace as one would an elderly relative or indeed a child.

'Lock my doors?' Grace was slightly taken aback by the notion, 'Out here?'

'Aye, especially out here. I had things taken a while back. Spade, fork, scythe and the like. All taken. Tinkers most likely,' Kitty sighed.

'I wouldn't have thought to lock my door out here, at least, not during the day,' Grace replied and was genuinely put out by the idea that her city routine had found its way to Connemara.

' ...'specially out here. And ...'specially when they know you're on your own.'

'On your own? Like you are?' Grace asked.

'Like we both are!' Kitty smiled and her stained and grossly uneven teeth were revealed for the first time. A major gap at the front also did very little for her. 'So make sure you lock your doors. Oh, and your windows whilst you're at it.'

They fetched their water in turns, with Kitty helping Grace each time, and they chatted about the prospects for the weather and where to shop in Clifden, if the need arose. 'The emigration' was also made the burning topic of that first encounter. Kitty was clearly distressed by the fact that too many young men in the area were having to leave. 'That it had always been so,' was their jointly considered conclusion. Kitty then went on to recount the tale of a recent returnee who had come back with an altogether 'sunken and unhealthy look' as a result of working in factories in England. According to Kitty, he had 'not seen daylight or breathed fresh air since he had first left'. Grace felt that she was more than slightly exaggerating on at least one of these scores but didn't say so. Now the boy was back home but still without work, he had 'picked up wonderfully' and was 'his grand self again'. Kitty continued, 'No-one should have to work indoors,' she rather fantastically proposed. Again, Grace did not challenge either the sentiment or the practicality of Kitty's suggestion. How could she, here in Connemara? Kitty apologised for keeping Grace who, in turn, made sure that Kitty understood that she had not done so at all. They vowed to meet again soon and that they would both lock their doors.

They gave each other a little wave as they went their separate paths.

'And your windows', Kitty shouted after a few strides back along the boreen.

————

JOHN FAHEY RETURNED to Keely cottage at the end of the week, driving a large, black limousine. Grace was struck by both the size and the inappropriateness of the vehicle in this setting. The car was both a statement and an ostentatious eyesore.

'John, is that yours?'

'I wish. No, it's a customer's. I thought I would pick ye up and take you to town. I have a van waiting for ye.'

'For me?'

'Who else? Can you get yourself in now, please? I'm running late as it is. I have to have this back.'

Grace closed up the cottage and remembered to lock the doors but forgot the windows. She got into the very expensive looking, up-market car which had leather seats, pile carpet and walnut trim.

'This is a great big car John. Its owner must be of some importance?'

'He is. That he is.' John was obviously reluctant to take the conversation further and he resorted to observations about the weather and the prospects for a drier Spring. Grace continued to survey the vehicle for clues about its ownership. There were none that she could see. Even the Rosary draped over the rear-view mirror, which was more compulsory than the road-tax in Ireland, offered no particular insight as to whose car it might be. When they reached John's garage, Eoin, his young apprentice fitter, was cleaning a motor-van on the forecourt. John took Grace over to the vehicle.

'It's a fine van now. Spick 'n' span and all,' John indicated. The boy's done a grand job on it,' he stated proudly.

The boy smiled and carried on shining the headlights. Grace thought she should try to engage in the technical details of the 'fine' van,

'What is it John?'

'It's a motor van,' John twinkled and winked at Eoin.

'I meant...You know what I meant!'

'Just pulling your leg,' John chirped. 'It's an Austin 7. But not just that, it's a pick-up and they're very rare in these parts. Look at the box on the back, you could easily get half a dozen sheep in there and in comfort I'd say. It's a working vehicle alright. You'll get almost anything in there and it'll still take you places and back.'

Grace went to the rear of the vehicle and the open box behind the cab was indeed capacious and potentially useful, although any talk of comfort she attributed to John's low opinion of the sheep's standards.

'16.5 cubic capacity and an 800 cc engine. It's big enough and powerful enough for you.'

'747cc,' Eoin sheepishly corrected his boss.

'Aye, 747cc and 14 bhp?' John was now looking towards young Eoin and waited for confirmation. The boy nodded and thought best not to revise any more details. 'And it has a four-speed box. Good tyres and a low use. The engine is practically new. Hardly used at all.'

'How old is it then John?'

'A few years and never been as far as Galway. And I'll look after it for you just in case.'

'1931,' Eoin offered much to John's annoyance.

'1931!' Grace was immediately troubled by its antiquity.

'Reliable...though. Built to last and now in tip-top condition thanks to us and the work we've put in.'

'You'll guarantee it then?'

'I will, if it's treated well that is.'

Grace was desperate to be motorised; the vehicle had a quirky charm and the sales-talk was ultimately convincing. They agreed there and then that she should be the new owner. John then began to outline the necessary precautions needed to drive safely on the local roads,

'Under the box, you'll find the spare wheel. You need to carry some petrol and oil at all times. There's few places to fill up. Spark plugs, do you know what to do with them?'

'I do John,' Grace lied about her ignorance. She had really forgotten.

'And an umbrella and spare coat and boots are essentials. They're always handy now. Have you got that?'

'It'll be full already John!'

'Plenty of room in there. Don't you be worrying about that.'

They walked around to the cab and opened the door. John continued,

'Now, on the road, don't be driving too far on the left. The sheep will be on the road and you'll knock a few over if you keep too close to the edge. Drive down the middle when possible. That way, you can go left or right if something doesn't see you coming. Don't drive through the puddles! They'll be full of holes and you won't know how deep they are. Drive around them whenever you can. And watch out for the crowd cadging lifts everywhere, especially the priests and the like. Never, never, take them to where they want to go! Always say you're only going to the next crossroads. That way, you can say you're going left if they want right, or you can go right if they want left. Don't let them be taking you where you don't want to go. Everyone will hear about it and there'll be no end to it. You'll be the local taxi before you know it.'

'Is that all John?'

'Isn't it enough to be getting on with? Shall we see how it sounds?'

The van started first time and the engine sounded brash and throaty. The thrill of having her own motor-van was now dawning on Grace. She sat in the driver's seat and randomly twiddled the various knobs. John sat next to her and watched her unschooled exploration.

'Sounds good John.'

'Are you sure you can drive this?'

'Yes of course. Shall we go?'

'Let's try it then,' John did not look so convinced. He turned the engine off. Grace tried to remember the wartime driving training course. The drill-sergeant who had been recruited to instruct the WVS women was now bellowing in her memory.

'Starter, Engage first gear! Look around! All clear? Indicate! Brake off! Proceed! Stop!'

On her first attempt, the van stalled and John jerked forward and held his head in his hands. Grace smiled at him and recomposed herself. She was now more determined than ever to achieve her motoring ambition. The van stalled again on her second attempt. Eoin barely contained himself from giggling and, by the way he shook his head, this only served to confirm his ideas about the inadvisability of allowing women to drive at all.

'A little more choke,' John suggested and Eoin concurred.

Grace went through the process of starting once more. Success.

'Engage. Proceed!'

'Ohhhh...slow down now!' John was a little frantic as they pulled out of the garage forecourt and on to the open road. Luckily no other vehicle was in the vicinity. Grace was near-ecstatic; the freedom of the road and all its possibilities beckoned. It felt like a coming-of-age.

———

GRACE SOON SETTLED into a routine as, much to her surprise, life in the isolated cottage demanded it. After waking, ablutions and breakfast, and regardless of the weather she took the first of her two daily walks on the foreshore. These walks were for the exercise, as well as helping to clear her mind for the day ahead. The days had passed slowly at first and it was only when John Fahey delivered her belongings that she began to feel that she could make a serious start on her writing. Her books, blankets, a few paintings and wireless had all made the journey unscathed. Unfortunately, she soon discovered that she was only able to choose her radio station on the rare clear day. So John volunteered to repair the cottage's much-rusted radio aerial and completed the task without delay. However, even he could do little about the weather and the wireless reception remained sporadic and often indistinct. Grace was desperate to hear music once more, especially her favourite Chopin sonatas. She had not realised how much she craved the company of the composer. A gramophone and some records were soon ordered.

Ideas for the book had been swirling around in Grace's head for some time and she had produced numerous rough sketches for the plot, characters and structure. As with all her previous novels, she had no idea of an ending. Looking at the jottings, she thought they had much in common with the clouds that had blanketed Connemara for the last three weeks; they often obscured more than they revealed. On some days her notes covered up all traces of the past and there were absences and confusion about time, places and action. Yet on other days, and even on the same day, a brief parting of the greyness would provide opportunities for a ray of sunlight to suddenly appear. On such days memories and insights came flooding back to her with such clarity that they were sometimes too painful to record. All this note-taking had been in anticipation of her beloved typewriter arriving in one piece. The small, portable machine was a trusty friend and had been a reliable companion on all her travels. Here in Connemara, she had felt disarmed without it.

After her morning walk, Grace went to the spring to gather water. Twice now she had run into Kitty although they had made no firm arrangement to do so. Their conversations seldom strayed beyond the weather and local gossip and Grace soon realised that Kitty was wantonly ignorant about the world beyond Connemara. It had, after all, little or no bearing on her daily struggle to exist. After gathering the water, Grace collected any post left at the end of the boreen by Eamon the postman. She planned to get to the first gate by 10am and catch a conversation. After mid-morning tea she would spend the remainder of the morning reading and only begin to write after lunch. Up until the arrival of her typewriter, these afternoon sessions had had a tendency to be cursory and she found herself being easily distracted. Now, armed once more, she felt able to commit to the book and the words began to flow.

4

LONDON DECEMBER 1936

THE NOTE TOM RECEIVED EARLIER IN THE DAY HAD BEEN typically brusque:

Monday, 17th December, 1936 Tea at J. Lyons' - The Strand
3.30pm?
I MUST, MUST meet you TODAY. YOUR VERY LAST
CHANCE.
Yours, M.G.M Deben

This was not the first such note to arrive, in fact it was one of several that had come his way over the last few days, each of which had become increasingly curt and desperate. To begin with he had dismissed the requests as a prank orchestrated by his fellow 'Scribblers', the band of struggling young writers he had fallen in with. As the notes continued to arrive he began to question whether they might in fact be genuine and became intrigued, even flattered, by the attention. He had no idea who his mystery correspondent might be and began to make inquiries. However, all he had uncovered from his local librarian was that she was 'a quite well-known left-wing author'. In Tom's cynical estimation, the 'quite' signalled relative obscurity and 'left-wing and well-known' sounded oxymoronic, unless of course you were a Wells or a Shaw. Added to which, M.G.M. Deben was a woman. She had certainly not drawn his attention nor that of his as yet, or indeed never-to-be, discovered circle of hopefuls. With the arrival of the 'last chance' note he felt he should meet her. He had very little to lose and her increasing desperation indicated that he might even have something to gain. M.G.M. had stated in one of her notes that she had read some of his recent 'journalistic pieces' and would welcome the opportunity to discuss them further. Without even trying, she made them sound as though they were broken glass. For Tom, those articles had been written largely out of hunger and the need to pay his rent arrears and, as far as he was concerned, they had little if any, literary merit. Nevertheless he comforted himself in the knowledge that he had at least one discerning reader.

For over six months Tom Lees had been trying to live in London as a writer but without much success. He wasn't really sure what kind of writer he was or even wanted to be. On Monday he might be a journalist, on Wednesday a novelist and at weekends he saw himself as an essayist. It was the latter that was to eventually bring him some notice. He had entered an essay competition in the *London Evening Standard* and won second prize, a most welcome and much needed five guineas. His near-successful essay was entitled *London's Peaks* and told of his attempts to 'bag' in the manner of climbers scaling the Scottish Munros, views of the capital from its tallest structures, its urban summits. This was to be the new sport of 'city mountaineering' - with the doormen of London's buildings replacing the game-keepers and gillies of the Highlands. In both its originality and prose it stood out from the crowd. Whereas the winner of the competition had written something about the origins and development of the London Underground system that, on its publication, had confirmed Tom's view that his own work was indeed far, far superior. And at least one of the competition judges, M.G.M Deben, agreed. However, she was also struck by the limited ambition of the author and had some forthright views about what would have made it 'a much better essay'. In particular, she thought the metaphor of London's Peaks had not been fully developed and the tallest buildings in London, St Pauls and the University of London's newly constructed Senate House, the twin peaks of Church and Academy were, in her opinion, ripe for greater exploitation. Alongside these obvious targets, Tom had also come to the conclusion that the best peak was in fact Parliament Hill, a natural viewpoint offering the grandest vista and one which was free to the general public, the masses. This struck M.G.M Deben as another missed opportunity to inject some social commentary into his composition. Nevertheless, she could see that the author had some raw talent and this was subsequently borne out by the various journalistic pieces she had sought out. Tom had no inkling who the judges were and the name Deben had not resonated at the time. With no money in his pocket, little idea about what she might want and even less expectation that anything would come of it, Tom set off to meet M.G.M Deben. The whole situation perfectly encapsulated his writer's existence. Little could he or anyone else know then, it was to be a meeting that was to determine his life and change hers forever.

Before coming to London to seek his fame and fortune Tom had had various jobs back home in the West of Ireland. He started his adulthood in Galway as an apprentice compositor and working with words was to be the leitmotif of his life. Quite how he managed to secure that rare initial opportunity he wasn't really sure. The print trade was a closed-shop and notoriously difficult to break into. Most apprenticeships were passed down through family connections, of which he had none. Therefore it could only have been a case of his being in the right place at the right time. At first he really knuckled down and relished learning a highly skilled trade, albeit in a very small Dickensian print shop. The work was long and hard for such a slight young lad and lifting the enormous cabinets of metal typeface, the forms, was often too much for him. The older hands took great pleasure at watching his largely unsuccessful attempts to shoulder the beasts and he was the constant butt of their horseplay and jokes. It was never crude bullying, only *stiffening the backbone*. This was how it was in the print trade; there were rites-of-passage and you did your time. The owner of the print shop also sincerely believed he was doing Tom a great favour by training him up. Consequently, his pay was paltry and he only just managed to get by. However he did learn a lot and his dexterity in composing words upside down and the wrong way around soon blossomed. It was indeed a rare skill. The trouble for Tom came when the words he was asked to compose began to reappear over and over and over again. He soon grew tired of the advertising for local shops, mostly small flyers and posters, and the fact that Sales, Reductions and Offers were becoming almost his entire workaday vocabulary. When he found himself enjoying the composition of wedding invitations, he knew that it was time to move on. He gave up his prized apprenticeship before being 'banged out' as a fully-fledged compositor, a decision that he sometimes reflected on with not a little regret.

Thereafter came a whole range of factory and menial jobs which he was always grateful to secure but just as quickly came to despise. He found himself drifting and unhappy and he began to miss composing words, even the simple everyday ones. Then, quite by chance, he applied for a job on the *Galway Observer* - running errands and being a general dogsbody. The pay was even worse than that of the factories but he did at least get to read a newspaper every day. It was also working with people who worked with words. The work was anything but demanding and most days Tom, if he hid in one of the outside toilets, had time to read. Whilst the Observer was only a regional newspaper, it had all the necessary ingredients - with the exception of foreign correspondents - for him to get to know how the news was produced by a combination of heads and hands. Without really trying, he accumulated a working knowledge of all the different departments and their functions. His general inquisitiveness was also appreciated by those who he often cornered and whose knowledge he skilfully extracted. He was well-liked and they saw in him a great potential. Unfortunately, he was also too expensive to keep on and the Observer dispensed with his services after just seven months. Everyone was sorry to see him go and they all wished him well. Although he was devastated, Tom took some consolation from the fact that he had found his vocation - he wanted to work with words.

The casual jobs also soon dried up and, in between looking for work around Galway, Tom tried his hand at writing. For reasons he could not fathom, he found that he couldn't get beyond pallid descriptions and well-used platitudes. The beauty of the words in his head never seemed to reach the page in the way he intended and most ended up in the fire grate as ash. After a while he became despondent and disillusioned about his own ability and stopped writing altogether. He needed a fresh start and it was then that he decided that he must move to Dublin or beyond.

The Jacob's Biscuits factory in Dublin was at least warm and it just about paid enough for Tom to survive in the capital. Unlike the city itself, the work was painfully dull and alienating. It did however provide enough income for him to enrol in an evening class in English Literature and Composition, which he found uninspiring and costly. However, he developed some discipline by being forced to write regularly. Most of his essays were on his experiences at Jacob's and the lives, some real and some imagined, of the people he worked alongside. His tendency towards realism began to take hold and he found that his preferred style, somewhere between factual journalism and short story fiction, was slowly developing. He began to feel comfortable in himself and with his progress towards becoming a writer. As a result, he decided to endure the classes and shoulder the expense.

His tutor, Michael Higgins, was appreciative of Tom's diligence but singly unimpressed and unmoved by his student's choice of subject matter. He found Tom's work unerringly 'dreary and like the rain, highly predictable'. Tom, in turn, cast Higgins as a failed writer in the Wildean tradition of 'Those who can, do, and those who can't, teach'. Nevertheless, he appreciated Higgins' critical perspective even when they disagreed, which was most of the time. Much to Michael Higgins' amazement and dismay, one of Tom's Jacobs' essays came tied fourth in the Dublin evening class' annual essay competition. Tom took this as a sign that he was on his way to bigger and better things and as a result was intent on taking whatever opportunities came his way.

His move to London was both hasty and ill-thought out.

Two of his Jacob's co-workers had heard about jobs in factories in Enfield, London and had convinced him about the lure of the mighty colonial metropolis. Although he had had thoughts about migrating to England before, he had settled into his new existence as the unofficial Jacob's Biscuits writer-in-residence and wanted to finish his course and above all prove Higgins wrong. In what was a rash and totally uncomprehending turn of mind, he joined the two men on the ferry to England. Somewhere in his subconscious he had estimated there was no point waiting around in Ireland and that his chances of becoming a writer were a lot brighter in London. And so it was on the 13th of May 1936 that he found himself in London.

———

THE STRAND WAS BUSIER than ever in the run up to Christmas and the afternoon was already condensing the notorious London fog and traffic fumes into the sclerotic lung that was the signature of the capital. It was also near-freezing outside and Tom was just glad to be getting out of the worst of it. Christmas was never his favourite time of the year and having no money or future prospects simply reinforced his antipathy to being Joyful and Merry. It was only at times like this that he seriously wished he was somewhere else, otherwise London, albeit crowded, dirty and English, was now his home.

As he entered the Lyon's Coffeehouse, he couldn't recall how they were supposed to recognise each other and it soon dawned upon him that they had failed to arrange a signal of any kind. As luck would have it, there was only one person sitting alone amongst an otherwise sociable set of customers. She was also the only woman without a hat or scarf. Rather small and prim, she was about thirty years of age with hair that was very dark and raised tightly in a perfect bun. She could easily have been taken for the archetypal, spinster librarian. Initially, she didn't look up from her papers and it was only after he had made two rather amateur dramatic style panoramas of the room that she deigned to acknowledge his presence with a question-mark nod of the head. Tom couldn't help but stare at her amazingly large, round, brown eyes. He could see that she already had her afternoon tea, so he ordered a coffee from a passing waitress in the full knowledge that his host would be paying for it. He then went to sit down at her table.

M.G.M Deben was fraught. She had been trying to make contact with Tom Lees for over a week and as she sat at the table waiting to see if he would appear, she couldn't help but think that her reliance on another man, especially such a young man, was already a horrendous mistake. After Walter, she had resolved never to be dependent on any man ever again - in fact, anyone, man or woman. Her success had come through her talent and creativity as a writer, plus her commitment to causes she believed in. And the difficulty and urgency of the situation she now found herself in was one that she was equally determined to overcome. Recruiting this young man was the only practical solution she had in mind.

Mary spotted Tom enter and watched as he looked all around. He was far from arresting; young in the face and lithe in body, he was poorly dressed with all manner of clothes in conflict. His checked shirt and jacket stripes were in a loud conversation with a Paisley tie. Nothing about him was coordinated and she thought his over-large scarf and a flat cap made him look as if he had come straight from a stall in the nearby Covent Garden fruit and vegetable market. When he took off his cap a shock of unkempt straw-coloured hair billowed outwards and upwards. He also had narrow, squinty eyes, the type that for many women signalled a man who was not to be trusted. He obviously needed glasses but like most men, especially Irish men, he probably thought them too unmanly. Mary kept her head deliberately low and made out to be reading as he approached her table.

'Miss Dee-ben? Pleased to meet you. I'm Tom Lees. I got your notes. All of them.'

He went to shake her hand but there was no recognition on her part of his intent. He quickly withdrew the offered hand by removing a non-existent glove. Do you shake hands with women? He wasn't sure. It had taken her no time at all to make him feel uncomfortable, even socially inept.

'It's Deben...like Devon', she snapped without looking up from the table.

She was not about to afford him the opportunity to take the initiative and already had doubts that he was suited for the task she had in mind. She needed to start as she meant to carry on and decided, in that instant, that he had to be put in his place, to know what-is-what and who-is-who. There wasn't much time and he needed to be tested.

'I'm sorry—,' Tom began to feel awkward and uneasy in her presence.

Addressing the table rather than Tom, she replied, 'There's no need to be sorry Mr Lees. Please sit down. It's just that it's not Dee-ben. It's Deb-en, like Devon. Although what's so hard about that, I really don't understand? And it's M.G.M. And that's nothing to do with the motion picture company! This afternoon I'm just 'M. Deben'.

Not once did their eyes meet as she continued to offer up her misgivings about how people had or had not, or should or should not, address her. She just looked beyond him, towards the door and then down at the table. In fact she looked everywhere and anywhere, except at him. All the while her words just flew past without making much sense and without ever coming to a resting place. They seemed to just flow out of her mouth and Tom had great difficulty trying to follow their direction, let alone meaning. In fact he had not followed some of what she had said as her voice was brittle and without inflection. Her philippic was entirely unexpected and unwelcoming and was not what he, or indeed most people, would take to be the way to start a conversation, if indeed that was what was meant. This woman was terribly rude and their meeting had not started at all well. He too was already beginning to feel that the decision to meet her may have been a mistake.

After taking a sip of coffee as respite, Tom asked, 'And this afternoon, what might 'M' stand for?' He tried not to let his tone sound too facetious, but for some reason he thought she deserved it.

'This afternoon I'm Mary...Mary Deben,' she replied without eye contact, 'Now, Mr Lees, can we begin, please?'

Tom felt that getting her first name was a minor victory, a concession of sorts. With no discernible movement she produced a list from under the spread of papers on the table and then went to take some reading glasses from a case, only to realise that they were already hanging by a lanyard around her neck. A quick glimpse was taken to see if Tom had noticed her faux pas; he had, and she knew he had. Both looked slightly embarrassed by the incident and in different circumstances it would have been the occasion for at least a smile.

'I'm not really sure what it is you want me to begin?' he

managed to respond. 'If I may say so, your notes, all of them, were far from clear in that regard.'

'Then why are you here?' she snapped.

'Curiosity ...and the coffee of course'.

There was no hint whatsoever of Mary recognising his attempt at defusing the situation. She simply re-focused on her list and carefully placed the reading glasses on her nose. Tom noticed that she didn't look through the lenses, instead she looked over them at the piece of paper and then, finally, at him. There was a pause as she appeared to use her finger to order the questions to be asked. By now he thought that everything about her was odd and not a little irksome. She, in turn, was confirmed in the thought that he was far too immature for what she had in mind. Could she mould him? Could he be trained up? She tried to think of the possible virtues that may come with his naiveté and lack of experience.

'Is Spain going to be a re-run of Ireland in '22? Does civil war solve anything? Or will it simply entrench the differences for future generations? Did it do any good in Ireland?' she burst forth as if she was speaking down a telephone line.

Tom was taken aback by the rapidity of the questions fired at him and before he could even begin to answer, another volley was on its way.

'And what about the role of the Catholic Church? Are they really Fascists in Spain? Will they side with Hitler and Mussolini if the war spreads to Europe? I have a hundred and one things I need to know and there simply isn't enough time,' her voice crackled in a strange, machine-like monotone.

Meanwhile Tom had wandered back to staring at her eyes and as a result only heard half of what she had just said. He tried to lighten the situation. 'Have I come for a history exam? I've no notes and I've not swotted up. If I had known what you wanted, I could have done some prep! I'm sorry.'

Although he thought he was beginning to come to terms with the strangeness of the situation, all that was happening was that her demeanour was undermining him and he was being forced to resort to quips and asides as a means of defence. He began to feel that she was in a deep conversation with herself and that his whole purpose or role was simply to be there and listen.

'No matter. I don't want your notes Mr Lees, I'd prefer your thoughts. That's why I asked you to meet me here today. Words often mean something completely different when they are spoken, compared to when they are written down. There's a world of difference between what you hear and what you read, and I'm sure even you will appreciate that fact one day. Therefore I'd rather know what you *think* about what happened in Ireland and how it might relate to what's happening right now in Spain.'

'Ireland? And what's happening in Spain? The coup, civil war, or whatever you call it? Do you always start with the easy ones? Could you not find on your list some harder question to start with? Before I might answer, why do you want to know what I think? There are plenty of experts out there, people who know an awful lot more than yours truly.'

This young man definitely needs to be managed, she thought. He was not what she had hoped he'd be and he didn't appear to be serious or even capable of being serious. And the hair! It was entirely distracting. His finger nails were also in need of a good cut and clean. His teeth were, however, acceptably straight and unstained. He couldn't be a smoker, which must be in his favour. In every other respect she thought he was un-honed.

Tom took a swig of coffee by way of making another pause for thought.

'And, if I might say so, what's in this for me? I don't even know who you are. We're complete strangers and I've no idea why I'm here. I'm not even sure I know what it is that you're after? If it's about civil war, Ireland and Spain, everything was in the pieces that I wrote. That's it. That's everything I know, which is really not a lot, if I say so me'self.'

Tom had no idea as to why he had suddenly become both modest and not a little a stupid. As a result of researching his articles, he did indeed know more than it was good for any one person to know about the current situation in Spain, and he already had a very good knowledge of recent Irish history. If he had a mind to, he could answer all her questions quite easily. Yet, after just a few minutes, she had made him feel ignorant and resentful of what he took to be her innate sense of superiority. He had begun to sulk and Mary recognised this. She started to think that he was little more than an overgrown adolescent and that it had indeed been unwise to choose him on the basis of the little he had written and, more significantly, the simple fact that he was Irish and available. On paper, he should have fitted the bill. Nevertheless, she was now desperate and felt that she had little choice but to persist with him. The decision was almost made.

'Work... I can get you work', she said in a now grave, matter-of-fact way. 'You want to be a writer but you obviously still have a lot to learn about how to write. I can get you work, as a journalist, if that's your ambition?' There was a pause, 'I also need a Secretary', she added. As if to reinforce and actively demonstrate her pressing need for clerical assistance, she began another exaggerated reorganisation of her papers.

'A Secretary?' Tom hadn't misheard her and really wanted her to say it again, just for effect.

'Yes, a Secretary or assistant if you prefer? What I need above all else is someone who actually knows about Ireland, the Irish and the current situation in Spain. You see, I'm planning to go there very shortly, Spain that is. As soon as possible in fact and I would like you to accompany me, as my Secretary ...or assistant. My publisher has already agreed to pay you a stipend and the promise of future publication... or at least consideration of your efforts. You'll be more than adequately recompensed I assure you. I hope you understand that I'm offering you more than just a job Mr Lees?'

That she had already agreed his immediate future with her publisher, served only to further generate Tom's resentment of her presumptuousness. How very English of her, he thought.

M.G.M. re-shuffled her papers and made yet another neat pile in a new, new order. Tom sat waiting for her to look up, but to no avail. At the same time and despite their lack of eye contact, he felt she was now actually getting inside his head, penetrating and beginning to mine his thoughts. For all his rather juvenile attempts at bravado, he began to feel that he was already her employee and that she was his new boss. He felt his resistance was all but crumbling.

'You don't know me from Adam and I don't know you! In fact, I haven't a clue who you are! I'm really not your man. I'm not,' Tom pleaded in his defence, albeit he was unconvinced as to what it was he was supposed to be denying or objecting to. He was currently unemployed and had no money in his pocket and here she was offering him some sort of job. And his self-doubt about becoming a writer had recently reached a new nadir, to the extent that his literary ambition had recently been lowered to applying for work in the local library. As with publishers, he didn't even get an answer.

M.G.M. was now genuinely worried that he had shown no real curiosity about her identity. If that were so, his self-centredness was not what she was looking for. Surely, he had tried to find out something about her, anything? She didn't expect him to have any knowledge of her work, but he must have had some interest in finding out who was sending him the notes? For the first time and for more than just a moment she looked Tom fully in the eye. There was another silence during which her mouth pursed and the eyes narrowed. She was trying to read his face, 'I had hoped you would be what I'm looking for, and I still think you may be. Did you attempt to find out about me? It would be odd to say the least if you haven't. You must have been curious to receive my notes? Have you really not looked me up? And you really don't know who I am?'

'Jeez, Miss...Miss Dee-ben...Deben, and forgive me, but are you some sort of crazy woman? Have I heard you right? You want me to go to the war in Spain with you ...as your Se-cre-tary? Will you pinch me and wake me up? Or better still, wake yourself up! That's a really crazy idea. Is this some sort of joke you'd be having? Have the Scribblers put you up to this? If so, I'm sorry...but—' Tom looked around the cafe and tried through his gestures to engage another customer, the waitress, anyone, to share his disbelief at her proposal. Shaking his head, no-one appeared to respond other than to look away from what could have been taken for a lover's tiff of some sort; she was the older, married woman and this was her young man with whom she was now ending their affair.

'The Scribblers?'

'We're a bunch of ... strugglers ...fellow writers here in London.'

'This is not a prank I assure you Mr Lees. I'm deadly serious', Mary paused, thumbed her papers and then resumed.

'As far as the authorities are concerned, I could be your secretary. You'll be a writer, a journalist or correspondent if you will, and I'll be your secretary if necessary. What passport do you travel under? You do have a passport, I hope?'

There was nothing in Mary's face or tone to suggest that her plan was anything but entirely sane and well-considered.

'Of course I have. I've a Free State one,' Tom replied still shaking his head vigorously.

'Perfect, I thought as much. That will help resolve any accreditation issues we might have. Now, I may even try to get myself an Irish passport, but I'm afraid that may take a while. By then, of course, it may be too late, the war in Spain could well be all over. What do you think?' She fixed a stare and then raised her chin in expectation of his response.

'Wait, wait up now Miss Deben. I'm not going to be yours, or any other woman's, Secretary. I've also no intention or inclination to go to Spain. I don't actually speak the lingo and that is a real, bloody war going on there you know! I don't think you should be running away with yourself and your plans. Secretary? Now I won't be after being called that, officially or unofficially, and for no woman.'

Mary was incensed by his response, 'Why ever not?'

The other customers began to avert their eyes from the unfolding scene.

'Because ...because it's not right!'

'Not right? For any man? Or just in your case? We have, after all, already got Secretaries of State, Secretaries for War, Permanent Secretaries, the Home Secretary?'

'That's not the same and you know it. A secretary is a secretary and being a secretary is not ...it's not a man's job, especially if...if his boss is a woman. Most right-minded people would say so.' Tom found himself struggling to put his argument together. He didn't actually like the term 'right-minded people' but he couldn't at that moment think of who else might support him. Even the 'man-in-the-street' and the 'man on the Clapham Omnibus' seemed somewhat distant allies.

'Have you ever really thought about the meaning of the word 'Secretary' Mr Lees? It means a keeper of secrets. Somehow and for some reason I thought you might be very good at that?'

'Thank you, but was that a compliment? No, I've not thought about the word before or the job ...until this very minute. I'm Irish and, as you might know, we Irish don't keep secrets, for very long at least. In fact I'd say we're downright hopeless at it. We have the gift-of-the-gab and all that. We're loquacious. Had you not heard?'

'That's not how you strike me, not at all. You're certainly quite loquacious but also somewhat secretive I'd say. You appear very reluctant, it seems, to say what you actually think, and even less what you actually know. You're guarded in perhaps a typically Irish way. There are probably more secrets and male secretaries in Ireland than you think. And those secrets, the ones you believe you are not very good at keeping, may in fact be ones that you deliberately let slip in order to protect the real ones. You see, I too have always found that that bit of the Irish that is inside me...yes, I'm half-Irish....is nothing like the Irish that is supposedly on the outside. What people see and who I am are most definitely not the same thing.'

'You're Irish? I'd never have thought it!' Tom exclaimed, shaking his head vigorously.

'Exactly, I always say I'm *half*-Irish...on my father's side.'

The way in which Mary had drifted seamlessly, as if on a wave of thought, into the subject of the Irish character intrigued Tom. For the first time he found himself trying to listen intently and agreeing and yet all the while trying not to agree with her. Her voice had also changed. It had mellowed and become almost ethereal as she developed her train of thought. But was she real, or was all this rehearsed? Is this some sort of game? he thought.

'If you don't take up my offer you will regret it and you may even do so for the rest of your life. This could be a once-in-a-lifetime opportunity; you may be on the cusp of attaining your ambition to become a writer, an author even. Believe me, I know, I was once in your position myself.'

'You've done this before? I can't believe that! Gone off to a war with a complete stranger?'

'No, but I got married. And yes, at the time, I suppose we were still something of strangers.'

'Marriage as war?'

'Yes. I think that, after a fashion, marriage can be a sort of civil war.'

'I don't get yer there. A sort of civil war?'

'Marriage can turn out to be civil war of sorts. Couples believe they have many, many things in common. They think they understand each other and they may even love each other. But that's not enough for a successful marriage, as I know from personal experience. You see, I think you can know each other too well. Total familiarity leaves nothing for the imagination. And it strikes me that it's just the same in a civil war. You can, it seems, know your enemy too well and as a result any differences, no matter how slight, are necessarily exaggerated. They become more pronounced than they really are. That's probably why they are often much more bitter and savage than other wars. It must sometimes feel like you are fighting a version of yourself.'

Tom was rather embarrassed by how forthright she was now being. She was also more animated.

'There now, you've just given me an absolutely brilliant idea. I could travel under my ex-husband's name! Yes, why not?' She looked away and then down at her cup and took a sip of tea. For his part, Tom could now hardly swallow his coffee. There was a pause and then she said:

'I'm sorry, but you have rather disappointed me Mr Lees'.

'Please, please call me Tom,' he feebly interrupted as a defence.

'Tom?' 'Yes, this morning ...and this afternoon. All day and every day in fact. It's Tom. That's short for Tomás...T.O.M.A.S. It's Irish.'

'There is no need for the sarcasm Mr Lees. It doesn't impress me.'

Despite her now many misgivings, Mary thought that she had little or no alternative but to continue with the task of getting him to accompany her. There was simply no time to find someone else. He could learn; he was quick-witted, if nothing else. But he would have to learn very quickly.

'I'm offering you an opportunity, an adventure and, as they say, a chance to 'record history in the making'. You'll also be earning some money, not a lot, but I would hazard a guess more than you earn now. As anyone and everyone in this room can in fact see, I'm a lot older than you. Well perhaps, not a lot older, but older nevertheless. I should say I'm also a lot wiser than you. I'm certainly a lot more experienced than you in o' so many things, politics, travel, love and life, to name but a few. I'm obviously a more successful writer than you, judging by our respective published titles. And I would say I'm better informed than you, especially perhaps about women? I may even be physically stronger than you by the looks of things. Moreover, I'm financially more comfortable than you, again albeit not overly so, I would hasten to add. In short, I can certainly afford you and I do in fact really need you. Will you come to Spain with me ...as ...my eyes and ears?'

'You can *afford* me?' Tom's exclamation echoed around the room to every onlooker's embarrassment. 'Now there's a nice way of putting it!'

The offence of the obviously carefully chosen word was already doing its work. His repeating of it only made him feel worse about his relative worth, in each and every one the departments she had enumerated. The idea of going to the war in Spain paled into insignificance by comparison.

As Tom shrank, Mary seemed to grow and occupy the high ground. Her diminution of his existence continued unabated and he couldn't fathom whether he was submitting or she was conquering. He found himself just listening to the implied denigration of his one undoubted achievement, that of getting this far in his troubled life. He had by then decided that he had never before met anyone, man or woman, quite like her and she had almost won him over.

'Yes, I can afford to support and teach you. I promise you will learn more from me than any man. I believe you would be more than a fool to turn down this opportunity. Please don't play the Irish fool.'

'The Irish fool? Is that really necessary?'

Tom objected to the slur on his national character, although he half agreed with the fact of the matter. He was indeed beginning to think he might actually be a real fool to pass up this extraordinary opportunity and this extraordinary woman.

'I speak as someone who has herself been more than half-an-Irish fool in the past. You have to admit, we Irish appear to have the knack of doing foolish things or, rather, doing things foolishly.'

He now felt the urge to say something that he hoped would sound equally, if not even more, profound by way of a reply.

'The fact that I'm Irish and you being half-Irish and all, doesn't actually mean that much to me. You see, Miss Deben, I'm not one of those people who looks back all the time. Really, I've no time for the past or harping back at history. If I had my way, I'd forget it all. What matters is what happens today. In Ireland it's always been myths and faeries and the like. We're great ones for the cock'n' bull stories. I'm sure we invented the epic, not the Greeks and it was probably in a pub in Limerick. The Free State hasn't changed any of that. I'd say it's made it worse. All the tradition, the freedom fighting, the pride and the piety is mostly, please excuse my language ...bollocks. We Irish are always fighting the war that started the century before last. It's hypocrisy. The Free State was only half-born and it shows no sign of ever cutting the umbilical cord to the British and growing up independent. In fact, it'll never grow up, in my view, whilst those who live with their noses in the history books are in charge. All they have is their mythical past. The real past was really very dark. Bad things happened and they continue to happen. But no one wants to tell the truth. They're so busy reinventing the past, they've no vision of a future. They've no time, especially when they're shackled to a Church that insists on blocking all vision. It's all about protecting their disinfected version of the past. They can't even face the present. That's why so many of us leave as soon as we can. Nothing changes back home. History just repeats itself, with the same crowd running things. It's only the rain, the Catholic Church and money that make the grass appear greener in Ireland ...but only for some.' Tom stopped and tried to gauge Mary's response. She just looked at him in a way that suggested he should continue, 'Do you know there are no moles in Ireland?'

'Moles?'

'Yes, the dark little creatures. It's not just snakes we've none of, although the human variety are still there alright! We've no moles and do you know why? We have the men dressed in black instead! And, as we all know, they are near-blind creatures; they only see what they want to see. They're voracious eaters as well. I'm told they consume their own body weight every day, whilst other little creatures go hungry or even starve. Everyone knows they're also incredibly destructive. They dig up any garden that gives pleasure, just for the sake of it. That's why we have no moles. We have the priests.' Mary remained just looking at him and Tom felt he should finish his diatribe, 'There, I've said it. I've no illusions about the Irish State or state of Ireland. In fact I'm glad to be away from it all. That's why I left the place because of all that fecking historical and religious shite. Again, please excuse my language! I'm sorry. It gets me going.'

'You're not such a fool after all. So you'll take the position I'm offering you?' she pressed him.

'I won't be after being called your Secretary.'

'As I've already said, as far as the authorities are concerned, I might actually have to be your secretary. You can play what you are - an 'up-and-coming' writer. I do want you to keep a secret however. My work and my sympathies are, if you had cared to inquire, too well-known for me to go to Spain as myself. The Government side, the Republicans, would not welcome me, least of all the Communist part of it, after my book on the Soviet Union. Therefore I have no choice but to go to the rebel, the Fascist side. They won't know who I am as I'm told they seldom read anything other than the Bible or Mein Kampf. In any case, it will probably be the winning side by the looks of things and it'll be less dangerous for that. They say 'only the victors write history', but I don't want that to happen. There's always at least two sides to it, if not more. Everyone has a story to tell.'

'So that's what this is all about? That's what you actually want to do, collect material for a book? Is it a novel? You want to collect some characters, a story-line, a context? You're the mad one alright!'

'Why else would I go? I'm a writer. The cause? Perhaps, but I'm really not sure what the great causes are any more. I believe in peace but I'm not really a pacifist. I was once a Socialist but could never be a Communist. I hate the Fascists but don't really understand what they stand for. I only know what they are against. I am however for the Spanish people and I'm against war. That's why I need to find out, for myself what's going on ...but I need your help. I'm a writer and I can write, but I need to know what it is I'm to write about before I can write whatever that might be. Do you understand what I am saying?' her head tilted to one side and rested with a quizzical raising of an eyebrow.

Once again Tom found himself floundering as a result of her intensity. He felt that she was at last showing something else, her real self? The withdrawn, cold and rude woman he had met earlier was now bathed in some warmth, even emotion.

'And what would I actually be doing at the war? Is that how you should say it, *at* the war? I don't want to be *in* it.'

'As a woman, I've been told that they won't let me go to certain places, especially to the front. I won't be allowed to speak to certain people, officers mainly, on the Nationalist side. Regrettably, I'm going to need you, a man, to do that for me. That's why you'll need to act as my eyes and ears.'

Tom tried to get back to the practicalities and the possible escape routes from the madcap adventure she had in mind.

'And how do you propose we get to Spain?'

'By train of course...via Paris and South to the border.' This was said as a statement of fact rather than an attempt at her own humour.

'I meant with the papers. Aren't there special papers? Accreditation or whatever it's called. Don't you need special permissions?' Tom was now trying to construct as many obstacles as he could to put in the path of the nonsense she was suggesting they embark upon. 'It seems mighty desperate to employ a stranger so that you can get to go to a war and just to write a bleeding book!'

'This is not just any war. What's happening in Spain could determine the future of the whole Continent and indeed the entire world order. I thought you, of all people, would appreciate that. It's not just Spaniards fighting each other. The Germans, Italians, Russians and even the French and the British could become embroiled very quickly. Who knows, this might be the beginning of the Second Great War? That's why I need to go there. I have to see for myself. We need to understand this madness now. Everyone needs to know what is going on if we are to do something about stopping it.'

'We? You want to go to a war in order to stop a war, only a bigger one? And you think you can do that by writing about it! Good luck to you! I may be a fool, even an Irish fool, but like Ireland I think I'm going to be neutral in all this.' He scoffed and continued, 'The Spanish Republic is already a right mess and the Fascists will be no better. I'll not be taking part in saving Spain from itself. We all need to save ourselves. Perhaps Russia will save them? All us Irish, even yourself, if you have any sense, should steer well clear of all that as well. Mark my words, nothing of any good can come of it. Spain will end up worse than Ireland ever did after our own senseless war. What comes of it won't just be half born, it'll be a monster, a Frankenstein. I think you are best off leaving it to others to write about it, I really do'.

'Frankenstein was the doctor, not the monster.'

'It'll still be a mess.'

Mary paused and Tom averted his eyes. There was a brief silence and the customers in the café appeared to be waiting for the next instalment. She then resumed the examination, 'Are you entirely apolitical? Do you not have an ideology of your own? Neither Left nor Right? You're not a Socialist or a Fascist? A Democrat? A Liberal perhaps? You must believe in something?'

'Plague on all their houses! I've no time for politics or politicians. They're all grafters...Left and Right. I don't get involved. Democracy is a shambles, everywhere. How can you have democracy when there's so much bloody ignorance?'

'You have no principles? Justice? Equality? Freedom? None of those matter to you?'

'This is no time for principles! We all have to look after

ourselves. Politics and politicians won't do that; we need to look out for ourselves. Everyone needs to know what's going on to start with.'

'Then you do agree with me? We need to know. I thought as much. I need my 'eyes and ears' not to be too contaminated and you fit the bill perfectly. I need an unbiased observer; and you're exactly what I need.' She looked at Tom and for the first time the faintest trace of a smile was on her face, 'The trouble is, you're also a bit ill-informed. You are simply and factually wrong about the Irish, they're not keeping out of it. Perhaps you don't know everything Mr Lees?'

Using his proper name was deliberately calculated to relegate him back to the role of the immature and ignorant listener. After taking the measure of this demotion, she continued.

'I said I was better informed than you and I obviously am. I'm told, as we speak, there are already hundreds of Irish volunteers for the Rebel side waiting to board a ship in Galway. They say it's a German, a Nazi, ship that's picking them up. The Irish 'Blueshirts' are being led by some IRA civil war hero - a General O'Duffy? Or had you not heard?'

Tom knew about O'Duffy and his Blueshirts, but did not want to signal this to Mary. This was largely because her tone had gone into what he thought now sounded like a sneering contempt of the Irish. Her voice struck him as dismissive of the idea that there could be a meaningful Irish intervention in anything outside of the island of Ireland. He thought she made it sound as if the whole thing was a caper, just another ill-fated and foolish Irish adventure. It was this conception of the Irish and their character rather than O'Duffy's insane mission that he really objected to. So much so in fact, he now wanted to prove her wrong, by going with her to Spain. His mind was all but made up. Mary had stopped for another sip of what by then must have been stone-cold tea. Finally, she confessed the main reason that she had chosen him.

'That's where you could be most useful to me. I want us to go with them...the Irish volunteers ...to Spain. I can get you accreditation from Ireland. You're hardly known there if at all. In fact, no-one I've spoken to knows of you or what you have written. I have contacts in the newspapers and you will be able to go as a special war correspondent, a freelance of course, but assigned to do some work for one of the nationals, the *Irish Press* most likely. I shall accompany you. If the Spanish authorities or the Rebels don't recognise my own accreditation as a correspondent, I'll go as your secretary. I shall travel under my husband's –my ex-husband's - name. It'll be Mary Porteus. Only, as we both know, I shall, in reality, be the writer and you will in fact be my secretary... sorry, my assistant. That, after all, is what secretaries do, they keep secrets. It'll be our secret.'

'Mary Porteus? Ex-husband?'

'Yes. We're not yet divorced. So I can still travel under his name.' Mary looked up and asked directly, 'Are you in any sort of relationship?'

Tom seemed reluctant to engage and looked around the café. Almost under his breath he replied, 'No. No sort of... relationship.'

'No-one at all?'

'If I was, I think that that would be my business.'

'There would be no ties then? No-one to chase after you?'

'No, no one... and there never has been.'

'No family?'

'No one.'

5

TIGHE

IT WAS STILL DARK OUTSIDE AND GRACE HID HERSELF BENEATH the blankets to await the dawn. The cottage was too cold to raise herself, even though she desperately needed to use the toilet. As the room brightened with the first rays of morning light, she could postpone the trip to the privy no longer. Casting on her heavyweight coat that hung on the door and slipping into her Wellington boots, she made her way shivering to the outside lavatory. Just before entering, she remembered that she needed to re-stock with toilet paper. After going back into the cottage, and in the interest of good time-management, she put the kettle on and collected her last roll of British No.3 Pure Tissue before braving the facility. After British No.3 it would be the *Irish Independent*, she told herself. Outside it was drizzling a mix of rain and freezing mist. The grey, rain-filled clouds were very low and the waves were small white horses riding the bay on the morning tide. The quiet and general stillness of the scene made it feel as if time itself had almost stopped. Even the sea gulls had stayed in bed this morning, she mused. The toilet increasingly beckoned as the cold began to make itself felt on her now hard-pressed bladder.

As she opened the toilet door a small figure unfurled itself from the old sack that she used to stop the toilet pan freezing over. It was a very young boy and he said nothing. He just stood staring at her and Grace was momentarily dumbstruck by the discovery. The young lad looked very frightened and began shaking his head from side to side in some form of involuntary reflex. He was very thin, even emaciated, rather dirty and obviously very cold. Grace forgot the reason for her outing and stood staring back at the creature. Eventually she said, 'And who are you? What're you doing here?' She spoke softly but firmly.

The boy did not answer and remained shaking. He quickly turned his face away from her.

'Who *are* you? What are you doing here?' she tried again, only a little louder.

The boy turned and went as if to make his escape. Grace held on to the door and stood across the entrance to bar the way.

'Sorry Miss. Sorry. Let me go...please,' he begged.

'Tell me who you are first and why are you in my toilet?' At which point she remembered her reason for being outside in the cold. 'Come out, now!'

'Let me go Miss. I'll go...I'll go.' He stayed on the spot and was now trembling.

'You still haven't told me who you are and what you're doing here.' Grace's bladder was now getting impatient.

'I'm from...my name's Kevin,' he stuttered. 'But they call me Tighe,' he said somewhat proudly.

'Tighe? Why Tighe?

'Don't know Miss. They just do.'

'Where are you from Tighe and what are you doing here?'

'From the village Miss.'

'The village? Letterfrack?'

'Yes Miss. Down the road.'

'Do you live there? Have you any family?'

'No Miss.'

Grace detected something amiss,

'You're not from 'round here are you? You're not local?'

'No Miss.'

'Where are you from?'

'Enniscorthy Miss.'

'Enniscorthy! That's a long way from Letterfrack!'

'Yes Miss. I know Miss.'

'Are you from the School?'

Tighe looked away and paused before answering, 'Yes Miss.'

Grace realised that this examination was taking some time and meanwhile she was getting colder and more in need of using the toilet. Her dilemma was whether to release the boy, let him run, or carry on the interrogation inside the cottage. His size posed no threat as, although he was also quite as tall as her, he was also very thin. His fearful manner and rigid politeness was enough however to reassure her that he was unlikely to do her any harm. She now looked at him more benignly and he reminded her of every Dickensian ragamuffin, waif or stray.

'Do you know how to make tea?' she asked.

'Yes Miss, I think so.' He looked at her quite quizzically, as if the question was really odd.

'Would you like some?'

'Yes Miss, please. It's fecking cold out here!' He let slip

the profanity and, realising it quickly covered his mouth. 'Sorry Miss,' he muffled behind his hand.

'You're right, it is *fecking* cold,' Grace echoed with half a smile. 'Come out. I need to go.'

He looked slightly embarrassed by her admission and possibly the very thought that women used toilets at all. The boy slowly and cautiously emerged and followed her into the cottage, where the living room was now full of steam and condensation from the kettle which had been boiling all the while.

'It's fecking cold in here!' he muttered.

'It is, and please stop now with that language,' Grace said firmly.

'Sorry Miss.'

'The kettle's boiled. The pot's there and the cups. The tea's next to them. You make the tea and I'll be back. Don't be touching anything else.'

Grace went back outside wondering what she might meet her on return. Would he still be there? Would he have robbed her? She went to the outhouse and relieved herself as quickly as she could. On her return Tighe had made the tea and now stood to attention by the long dead fire.

'Would you like me to light it?' he indicated the ash lying in the grate.

'No, I'll do it myself. You pour the tea and while you're at it, tell me why you're here.'

He gave her a pitiful look and she could see that he was thinking as to whether he shoduld divulge his motive. He started to pour the tea.

'I was going back to Enniscorthy and I got lost up the road there. So I thought...I thought I'd take some shelter out of the rain,' he said, not looking at her but focussing on filling the cups.

'In my toilet?'

'Yes Miss. But I didn't use it, I promise.'

'Now tell me why you are *really* here?' Grace asked more intently, sensing that his story was just that.

'I *was* trying to go home. But I didn't know the way and I got lost. Really, that's the truth, I *didn't* mean to come down here I promise.' He stopped his pouring and looked at Grace.

Grace thought that she should try another tack.

'But where have you come from? Letterfrack you say? The Orphanage?'

'Yes Miss. The School they mostly call it.'

'You've run away?'

There was a pause. 'Yes Miss.'

'Will they know? Will they know that you've gone?'

'Yes Miss. By now they'll be after me alright. At Mass or at breakfast they'll see I'm not there.'

'Then you had better go back.'

'No...No Miss, I'm not going back there. I'd rather...I'll throw myself in the sea before that. I'll hang myself first! I can't go back.' His agitation forced him to put his cup down.

Grace rebuked him at the very thought of harming himself. 'Don't be so stupid! You'll have to go back. They'll be looking for you. You've nowhere else to go.'

'No Miss, please. Please don't send me back,' he begged through a loud sob.

She looked at him and couldn't help but feel sorry for his utter desperation.

'Why? Why did you run away?'

There was another long pause and they both took some tea. He was about to answer but then hesitated. She thought it best to let him think awhile and began to attend the fire. There was a long pause before he spoke.

'They'll beat me Miss,' he said meekly.

'What?' Grace looked up and was obviously surprised at what she thought she had just heard.

'They'll beat me Miss.'

'Who will?'

'The Brothers ... they'll flog me alright.'

'Beat you? Why would they do that?'

'All sorts. They do all sorts, especially if you'd run off like.'

'I'm sure you are exaggerating. Of course, if you cause them the trouble, you should expect some punishment, don't you think?' Grace said.

'Yes Miss....but—,' he was momentarily lost for words. 'I ran away because they beat me and do other things. You get beaten if you run away and you get beaten if you stay. Makes no difference. That's why I bunked off. I'll get another flogging I know it. They all do it.' The boy looked away and clutched his hands very tightly, as if imagining the strokes that were coming his way.

Grace could see he had tears in his eyes. They were welled and when he thought she had noticed he looked down and away before wiping them on his sleeve. There was another silence. Grace busied herself with the fire and managed to light the kindling. Tighe cuddled his tea cup and watched her every move. He was becoming more wretched by the minute and had also started to shiver and shake again. Grace fetched a blanket from her bed and wrapped it around him. He smiled his thanks.

'Are you hungry?' she asked.

'Starving Miss!' He had an outsize mouth which gaped at the thought of food and all Grace could see was a very hungry young boy. In that moment he appeared to have forgotten his plight.

'I'll make you a sandwich. Do you eat eggs?'

'Yes, anything Miss. I'll murder an egg, if you have one?'

She prepared them both a fried egg sandwich and they sat around the hearth to eat them. He ravaged the food and she scolded him to slow down or get indigestion. He ignored her and the sandwich was no sooner in his hand than gone. She made him another. More tea was poured and she began to think about what to do next.

'What if I take you back? I could explain to them.'

'No Miss, please. Don't take me back. They'll still kill me,' he pleaded.

'They'll not kill you. But you have to go back. Where else have you to go?'

'Anywhere. I'll make my way home.'

'Don't be silly! How old are you?'

'Twelve Miss. I think I'm twelve.'

'Twelve? You think?'

'Don't rightly know. I've forgot. They don't let us have birthdays and I can't remember the last.'

'What d'you mean, 'they don't let you have birthdays'? Grace couldn't comprehend the idea of not being allowed a birthday.

'They just don't.'

'The Brothers?'

'Yes Miss. There's only one birthday that counts they say, Jesus Christ's!' He broke into a broad smile and shook his head at this edict.

'Do other boys run off?' she asked.

'All the time. Some get away, most don't.'

'They're caught and returned?'

'Yes Miss. The Garda usually catch us.'

'And what happens when they come back?'

'Like I said, we get beaten rotten. Head's shaved and

other stuff. The hose, marching...working...all sorts. It depends on the Brother. Some are hard, others just give you the leather.'

'They shave your heads?' Grace was genuinely shocked at the thought.

'All the time. It marks you and they all know you've done a runner if you've no hair. And you get belted and all. It goes on for weeks, 'til you hair grows again. They don't let you forget. They think you'll not run away again 'suppose.' This was all recounted by the boy as a matter-of-fact.

'Have you lost your parents? Are they dead? Is that why you're at the Orphanage?'

'No Miss! I only lost me Da. Well, he ran off before I knew him. But I've me Ma. She's back in Enniscorthy.'

'So you're not an orphan at all?'

'No parents you mean? Most of us aren't. Most have a Ma somewhere. Some have both still. They got a Da and a Ma. I've only got a Ma.'

'Then why are you there? How long have you been at the School?'

'Don't know Miss. I've forgot. Long-time though,' he was shaking his head in an effort to remember.

'And you've no idea why you're there?'

'Must have done something wrong...but I don't know what it was. No-one says. I don't remember doing anything, but I must have. I thought I might have stolen something. If I did, I can't remember what it was. So it can't have been much, can it?'

'When did you go there? How old might you have been?'

'I don't know. It was years ago and I just remember being small. Could have been six or seven or, I don't rightly know Miss.'

'Some time ago then?'

'Don't know Miss. I was too small to remember.'

Grace was feeling ever more distraught as the boy's story unfolded. Her dilemma as to what to do next was growing, as was her wish to simply enfold him in her arms. She had not had such a feeling since Tom.

Suddenly, there was a loud knock on the door. Tighe froze and Grace was also taken aback.

'It's them', he trembled and went as if to hide behind his chair.

'Stay there. Don't move. Let me see,' Grace whispered.

'It's them!' He struggled once more to hold back the tears. 'Don't send me back. Please Miss. Please.'

The knock on the door was repeated, even louder this time.

'Stay there. Be quiet. Let me see who it is.'

Before she could get to the door she heard John Fahey's voice,

'Miss Grace, are you there?'

She turned to the boy and tried to reassure him.

'It's just a friend. It's alright. It's a friend.' Tighe was not convinced and shook his head by way of appealing for her not to open the door.

'John, you're early?' Grace tried to normalise things as best she could.

'Where is he Miss Grace, the boy?' John inquired quietly and all the while trying to peer over her shoulder into the room. She stepped closer towards him and cut down his view.

'What boy?' she pretended. 'What are you talking about?'

'He was seen coming down here and they haven't seen

him come out. He's here isn't he?' Grace knew he had the boy's scent.

'He says they'll beat him if he goes back,' she said in a whisper.

'That they will,' John said without any emotion. 'That they will.'

'But—' Grace was lost for words.

John made his way past Grace and into the kitchen. Tighe stood quite still. Fleetingly, he made to look for an escape route but John was already upon him.

'Now lad, you'd better come with me.'

'No Miss...don't...don't let him,' he cried out to Grace.

'You must—' Grace couldn't think of anything else to say. She simply nodded to John the necessary permission to take the boy. 'I'm sorry. You must go back. You can't stay here,' she eventually managed to utter the words she did not want to hear herself say.

'Just let me go. Just let me go. I'll not bother you. I promise.'

'They're waiting up the road,' John said. 'It's too late. She can't let you stay. They know you're here. That's why they sent for me to bring you out.' He moved on the boy.

'Please.....please Miss,' Tighe screamed in real anguish.

'Tighe I can't—'

'Tighe is it?' said John as he took hold of the boy's arm. 'Come on now, let's not be causing any more trouble for the lady.'

Tighe tried to resist John's grip but couldn't. As he was being led out he turned to Grace and in a voice which belied his years shouted into her face,

'Bitch! Fecking bitch! You're all the same. Fecking bitch!'

John slapped him once around the face and shuffled him past Grace who was terrified by his outburst. She stood frozen and watched them leave the cottage. Almost immediately John came back still clinging on to the boy and threw the blanket Tighe had had around him onto the floor. As he was marched to his cruel fate, Grace watched from the window and felt completely helpless, even complicit in what might happen to him next.

6

INTO SPAIN

Tom felt like he was being corralled into the front car of the Press corps convoy that was heading towards Cáceres, where the Irish Brigade were currently stationed. There were five other vehicles in the convoy, plus a Nationalist military lorry which had been temporarily decommissioned in order to carry their luggage across the border. Mary had joined one of the cars at the rear as her request to travel with Tom had been refused, albeit politely, on the grounds that all the women must travel together. This made little or no logistical sense but both Tom and Mary were keen not to create a fuss and stand out from the crowd. They complied with the instruction. As they were parted for the first time since leaving London, Tom felt strangely alone and vulnerable. The journey was to take an arduous twelve hours and, if all went according to plan, there were to be stops in Burgos, Valladolid and Salamanca, all recent Fascist conquests.

Opening the passenger side door, Tom came face-to-face with one of the most renowned war correspondents of the age, Captain James McIlroy. Leathery-faced and with deep, sunken eyes, this veteran reporter looked even older than his sixty-seven years. Whilst not completely wizened, he certainly looked reptilian. From gossip at the hotel bar and elsewhere, Tom already knew of his reputation and was unnerved at finding himself in this particular man's company. This already felt like it was going to be a very long journey.

McIlroy was a veteran in every sense of the word. He was a veritable encyclopaedia of conflict in the twentieth century, albeit his accounts had become increasingly jaundiced of late. As if having covered the Russo-Japanese war of 1904, the Turkish civil war of 1909, the Portuguese revolution of 1910, a whole handful of Balkan wars, the conflict in Morocco and the Italian invasion of Tripoli in 1911 was insufficient, he went to the Eastern Front and served with the British army in Gallipoli in the Great War. And as if that was still not enough conflict for one man in one lifetime, he then returned to Russia and covered the Bolshevik revolution and the Siberian 'Intervention' by Allied troops in 1918. Later, he also managed to get himself arrested by the Red Army. Insatiate or by then simply mad, he then reported on the civil war in Mexico in the 1920s and it was there that he had honed his belligerent defence of the Catholic faith and his virulent anti-Communism. By the time McIlroy had arrived in Spain, the gnarled, old reporter had been contemplating retirement. Now, he appeared to be less committed to the art of reporting and was more intent on pursuing a mission to 'Defend the Faith'. Nothing, it appeared, was going to keep him away from the current conflict.

McIlroy was already drawing on a cigarette and Tom thought he smelt of last night's whiskey. Surprisingly, the veteran reporter broke the ice.

'Did you see her, Carney?' he inquired in his broad Anglo-Irish accent. He was not looking at Tom and was instead struggling to peer out of the rear window of the car. His large frame made the task nigh on impossible.

'No, sorry...who?' Tom replied, trying to move out of his way.

'That tower of shit.' McIlroy snorted. 'That huge fecking tower of shit following me around everywhere.'

'No...sorry...I don't know who—' Tom was completely at a loss to know what or who the old man was referring to.

'That bloody bitch on stilts. You must have seen her? You couldn't have bloody missed her! How could you miss her? Carney, that huge pile of shit! There, in the car back there! She's in the car back there! I can see her. Look! You can't bloody miss her! The damn woman has no right to be here! She's not qualified. She's no experience of war and she can't write to save her life. She's never been to a boxing match let alone a fecking war! And that stupid shit of a man, Geary, only sent her so he could get away from her! It's a bloody scandal that she's here! Do you know what she writes? A fucking Women's page. A Woman's page! So Geary, the sheep's arse of an editor of the *Independent,* sees fit to send her here, to the fecking front...with me! With me for Christ's sake! What is the world coming to? It's insane. It's more than bloody insane, it's fucking demeaning!'

Tom looked even more bewildered on hearing the volley of vitriol that had just been sent his way. He knew that he needed to change the subject fast.

'I'm Tom Lees'

'McIlroy' he said as he tried to turn towards the front, 'James McIlroy.'

'Yes, I thought so,' Tom replied.

McIlroy had managed to turn and face towards the front of the car at last. 'Lees? Who you with Lees?'

'I'm freelance, but mostly working for *The Press*', Tom said proudly. It felt good to say he was accredited.

'The fecking *Press*! De Valera's pap? Come to do his bidding eh? I didn't think they had anyone over here? On the other side perhaps, but not here, not with this fecking rabble! You're on the wrong side my boy! You should be over there, with the Reds!'

'I chose to come here.'

'What the fuck! Some choice! Sending boys to do a man's job now are they? You're new to the game I'd say? You actually look green my boy. Shitting yourself? Your first war? Make the most of it sonny, it could be your last', McIlroy snorted. The old man was already warming to the task of mocking his young passenger, 'Tom you say? Green Tom I suggest.'

'Yes, I am...but no...I'm not ...shit...Yes, I'm new to it,' Tom tried to respond but gave up when the words tumbled out.

'I suppose you can't be any worse than that towering turd Carney!'

For the remainder of the journey, and interrupted only by a regular and always vicious criticism of Ethel Carney, McIlroy continued with a diatribe against Spanish drivers, Spanish roads, Spanish food, Spanish wine; in fact all things Spanish and especially their tendency to bath *'everything'* in olive oil, *'if they bathed at all'*. Tom tried not to listen but McIlroy's penetrating voice made this impossible. In any case, he soon realised that here was a man one should not make an enemy of because he was obviously not averse to slicing everyone and anyone into tiny pieces and feeding them to whoever cared to listen. Once or twice he thought he caught a glint in old man's eye when he passed on an indiscretion about one or more of the other correspondents in the convoy. Tom had discovered that McIlroy was an incorrigible gossip.

Thereafter the journey became an extended lecture on 'journalism according to the principles of McIlroy'. Tom was learning and learning fast. His first lesson was that he knew he did not want to become what McIlroy had become, a narrow-minded, cynical and distorted purveyor of mistruths and untruths. As they rattled along the broken roads and through the war torn landscape, Tom's increasing dislike of what McIlroy had become as a journalist was met in equal measure by a grudging admiration for the miserable old sod's indefatigability. Unlike his caustic denunciation of virtually all the other foreign war correspondents, McIlroy actually refrained from offending the young man sitting next to him. Perhaps the veteran saw something of his former self in 'Green Tom'? Whatever the reason, Tom took it as a rare mercy not to be on the end of his sharp, vicious tongue.

Tom soon noticed how McIlroy would fly the Irish flag for convenience whenever it suited. Judged by his inter-changeable 'fecks and 'fucks', he was equally at home with being Irish one minute and English the next. It seemed to depend on the personal or political advantage that could be gained and writing for both the *Irish Independent* and the English *Daily Mail* perfectly mirrored his national transposability.

'We're on a Crusade young man and you're with the new Crusaders here. You know that don't you?' McIlroy exclaimed. 'I presume you're a Catholic?'

'I was brought up one,' Tom admitted.

'Brought up one? That sounds more a lapsed-Catholic that I'm hearing?'

'Lapsed? Yes, I suppose I am. I'm not regular,' Tom was

reluctant to answer as he sensed the direction of the discussion.

'You won't be after you've seen what the fecking Reds have done here! My God, you'll find your faith again I bet you! Have you any idea as to what they have been up to? They're out to exterminate all Catholics, all Christians...all religion! The Communists want atheism to rule and murdering the clergy is just the start. They'll have to murder all believers. I saw that for myself in Soviet Russia and Mexico in '26. The Devil himself is behind all Bolshevism.'

'The Devil himself?' So that's why it's a crusade?' Tom replied trying not to sound facetious.

'That's right. We're here, the Irish are here, to 'Defend the Faith' just like the Crusaders did. Just like the Wild Geese did. Mark my words, the very survival of the Church is the prize. This is going to be no ordinary fight. It's Godless tyranny versus our duty to God! For once, it couldn't be any clearer. And you're here to witness it. You don't know lucky you are my boy, if you survive that is.'

'You actually believe it is as simple as that: Communism or Catholicism?'

'Catholicism or Communism, yes. What else? Spain has been chosen and we shall be God's witnesses.'

'And the Fascists and democracy?' Tom knew he was heading into deeper waters and was now in danger of simply provoking the old man.

'Bollocks! Makes no difference. There's certainly no democracy under Communism. Spain doesn't know democracy, never has. It makes no fucking difference what system they have. This is bigger than Spain. It's being free to practice your religion that counts, not how you vote or how much bloody tax you pay. Freedom of conscience is all that matters. Freedom to practice your faith. They'll be no call for voting in heaven.'

'And the Fascists? Will they let people pray the way they want? Will there be freedom of conscience once they're in power?' Tom knew he was beginning to goad the old man.

'The Fascists are simply a means to an end, that's all. God's chosen instrument to rid us of the Reds. We Catholics can live with the insurgents for the time being. As long as they let the people practice their religion without interference, they might as well support Franco. He has to be better than the fecking Communists. He's a Catholic.'

'A lapsed one some say.'

'Lapsed or not, he's still a Catholic. And like you sonny, he always will be. Once a Catholic—'

'A Catholic-Fascist or a Fascist-Catholic?'

'Catholic first and last. That is most important thing. That's all that matters. That's all that matters.'

Their conversation expired on a note of mutual incomprehension. Tom pretended to doze and, by the sound of his snoring, McIlroy fell into a deep sleep. Time, the increasing consumption of whiskey and the nature of modern warfare were catching up with him.

In many ways the war in Spain was to be the zenith of McIlroy's career. All his other wars, it seemed, had been leading up to this great war of ideology. Armed only with the lens of a religious zealot, the social, political and economic factors could and were obviously being discounted as having any bearing on the conflict. In McIlroy's estimation it was simply and straightforwardly a Manichean contest between Catholicism and Communism. His defence of Catholicism involved, in effect, demonising all things 'Red' by employing as much gory detail and using the most intemperate language he could muster. Such was his desire to destroy the 'atheist menace' in Spain, it appeared as if he was preparing himself for the priesthood that he had once trained for in his youth. That Franco and the Fascists were on the side of God, McIlroy believed, meant that his sympathy for their Nationalist cause was simply an unintended consequence. This was to be reflected in his reporting and ultimately in the problems he caused for both his editor at the *Irish Independent* and the Press Office in the Nationalist zone, especially in the shape of Captain Bolín. In effect, he had no thought for his future employment and was therefore determined to pursue his own path which, if it coincided with that of the Nationalists was, as far as he was concerned, simply fortuitous. Unfortunately for McIlroy, the Nationalists did not see it that way and he was soon to make an enemy of both Bolín and O'Duffy and nearly everyone in between. This was despite the fact that his dispatches were never anti-Franco, always anti-Red and without exception profoundly pro-Church. Apart from the questionable quality of O'Duffy and his men, the substance of his dispute was the nature of the censorship which he believed was being unnecessarily and counter-productively imposed by Bolín's office. The veteran reporter had always been 'a rebel', 'a loner' and had now added the proverbial 'loose cannon' to his signature.

From the beginning, Tom's relationship with McIlroy was destined to be complex and ambivalent. The experienced man was a role model, the fabled 'intrepid' war correspondent. He was also clever and complicated, particularly in terms of his antipathy towards newspaper owners as a breed. McIlroy was disinterested in the minutiae of politics and instinctively focussed on the broader picture as it affected what he called 'the common crowd'. However this expansive vision, which Tom shared and indeed aspired to, was never matched by the experienced man's willingness to see all sides of the situation. He also had no concern that his partiality was overt and there for everyone to see. For McIlroy it did not matter 'a shit what others thought'. He was on the side of God and the Catholic Church and they were the only editors that really mattered to him, especially at this seminal point in a long and, if not distinguished, then very distinctive career.

Meanwhile, at the rear of the convoy, Mary found herself sharing a car with the impossibly tall and abundant Ethel Carney. Carney smiled and hauled herself closer to the car window, thereby making more room on the seat. Far too much room Mary thought. The gesture seemed more about Carney trying to downplay her size and her exaggerated movement appeared to be designed to show that she was *not* taking up too much space. That they had been assigned the same vehicle was not, Mary soon realised, a coincidence. This was confirmed by Carney's air of expectancy.

'Ah, there you are! I've been waiting to meet you. I'm Carney, Ethel Carney.... *Irish Independent*. And you must be?

'Yes, hello...I'm Mary ....Porteus...nice to meet you.'

'Who are you with my dear?'

'The *Rangoon Times*.'

'Oh my dear, you are a—'

'...a long way from home?' Mary interjected rather wearily to what was becoming a rather hackneyed phrase.

'Why on God's earth are you *here*?' Carney asked.

'We could all ask the same thing, couldn't we?'

'You're quite right my dear, especially given the state of the hotels, the restaurants and the food! Not to mention the shopping and the women! Oh my God, how frightfully ugly they all are! This has not been my favourite assignment I can tell you. And it looks like getting worse! God help us.

Where are we off to this morning? I've lost all track. The whole country looks the same to me. It's so, so depressing.'

'Cáceres. We're off to Cáceres', Mary replied.

'Oh yes... Yes...of course. I've been there already. What a *dump* of a place! It makes Navan look like well, Biarritz!' She chortled at her own joke and Mary just smiled politely.

'I can't wait to get to Madrid, or what's going to be left of it. Poor thing, you must be missing Rangoon terribly?'

'No...Not at all. I'm the Europe correspondent. I don't actually live in Rangoon. In fact I've only been there once. I travel all around Europe. I suppose I'm more of a gypsy correspondent.'

'Oh you poor gypsy! How drab is that? What with Europe on the precipice and war, war, war! It seems that is all we have to look forward to. It's all so terribly depressing don't you think my dear?'

'I think it's quite scary but also interesting?' Mary suggested.

'Interesting? That's not what I would call it. If you came from where I came from, men fighting is never 'interesting' my dear! It's simply what they do.' Carney paused and eyed Mary intensely, 'Are you a virgin my dear? As a war reporter I mean. You must be?'

Momentarily taken aback, Mary stumbled a reply, 'Yes, yes...this is my first war.'

'And mine! We shall be deflowered together! How nice! We should try to get along and enjoy whatever we can, don't you agree?' Carney placed her hand on Mary's knee and gave it a gentle squeeze.

Carney proclaimed that she was renowned for her weekly column in the *Independent* and that she circulated as a 'courtly diarist' amongst the Dublin social set. Mary soon felt unsettled by this information and in particular the possibility that this woman might uncover her identity. Women writers, especially progressive women writers, might easily have been the target of one of her columns. Had she heard of M.G.M Deben? Mary thought, anxiously. The very notion of 'enjoying' the war struck her as rather odd, even obscene. Consequently, the word stayed with her for the rest of the journey. It also informed her initial estimation of Ethel Carney who, at first, she thought had a vocabulary only fit for the Society pages. In fact it was difficult to fathom whether Carney could be more than superficial about anything.

IT WAS ONLY in Cáceres weeks later, when she offered Mary a copy of an article she had written on the position of women in Hitler's Germany, that Mary had cause to revise her opinion. Ostensibly, the piece was given as an example of 'foreign correspondence' for Mary to emulate. This was entirely in keeping with Carney's general manner and the fact that she had not one ounce of modesty. However, her intention had been to signal a genuine interest in women and women's issues. She could write seriously it appeared, especially about those things that were close to her heart. It also transpired that Carney's public persona, that of a light-headed Hedonist, was only for the gallery and, it seemed, for denigrating the opinions of men, often without them realising.

Overall, Carney cut a rather solitary figure and Mary was to witness how she craved company, often demonstrably so. She always gravitated towards women and had a proclivity to embrace and touch them at every opportunity. This was something that Mary found particularly disconcerting. She surmised that Carney was almost certainly a lesbian whose sexual desires may have never been successfully consummated. Hence she appeared as if she was forever stalking. Despite this, Mary had a grudging admiration of her. She was a woman with her own agenda and *modus operandi.* That, in itself, was a very rare thing in the circumstances and indeed in society more generally. However, Mary's forbearance was to be tested as time went on. She soon learned that Carney's agenda was also horribly distorted and that the war in Spain was some way down her list of priorities and indeed interests. She had no doubt that Carney's ambition and private desires were always uppermost. And it was only later that she would come to loath Carney's type of self-confidence and the way in which it easily transmuted into pure self-centredness.

Ethel Carney towered over most Spaniards and not a few of her male foreign correspondents. For that reason the Spanish men appeared to view her either as an object of awe or pity. You could see it in their eyes: 'How could a woman be so malformed, disfigured and ill made?' On the other hand, Mary came to see that Carney was in fact entirely comfortable in her body and she moved, for such a large person, with an unexpected litheness. She also appeared to revel in her physical conspicuousness and knew how to manage the difference between what others might see and how she saw herself. She was always immaculately turned-out, regardless of the need or occasion, and was said to travel 'heavy' with three large suitcases, all full-to-brim with the appropriate attire. She never went anywhere without her Irish tweed twin-sets. Her long, curled and patently coloured hair also appeared to encounter everything and anything that was proximate. As a result, it was the hair that often announced Carney before she could do so herself. She was loud in company and her Armagh drone, which had long since been buffed into a middle-class, Dublin-ish sounding lilt, surfaced in proportion to every increase in volume. Yet, in private, she was disconcertingly quiet and spoke in little more than a whisper, to the extent that Mary often found herself craning to hear her. Whilst Carney did not dominate conversations, she was also never going to be dominated. This was due to her size as much as anything else. She was a mature woman in what was a man's world and that appeared to frighten most of her male colleagues.

Carney willingly wrote for the public whatever she was asked to write. For the most part, her articles were to be nothing more than homilies to the 'brave boys' of the Irish Brigade. Her dispatches were everything the editor of the *Independent* had asked for and her readership no doubt expected. As a result, the Nationalist cause and atrocities were seldom mentioned, let alone examined. The Reds were 'naturally evil' and the 'Defence of the Faith' was the one and only cause worth fighting for. Her articles could have been written by McIlroy. Conversely, she could and did think for herself, but only if she chose to and, more impor-tant, if it served her immediate interests. She was something of a Jekyll and Hyde character and that is how she had survived and indeed prospered as a woman journalist. Mary understood her approach, but it was the antithesis of how she felt it should be.

7

SISTERS OF MERCY

BEFORE SHE HEARD THE KNOCK AT THE DOOR, GRACE SPOTTED Kitty's dogs, Saoirse and Cap, playing on the shoreline. Kitty was soon stood at the porch, out of breath and taking in gulps of air before she could say anything. Grace realised her predicament and waited.

'I heard...about the lad,' Kitty panted. 'Are you okay?'

Grace was surprised by the speed at which Kitty had come over, 'I'm grand,' she lied. 'I'm fine. You'd no need to trouble yourself. It was nothing, really. Come in, have some tea whilst you're here. You look like you could do with a bit of sit down. The kettle's boiled.'

'I've got me muddy boots on.'

'Look at mine! Don't be worrying about that. Come in, sit down.'

Grace went to make the tea and could see that Kitty was really struggling with her breathing. As she placed herself in the 'comfy' chair by the hearth, the normally strong woman looked weak and fragile.

'I won't be staying long now.'

'You stay as long as it takes. There's time enough as they say,' Grace replied. 'The tea's almost ready now.'

'Was he here long? The boy?'

'No...well, I don't really know. I found him out there. He was sitting on the lavatory! He gave me the shock of my life. I hadn't been expecting that, I can tell you. And there I was dying to use it!' Grace handed Kitty the mug of tea.

'Did he go for ye?' Kitty looked concerned and her voice had become a grave whisper. She took a gulp of the tea and winced because it was too hot.

'Go for me?' Grace was surprised at the very suggestion.

'Did he get violent with ye?'

'No, not a bit of it. I think he was more frightened of me than I of him. I thought he was going to pee himself there and then. He was very scared...and very cold.'

'And John Fahey came and caught him?'

'I wouldn't say he caught him. He was about where you are and having a sandwich. He started to cry when he saw John and was begging me not to send him back. It was really pitiful.'

Grace reflected for a moment and looked away from Kitty. The thought of the young boy swearing at her replayed in her mind and she couldn't help feeling somehow responsible for what had happened. Kitty, too, looked mournful and not a little upset at the thought of the boy begging to be let free.

'Are you alright Kitty? You look mighty upset by all this. I'm perfectly fine, really.'

Kitty got up and went to the window. She made as if to look for the dogs on the beach and remained staring out.

'Kitty, are you sure you're alright?'

She turned and looked at Grace.

'Miss Grace...'

'Kitty! Call me Grace...*please*. It's Grace.'

'The young lad, do you know what will become of him?' She looked directly into Grace's eyes with an intensity that had not been apparent before.

Grace thought about what to say.

'He said...he said he would be beaten. Do you believe that?'

'He will.' Kitty muttered under her breath. 'He will.'

'How can you be sure?'

'Everyone knows it. That's what happens to them.'

'They get beaten...for running away?'

'Not just running away. They beat them and worse, for everything. I've seen them after. I've seen the marks. They beat them something fierce. He'll be beaten alright.' Kitty covered her mouth and looked away.

Grace felt a terrible guilt and stumbled to get the words out.

'And worse? You said they get worse?' her voice became more fractured and all the time the vision of the frightened young boy kept coming into her mind. She could hear Tighe begging once more.

'Kitty, how do you know all this?'

'Everyone knows it happens.' Kitty repeated.

'Who beats them Kitty?'

'The Brothers...who else? We all know that.'

'Then why doesn't someone say or do something?' Grace was getting more and more perturbed by what she was hearing.

'You can't. It's the School. They...*we* all depend on it. You can't say a word. You mustn't!' Kitty exclaimed.

'Mustn't?' Grace echoed.

'You mustn't. It's the work. Everyone needs the work from the School. I do.'

'And the beatings?'

'There's worse. 'Tis said they starve them. They turn the hose on them and shave their heads. And even worse things, it's said,' Kitty added and immediately turned away so that Grace could not see the tears that had welled in her eyes.

'Everyone knows this...but nothing is done?'

'Aye. You can't. You musn't.' Kitty turned back and sat back down in the chair.

'The hose? He said something to me about a hose, and the hair shaved,' Grace recalled in a whisper to herself.

'And they work them 'til they drop ...the poor creatures. Even the very young 'uns. I've seen it myself on the farm down there. There's been some terrible accidents on that farm over the years. Terrible goings on altogether.'

'Who's letting this happen Kitty? Why is it allowed? Under our noses...Oh my God. This is a terrible. Someone has got to do something. I've got to do something. We can't just let it happen.'

'No, no you can't. You mustn't!' Kitty raised a voice from within that was now a lot more agitated. 'Everyone depends on the School. The whole village needs it. No-one will say a word. You'll not get anywhere.'

'And that includes you Kitty?'

There was a short pause before Kitty answered, 'I'm the same as everyone else.'

'And John...John Fahey?'

'John's in need of the business like everyone else.'

'Oh my God! Is there no-one who has any courage?' Grace was exasperated by the thought.

'We can't do anything. It's not courage. The men have no balls in any case, 'cuse my French.' Kitty replied in a resigned, half-swallowed mumble.

Grace took some tea and stared at the floor. She was trying to think what to do.

'What about the local priest? Surely he can't condone it?'

'My God Grace...are you are really so green? Don't you think Father Boyle knows what goes on in these parts? He knows everything. He's the all-seeing one. That man is in the middle of it...he knows alright. He makes his way by it and he's plenty of good reasons not to stop it. You should not be crossing him in a hurry. He'll chase you out soon enough and you'll not be wanting to stay if you cross him.'

'What do you mean, he's at the heart of it?'

'He is. He dishes out the work. Boyle decides who gets the jobs, rakes in his share and turns a blind eye to how it's made. He's in cahoots with the rest of them. He's one of them. He's the Boss.'

'The Boss?'

'Along with the Superior.'

'The Superior?'

'The School Principal or Head or whatever. The Head ... Brother Marcel. He's the hand in Boyle's glove and the foot in his shoe, I'd say.'

'How long has all this been going on Kitty?'

'Ever since.'

'And nothing's been done?'

'As I said, you can't.'

The shine of her Connemara existence had left Grace and she stared into her cup. She thought before asking.

'Do any of the boys come to your place?'

''They have. Not many...but some get lost and end up down the boreen.'

'And did you return them?'

'I did. Oh Jesus help me, I did. I regret it...every one. I know what happens to them. But you couldn't have...so you have no need to feel sorry about it. I knew and I still sent them back. God help and save me.'

'We've got to do *something* Kitty. We really must. It can't just be allowed to continue. Someone has got to do something. It's wrong. It's terribly wrong and everyone knows it.'

'Grace...don't. Please don't get yourself involved. You're a stranger here and you're not part of it. You can go. We're stuck here and we have to work for the School. We have no choice. We just have to live with it. We can't do anything.'

'But the boys?'

'They learn to survive...most of them do at least. Just like we all have to.'

"Kitty, it's wrong. It's evil.'

'There's so much that is wrong in this world. We've seen that with the war. And this is but a wee bit more.'

'But it's the Church. It's the whole community.'

'It is...but you can't touch them. They are mighty powerful and they have friends all over.'

Grace paused to digest what she had just heard. Her reaction was instinctive.

'I'm going to do something. I can't just live here and know that that is happening on my doorstep. I can't live with that....and I don't think you or anyone else should.'

'Grace no, please. I beg you. You'll upset everything. You'll upset everyone...not just me...but *everyone*! For the love of God, don't be getting yourself involved.'

'But think of those poor boys?' Grace implored.

'They'll suffer even more if you go getting involved. You'll not achieve anything much and the lads will be punished even more I tell you. It's just no good Grace. They're too strong and you'll end up hurting yourself. They're like the wasps, everyone gets stung if you stir them up.'

Grace saw in Kitty more than the self-interest that she had admitted. The rawness of Kitty's expression suggested that she was harbouring her own grief and pain and that this was somehow related to the experience of the young lad. Kitty actually appeared to have shrunk before Grace's eyes. She was huddled once more in the comfy chair and turned to look plaintively out of the window in order to avoid Grace's stare.

'I'd better be collecting the dogs.'

'Sit there awhile Kitty. There's plenty of time. They'll not be going anywhere without you.'

'But I'm stopping ye—'

'Stopping me what? I've the rest of the day and there's always tomorrow. Have another cuppa.' Grace smiled and sensed that Kitty was still burdened by things not yet said. 'Is there something else you want to tell me?'

Kitty thought before answering. She rose from the chair, took her cup to the table, turned and stood before Grace.

'I know what it's like,' she said softly.

'What?' Grace replied.

'I was in one myself for a while. Back then,' Kitty continued in barely a whisper.

Grace at last understood what Kitty was referring to. She took a deep intake of air. 'In one of the Schools?'

'Yes, the School for us girls in Clifden. Another St Joseph's…just like this one. Only they're not a School, more a prison or workhouse I'd say. A workhouse is what they really are. My Da was killed at the end of the war and I was put there with my baby sister, Margaret. I was nine or ten thereabouts, Maggie was six. They took us to the court one day and the next thing we know we're crying our eyes out, both of us, and they just drove us off without even saying goodbye to Ma. She wasn't crying...I don't think she could. She was so sick with the shock of it all.'

'Oh Kitty... you poor thing. Why did they send you away?'

Kitty seemed relieved to unburden herself and continued.

'She couldn't cope they said. They said that... but it wasn't true. They kept on telling us that but it wasn't. It was really the fella she had living with us. He'd stay at the house and them not being married and all. I think the priest caused it. I know he did. He reported on Ma and that was it. They said she was not fit to bring us up right. But I know she did her best. I know she loved us. She looked after us the best she could. We hadn't much but it was enough. That's why they sent us away... because of the priest.'

'And what happened? What's happened to Margaret? Where is she now?'

'Maggie passed. She was never very strong and caught pneumonia in the School, a bad cold they said, and the next thing...she was gone.'

'I'm sorry Kitty. It must have been dreadful for you?'

'It was. But that was not the worst of it. They also beat us and starved us. They kept us in the cold and they worked us. God did they work us!' Kitty stopped and looked up at the ceiling as if it was heaven above, before continuing.

'Worst of all... they stole... they stole our childhood, our innocence... little Maggie's innocence. She had done nothing to no-one. We never had a chance to be children. We had to stop being children otherwise you'd never last. We had to grow up before our time. I think that's what killed Maggie. She couldn't grow up fast enough. She was just a child.'

'Who did this to you Kitty?'

'The Sisters of Mercy! God help us, isn't that the most stupid fecking name for them! Mercy... they never knew the meaning of the word. They did it... with the Church's blessing and that of the priests.... and the Courts and the rest of them. They were all in it and I think they got their pleasure from it as well. They seemed to enjoy hurting us. The harder they did it, the more pleasure they got. They were sick... all of them.'

'Then what happened to you?'

'I was let out. I survived. I grew up with a great hatred... which I still have.' She took a sup of her tea and looked directly at Grace.

'In the end they let me go. And when they did, I vowed that I'd never bring any children into this world. Not while they were still around. I wouldn't want them getting their hands on any child of mine. I was let out only if I married straight away. That was the price. I was to be let out if I married old Patsy. I had no choice.'

Kitty paused and held her chest tightly, 'Thank God he didn't last!' A great smile came across her face on the reflection of the late Patsy's demise.

'Who else knows about all this Kitty?'

'Everyone. There's no secrets around here.'

'What happened to your Ma?'

'I never saw her. One day they just told me she died. She drank herself to her death...with her man...or so they say. Not even that she had gone to heaven. I suppose that's because there isn't one, a heaven that is, and they know it! I know it and I expect everyone knows it, but they just don't say anything. Anyways, I was left on my own and I had not a soul on this Earth to turn to. So, after darling Maggie, I've never loved anyone. No one. And I never shall. I've no love left in me for anyone. I've learnt that you can't afford to love anything on two legs. Now I only love those dogs out there!' She paused and looked out of the window, 'And them being dumb animals and all, I can't even be sure they love me back. And that's fine, I can live with that.'

'Don't say that Kitty!' You can be loved and will one day. We all need to love. You'll find love.'

'Out here? You must be joking. And you Miss... sorry, Grace?'

'I've had my share Kitty. Probably more than my fair share of love and I've wasted it, like many of us do. I've not really appreciated it and I never realised what I had at the time. You don't and that's the pity of love. But I still need it and I want to feel it again if I can. Next time, I'll appreciate it for what it is... a precious gift.'

'A gift? Don't you have to earn it? What good can it be if you are given it?'

'Perhaps you're right? Maybe that's where I went wrong? You *do* have to earn it. I just didn't try hard enough.'

'And now? You being here and all? There's no love for you to find here, I can tell you that for nothing. The men that are still here are mostly feckless or drunk or both. All the best ones go. What's left aren't worth having. They bleed us women dry... if we let them. You'll not find love here that's for sure.'

'That's probably true. But I have my memories. I can recall how I felt when I was in love. It's a special feeling and sometimes that's enough.'

'That's what you write about in your books?' Kitty said pointing to the books on the shelf.
'Sometimes. Yes, I try to remember how I felt or how I should have felt.'

'Writing won't bring it back.'

'Oh... I think you're wrong Kitty. I have felt it and it does come back. It's not the same as the real thing, but the writing definitely brings back the feeling that you were once in love. And that's worth it I think. Some days I'm probably like you Kitty, I tell myself that it's all past me now and then I write something and it gives me hope again.'

'Not all of us have your gift for the words.'

'Nonsense, you could if you tried. It's not that difficult. It comes like everything else... with practice. I'm sure you'd have a few good stories to tell?'

'I'm trying to forget them.'

'But you can't?'

'No... you can't. They won't go away that's for sure. No matter how much you try. But you...you still have a life in front of you. Mine's over, it's in the past. I'm not going anywhere or about to do anything tomorrow that I haven't done every day these last ten years. You can leave tomorrow if you like. You have your writing and you still have your looks. You'll find a man somewhere if you care to look. But he'll not be in one of your books.'

'But I don't want to go anywhere. I have this place. Yes, I have my writing... and I want to stay with people, neighbours like you Kitty. Why would I want to go anywhere else? I've already been around the world or thereabouts. I'm beginning to feel this is now my home.'

'Home! With neighbours like me?'

'Yes Kitty, like you. I need to have the company of people like yourself.'

'Stupid people like me?'

'No! Decent people. You're how people should be with their neighbours. We get on. We meet, we chat, and we help each other if we can. We keep out of each other's business. We're there if you want something. And that's the way it should be. That's what I like about you, about being here.'

Kitty appeared to be embarrassed by what she had just heard and moved to the window. She made out to look for the dogs and whilst not looking at Grace spoke gently.

'But that's because you're different. Being a stranger lets you think that. But the people around here aren't all friendly and believe me they will rob you as much as look at you if they could. It's not true they're there for you. Look at what they're doing about the School. You said so yourself. And they all say you're 'crazy' behind your back. The 'Mad Englishwoman' they say.'

'Half-Irish please!'

'Half-mad more like. And half-English. And the way you drive that van!'

'Drive my van?'

'Aye...the van. The 'Killer Van' they say when they see it. 'Watch out, she's about' they shout.' Kitty turned to look at Grace.

'Don't trust them, that's what I say. Don't trust anyone. Look out for yourself. Don't get involved. For your own sake, don't get yourself involved Grace.' She then slowly made her way to the door.

'Lock your doors...and your windows.'

———

FOR THE REMAINDER of day Grace went about the cottage in an inner turmoil. The usual antidote to her writing block-age, a walk down to the foreshore, did no good and she found herself unable to concentrate on writing or indeed anything else. The incident with the boy had set in train all manner of thoughts about the nature of 'causes' and how she had once embraced the notion that it was her moral duty to get involved and to help those less fortunate. But what was the cause here? Was she, as an outsider, obliged to get herself involved? Was it her business? She was indeed a stranger and perhaps it was none of her business? And what good would it do in any case? Would it stop the abuse and save others like Tighe? How could she get involved? What might it do for her own cause, the reason she had come to Connemara, her writing? Such thoughts went around and around.

After Spain, she had had no such thoughts about getting involved, even if only in her writing. However, residing somewhere amongst the ruins of her previous existence lay an ember of her social and political consciousness, one that impelled her not to turn a blind eye to the suffering that was now a near neighbour. How could she remain neutral, uninvolved, after what she had just heard and witnessed? Amid the conflict and doubt was a frisson of the spirit that went by the name of M.G.M. Deben. Passivity was not the same as ignorance, and neither was it morally right in this case. How could it be? There was no escaping the necessity that she should and could do something, anything. By the end of the day she had decided to take up the cause of the boys in the School and, if she possibly could, rescue Tighe. Her Spanish novel would have to wait.

8

———

THE SCHOOL

GRACE WAS EXTREMELY NERVOUS ABOUT VISITING THE SCHOOL and as she entered the grounds she spotted two young boys in a very large playground sweeping up leaves with hand brushes. They were no more than seven or eight years of age. It seemed rather odd that they had no brooms, although their meagre frames were such as to question whether they would have had the strength required for tools that were any larger. Their industry was also obviously in vain, as the wind was constantly displacing their attempt to pile their efforts into manageable loads. One of the boys made to look up as she passed but appeared at the last moment to think better of it. They carried on with their futile task. Whilst not a particularly cold day, the fact that they were only wearing cotton shirts and short trousers, simply added to the general distress the sight provoked. As she passed and looked back at them, and as they struggled to recapture the leaves that blew back from whence they came, she saw that their Wellington boots were also several sizes too large. There was, however, nothing clownish about their predicament. She soon realised that the scale of their task relative to their size, the inhospitable conditions and the obvious inadequacy of their clothes and tools, meant that she was in fact witnessing some form of punishment.

Grace was met at the main entrance by a Brother Avenall, a small rodent-like man, who was polite but wholly unwelcoming. He looked at her as one might a shop manikin, without life or human emotion. The atmosphere inside the building was a strange mix of disinfectant and absolute quiet; it was more that of a sanatorium than a school. Grace's shoes echoed on the parquet flooring as she made her way along a gleaming corridor to the Superior's office. On one side of the corridor she was suddenly alarmed by the unexpected sight of classrooms full of boys from which there was not a sound. It was totally and eerily silent. The Brothers at the front and to the side of the class stared intently and unflinchingly as she passed. All the boys without exception either had their heads down or faced the front of the class and none passed even a glimpse her way. At the end of the passage she came across the reason for the gleaming floor. A small, pencil thin boy with what seemed like a giant buffer device was trying to negotiate the corridor without much success. He looked as though he was trying to wrestle a dragon. He could hardly turn the head of the buffer, let alone lift it. A rather forlorn face was momentarily lifted and then sunk as the rat-faced Brother Avenall turned the boy to the wall as they passed. Grace's unease was turning to anger with every step she took.

The Superior, Brother Marcel, was sitting behind an imposing desk and his office was suitably adorned with all the religious iconography one would normally expect and more. He did not raise himself as Grace was shown into the room and the rodent Brother Avenall crept out without a sound. The Superior continued to write in what looked like a file that was open before him. She walked further into the room and was immediately in two minds whether to stand or sit as the chair in front of the Brother was strategically placed at least three feet away from the desk, a distance that suggested that it was intended for an audience rather than an interview. She sat down and waited for the Brother to acknowledge her. He continued to write. Eventually, he closed the file and slowly re-housed his fountain pen.

'Miss Deben? Welcome to St Joseph's. I'm Brother Marcel, the Superior.'

Grace cringed on hearing the title and wondered what he might be 'superior' to? His voice was formal, exceptionally sonorous and perfectly matched to his physical self. He was a very large, elderly man with flecks of grey wispy hair on an otherwise bald pate. Dressed in a black habit adorned by a large silver crucifix, he filled his chair as a king might a throne, or a dictator a dais.

'Thank you ...Superior.'

'And how can I help you today?'

'I would like to offer my services to the School. As you may know, I have come to live in the area and I have time on my hands which I could put to good use. I'm a writer.'

'A writer? Yes, I had heard that we have a *famous* author in our midst. There are very few secrets to be had around here. Everyone knows everyone else's business, as you will soon discover.'

'I wouldn't say I'm famous exactly. I'm just a novelist and a travel writer who has had a little bit of good fortune.'

'A novelist, indeed. *Fiction* is it?' There was more than an air of condescension in his response. Grace also found the overwrought inflection in his speech unnerving.

'I could teach reading and writing to the boys.'

With his head slanted and eyes bulging, the Superior cut a false smile.

'That is very kind of you,' his voice moved into a new patronising tone, one that appears to be second-nature to many priests. 'And, if I may ask, why would *you* want to be being doing that for *them*?'

'I have the time and I would like to contribute the best I can.'

'But what makes you think we need your *best*? Surely, you'll be too busy writing your *fiction* books?'

'I shall, but I have more than enough time. And I'd be happy to give it freely,' Grace had detected his reluctance or was it disinterest?

'Freely?'

'Yes, of course.' She immediately recognised that the use of 'freely' was entirely unnecessary and by suggesting payment or reward of any kind simply added to his all too obvious disinclination to engage her.

The half-smile on the face of the Superior appeared to be unnaturally fixed and Grace quickly gathered the impression that he was humouring her. Slowly, he rose and walked over to the window and, squinting, appeared to spot something untoward. He returned to his desk and reached across to a small button which he pressed. There was no sound. He continued to look at Grace but said nothing. Then, in almost an instant, Brother Avenall appeared. The two men went to the window and murmured an exchange, obviously instructions relating to the situation that must have been unfolding outside the window. Brother Avenall swiftly left the room in his scurrying, rodential manner. Such was the atmosphere of the place and without any real grounds for doing so, Grace surmised that the two boys she had seen in the playground were in yet more trouble.

'I'm sorry, but I don't get much of an opportunity or time to read any *fiction* or the like. I'm sure you understand. And what sort of *stories* do you pen Miss Deben?' The belittling of her craft that was implied in his response did not pass unnoticed.

'I tend to write about modern themes. In today's literature I believe we need to address current issues, modern themes and contemporary life.'

'*Modern* themes and *contemporary* life? Now what would they be and what would that include, exactly?' Not looking at Grace, he fingered the file in front of him and turned a page.

'War and peace?' Grace offered with no pun intended.

'War and peace?' he seemed to appreciate the unintended pun nevertheless. 'Big issues indeed. Political by the sound of it?' He paused, 'And not perhaps for our boys, I would suggest?'

'I wouldn't be teaching them current affairs or politics Superior. I'm sure some basic reading and writing would be what they need.'

'Indeed. They've cause for very little else.' He walked to the window once more and spoke to Grace whilst continuing to look out.

'All the troubles of this world, Miss Deben, are, as I'm sure you'll agree, resolvable through faith. Modern society and *contemporary life* need to be tempered by the calming influence of the Church. In fact the whole political system is in need of being recast wouldn't you say?'

He turned and came back to his desk but did not sit down. Instead he hovered menacingly behind Grace. She steeled herself from rising to his bait and he carried on tempting her.

'It all needs a good shake up. This country needs to

develop its own system of government. I'd have liked to have seen that happen before the Emergency. But let us not forget, Miss Deben, that no amount of political tinkering can overcome the Original Sin.' He returned and sat at his desk and Grace felt far more comfortable with him in front of her and in full view.

'We need the vocations to be the way forward for the country. Even *fiction* writers such as yourself, might have a part to play. What do you think?'

'The vocations?'

'The experts and their like. Leaders drawn from the professions and so on. And of course a few men of the cloth to guide the moral side of things. We won't get any change in this society with the current crowd. Contemporary life, I'd say, is not always better than the past. It's not always progress to change things for the sake of it. We need to look to the Holy way but with a *contemporary* twist.'

'Wouldn't that be what they call ...Corporatism?' Grace narrowly stopped herself saying Fascism.

'Corporatism now. Is that what it is? You'd know better than I. A fancy name for something quite simple, I'd say.'

Grace knew he knew what it is and let him continue.

'Call it what you will. Have you read Pope Pius XI's *Quadragesimo Anno* Miss Deben? I'd recommend it. You will see in that that the Church has criticised both socialism and free-reign capitalism. We're not taking sides you see, but we'd like to think we too are seeking the answers to the economic and social ills of the country. We can't help but be engaged in *this* world and not be just concerned with the next. It's not political at all.' he looked directly at Grace and waited for her response. She declined and he continued.

'I think you'd agree, Parliaments and politicians are all very well, *if* they get things done. The present crowd doesn't unfortunately. It's all about the elections and self-interest. Abolish them all I say! Workers and employers, and the Church of course, we are all in it together. We all have common interests at the end of the day. That's why the vocations would work here in Ireland. I'd go so far as to say, there's no real need for a state at all. I've found that most people can govern themselves, with a little guidance from above and the suitably educated of course. Look at us now, we have a strong community here; good hard-working people and that should be the basis of any government. Keep politics out of it, I say. It's just common sense you need. Of course, it goes without saying, we also need to conserve and protect our traditional Catholic values.'

Grace had an instant recall of the many speeches she had heard in Spain on the Nationalist side. She recognised the direction of the Superior's diatribe and was wary of responding in kind. Franco, Fascism, the war against Nazi Germany could all have easily been invoked to counter the Superior's arguments, but she thought better of it. In any case, he quite suddenly and unilaterally changed the subject.

'Have you any idea as to the mental calibre of the boys we have here Miss Deben?'

'A good number must be in need of knowing how to do some basic writing?' she replied.

'Miss Deben, to be frank, the average level of intelligence of the boys in our charge is well below that of even the average farm child in Connemara, if not their sheep on the mountains. Their sheep dogs have more brains...and are far less trouble! Although they may all be God's creatures, they are little more than cretins. We find it impractical to divert our energies and scarce resources to their *education*. It is best that they learn a trade or parts of a trade. We are a vocational school first and foremost. May I remind you that it is St Joseph's *Industrial* School? I can't see them missing out by not having read *War and Peace*!' He guffawed to himself and clapped his hands.

'But they need to be able to read and write? Surely, they need the basics to practice a trade? And to read the Bible?' she added strategically.

'They do...they do...but only in some cases. Most will be content to let others do all their thinking. Being good with their hands and working hard will stand them in good stead. Reading and writing will then follow, if need be. They're not cut out for much else I'm afraid,' he looked at Grace and smiled. 'Now then, I won't waste any more of your precious time, not with novels on *contemporary life* to be written.' As he rose, he again pressed the button on the desk.

Grace rose from her chair and went to walk to the door. She turned.

'Superior, the two boys in the playground...have you no brooms they could use?' she asked.

'Two boys?' He feigned ignorance.

'There are two young boys trying to sweep the leaves on the playground with only hand brushes.'

'Are there now?'

'Yes, and they have very few clothes on.'

'Miss Deben—,' he interrupted. 'Will that be all? Brother Avenall will show you the way. Thank you for your kind offer. I wish you well in your literary labours and your stay in our community. Now, good morning and May the Good Lord be with you.' He returned to his desk and began to un-house his fountain pen.

Brother Avenall entered the office and opened the door wide so as to indicate the audience was over. Grace looked at the Superior and in that moment decided she was not going to give up on the boys. Now, more than ever, she would make it her mission to save them.

'Good morning Superior...and May God help *you!*'

Grace marched out of the office and back along the corridor. The small boy was still losing his fight with the Beast of a buffer and as she passed she gently and symbolically touched the unfortunate's head in full view of Avenall. Stepping ahead of Brother Avenall all the way back to the main door, Grace felt good about keeping him in her wake. She walked straight out of the entrance without looking back.

The two boys were still trying to fight nature, the School, the Catholic Church and perhaps the Irish state itself. Their plight was now made worse by the rain that had started to fall quite heavily. The wind had not abated and the swirling leaves continued to torment the young inmates in their own version of the punishment of Sisyphus. Grace wanted to stop and take them home with her, instead she began to cry inside. As she came to the main gates she had a vision of the Brother Superior, only it was the Irish Brigade Chaplain, Muldoon, who appeared before her.

9

———————

CÁCERES, SPAIN

CÁCERES WAS BOTH AN INTRIGUING AND A DEPRESSING destination. It rested on an undistinguished promontory that lifted what remained of its medieval walled-centre barely above the monotonously flat, surrounding country-side. A minor administrative centre in the vast Extremadurian plain, its historical virtues did their best to hide themselves amongst cramped alleys and passage-ways. It was once a semi-prosperous market town. More recently it had become the headquarters of Franco's advance and as such it felt and acted very much like a town under enemy occupation. The townsfolk did not congregate, huddle in cafes, or linger over the makeshift vegetable stalls in the manner of ordinary life in an ordinary Spanish town. It was strangely and threateningly quiet.

Tom was struck by the similarities between the poverty of the Spain he was now witnessing and that which he had known in the West of Ireland. The weather only served to reinforce his view, it was both cold and very wet - more Irish than Spanish. And just like the Ireland he had left, he couldn't imagine this country ever being developed in any sense: it was a land that time appeared to have abandoned. It was obvious that the desire for change and an attempt to maintain tradition lay at the heart of the conflict. Everywhere the dominance of the traditionalist, ultra-conservative Catholic Church was apparent, not least in the grandiose churches that, in even the smallest and impoverished of hamlets, dominated the skyline like mighty surveillance watchtowers. Yet, for all its prominence, Tom had also witnessed many of the inhabitants appearing to pay lip-service to the theocracy and a dark cynicism regarding the Church and the role of the priesthood appeared to be widespread. Whilst he could not evidence this, he somehow knew it to be the case. There was something about the manner in which the locals appeared to freeze in the company of the clerics. The otherwise animated and friendly became statues in their presence. And just as in Ireland, for every true adherent the Catholic Church produced it also spawned an informed disbeliever. Tom saw himself as evidence of this phenomenon. One major difference between Ireland and Spain was that the Spanish ruling class appeared to be more ruthlessly intent and capable of holding on to their power. And its attempt to retain a subordinate population was also clearly tied to the power and destiny of the Catholic Church itself, despite the pretensions of the fascists to be a force for modernisation. As a result, the Nationalist zone appeared to be run entirely by men in dress uniforms or vestments. There seemed to be an Officer for every private and a priest for every platoon. And nothing seemed to irk the priests and the officer class more than the absence of deference, which they took to be their birth-right. Hence their proclivity to resort to inhuman retribution on those who failed to show the respect that they thought their God had reserved for them. When it was said that they treated their animals better than the peasants, it appeared to be no exaggeration. Tom found his animus towards the ruling caste and especially the clergy, growing daily. They were a constant reminder of his childhood, schooling and a previous life in Ireland.

The military occupation was only made noticeable by the occasional convoy and the unusually wide berth given by the locals to the relatively few uniformed personnel who patrolled the narrow pavements during the day. This low-key physical presence of the Nationalist forces helped create a claustrophobic atmosphere, one that was made worse by the suffocating low grey clouds that sat motionless over the town. Life was carrying on, but nothing was anywhere near normal. Strangers were met with understandable suspicion and street exchanges were often undertaken with one eye on avoiding being seen as an informer. Civility was all but extinguished and simply staying alive appeared to be upper-most in everyone's day to day routine. Surviving night time was however an even greater challenge for most of the inhabitants. The full force of occupation was exercised under cover of darkness and the eeriness of the day turned into the terror of the night as the execution squads routinely went about their business.

Mary and Tom had arrived in time to witness the dedication of a plaque to the Irish Brigade in the local church, San Domingo's. The occasion was orchestrated to publicly mark the commitment and designation of the Irish volunteers as true 'Defenders of the Faith'. It produced a major turnout and the Brigade, in full marching order, was met by a respectable but relatively muted crowd of genuine well-wishers and the otherwise curious townsfolk. The entrance to the church was bedecked with sodden tricolours and Nationalist flags of all descriptions including, rather incongruously, the skull and crossbones of the Spanish Foreign Legion, the *Tercio*, which the Brigade had been assigned to.

The Irish Brigade looked impressive and well-drilled. Their recently acquired olive green uniforms had been supplied by General Yague's Central Command along with some of the latest German rifles. The effect was to produce regularity in what was in most other respects a highly irregular, even dysfunctional force. The fact that the uniforms were German Army surplus from the First World War did nothing to detract from the superior quality of their material. Only later were the weight and the unnaturally efficient moisture absorbency of the cloth recognised as the most likely reason the Germans had discarded the product in 1916.

On parade, the officers of the Irish Brigade looked particularly smart and even exuded an air of military experience, even competence. They were also noticeably older by some distance from their rank and file and this only added to their authoritative bearing. General O'Duffy was obviously the pivot around which the whole performance had been carefully choreographed and he took especial pride in his especial uniform. So much so in fact, it looked as if he was constantly searching in the audience's eyes for his own reflection. Either that, or there was an invisible barber holding a full-length mirror going from side to side of the preening General. He was entirely fixated with his own impression. Saluting the local dignitaries as leading man, he took centre stage and unveiled the plaque. In a high pitched Monaghan accent, he slowly but precisely proclaimed, 'On behalf of the officers and men of the First Bandera of the Irish Brigade, I unveil this tablet to the glory of God and the honour of Ireland.'

As for the ranks, it was clear to all that their devotions

were mostly genuine. They were ardently committed to their mission of 'Fighting for the Faith'. Although many had been Church-schooled and perhaps knew little else, they nevertheless had vigour in their supplications which could only have come from at least some measure of genuine conviction. It was as if the faith component of their brain was a frozen area, one that was impervious to the modern human or political condition. Their faith appeared to be as rock solid as any of their erstwhile Crusader forbearers and they undoubtedly saw themselves as first and foremost Christian Soldiers. This did not extend to the Officers however; they acted as if they had more important matters to attend to. It was evident that what mattered to them, above all else, was simply being seen. As a result, their contribution to the service appeared entirely perfunctory and none more so than O'Duffy's.

For days that turned into weeks after the ceremonial, the Irish Brigade did little but parade and perform drills in and around their garrison. There was hardly anything for Mary or Tom to write home about. They did however get a chance to learn something of the men and what struck them both was the extra-ordinariness of the Volunteers. There were men from all the Provinces, the four corners of Ireland, and no individual county or major town was unrepresented. From the West came the rural devout and the dispossessed - the second, third, fourth etc. sons of the land. From the East came accountants, clerks, bachelors, widowers, the jilted, and the usual clutch of semi-and-would-be felons. The North and South were conjoined as comrades-in-arms and former IRA, Treaty and anti-Treaty, footmen abounded. These were 'old soldiers', men who often had fond memories of life with a gun, a song and a cause worth fighting for. A number of these men had also gone into black market entrepreneurship in the Free State and were now on the run. Others had resorted to being mercenaries in Central and South America and now claimed this as their qualification for a stripe or three. Nearly all of these men were simply tired of living in or on their pasts. And finally there was the odd adventurer, the misfit, the dreamer, the clinically insane and the previously institutionalised, the n'er discovered poet and even a self-confessed bigamist, Sergeant Pat Hogan from Drumshambo. They were a disparate and mostly troubled and troubling crowd.

As far as Tom or Mary could discover, few, if any, of the rank and file were ideologically committed to the Fascist credo, and fewer still had any knowledge of or empathy for the Spanish people as a whole. That is not to say they had no idea as to why they were in Spain; only, too often, they had no *good* reason. Many of the younger 'volunteers', many of whom were no more than adolescents, had been conscripted by their mothers and the local priest, whilst others had joined the Crusade out of the sheer monotony of their life in rural Ireland. As a result, the Officers in the Brigade had no need to dragoon these men, as they were more than willing to see action. And neither were they entirely ignorant of the real politics of the war they had signed up for; they were simply uncommitted to any of the myriad Parties involved. For the most part, they had little or no knowledge of the kaleidoscope of competing groups who they were either sometimes and supposedly in alliance with or indeed against. They tended to get by on the basis of the broadest of generalisations as to who their enemy might be, the 'Reds'. Thus, whilst there were any number of racists, Catholic zealots, Irish Nationalists, anti-Communists, Republicans and Monarchists in their ranks, it was almost impossible to find a conscious or coherent Fascist ideologue amid these foot soldiers. It was enough for them to be fighting *against* something, rather than fighting *for* anything in particular. It was only the Irish Officer class who could begin to articulate something approaching a consistent Fascist doctrine, but even here they were the exception rather than the rule.

There was little chance of anyone missing Father John Muldoon, the Brigade Chaplain. He was a very large man with peas for eyes, a booming voice and a general physical awkwardness. He looked as though he had just been inflated by a tyre pump. He also had a penchant for picking his nose, scratching his privates in public and sweating profusely, even in the cold. These traits, amongst others, made most people feel uncomfortable in his presence. He was a predator and one that liked to first bully his victims before assaulting them. His prey were mostly the young men 'from the bog', the countryside, who he tried to put the Fear of Christ into. Whereas in fact it was the fear of Father Muldoon that most experienced. As the official Brigade censor he also had unparalleled access to their private thoughts, if they were literate. He read their letters home with a curiosity that was obviously as much a prurient interest as anything military or religious. Resorting to his role as priest, he used their confessions as the means to collect useful information against his charges, especially on matters of intimacy, which they soon realised he was overly interested in. One of the first things Muldoon did was to issue attendance slips to all the men of the Brigade for Sunday Mass, such was his desire to be controlling. The impenitent who failed to attend were thereby more easily identified and thereafter targeted, including the Officers who he regularly undermined and humiliated in his sermons, especially on those occasions when the Spanish

Liaison staff were present to witness his authority. He managed to alienate everyone, with the exception of General Eoin O'Duffy.

Unsurprisingly, Muldoon and O'Duffy were in many ways kindred spirits. They spent a lot of time in each other's company in Cáceres, although they also appeared to dislike each other. Unlike O'Duffy, who always stood a measured distance from actually inflicting pain, Muldoon took every opportunity to exercise it for himself. Muldoon was also the antithesis of being dapper. They were both scheming and egotistical and this put them on a collision course with Captain Thomas Bannon, O'Duffy's *aid-de-camp* who, in turn, appeared to detest both O'Duffy and Muldoon in equal measure. The only common denominator between Muldoon and Bannon was their rivalry for O'Duffy's ear. Like Muldoon, Bannon had no real interest in the Brigade and even less in the welfare of the men. His sole concern was ingratiating himself with the Spanish High command. This Irish *ménage-a-trois*, Muldoon, Bannon and O'Duffy, had more than enough self-centredness for an entire Brigade.

Tom walked into the Hotel *Alvarex* and into the presence of O'Duffy's camarilla who were sitting around a table with drinks and maps. Dalton, the second in command, Muldoon and last but not least, Bannon. Tom went to the bar and ordered a coffee. He fixed his eyes on Bannon, who appeared and sounded to be arguing more and louder than anyone else.

Bannon had an oddly shaped balding pate which made his skull appear elongated and his head over-large in relation to his body. His uniform could have been taken for a child's attempt at dressing-up as a soldier; nothing seemed to fit as it should. His shirt was enormous and the cuffs were rolled back several times, as was his belt which was wrapped around his waist more than once. He had the air of an undertaker. His wiry hands were never still and he waved them, almost Spanish style, whilst remonstrating with the others. Every now and again he would also run his hands over what remained of his hair, as if to re-plaster it back to his head. It also looked as if he dyed what was left of his strands, as they were an unnatural shoe-polish black in contrast to his grey eyebrows. Bannon could have been taken for Stan Laurel sitting next to the grossly fat Oliver Hardy in the guise of the portly Chaplain Muldoon. Such was the contrast in their body matter it made for a truly bizarre sight.

How or why Bannon's aggrandisement to the rank of Captain, albeit 'honorary', had come about was also a mystery to all concerned. Tom had learned that Bannon had held various positions within the Fascist National Corporate Party and the Blueshirt movement back home in Ireland. Before that he had trained as a priest in Germany in the early 1930s and had first-hand experience of the Nazis, whose ideology he was now unapologetically attracted to. Like so many others, Bannon decided against joining the priesthood and returned to Ireland where he worked as a journalist, rising to the height of editor of *The Standard,* a weekly Catholic newspaper based in Dublin. Therefore most people could only attribute his promotion in the Brigade to the simple fact that he had been a long-time acolyte of O'Duffy and that he could speak Spanish fluently. However, it now seemed that everything he touched was destined to turn to dust. Ethel Carney had told Mary, who in turn had told Tom that Bannon was also a heavy-drinker with a younger wife-problem. The rumour was that she was currently being put up in an expensive hotel in Lisbon and had a standard of living which he was struggling to pay for. Yet, in Cáceres, O'Duffy had seen fit to put him in charge of the Brigade's finances.

Tom had also discovered for himself that Bannon was one of the few bone fide fascists amongst the Irish Brigade. The views he espoused were carefully considered and consistent in their promotion of both Hitler and Mussolini, corporatism and anti-Communism. His anti-Semitism was also both explicit and pronounced. As such, he was entirely and comfortably at one with the Fascist-Nationalist cause. His open complicity with their Officers led many of the foreign correspondents, especially McIlroy, to suspect that he was in fact their spy. McIlroy also believed that Bannon was The *Independent's* insider in the Brigade. Copy was appearing, without a by-line, which neither he or Carney had written. Added to which, everyone knew that it did not pay to have a private conversation with Bannon as he was universally disliked and distrusted.

Tom was in the hotel for a press briefing and had the misfortune to take his seat at precisely the same moment that Captain Luis Antonio Bolín, the man with overall responsibility for policing the foreign correspondents, entered the room. Bolín was dressed as a Captain in the Foreign Legion. This had been his reward for organising, whilst he was a correspondent for the Spanish *ABC* newspaper in London, the plane that had taken Franco from the Canary Islands to Morocco. That is, for effectively enabling the start of the insurrection. Not only did Bolín, being very short and stout, not have the comportment to carry his uniform, his chosen accessories of high boots, breeches, leather gloves and riding crop, also made him appear a comical figure. It would later transpire that there was absolutely nothing humorous about this man and he was anything but comical.

The first thing Bolín insisted upon in the press gathering was that all the journalists stand in his presence. Thereafter all the chairs were subsequently removed from press meetings which he organised. Ironically, as Bolín stalked the floor of correspondents, nearly all appeared to tower over him and this only served to reinforce how inappropriate his stature was for a supposed Legionnaire officer. In fact he exuded all the signs of having a severe Napoleon complex. In his inspection of the Press Corps, Bolín paraded through their ranks and intermittently stopped along the line. He would then demand, in his most affected Public School English, to see some accreditation, in much the same way as a rather pompous, over-dressed ticket inspector might do on the 7.15 train from Guildford; only the consequences of not having the correct ticket were far more sinister in this instance. It was already well-known that he frequently and with actual intent threatened to have correspondents shot if they disobeyed the rules he invented or wrote things that he considered were treasonable to the Nationalist war effort. Tom, like most other correspondents, quickly realised that this man was not just egotistical but also powerful and extremely dangerous. Only the previous evening in the hotel bar, Sir Percival Phillips of the *Daily Telegraph,* who was renowned for his Francoist sympathies, suggested to Tom that Bolín was 'pure poison' and that he needed to be very careful when dealing with him. Kim Philby from *The Times* had, in passing, also warned Tom to 'keep his young head down'.

O'Duffy was at the centre of all things and appeared to have a uniform for every occasion. Such was the sloth-pace of the deployment and the surreal nature of the situation, the only real highlight came at the pantomime General's many press briefings. This one was to be no exception. Renowned for his involvement in all things Irish, especially the GAA – the *Gaelic Athletics Association* – O'Duffy was asked by the 'famous' American correspondent, why he had not engaged his men in sports whilst they were waiting to go the front?

'General, as a great supporter of sport, can I suggest that the men play a game of soccer against the locals? The Spanish are mad about soccer and I know they would be keen to beat your men!'

O'Duffy thought for a moment and then paraded up and down the front of the room. Gathering his thoughts, he puffed out his chest and responded.

'Mr Knickerbocker, you obviously know very little about our sports. Association football, or 'soccer', as you call it, is *not* the Irish game. My men will not be playing it, against the Spanish or anyone else, here or anywhere else. In any case, and contrary to what you are told, football is an Irish invention. And as with so much of our culture, the English purloined it as their own. Do you know that there was football played in Galway in 1527? Of course not, how could you? We, the Irish, also invented Rugby. Again, this is probably something most of you have been denied any knowledge of. Yes, it was at Rugby School in England that the football was placed in the hands for the first time, but it was by a boy from County Tipperary, William Webb Ellis. I think we may assume he was merely reviving the Gaelic game. It was obviously in his blood and nature to play the game the Gaelic way.'

'General, are you claiming that the Irish invented both soccer, sorry, football and rugby? Is that right? Did I hear you right?' Knickerbocker dared to ask.

'You heard correctly Mr Knickerbocker. And it is not a claim, it is a fact I assure you. The foreign games my countrymen have had to endure have all been imposed. They were meant to undermine our sense of ourselves, our nationality. We were supposed to play English games in order fit into their Empire. We will not submit ourselves to *their* codes of *our* games.'

'But General, in the interests of local harmony, wouldn't it be a good idea to have some sort of sport with the locals?' Cardozo of the *Daily Mail* intervened.

'Sport is all very well Mr Cardozo, but as you will have seen, the Irish soldier is already a superior specimen. Just compare them with the Spanish men here. It would not help the locals or harmony if they were to be subjected to our obvious superiority. It may be very demoralising for them and indeed not much use for my men to expend their energies in that way. You can see for yourself, the Irish Celt is taller, stronger and in far better condition, mentally and physically, than the local population. A life-time of Gaelic sport has prepared my Brigade for its role here in Spain. The endurance, speed and quickness of thought instilled by our native games are ideal preparation for what will be coming our way. The enemy had better be ready. We are altogether better athletes and manlier I'd say.'

Bolín's reaction to O'Duffy's diatribe was instantaneous.

'Gentlemen, I think the General has said enough on this subject. Please, no more questions about sport.'

The Spanish captain was more than livid and it showed. It appeared that, for Bolín, the characterisation of the Spanish as an inferior race to the Irish was tantamount to a declaration of war. Whether O'Duffy intended to upset his host is debatable. His tenor was entirely in keeping with Bolín's own doctrine of the 'survival of the fittest', something he had himself already used as a legitimation of the Francoist mission. Nevertheless, it was a diplomatic disaster for the Irish leader to have used this in the presence of his nominal ally.

For Tom, the claims by O'Duffy were not just some Mad Hatter musings about the origins of certain sports, they were also a disturbing first sign that the Irish leader was already losing any sense of reality. What had started as a simple chauvinist outburst had soon transmogrified into a parody of the extant fascist leadership style. O'Duffy was trying to ape, albeit unconsciously it seemed, Hitler and Mussolini, not to mention their infant bastard Franco. In a uniform with over-size epaulettes and fancy piping, one that looked as if he had come straight from the rehearsals of a Gilbert and Sullivan operetta, the increasingly rotund, red-nosed, balding figure of O'Duffy, did little to assuage the impression that he was the very poor relative of the Fuehrer-Duce-Generalissimo ménage. Whilst he was already a stranger to the General's worldview, O'Duffy's claims further reinforced Tom's sense of estrangement from his fellow countrymen. He desperately wanted to broadcast the fact that he was embarrassed by this clownish performance. More important still, he wanted to ask the question, 'what might this mean for the men under O'Duffy's command?' However, Tom was not so naive as to even broach the question. Within a few days of arriving in Spain he had quickly recognised that trying to write truthfully about what was happening in the Nationalist zone and in relation to the Irish Brigade in particular, was going to demand both all his skills as a writer, plus a good deal of patience. He also had increasing doubts as to whether he was equipped or up to the task. At the same time, he was more determined than ever to prove himself to Mary.

10

———

IF THE TRUTH BE TOLD

There is chaos in every war zone and the unexpected is always expected to happen. Yet nothing had really prepared either Mary or Tom for the menacing lunacy that encircled the foreign Press Corps in Cáceres. It was as if they had been committed to a mental asylum where it was impossible to distinguish the staff from the inmates. It was a surrealist nightmare in which they found themselves surrounded by so-called colleagues who were every bit as abhorrent as the Nationalist press officers. The one exception was Lieutenant Manuel de Lambarri y Yanguas.

Manuel Lambarri was different from all the other Nationalist officers in the Press Office. He always looked uncomfortable in his uniform and in himself. And from their first encounter, this had enamoured him to Mary. Short and stocky and about thirty-five years of age, she thought he was far too pallid for a Spanish military man. He shuffled his body but was remarkably light on his feet and danced around the office in a manner that suggested he was the lead actor on a stage. He had none of the stiffness or officiousness of the other censors and was certainly less concerned than most to cross every 't' and dot every 'i'. The Press Corps soon realised that this was due to his written English not being up to the task of correcting or in some cases understanding their despatches. As a result he became the correspondents' censor of choice. His trademark approach to signalling his approval of their copy was to append a sketch in blue pencil to the top right-hand corner of the cover page. He drew Big Ben on Mary's first cable. She later discovered that he had been a graphic designer and had worked in London for *Vogue* magazine. Lambarri, she came to think, was the only human being in Bolín's office. Why then was he in the Nationalist army? Was it a safe haven for a man of his sensibilities?

It was a minor incident, as many of what later turn out to be significant events often are. Lambarri had returned the first article Tom had submitted with just one note in blue ink: *'the term insurgent is not permitted.'* There was no sketch in the top corner of the sheet. It was the first time Tom had encountered censorship and he did not take it well. Despite Mary's counsel, his first instinct was to protest.

Tom arrived in the Press Office raising his voice and waving his rejected copy in the face of the ever-frenetic Lieutenant. Lambarri was already in one of his usual panics yet, to his credit and contrary to his nature, he tried to calm the young man and asked that he wait until he had a moment to spare. Tom, however, was in no mood to be compliant and insisted that Lambarri immediately approve his copy as written.

'Orders...I can do nothing. It is orders,' was all Lambarri kept saying as he flitted between tasks and stamped documents in a crescendo of officialdom. Far from placating Tom, this infuriated him still further. Consulting his notebook, he continued to remonstrate. 'Look, I have the OED definition. It says: *insurgent*, a person who revolts against civil authority or an established government. It's the correct term. That's what you are: *insurgents*.'

Lambarri was singly unimpressed and simply shook his head in the best traditions of the bureaucrat and carried on stamping,

'It may be what we are - in your opinion and even the OE...or whatever is your dictionary definition, but we have our own. It is not permitted to use the term. I have my orders.'

'Orders?'

Lambarri stopped stamping and looked up,

'Yes, orders Mr Lees, from my superiors. This is the Army,' he replied. And looking directly into Tom's eyes suggested, 'I can arrange for you to see Captain Bolín about the matter, if you would like?'

Tom knew that this was nothing less than a threat and soon realised he was getting nowhere with the usually compliant junior censor, 'What should I use instead? Any suggestions?' he said flippantly.

'That is your choice Mr Lees... A Thesaurus would help perhaps? But not *insurgent*.'

'Then it isn't my choice!'

'Mr Lees, I just take my orders. The word is not permitted and I cannot help you. See Captain Bolín if you wish to discuss this further.' Lambarri's patience was by now already exhausted and he resumed his stamping of documents with obvious frustration.

'Do you even want to...help?'

Lambarri pressed his top lip and did not answer. Tom gave up trying to convince him. His use of a single word had sabotaged all the others he had written and there was nothing he could do about it. It was a powerful lesson regarding the importance of words and the nature of truth in the context of a war.

Tom had come to Spain with the simple belief that his duty, as a journalist, would be to report the facts. He really believed he could and should tell the truth wherever possible. He had no time for politics or sentiment and felt that these only interfered with and obscured access to the truth. He saw his priority as not writing a record for posterity, but informing the readers of the day. This was especially important given that they were currently being fed what he now knew was little more than a diet of half-truths and outright lies. Since the start of the war, he had already seen for himself that the tide of articles that had made its way to the newspapers in Ireland and elsewhere were mostly of a lurid propagandistic nature. The Nationalist 'Crusade' was being portrayed as a necessary antidote to the 'Red Menace, Bolshevik Bestiality' etc. All manner of stories about the atrocities committed by the blood-thirsty 'Red atheists', especially against the clergy and nuns, had been prominent on the front pages of the major national dailies, including McIlroy's efforts for *The Irish Independent*. Tom now found himself surrounded by some of the most prolific fabricators of those self-same stories.

The Press Corps were far thirstier for blood than any of the men who were going to do the actual fighting. Their articles, often lathered with gory details and intimate accounts of the many heinous deeds committed by a sub-human enemy, left one with the impression that 'Red' Spain was populated by vampires and ghouls of every description. Tom had half-joked that Bram Stoker could have been their main inspiration and Dante could also be called upon if necessary. To his growing dismay, he soon realised that many of the correspondents were hacks, drunks, or both. Also hidden in their number were failed fiction writers, Baedeker guidebook-totting 'Sons of Gentlemen' on the path from leaving Public School to joining 'the Bank', and a sprinkling of Fascist-inclined academics, mostly historians, on sabbatical and in search of confirmation of their pet theories. The overwhelming majority of the foreign and war correspondents were, whether by dint of their newspaper's political orientation or their personal politics, nakedly partisan in relation to the Francoist cause. Whilst not entirely unexpected, it was their unconcealed lack of commitment to the truth that disturbed Tom and made him more intent than ever on not becoming one of their number.

Both Mary and Tom found the atmosphere surrounding the Press Corps toxic and intensely threatening. She likened it to drowning slowly in a cess-pit full of snakes. She also felt that her real identity was far from safe in their company. Tom also soon realised that keeping Mary's identity secret was no longer a game and it was now deadly serious. The male foreign correspondents were mostly middle-aged and acted as a chauvinist cabal. They often formed huddles and whispered to each other over any number of glasses of liquor. Many a story, or simply gossip, was communicated in the gentlemen's lavatories and other such exclusive locations. Tom, acting as Mary's eyes and ears, was becoming indispensable. The pack instinct of the correspondents was, if at all possible, to exclude women, of whom there were very few. Apart from Ethel Carney and Mary, there were just two other women journalists in Cáceres. They were both American and looked impossibly young, Tom's age or even less, and improbably pretty. It was said of one, she could have '*been taken for Lauren Bacall*'. They were 'assistants' to Cardozo and acted as his 'runners', as well as being trophies for the stunted reporter. Mary thought they had no right to be in the midst of all this, especially with these men. Yet, both the American women appeared to be very relaxed about their lot and, if anything, it was only Carney's inevitable advances and constant touching that they seemed to find disturbing.

It was not just the correspondents' politics that Mary found especially repugnant, it was also their profound moral cowardice. Having taken sides, they appeared to relish their own self-righteousness and, more so, the increasing likelihood that they had chosen the winning side. Mary's own partisanship precluded any criticism of their lack of objectivity and she never expected them to do anything other than to support Franco and the insurgents' cause. As such, she had no grounds for complaining that their accounts were little more than propaganda. However, it was their feigned indignation at the death of ordinary Spaniards - but only when it was the result of Republican atrocities - that marked a hypocrisy too far. For Mary, it was their refusal to face up to the depravity of their Fascist allies and their willingness to legitimate the massacre of innocents as a *'necessary but unfortunate'* bi-product of the 'Crusade' that placed the majority of the Press Corps on the side of evil. She felt her body and soul were being violated by just being in their company and was afraid that Tom may become contaminated by the cynicism of the older hacks. It was not long before she began to regret embroiling him in the folly of the whole venture.

'Tom, you are never going to have a 'God's eye view'. There isn't one. You can't sit on the fence in a war. You'll get your head shot off. On the fence is where the Devil wants you to take tea. It's true what they say, '*Truth is the first casualty of war*', she kept reminding him.

Mary also came to recognise that most of the journalists were also pitifully lazy. Rather than seek out their stories or corroborate those of others, they simply ate off the platter served up by the Nationalist Press and Propaganda Office, the second part of whose name they never seemed to acknowledge. They had become little more than ciphers for the insurgents' cause. In their mitigation, it could perhaps be argued that, in some respects at least, these were inmates simply responding to their guards. Bolín's office had most them on a very short leash and as such they were genuinely fearful of transgressing his edicts, whether by accident or design. They also soon discovered that the physical threat he posed was indeed real and never to be under-estimated. Very few, if any, had any inkling that worse still was yet to come in the shape of Captain Gonzalo de Aguilera y Munro.

Although he thought his commitment to objectivity was stronger than Mary's, Tom shared her perspective on the foreign correspondents. That is, that most of the correspondents in Cáceres were either repugnant or indolent or both. Like her, he had no great expectation that they were dedicated to professional truth-seeking or any such ideals. His conversation with McIlroy had confirmed as much. However, he also thought they were incapable, even if they wanted to, of uncovering the truth amongst the dung-pile of lies and propaganda that was constantly being flushed out of the Nationalist Press Office.

It had taken no time at all for Tom to become sensitive to the subtle but critical distinction facing all the genuine correspondents: do you try to tell the truth or simply try to avoid telling untruths? Thus, whilst he had yet to witness any atrocities, there was overwhelming and incontrovertible evidence from many of the correspondents that gave lie to the claim that the Nationalist insurrection was to save their faith or indeed to save Spain. Everyone on the ground could see that they were engaged in a war of extermination. It was not long before he realised that he was bound to be caught in the crossfire between attempting to tell the truth and producing propaganda that might be useful for one side or indeed the other. After just a few weeks amongst the Nationalists, such doubts had already begun to challenge his initial idealism. Whereas, for Mary, there was no point being a writer unless one actually supported the cause of freedom and justice or similar progressive values. Both by upbringing and conviction, she had set herself to promote the cause of democracy and that meant, in this case, supporting the democratically elected government of the Republic. Almost instinctively she knew that she could best do this by writing about the threat the Fascists posed for all the disempowered, and not just those in Spain but throughout Europe. There also had to be some meaning in what she was doing and her writing had to have some moral grounding. She did not value or even have time for the notion of objectivity, especially 'objectivity for the sake of objectivity'. In her view, neutral or objective reporting was simply a way of maintaining or failing to challenge the perspective of the most powerful; it helped maintain the status quo, albeit, as in Tom's case, this was sometimes unintentional. She thought that the best that he might do was to recognise a reality of all wars; that it was a deadly competition *between* different versions of the truth and protagonists who were not averse to fictionalising their gains and losses. Therefore she not only believed that not taking sides was impossible, but that it was also more than a little self-inflating for Tom to pretend that he could do otherwise.

It was almost impossible for those like Tom to do their journalistic best, let alone those that had no time or indeed intention of upholding 'the freedom of the press'. He thought that the vast majority of the journalists had become mere 'hacks'. Indeed, what appeared to matter was getting their story out and being the first to publish. Their egos and competitiveness meant that even the most hackneyed story was fought over in terms of the importance of being first to print. They appeared to act on the basis that the substance of the copy was largely being prescribed and therefore felt no need to adjust or even embellish that which emanated from the Press Office. Their articles were, in effect, facsimiles of the official accounts. The correspondents' common cause with the Nationalists was nevertheless fragile. There was internecine warfare going on, as well as all manner of subterfuge associated with getting the story out. It was well-known that at least one of Cardozo's young American 'runners' was acting as a conduit for despatches going to the French border, thereby avoiding the interminable delays caused by the Nationalist's censorship process. And it was no secret that a place in her corset was in constant demand.

No matter how hard Mary tried or how cogent her argument, Tom continued to be convinced that there had to be a real distinction between fact and fiction. Despite his willingness to concede that his perspective and personal values would inform what he saw, his subject and choice of words, he maintained that his mission was to seek the 'truth', despite the cacophony of competing voices in the conflict.

'By all means sympathise but that shouldn't get in the way of telling the facts of the matter. Would you stop yourself writing about something if it didn't favour your cause? We both know there have been atrocities in the Republican zone. There have been thousands of executions and many innocent people have been murdered in the name of 'revolutionary justice' and 'the cause'. Would you not write about those things if you were in that zone? Would you censor yourself for their cause?' Tom asked in an increasingly accusatory voice.

Mary had already found herself wondering what it would have been like if she had gone to the Republican side? By most accounts, the censorship was far more arbitrary, even haphazard. Naturally, this did not help the Republican cause as stories emerged of wrongdoing, executions, murder, mishaps and general misery, all of which came to reflect poorly on the government side. Similar stories were not tolerated and certainly could not be ventilated on the Nationalist side.

'No, of course I wouldn't. I wouldn't stop myself from reporting crimes or injustice or even just mistakes ...committed by ...well, anyone... but especially by those I support. In fact, more than most, they should be made aware of the right thing to do, morally that is. But we also have to understand their position and why they might do things that we disapprove of or find reprehensible. When we do that, we are likely to find that they thought they had good reasons. So it's also our responsibility to try to understand and report those reasons. If that means in order to understand we have to empathise with them, then I'm willing to do that. In which case, I'll inevitably appear as sympathetic to their cause, their situation, their explanations and against the versions of those in power. So be it. But that doesn't mean I approve regardless of what they might do.'

Her eyes lit up even more than usual when she was in full flow and Tom was captivated by their intensity. In order to stop his submission to her argument, he averted his own stare and summoned up a deliberately provocative response.

'You sound just like all the others. Just like McIlroy and Carney.'

Although he intended the barb to repress his growing attraction to his mentor, Tom also knew his particularly low shot would hurt her. Immediately recognising and regretting the poverty of the insult, he hastened to re-elevate the discussion.

'But what if their reasons are genuine but mistaken or simply wrong?'

Still feeling the insult and thinking how to respond, she paused and stared at him intently. Eventually she decided she would not stoop to his level.

'It depends on the reasons. We all make mistakes - even you? We all think we are in the right sometime and we all justify our actions, usually after the fact. Everything depends on our motives and our values. They should cause us to ask whether what we did might, in some way, at least be understandable.'

'Saying something is understandable is not the same as saying that it's right or wrong. I'm sure we can all understand Franco's motives, but that doesn't make them right,' Tom replied.

'No, but understanding helps us to make that judgement, which we all need to do for ourselves. It's the values behind our reasons that guide us. That's why I know which side I'm on in this war.'

'The losers by the looks of things! Tom chided.

Again, he had not meant to be facetious but his defence mechanism had once again overruled his reason.

'Will there be any winners?' Mary snapped back.

'Oh yes, most definitely. Just look around', said Tom. 'Us, if we survive. We stand to gain from this.'

Mary was getting increasingly agitated with his unwillingness to countenance the idea that, winners or losers, there were principles at stake.

'In that case representing the view of the losers becomes even more important. Who will tell their story? Where will your truth be when the Fascists have won?' she almost shouted at him.

'But who are your losers? The Communist Party? The Anarchists? The workers? The Republican government? All of Spain? Are we to hear *all* of them? And are we to believe them *all*? How are we to believe any one of them, if we have to believe *all* of them? They can't all be telling the truth.'

'And the Fascists? They too will have their version. At the moment, it's theirs that looks like being the one that dictates what the truth might be, especially here and now. And, more than likely, it'll not be yours or mine that matters in the long run. Don't think you can find *your* truth without contesting *theirs*. If they win, they will decide what is true or not, and you and I will hardly be in a position to say otherwise. They will have the power. Surely you've witnessed that already? They won't let you tell anything but their truth and you either go along with them, like most of the so-called journalists in this Hotel, or you become their enemy. You'll not choose, they will.'

'Go along with them? I've no intention of doing that. But I am going to tell the true story.'

'Tom, they're not playing games here! These people are dangerous. Bolín is very dangerous. You can't play games with them.'

'There must be a way of finding and telling the truth. I will find it. I will and I must.'

'Then you really are a fool. I should have never brought you here. This is no place for dreamers.'

By now Tom was also getting increasingly exasperated by her arguments.

'Then why are we here? Why *are* we here? If all we end up doing is telling their version and it's all lies, what's the point?'

'All we can do is bear witness and live with the hope that someday the opportunity to tell our stories will come along. We're like squirrels collecting nuts.'

'I want to tell the story of what's happening here and now, not last month or last year! I don't want to write history. I'm not interested in history. In any case, squirrels always forget where they put their fecking nuts! They're bloody stupid creatures and that's why they are always so damn busy.' Tom paused before resuming, 'And if we don't try to tell the truth now, it'll be lost and perhaps lost forever. Nothing can be true about old news. Truth is in the moment.'

Tom thought that Mary's approach to the truth was distorted by her natural sympathy for the oppressed, the workers, the downtrodden and a myriad of other victims of the military coup. She was unable and unwilling to look at the situation dispassionately and as a result failed to see what was actually happening, as opposed to what she thought *ought* to happen. He thought she would end up writing only for the converted, or escapists, and that was not what 'serious' writers do. In his view, it was also a denial of herself, her being, and a form of self-censorship. Worse, it relegated her work to mere propaganda and as such placed her in the same camp as that of the most wretched of sycophants in the Press Corps, the ones he was trying so desperately hard to avoid becoming.

Although she disagreed with Tom, Mary couldn't help but be impressed by the intensity of his new found conviction. His transformation, almost overnight, from being a rather light-weight, flippant, care-free and insolent Young Turk, to this serious seeker of The Truth, was entirely unexpected. She also knew, however, that his ideal of telling the truth was going to put him in enormous danger in this context. Yet, there appeared to be no way for her to breach his new found faith and indeed a part of her didn't actually want to. She found herself deeply attracted to his passion and couldn't help but recognise how he was recharging her conscience and rekindling a sense of being alive to her emotions. Their differences were enlivening and fuelling a recovered sensitivity and awareness of others, as well as each other. At the same time, she was also frightened as to what this might mean for both of them.

This debate about the nature of truth and the role of fiction had been building up since leaving London. Mary had dominated these discussions and in a rather maternal manner she had tried to make Tom more worldly wise and realistic. For the best part of the outward journey he had travelled with his mouth agape and in thrall of the whole experience of foreign travel. Only now, in Cáceres, had the initial shock of being abroad given way to the realisation that he was in a real war zone. In the course of their journey she had also sensed that there was some underlying, unstated reason for his obduracy and insistence on the need to search for the truth, to reveal all and have no secrets - save that regarding her true identity. Her intuition told her that it must have something to do with his childhood, of which in their entire time together he had made no reference whatsoever. From the little he had said about his upbringing, one would have thought he had been born sixteen years of age. She gathered he had no father, no mother and no siblings; an even more immaculate conception than Christ himself. She was convinced that Tom's belief and commitment to the truth, whilst misplaced and illusory, was born out of some early experience back home in Ireland.

11

DIAMOND HILL

Grace waited in her van in a small lay-by opposite the gothic monstrosity of Kylemore Abbey, the girls' boarding school on the road just beyond Letterfrack. She had time to ponder and decided it was peculiar, to say the least, that no one ever mentioned the girls' school. She thought that this might be explained by the fact that the girls were seldom, if ever, seen in the village. Were they prohibited from going into Letterfrack? Whatever the reason, the contrast between the two Schools was stark and, save for the hideous pile and its adjoining farm, the very existence of the girls could well be doubted. They were an unseen presence and she thought this could be said of most of the women of Ireland.

The mist and rain cavorted across her windscreen and Grace had difficulty viewing the approach from the farmstead, where any troop of boys would need to emerge. She was worried that her distinctive vehicle would attract the attention of those who could not resist whiling away their time with local chit-chat. The last thing she wanted was an uninvited conversation about the dreadful weather, the price of eggs and how Dublin is full of thieves who kept ponies in their tenements. She kept low in her seat and at the first sign of life ducked down below the dashboard.

Looking out at Diamond Hill she could see the clouds parting and the mountain began to live up to its name. Very slowly, a small ray of sunshine appeared through the otherwise grey blanket of cloud that surrounded the peak and a funnel of light reflected off the schist sending a searchlight beam high into the sky. It was little wonder that heavenly forces were often invoked on such sightings. Divine intervention would be most welcome she thought. Of course it didn't materialise and she resumed her vigil as a confirmed atheist.

Towards the middle of the morning she began to doubt whether she should continue with the vigil and was ready to abandon her mission when a worm of small figures appeared. They were boys from the School being led by a Brother. She sunk down in her seat and watched as they passed on the other side of the road and crossed to join the path leading to the hill. Mercifully, she thought, the rain had stopped temporarily. The boys already looked bedraggled and by their step she could tell that this was not an outing they were looking forward to. They all had some form of homemade poncho-like cover over their bodies, but their legs were bare, save some knee length socks that were already around their ankles in most cases. Some had Wellington boots, others wore plimsolls. They looked like a column of wet rag dolls and made for a pathetic sight. The Brother was dressed in a raincoat, a flat cap and a scarf covering his chin. He carried a wooden staff and a haversack. From where Grace was hiding, it was difficult to make out his age or identity. All she could do was watch as they snaked their way down the footpath to the first hillock and beyond.

Giving them good time to start their ascent, Grace secured her van and set off in pursuit. She had no idea as to their likely pace or her own stalking skills. Keeping a distance would be difficult, especially on the initial climb which was a steep grassy verge that rose slowly to a minor ridge. She thought she would be spotted sooner rather than later and began to rehearse her introduction. After twenty minutes of uphill slog, the boys had disappeared. She stood and surveyed the horizon without success; they were nowhere to be seen. Then she heard them. An indistinct but obvious sound of crying and shouting could be heard from directly above where she stood. Slowly, she kept low to the profile of the hill and finding suitable rock cover peered over the line of the ridge. The boys were standing in a circle with the Brother at its centre. Two small boys were sitting on the edge of the circle and it was from them that the sobbing could be made out. The other boys were haranguing the Brother and indicating something about the two boys who were in distress. He was leaning on his staff and appeared to be rebutting their dissent. Grace watched as the scene unfolded. The Brother made an attempt to organise a hand-lift for the stricken boys by two able-bodied boys crossing their hands and placing one of the casualties in the seat that was formed. They attempted a lift. They were unsteady and slipped and fell almost immediately. Grace could see that their footwear was the problem. The poor victim of the botched effort let out another almighty scream in agony and Grace took this as an invitation to announce herself. She clambered down from the ridge.

'Can I help?'

'Good Lord! Where did you come from?' the Brother looked genuinely alarmed by her sudden appearance.

'My Goodness yourself! Weren't you on the Galway bus?'

'I'm sorry, I don't—,' he looked every inch puzzled and confused by this opening exchange.

'You were on the bus from Galway. I sat behind you.'

'I don't rightly recall. I'm sorry.' He was as meek as she remembered.

'What's happened here? Can I help?'

'We have a couple of ...well, they are a bit poorly, they say. I'd say they're swinging-the-lead. Malingerers more like. I think they're beyond help.'

'These two?'

'Yes, Nye and Doyle. Stand up boys when there's a lady present!' he shouted at them. His voice sounded as if it had only just broken and was little different from that of his charges.

'No really, there's no need for that,' Grace intervened. 'Really. Sit. Stay there. Do you mind if I take a look?'

'There's nothing to see...but by all means, help yourself. We can't be standing here all day. The rain's coming any time now. Stand back boys. Let Miss through now.'

The boys broke the circle and Grace entered the ring. The smallest boy sat holding his leg and had managed to streak his face with the black of the bog turf. He looked like a Victorian child chimney sweep. His companion in pain was a little older and cleaner. He too clutched his leg about the ankle.

'Can I take a look?' she asked.

Grace gently lifted the first boy's wet and freezing cold hands off his leg. There was nothing but skin and bone on what were twig-like appendages protruding from his shorts. They were also full of scabs and sores, some of which had opened up and rivulets of blood, now dried, had streaked down onto the top of his socks. She could now see and feel his pain. Grace then moved across to the elder of the two boys. He too was painfully thin and his elongated limbs and oversize Wellington boots made his lack of thigh muscle an even more disturbing sight. It also made his boots appear as if they were those of a puppet with strings attached.

'Where's the pain?' she asked.

'Me ankle Miss,' the boy replied and his eyes filled with tears.

'Can you take your boot off?'

'No Miss. I can't...it hurts too much,' he sobbed.

'You need to try. We might be able to wrap it and give it some support, so we can get you down. You need to try. Let me pull your boot and you just stay still.'

'It really hurts Miss. Please—'

'It will hurt, but we need to see what the damage is. Father, could you just hold the boy while I pull his boot off?'

The Brother stayed his distance and was clearly reluctant to help. 'I really don't think this is necessary. I'm sure we'll manage now. Really, thanks and all but we need to be getting back now. If you take it off, it may never go back on again.'

'Father, hold the boy please. I have a van back at the road. If we can get these boys down, I can drive them back to the School or, better still, the doctor's. Just hold him please while I take off the boot.'

The young cleric relented and took hold of the boy around his shoulders. Grace slowly pulled the boot and the boy let out a scream. She quickly pulled the remainder of the boot off whilst he was still emitting his agony. His ankle was swollen and the bone stood out at an unnatural angle. It was crimson, blue and black and even to her untrained eye she could see that this was an old injury.

'The School. We have to go back to the School. We have

our own infirmary. But this really is not necessary. They'll be fine in a minute and we can walk ourselves back.'

The Brother was now almost in a panic and nothing he said made any rightful sense given the evidence that now confronted him. Grace could see that the young man was more than just unwilling to allow her to help; he was scared. She stood and took him by the arm and led him away from the boys.

'A word please Father?'

'It's Brother. I'm not a priest. I'm Brother Noel.'

It had already grated on Grace to be calling the boy Father and she was only too ready to be relieved of the anachronism. '*Brother*, these boys should not be on this mountain. They are in no state to do this exercise and you are endangering them by doing so. Both the boys are hurt and in my view they need urgent medical attention. And those wounds do not appear to have been caused today.'

'I wouldn't know about that.'

'The welts on the small one, did you not see them?'

'I did not.'

'And this boy's ankle is nearly broken! You couldn't see he was struggling?' Grace was becoming more irate at his obvious faux-ignorance.

'It's not my job to give them a medical inspection before we start!' he pleaded. 'As far as I was concerned, they were fit for the walk. They didn't say anything, so how was I to know?' His defensiveness was growing and he started to avoid her eyes. 'I thank you for your concern but I now need to get back to the School. We'll manage between us I'm sure. You have no need to concern yourself any longer, Miss?'

'Deben. Grace Deben.'

'Miss Deben.'

Grace reasserted her hold on his arm and decided that this

would be the most opportune moment to broach the main subject. She lowered her voice so the boys could not overhear.

'What's going on Brother? Why are these boys on this mountain? Is it a punishment? I've heard that you beat these boys ...and worse.' Grace stared directly into his disbelieving eyes.

Obviously shocked by her bluntness, he tried to untangle his arm but then noticed that all the boys were watching intently and decided to remain in her grip. In an exaggerated whisper he tried to answer her, 'I don't know what you are talking about! I don't beat the boys! How dare you suggest such a thing? Who are you?'

'I know all about your so-called 'School.' There was more than menace in her tone and the cleric tried once again to escape her grasp.

'Let me go please. The boys are watching.'

'Is this a punishment? Shall I ask the boys?'

'You'll do no such thing! It's not your business. Now, if you'll let me go, I'll get them back.'

'What's to stop me asking?'

'There's nothing to tell. This is normal physical exercise. We do this all the time and some boys are just laggards who want to avoid it. That's what you see here.'

'Laggards? Those boys are in no condition to do any exercise, let alone climb this hill. They are not even dressed for it. Why are they wearing plimsolls and Wellingtons?'

'We're a poor School. That's all they have.'

'And that's a poor excuse Brother. Look at them! How many do you think want to be up this mountain? Do they look like they are enjoying themselves? This *is* a punishment of some kind *isn't* it?'

'Whether they like it or not they need fresh air.'

'Then I'll ask them.'

'No, please ...please do not interfere! Yes, this is a punishment...but a healthy one. It's for their own benefit.'

'If they're injured?'

'Obviously not. I didn't know they were injured.'

'Why then are they being punished? What have they done to deserve this?'

He paused before replying, 'Bed-wetters, all of them.'

Grace could hardly contain herself, 'My God! You're punishing them for wetting the bed!'

'The fresh air is a good remedy. That's the advice we received. Now, can we get going please? If you're worried about them, then you'll be wanting us to get them down, right now.'

'Bed-wetters?' she still couldn't comprehend the justice of the case.

'Yes, bed-wetters. 'Little sailors' we call them. We should be going now.'

Grace turned towards the boys and, seeing their pitiful faces, decided to stop expressing her anger.

'Yes, of course. Let me help. I can take them back in my van.'

'Let's see if that's necessary when we're down.'

Grace found a scarf in her haversack and wrapped it around the ankle of the taller boy. His oversize boots enabled her to gingerly place his foot back in the fold and two of the larger boys took his shoulders and he stood, painfully. She then spotted a clump of sphagnum moss and had a moment of inspiration. Pulling up a large handful of the wet sponge, she gently rubbed the plant down the younger boy's wounds. As she did so, he looked at her as if she were a witch.

'It's a medicine,' she said. 'It'll do it good. You'll feel better. Tuck it in and pull up your socks.'

Two of the remaining boys took the youngster by the arms and they proceeded to start the descent. Before they had travelled fifty yards the drizzle descended softly and continuously. The slope became even more slippery and one boy tumbled, then another and then another. Even Grace in her sensible hiking boots had trouble staying upright. Brother Noel also took a fall and several of the boys smirked and giggled at his plight. The back of his raincoat was muddied and sodden and they remarked out of his earshot that he had 'shat himself.'

Grace attempted to re-engage the Brother before he escaped. She sensed he was very much troubled by his role and she wanted him to confide in her. Calming her anger as best she could.

'Brother Noel, can we talk please? I'm sorry about my manner earlier. I was upset by the boys' injuries and ...this punishment business. I can't help feeling that there is something more amiss here? As I said, there are rumours, some say more, about the School. I had one of your boys who had run away turn up at my cottage not so long ago.'

'Is that so?' he said, still disinclined to look at her.

'The boy told me he was beaten, regularly. He said that he had a hose put on him and—'

'You shouldn't be believing a runaway. They say all sorts. Did you get his name?'

'Tighe, they called him Tighe.'

'Ah Tighe! Yes, a bigger liar you'll not find in the county.'

'Is he still at the School?'

'He is, I believe. Still lying of course.'

'And would he have had his head shaven for running away?'

There was a silence as the young cleric tried to decide what to say,

'Perhaps, but only to check for the nits ...because you never know where they get to on the run.'

'And the hose?'

'They enjoy that in the summer. A wash down.'

'And winter? And worse?' She stopped on the track and tugged his raincoat.

'And worse?'

'Are they interfered with?'

'I've no idea what you are talking about!' he tried to walk on but realising the slipperiness of the slope, slowed and placed his staff in front as a prop.

'Really? What else goes on with the Brothers? I've heard—'

'You seem to have heard a lot of nonsense gossip Miss. They say people in these parts have very fertile imaginations. It's due to the weather and the like. They have to be able to think themselves out of the dreariness of it all. There's nothing going on around here you see.'

'Are boys being abused Brother?' Grace was not diverted by his response.

'I've no idea what you're getting at and I'd say it was no business of yours in any case. You're not from around here.'

'Not my business? Surely it's all our business! If these boys are being abused by your Brothers, we all have a responsibility to stop it?'

'If, if, if... There's no proof of anything you suggest. The fantastic imaginings of a young lad, I'd say.'

'Brother, I don't need further proof. I can see it in these poor mites.'

'They're rough boys. They come from terrible homes, or no homes at all. They were worse off in some cases before they came here. This will help make them. Yes, we may discipline them, but it's for their own good. A beating from my father never did me any harm. In fact, I think it sorted me out alright. That's why I am what I am today.'

'And were you interfered with?'

The Brother was shocked by the question and stopped in his tracks.

'How dare you! Of course not! I came from a loving family. How dare you suggest such a thing? What are you, mad?'

'So you do know what I'm talking about?'

'Miss... Deben, can we stop this interrogation, please? I'm not at liberty to tell you anything. I don't know why you are persisting with this. The School is there to protect these vulnerable children. That's what it does.'

They resumed the descent and Grace trailed keeping the Brother within earshot.

'Then why do they run away?'

Without turning to look at Grace he offered, 'Adventure? The grass is greener? Who knows what goes through their heads?'

'Then why are they so fearful about returning?'

At last he turned and faced her.

'Because they've caused a heap of trouble and inconvenience and they know it.'

'And the beating? You sanction that yourself? Do you hit them?'

'I'll answer no more of your nonsense questions. Can we end this please?'

Again, he went to walk ahead of her at a pace and slipped on the sodden turf. He scrambled to his feet and turned his back on Grace as she approached. She called to him, 'Have you no conscience Brother? Not to mention a duty to actually protect these boys from whatever?'

Not waiting for her to reach him, he approached her.

'My conscience? *My* conscience is clear, I assure you.'

He did not sound at all convincing and Grace thought she had detected a fracture in his defences. She decided to drop her accusative tone for the time being,

'What about the other Brothers?'

Noel did not answer.

'We're nearly there. My van is in the corner by the gate. Let me take the injured boys back?'

'I don't think that would be a good idea. Questions might be asked and I would have to report what has been said.'

'Why?'

'Because the boys would be the first to make up a pack of lies. I should imagine they would say we were having...or something ludicrous...and then we would all be in trouble explaining why you were on the mountain with us. The inquiry would go on forever. I'd rather I take them back and explain a bystander helped dress their wounds.'

'Which I did.'

'Which you did and we're grateful. As for your inquiries, your accusations, I think we should just forget those.'

'Do *you* want to do that?'

'I think it's for the best.'

'For whom? For yourself? Or these boys? The School? The village? Who's it best for?'

'Everyone, yourself included. No good can come of it. You'll be getting beyond your—'

'Business? What about your business ...as a servant of Christ?'

'My conscience ...is my conscience. God will be my witness.'

'And theirs?' She indicated the boys.

'Yes, and theirs.'

'Meanwhile, they'll continue to suffer?'

'As we all do on this earth Miss Deben, as we all do.'

'And must?'

'Perhaps.'

'But these are just children Brother. Innocents. And you can help them, if you really wanted to.'

'I do my best. I do my best.'

Noel looked to the sky and then at the boys. Grace thought he was about to cry.

'Let me help?'

'Help?'

'Yes, let me help *you* put an end to their suffering.'

'How? How can you help? What might you be able to do that others can't?'

'I'm a stranger here. I have no ties or interest to protect. I'm also a writer. I can tell their story. We can tell the world what's going on here.'

'Ahh...I thought so, this is all about you. You want a story. *Their* suffering is *your* story. That's what all this is about. I knew it. It's not about them at all.' Noel began to walk away. Grace caught up and grabbed his arm.

'No, that is not true. And even if it was, what is happening to them needs to be stopped. If a story helps, it would be worth it. I am not seeking fame or fortune. I have no call for that, I promise you. My concerns are genuine, I assure you.'

Grace looked straight into his eyes and could see that he was in some form of turmoil. He went to reply and then stopped himself. They walked on and allowed the boys to create some distance between them. And then he stopped and permitted himself to speak.

'People don't believe what they read in the newspapers.'

Grace was pleased that he had decided to engage her.

'Some will sit up and take notice. The press *can* make a difference.'

'Not always for the good.'

'True, but not always for the worse either. Please Brother, consider these boys...and...let's meet to discuss this again?'

'That's not possible.'

'Please?'

He did not reply and as they reached the last hummock on the hill Grace pointed to a mound that lay to their right.

'That's a children's graveyard,' she said.

'I didn't know that,' he was clearly disinterested and now eager to leave her company. She could sense that he was trying not to submit to her.

'It was for children born out of wedlock or the unchristened, or both. They were denied a passage to heaven not because of what they may have done, far from it. They were innocents all. Yet, your Church punished them, as God is their witness you might say?'

The young Brother simply raised an eyebrow and nodded his farewell. The ragged boys followed their shepherd meekly down the path away from the farmstead and in the direction of Letterfrack. Grace went to the van and sat with tears in her eyes at the thought of what awaited the 'little sailors' back at the School. She was also minded of her first meeting with Tom and his reluctance to go with her to Spain.

12

CAMPAIGN

Letterfrack looked its normal languid self. The stiff wind that blew down the Clifden road had picked up and the leaves from the large oaks on either side had been scattered everywhere making the intermittent pavements especially slippery. Grace was in no hurry and carefully picked her way through the now slimy foliage. Almost at once she was stopped in her tracks by the sight of two boys who were sweeping the front of Geoghan's General Store. She was relieved that they were not the same boys she had seen at the School. She approached them quite furtively and they did not see her until she was nearly upon them. They stopped their brushing and moved aside to allow her to pass. Again, she could not help but notice that they were hardly dressed for the task. Their Wellington boots and short trousers provided no protection for boney knees that appeared to have been chaffed in the wind and rain. They wore woollen jerseys over cotton shirts and had neither hats nor gloves. They were no doubt grateful that the leaves that they had already arranged in neat little piles were so wet it meant that they generally remained where they were placed.

'Are you from the School?' Grace asked as she passed, knowing full well they must be.

'Yes Miss' the older one replied.

'You're working here for Mr Geoghan?'

'Don't know Miss,' replied the junior.

'Mr Geoghan, the owner here?'

'Don't know Miss,' the number one boy echoed.

'Then who *are* you working for?'

'The School Miss,' chipped in the number two boy.

'The School?'

'Yes, we're sent here... they tell us where to go.'

The boys looked keener to resume their task than answer questions, no doubt for fear of being seen to be idling. Grace recognised their predicament and went into the store. Inside, another School boy was stacking sacks of something into a trough that was being used as a container. He was older and looked stronger than those outside. As she passed him he volunteered a 'Good day Miss'.

'Are you from the School?' she asked.

'I am Miss.'

She did not pursue the line of questioning.

'Mr Geoghan will not be long,' the boy volunteered.

'Thank you.'

Grace toured the shelves and decided on a number of items she wished to purchase. As she did so, she noticed that the boy was watching her closely and this unnerved her. She thought she had found her way around to a point in the shop where she could no longer be seen when his head suddenly appeared from behind a shelf.

'What would you be after Miss? Can I get you something?'

Grace was now made to feel even more nervous by his abrupt appearance.

'No...no thank you. I'll come back in a minute or so. I have an errand to run and I'll...I'll pick up what I want on my return.' With that, she quickly left the shop.

Outside, the boys were continuing to sweep and one gave a toothless smile as she passed. She moved down the road, only occasionally looking back to see the boys were still hard at work.

Finnan's, the butcher-cum-greengrocer was her next destination. Earlier in the week she had ordered some fruit and was expecting to pick it up. Entering the shop she stopped when she saw that two more small boys from the School were pouring buckets of potatoes into large canvas bags. They were obviously struggling with the weight and it took both of them to lift one bag onto a trolley. Finnan, dressed as a butcher, came to the counter. He was a very large, ruddy, unkempt man whose butcher's hands were puffed, bloated and as pink as poached salmon. To complete his unsavoury appearance, he wore a Boater straw hat that was at least two sizes too small for his large head and a blood-stained apron that only just circumnavigated his enormous stomach. Grace tried to stop herself thinking that he looked more pig-like than the produce on his counter as this was both disrespectful of the animal and unappetising given her fondness for bacon.

'Good morning Miss. What can I do you for today? Oops, sorry, I meant, what can I do for you today?' Finnan had an exaggerated mock joviality and false informality in his voice.

'Good morning Mr Finnan. I don't suppose you have been able to get the fruit I ordered on Monday?'

'Oh...Miss Deben it is.' There was a pause. 'I'm terribly sorry...no luck I'm afraid. They're right out in Clifden. I'll have to order some from Galway and all. I'll do that today and you may get it by...Friday next?' He had obviously not got around to ordering Grace's 'exotic' fruit – oranges and bananas – in the first instance.

'Friday next?' Grace was unbelieving.

'Friday at best.'

'Have you any fruit in now?' she asked.

'I have...a few late apples and a few...' Again a pause and an attempt to look beyond her into the shop, 'no...they're all gone as well.' He looked again to the front of the shop and shouted at the boys, 'Apples! Get the lady some apples. Now!'

Grace could not see where the boys got the apples from but they were on the counter in a split second. They had only brought a small handful each.

'That's not enough!' Finnan bellowed. Both the boys now looked like scared puppies. They rushed back to collect more apples and returned with several wrapped in their jerseys doubled over as a carrier.

'Stupid...Eejits all of them!' Finnan made sure they heard. 'Is that enough now Miss? Will you be taking them all?'

'I will. Thank you.' Grace looked about the rest of the shop. 'Can I have some bacon? About six rashers will do.'

'You can.'

Almost as an aside, Grace asked,

'Are the boys from the School?'

Finnan looked up from wrapping the bacon. 'They are. I try to help them out when I can.'

'Help them out?'

'Keep them busy and all.'

'And they help you?'

'Oh...I wouldn't say that now. I have to keep an eye on them all the time. They steal if you let them. I've had a lot go missing. Little thieves they are alright.'

'Do you pay them at all?' Grace knew this was a question that would declare her real interest and tried to make light of it. 'I mean, do you give them anything for their work?'

Finnan was already suspicious and declined to answer.

'Will that be all now?' he said, handing over the bacon.

'It will. Thank you.'

'Now, will you be paying today or later?'

'I'll pay now if you like.' Grace replied and pointedly added, 'I like to pay my way as I go ...especially those who do a job for me.'

Finnan was not slow in understanding the real meaning behind Grace's remark. He took the ten shilling note she had in her hand. 'Have you nothing smaller?'

'I'm afraid not.'

'Then pay me later,' he gruffly responded and returned her note.

'Perhaps on my way back from Geoghan's. I need to pick up a few things there.'

'If you wish. Or Friday next?'

'Oh yes, when the fruit arrives, I'll see you then.' Grace had decided that she had no wish for a further encounter with Finnan today.

Her last stop was at McCready's Post Office shop and bar. The possibility of purchasing a newspaper that was less than two or three days old was too good to pass over. She entered the bar and was only half surprised to see two more boys from the School. They were vigorously polishing the tables and stools and very briefly turned to look at Grace as she entered. They then looked fearfully towards the bar and quickly resumed their buffing. There were only two old men in the premises and they were sitting together in a corner snug with near-identical flat caps and still-fastened rain-coats. Both were smoking pipes and their sheep dogs were stowed obediently under their chairs. The aged farmers sat gazing at two half-filled pints of stout which had draught rings that clearly recorded their every mouthful. No words were being spoken and it looked as if their conversation had probably run its course some years ago. Grace thought they had to be brothers.

She went to sit at the bar and both the farmers gave her a look that suggested she was a street-walker. Obviously, in their experience, only a prostitute would drink alone during the day. No-one appeared at the bar to serve her and she waited. One of the boys then left his labours and ran through to the Post Office section next door and it was not long before the Landlord-Post Office owner appeared. Middle-aged, slight, with greasy matted hair, he looked as if he had slept in his clothes and had not seen a razor in an age.

'Sorry to keep you there,' he said.

'Not to worry,' Grace replied. She then turned to the boy who had fetched the man, 'And thank you.'

The boy blushed and carried on polishing. The other boy pushed him in a mocking way for being so considerate.

'What can I get you now?' The landlord asked.

'I'll take a small shot of Jamieson's.'

'Anything else?'

'Have you any newspapers?'

'I don't know.' He then turned to the boys and told one to go take a look, 'Look on all the shelves', he instructed.

'What paper would you be looking for?' he inquired. 'The local?'

'I'd prefer the national. *The Times*? Or the *Independent*?'

'It's Miss Deben isn't it?'

'Yes...and you're Mr McCready?'

'James McCready, Postmaster ...and Publican. We don't see you much in these parts? I hear you're busy, a writer of novels I'm told?

'I am. It's difficult to tear myself away from the cottage. Once you're in, it's hard to come away again, especially on these wet days.'

'That'll be most days then!' He passed her the whiskey. 'Where's that boy got to?' He turned towards the Post Office door and shouted, 'Where are you boy?'

The difference between his otherwise convivial self in relation to Grace and the tone of his voice aimed at the boy was striking. The boy soon came rushing back into the bar carrying a pile of newspapers. Obviously frightened, he clumsily slid them onto the counter and a few continued their journey and fell on the barman's side.

'You little eejit!' McCready went to swipe the boy around the head only, at the last moment, on seeing Grace's look of alarm he held his hand back. 'Get back on the tables!' He reached down to pick up the fallen newspapers and thus avoided Grace's stare of disbelief. She took a draft from her glass.

Picking up the fallen newspapers McCready spread them on the bar top. '*The Times*! There you have it. This Tuesday and all. And *The Independent*! Only Monday's I'm afraid. There now...both just waiting for you to come in.'

'Are the boys from the School?' Grace asked whilst McCready was still reflecting on his sale of yesterday's news.

'The School? Oh...them...yes. I let them in and keep them busy. They might actually learn something...but... you've seen yourself now...they're mighty slow. Not much there I'd say,' he pointed a finger at his forehead.

'But they do the work for you?'

'For me, no. No, it's for the School really. I just help them out when I can.'

'Help them out?' Grace knew she was near to the edge in terms of the questions but he seemed willing to divulge and she was determined to press him.

'I give them a bit. A donation like. It helps them out. The lads then do a bit for me...or they're supposed to! Lazy and all. Look at them. Half asleep most of the time. Hey you's two, wake up!' he shouted at the boys. The old farmers' dogs retreated further under their table and the old men half-smiled, grins that revealed that they had barely one set of employable teeth between them. Grace said no more and McCready went back into the Post Office. She watched the boys over the top of one of the newspapers that she had begun to scour. She felt sure they had already cleaned the same tables at least twice since she had entered. The wind on the window of the bar brought the patter of yet another heavy shower of rain.

Not wishing to think about the dire state of the economy or the various horrors still being uncovered in the aftermath of the war, she turned to the Letters page for some light relief. It was always good sport to see if anyone she knew had had a letter published. It was not to be. Turning to the *Independent,* she could not help but flinch and catch a breath when Ethel Carney's name jumped off the page. This was not the first time she had rediscovered her old acquaintance, nevertheless it sent a shiver of recollection through her. The current Carney article concerned, as far as she could make out, the growing '*problem of migration from Ireland*', especially of young women. Rather ungraciously, she deduced that Carney's interest in young women had not yet waivered in the slightest. It was a pleasant surprise to see that she was writing about something other than who's in town, who's wearing the latest hats, and what this season's colour was etc. She could not bring herself to finish Carney's article and picked up the *Times* and sought the Correspondence with the Editor pages. It was to be a day of coincidences. She was disbelieving when she saw the first heading on the letters page, '*Industrial Schools Defended*'.

She began to read, '*Last year Monsignor Flanagan turned up in this country and went galumphing around and read a book and got his photo taken a great many times and made a variety of speeches to tell us what a wonderful man he was, what marvels he had achieved in the United States . . . and then he went back to America and published a series of falsehoods and slanders...*'

'*...farrago of ill-informed nonsense*'...

'*...when a Catholic Monsignor uses language which appears to give the colour of justification to cartoons in American papers where muscular warders are flogging, half-naked fourteen year-old boys with cats-of-nine-tails, I think it is right to say in public of that Monsignor that he should examine his conscience and ask himself if he has spoken the truth...*'

'*If he finds that the substance of what he has alleged to have said is grossly untrue, then he should have the moral courage to come out in public and say so, and correct in so far as he can, the grave injustice he has done not only to the legislators of this country, but to the decent, respectable, honest men who are members of the Christian Brothers.*'

Yours... James Dillon T.D. Fine Gael

It was as though she had come into a conversation at midpoint and had trouble trying to comprehend the substance of letter. Nowhere could she see the expected defence of the Industrial Schools indicated by the headline. She did however manage, from the subsequent letters, to glean that the target of the abusive letter was an Irish-American priest, Father Edward Flanagan and he was famous, she gathered, for being the subject of a Hollywood film entitled *Boys Town*. This had been based on his experience of setting up a home of the same name for delinquents. And it was his story that had subsequently been turned into the film starring Spencer Tracy; a name Grace had heard of. Indeed, Tracy, she read, won an Oscar in 1938 for playing Father Flanagan whose catch phrase was, '*there is no such thing as a bad boy. There is only bad environment, bad training, bad example and bad thinking.*' Her training as a copywriter told her that this was far too long for a catch phrase and she read on.

At last, she came to the vital piece of the jig-saw. Father Flanagan, it transpired, had been in Ireland the previous year and had castigated the Industrial Schools as a '*disgrace to the nation*'. And this correspondence appears to have been in train ever since. Hence, the defenders of the system were now hitting back at the '*...ignorant yank*'. The good Monsignor had, it appeared, also had his nationality changed a few times during the ensuing exchange. In some letters he was 'the American', in others the 'Irish-American', sometimes he was just 'Irish', and finally in the few cases that were more discriminating he was 'from Roscommon'. However, it appeared that the latter was employed as either a positive or negative attribute depending upon ones view of the county rather than the man. At the foot of the page was the response Grace was hoping for, a letter from the man himself:

'I don't seem to be able to understand the psychology of the Irish mind....'

She thought that this was not perhaps the best way of endearing himself to the Irish readership and that he would need to recover their confidence if he were to be convincing.

'...the institutionalisation of little children, housed in great big factory-like places, where individuality has been, and is being, snuffed out with no development of the personality...and where little children become a great army of child slavery in workshops, making money for the institutions which give them a little food, a little clothing, very little recreation and a doubtful education....'

Grace looked over to the two boys who, starting at opposite ends, were now wiping and burnishing the bar counter. She thought it best to gather her things and went to sit at one of their gleaming tables. One of the boys helped her with her drink and took the opportunity to inhale its content. She didn't think much of his kindness after that.

She sat and continued to read Flanagan's letter:

'Your great country...' Mary noticed the distancing in this phrase.

'...that is sending forth missionaries into foreign lands...might well learn to begin at home to do a little missionary work among the unwanted, unloved, untrained and unfed children, who are suppressed and have become slaves because of the dictatorial policies of those in power. What you need over there is to have someone shake you loose from your smugness and satisfaction and set an example by punishing those who are guilty of cruelty, ignorance and neglect of their duties.

Grace paused to take a drink and thought it quite incredible that this had even been published. She continued to read.

'Who is going to fight this danger? Not you and I, we are getting too old for that. It is the little children that we pick out of the gutter . . . these are the people who will fight against Communism, Hitlerism and dictatorship...We have punished the Nazis for their sins against society...'

Grace stopped and said quite loudly, 'But not Franco, your Catholic friend!' Realising what she had done, she looked around at the two old shepherds. They could not or had not heard her. However, the boys from the School stopped their work at the bar and looked at her. They raised their eyes at each other and one revolved his finger at the side of his head to indicate her possible madness. He laughed when Grace, noticing his action, pulled a face at him. She returned to finish what by now she thought was a quite extraordinary letter:

'...I wonder what God's judgement will be with reference to those who hold the deposit of faith and who fail in their God-given stewardship of little children?

Yours Fr. Edward Flanagan. Nebraska, USA.

She took another sip of her whiskey and sat absolutely stunned. She had no idea that the issue had had such a wide resonance and it was obviously a case of only seeing what you are looking for. And here she sat, within touching distance of just one of its manifestations: two young boys being forced to work when they should be in school. She then thought about all the other boys just down the road; the two young sweepers in the playground, Tighe and the boys on Diamond Hill. Suddenly, it was all rather surreal, as here she was, quite unintentionally, sitting in one of the centres of this *'national disgrace'*. Furthermore, she was a stranger who already knew and cared too much.

'Okay lads! Let's be going.'

She was jolted out of her meandering thoughts by the recognisable voice of the young Brother Noel. He came through to the bar from the Post Office side. The two boys immediately tucked the rags they were using to polish the bar into a small box carrier and then, quite spontaneously, turned to Grace.

'Bye Miss!' They even gave her a cheery wave.

The Brother was stopped in his tracks when he eventually recognised Grace as the recipient of the boys' address.

'Wait outside boys. Don't be going anywhere now. Wait for me out there.' He manoeuvred them through the bar door and returned to stand at Grace's table. 'Miss Deben...I wasn't expecting to see you here.'

'And I you Brother! We seem to have a knack of bumping into each other. Are these also your charges, the boys?'

'They are.'

'Working in a bar, is that another healthy punishment for 'little sailors'?' Grace raised her glass and pointedly took a drink.

The Brother shook his head and in immediate umbrage began to walk away.

'Brother! Brother Noel...please, take a look at this.' Grace held up the *Times* page. 'Please, just second of your time. Please read this.'

'I have no time Miss Deben, not for you or reading the newspapers. If you'll excuse me now? I'd better be after the boys.'

'Please Brother, just read Tuesday's *Irish Times*. The Letter's page.' Grace implored.

'If I get chance, which I doubt, I'll do my best,' he said unconvincingly.

'Please do,' said Grace. 'I'd very much like your opinion.'

The Brother had stopped his exit and returned to her table. 'My opinion? On what exactly?' There was a touch of anger in his voice and his boyish tone had been replaced by a mannish impatience.

'The School system you run, or rather you and your Brothers run, is coming in for some criticism I see. It's not just me you know. You should read it.'

'As I said before Miss Deben, I wouldn't know about that. And I don't think you should be pursuing this either. It's not—'

'My business? Yes, I know. Yes, I've already heard that said to me before now. But just look at this...it is now everyone's business it seems. Just read this.' Grace held up the page once more.

Noel leaned on the table with both hands and looked Grace straight in the eye. 'What do you really want Miss Deben? Is this just another story for you?'

'No...' Grace looked around at the two old farmers who were now both staring in their direction. 'No Brother...I want to help those boys. I want to stop the punishments and the slave work you're making them do. It's not right and you know it. And God only knows what else you do to them?'

'Good Day Miss Deben.' He turned and went to leave again.

'Glassilaun Brother? Meet me on Glassilaun beach. I shall be there on Saturday afternoon, about one. We must talk. I'm not going away.' It was a desperate and rather forlorn final plea.

Brother Noel looked back momentarily and made no acknowledgement of the request. The door to the bar closed after him. The farmers nodded in unison at Grace as if to say, *'That's the clergy for you!'*

Grace quickly gathered her belongings and followed the

Brother out of the door. There was no sign of either him or any of his boys. She had no wish to return to Geoghan's and instead went straight to her van where she started to re-read the Flanagan letter, only this time she imagined it being read in the voice of the young Brother, who sounded remarkably like Tom.

13

FIASCO

As Mary waited for Tom at Cáceres railway station, her every passing minute was becoming more pained by the fact that permission to go to the front had, inevitably, been withheld by Bolín. The embarkation of the Irish Brigade was proceeding with the usual mix of chaos and excitement. No-one, it appeared, was in control of the process and men who had passed Mary not two minutes earlier were reappearing and being reallocated to different parts of the troop train. She stood back from the turmoil and reflected on the sheer magnitude of the task of getting people to a modern war. The scale of the operation and the energy being expended on sending people to their possible death was not only an irrational waste of human resources but also a reason to question the whole notion of the 'march of civilisation'. The same scene had obviously been repeated down the millennia, only now, she thought, we had the marvellous technological advances of the locomotive and the aeroplane to hasten the madness of it all.

Everyone looked as if they were in holiday mood. Weeks of inactivity and the prospect of real engagement with the enemy were a heady mix, especially amongst the young recruits. They were mostly all smiles and many took Mary's presence as some sort of good luck sign, a piece of shamrock, and she was royally acknowledged as they trooped to their carriages. All the while, she couldn't help but wonder how many would never return or, if they did, how they might be changed by the experience?

Just as Mary thought that she was the only woman on the platform, Ethel Carney's head and shoulders appeared above all the others at the far end of the platform. She appeared to be in deep conversation with Bannon and from the animation of Carney's arms, Mary could see that she was remonstrating with the Irish officer. Just for a moment she thought that Carney may have succeeded in inveigling her way onto the train and a flush of jealousy ran through her. Then, in a more sober moment, she thought that that was probably the last thing Carney would actually want to do and, in any case, she was hardly dressed for the part. In a bright, straw-coloured raincoat and with her florescent red hair she might well have been designed as target-practice for the Republican aviators. She stood out in every sense and in every direction.

Tom arrived looking very nervous. He had his raincoat tucked around his haversack and Mary was glad to see that he had his stiff boots on. As she inspected him closely, she felt older than she had previously felt in his company and more like a mother sending a child to school.

'Have you got some water?'

'I have...in the pack.'

'And food?'

'I have some biscuits. And I've got some sausage and an apple.'

'An apple? Is that all?' Mary chided. 'And your hat? You'll need a warm hat. And spare socks?'

She soon realised that she was being overbearing and when he refused to reply to all the questions, she just smiled at him. At that moment the train's whistle sounded and the already existing commotion was immediately doubled and became a frenzy. The train's whistle began to sound again and again and Mary and Tom couldn't make out what was happening. Just then, Tom Hyde, a fresh-faced young Lieutenant, came past and they asked him about the confusion. Apparently, the train driver had disappeared and a replacement had to be found. There would obviously be some delay, he said.

'A great start!' Tom muttered.

Mary was thankful for the delay and wanted the whole exercise to be abandoned.

'You'll be careful?'

'I will. Of course I will. I'm not doing the fighting.'

'I didn't mean the fighting, although you need to be careful of that. I meant Bolín and the rest of them. You've got to keep a watch on them all. Remember, they're dangerous and I don't think he likes you one bit. Keep an eye on your back and don't say anything without thinking first.' Mary's maternalism had returned in her tone.

'Keep an eye on my back? Now how do you suppose I do that?'

'You know very well what I meant,' Mary gave Tom a gentle push and continued to lay her hand on his breast.

'I know. I promise. I'll be careful. Will you stop now?' Tom tried to acknowledge all the practical advice but he continued to shake his head in a sort of disapproval, as much about the volume as the substance of what he was being offered.

Mary withdrew her hand and reached into her bag.

'A present,' she held out a small paper parcel.

'For me?' Tom took the bag and looked inside. 'Toilet paper! You think I'm going to shit myself?' He smiled broadly and gently touched Mary's hand. This time she withdrew it almost instantly. This was the first time Tom had experienced any sense of humour on the part of his employer, albeit characteristically it had a practical aspect.

'I thought you might need it!' Mary returned a smile. She reached into her bag and took out a small book, 'Actually, this is what I want you to keep.'

'What is it, something of yours for me to read? It had better be good? Do you know that I've never actually read any of your books?'

'You'll have plenty of time for that. No, it's a diary. I'd like you to keep a diary. I know it's a chore but it might help. You needn't think when you write it. It's your letter to yourself. Just be as honest as you can.'

'If it's for me, why do *you* want me to keep it?'

'So that when you return you'll be able to remember and tell me of course. You're my eyes and ears. My Secretary!'

'Don't be bollocking me now! I'm not your Secretary. Never have been, never will be! I hope I'm more than that?'

Mary didn't respond. She was unsure how to. Instead she resumed on the function of the diary.

'I'm sure you'll forget some things if they are not written down. It is often the small things that need to be remembered most. We all have a habit of blotting out things that we don't like. Don't we?'

Mary paused and Tom immediately took this as some indication of her suspicion about his own past, his secret. The train's whistle sounded once more.

'It's an aide-memoire. Keep it and please use it.' Mary

took Tom's hand and placed the small red leather bound notebook in his palm. She slowly closed his fingers around the diary. The physical interaction was again fleeting but memorable in terms of their developing relationship. Both now seemed to be regretting the impending moment of their parting. She was conscious of her feelings growing and he was conscious of not having told her the story of his past. Both had things to say and both had regrets about not saying them.

The train's whistle sounded one long, last blast and all the carriage doors began to be slammed closed. The billowing grey smoke from the locomotive engulfed the station and there were signs that its departure was imminent. Tom boarded the carriage that had been reserved for the Nationalist Press Office and Foreign Correspondents. As he had dreaded the most, McIlroy was already ensconced in the window seat, along with Dauban from *Figaro* and 'the famous' and now more than ever inappropriately named Hubert 'Red' Knickerbocker of the *Hearst Press*. The Red moniker was on account of his flaming hair colour rather than his politics, although he had been expelled in '33 by the Nazis in Germany. They were soon joined by Harold Cardozo, 'the Major', of the *Daily Mail* and the American Webb Miller of *United Press*. Tom felt he was entering Mary's nest of seasoned vipers. He had little choice but to navigate a seat that was uncomfortably vacant between McIlroy and Cardozo, both of whom did their best to ignore him. He was by far the youngest, the runt of the pack, and he very much looked the part. The older men simply sat and scrutinised the upstart, much like an appointment panel at the start of a job interview. Before he could locate his haversack in an overhead basket, the train began to shuffle and jerk its way out of the station. Tom caught Mary's eye through the carriage window and they smiled at each other. Then, quite unexpectedly and entirely out of character, she blew him a kiss. He was acutely embarrassed, as he noticed the others had also noticed. No-one, save McIlroy who swore under his breath, said a word as the train trundled past the platform end where Ethel Carney could be seen in her candescent raincoat still conversing with Bannon.

Tom began to reflect on the first signs of Mary's affection which he had just experienced. He was bemused as much as surprised. He had hardly expected it from her, especially at that moment and in full view of the other correspondents. He pondered the possibility that she had done it on purpose - to signal to the others to 'look after my boy'? Or was it an entirely spontaneous gesture? Or simply the mothering instinct getting the better of her? Or was it something else? Whatever it was, he found it comforting and was now more than ever intrigued to find out what might lay behind it.

After thirty or so minutes the pace of the train picked up and it was now moving quite freely through the vast Extremadura plain. The overcast skies and the light drizzle made the countryside appear even flatter and more indistinct than it actually was. It resembled a vast billiards table. The reporters were nearly all reading newspapers or writing notes and hardly a word had been exchanged since the train had departed. They threw knowing glances every now and again and appeared to be saving all their words for their copy. McIlroy looked as if he was asleep, whilst Cardozo, wearing his ever-present over-size beret and thick-lensed horn-rimmed spectacles, pulled his collar up over his chin so that his incredibly beaked nose was left outside, overhanging the precipice. He looked every inch the archetypal spy. It was also strange to see him without the company of at least one of his glamorous young American assistants. He looked positively undressed without them by his side and doing his reckoning. Only Knickerbocker appeared agitated and kept glancing anxiously out of the carriage window. Eventually, he could restrain himself no longer and pulled down the window and attempted to look out towards the front of the locomotive. He peered back into the carriage with real consternation drawn across his face. Looking at the others and not getting any reception for his obvious anxiety, he sat down again and began to rub his hands vigorously. Tom felt unnerved just looking at him. The train continued to jolt the passengers in their seats and soon the movement began to feel most unnatural. In a moment of collective unspoken insight, everyone in the carriage began to sense and could in fact now see that the train was getting faster and faster, and uncomfortably so.

'There's something wrong....this isn't right,' Knickerbocker exclaimed and once more went to the window.

'What's wrong?' Cardozo replied, and stood next to Knickerbocker trying to look out of the carriage towards the engine. He nearly lost his beloved beret in doing so but somehow managed to cling on to it at the very last moment. Suddenly, both men were thrown sideways and Knickerbocker was thrown to the floor. Cardozo landed in the sleeping McIlroy's lap and with his eyes still closed, the veteran reporter shouted at the intruder, 'What the fecking fuck?'

'Jesus Christ!' Knickerbocker bawled as he tried unsuccessfully to regain his feet.

The train was by now at breakneck speed and the violence of its motion on the tracks increased even further. Between the outside world flashing by and the passengers inside becoming frozen in their seats by increasing fear and uncertainty, it felt as if time itself was being transgressed.

The train seemed to be flying through space as much as travelling on the rails. The countryside had become all but a blur and the buffeting from side to side became more extreme by the moment. Shouts could also now be heard above the din from the adjacent carriages. Everyone grasped that there was indeed a problem, a major emergency in fact. Very quickly they all realised they were now on a runaway train. Tom sat completely inert as the scene before him had more than an air of the surreal. He felt strangely excluded and above the situation, as if looking in from above, and he could not believe it was really happening. He was in a story he might have wished to write.

'It's out of control! I don't think there's anyone driving this thing!' Knickerbocker continued to provide the only commentary as he tried to regain his feet.

'Don't be daft!' McIlroy interceded. It's a bloody Spanish driver! What do you expect? Sit the fuck down man, before you fall down again!'

'This isn't right. The train shouldn't be going this fast. We're gonna come off the rails if —'

Before Knickerbocker could complete his sentence, there was an almighty screeching of the brakes and he was once again thrown from his feet. Under normal circumstances such a fearsome noise would not have been welcome and one would have expected the worst, a crash of some sort. However, the perceptible slowing of the train that accompanied the sound of the grating and chewing of steel on steel, was embraced as a sign that their salvation might be at hand. And, just as quickly as the train had accelerated, it now came to a shuddering, crunching halt. For at least a minute Tom sat dazed, as did the others, and everyone simply looked at each other. The smell of burning metal wafted into the carriage. Dauban lit a cigarette and most of the others followed him. Moments later, one of the Spanish interpreters, Bove, entered the carriage waving his hands up and down in a 'be calm' motion.

'Gentlemen, please, do not worry yourselves! We have complete control. Everything is now in order. We will start again very shortly. Please be calm. Everything is now in order.'

'What happened?' Cardozo inquired.

'We're not sure at this moment. Maybe sabotage...but be calm gentlemen. We have complete control now. There is no problem. No danger at all.'

'Sabotage!' Knickerbocker exclaimed. His American accent boomed as he mouthed the word.

'Maybe...Gentlemen, please, it is over. We have complete control and will be starting again soon,' Bove insisted.

'No...you just said 'sabotage', Cardozo intervened.

'The driver may have been a Red.' The interpreter shrugged his shoulders and held up his hands.

'A Red?' McIlroy huffed. 'Now, there's the story! My God, we haven't been gone an hour and already we have our story!'

'We could have all been killed!' Cardozo was now in a state of cold realisation and shock.

'We might still be,' McIlroy replied. 'At last, we're in a fecking war gentlemen, in case you had not noticed. These things happen. You should expect them to happen. I've had a lot worse.'

'Sabotage?' Knickerbocker muttered to himself again. His face had turned ghostly pale and he continued to rub his hands together uncontrollably.

Tom sat and watched the correspondents trying to make sense of the situation. He imagined that they were already writing copy in their heads. He could just see the headlines,

'*Reds try to murder Irish heroes*', '*Reds sabotage Irish crusaders*', Webb Miller, ever the professional, had his notebook in hand and had already begun to jot some notes. Like Tom, he had said nothing during the entire episode, as did Dauban who had also sat motionless and mute. Cardozo now held his head in his hands and stared at the floor. Only McIlroy re-assumed his place in the corner and looked the least perturbed of them all. However, Tom thought he could well have been saying a silent prayer.

It was thirty minutes or more before the train started to move. They had been ordered to stay in the carriage and as a result the smokers began to rapidly replace the air with their smoke. Tom made for the corridor to try to escape the fog of the tobacco, especially Dauban's French cigarettes which he found the most pungent and unbearable. Outside, it had begun to rain heavily.

The remainder of the journey to their first stop, Plasencia, was entirely uneventful. On arrival at the middle-of-nowhere junction, the acrid smell of explosive was in the air. The town had just been bombed. It was soon surmised, especially by the increasingly fertile mind of Cardozo, that the sabotage of the train had been intended to speed them to an appointment with the bombers and the Grim Reaper. The track had been damaged, as had most of the railway station, and yet another delay was necessary. Tom wistfully acknowledged both the ingenuity of the plot and the accuracy of the pilots, albeit their intended target, the train, had mercifully not been found. Perhaps damaging the track and delaying the deployment of the Irish was the best they could do in circumstances. It soon occurred to Tom that his war could have been over if either the train had left the track or the bombers had found them in the station. All this, and he was just two hours into being a *real* war correspondent. The luck of the Irish?

Their next stop was Torrijos, another desolate and featureless railway junction. Here they changed train and made their way along what must have been one of the most minor of minor tracks to their eventual destination of Torrejón de la Calzada, a place with more letters in its name than inhabitants. The disembarkation was just as chaotic as the embarkation, only more so as the enthusiasm of the ranks was depressed by the thunder and lightning that met them. Indeed, the sound of the initial thunder claps had sent some of the youngsters diving for cover. Although they attempted to laugh at their mistake, you could see in their eyes that they had real fear. Theirs were very nervous laughs, the sort that come whenever men are prohibited from crying.

By mid-afternoon, and now in persistent rain, the Brigade assembled in marching order. Dalton and O'Sullivan, the senior officers, inspected the ranks and the four Brigade Companies were divided into separate files. The foreign correspondents, left under the charge of the always flapping Lieutenant Lambarri of the Press Office, were told to remain behind for at least thirty minutes. They were to march for the rest of the day in the direction of a township called Valdemoro. McIlroy and some of the others had not realised that they too would be required to proceed on foot. Most, with the exception of Tom and Webb, had casual footwear and looked out of condition. Lambarri tried to assure them that the march would be possible, if they took their time. Cardozo and Knickerbocker were again at the forefront of the complaints about the lack of foreknowledge of the intended route march and in concert they refused to move. Dauban and the others similarly began to question the feasibility of the march. Only Tom had no reservations about doing his shift. Lambarri suggested they all wait until transport could be commandeered, however, 'that may take a day or two,' he hinted. The prospect of staying in Torrejón de la Calzada overnight did not go down at all well with the older men.

'Is there a hotel nearby?' Knickerbocker rather grandly and quite ignorantly inquired.

'No Senor. Perhaps a tavern?' Lambarri apologetically replied.

'A tavern? Where? There's fuck all here,' McIlroy sneered.

'The main town is just down the road there. There may be a tavern or a pensión. I don't know myself.' Lambarri plaintively offered.

'How far down the road?' barked Knickerbocker.

'I'm sorry gentlemen, I don't know. On the map it doesn't look far. Certainly you should be able to walk there. If there is nowhere for you to stay, you could return to Torrijos. There is a guesthouse in the station there. If you like, I will ask the train driver to stay until dark. And then, tomorrow, I can arrange transport for you.'

After much muttering and cursing at all things Spanish, the correspondents agreed that their preferred option was to go back to Torrijos immediately. It was obvious that they had no thought of marching or even walking into the unknown and that they would rather catch up with the Brigade the next day. It was agreed they would get back on the train. Tom was the only dissenter. Quietly he asked Lambarri whether he could go ahead as originally planned and follow the march of the Brigade. Lambarri refused to sanction this, as he himself would now have to accompany the other journalists on the return journey. They had to keep together at all times and that, he emphasised, was a direct order from Captain Bolín. After watching the last line of the by now already sodden Irish banderas leave the station, the correspondents climbed back on board the waiting train.

Once back in Torrijos they discovered that there was insufficient room at the inn and Tom, as the junior, was relegated to sleeping on the innkeeper's living room floor. And sleep he did, as the tension of the day had taken its toll. His only real disturbance was a sniffing flea-bitten dog that occasionally made the rounds during the night.

Almost inevitably the transport Lambarri was meant to arrange failed to materialise until well after midday the next day. He insisted that local flooding on the roads was responsible for the late start. The execrable state of the vehicle he had procured did not feature, although everyone could see for themselves that this was the more credible reason for the delay. It was a lorry that had been converted to a local bus, perhaps twenty or even thirty years previous. Its canvas roof was pitted with holes, the 'seating' consisted of orange boxes nailed to the floor and the engine, like the driver, sounded tubercular.

It was already dusk by the time they eventually arrived in Valdemoro and the Irish Brigade were nowhere to be seen. The 'bus' journey had been everything they had feared –slow, painful and immensely frustrating. The sight that greeted the correspondents was entirely unexpected. General O'Duffy's car was outside the railway station and the man, as usual, was nowhere to be seen. A number of his camarilla were standing over what appeared to be four sacks laid out on the steps of the ticket office. As the correspondents made their way to the entrance of the station it soon became clear that the sacks were in fact bodies, two wrapped in sheets and two in tarpaulin. Fresh blood could be seen seeping from the sheets. Bannon came to meet the reporters.

'Welcome to the war gentlemen.'

'Who the fuck are they?' asked McIlroy, indicating the bodies.

'Ours,' replied Bannon. 'This morning—'

'This morning?' Cardozo interrupted.

'Yes. It seems there was some misunderstanding...about seven kilometres from here. An accident you might say,' Bannon already appeared to be struggling to explain the situation.

'An accident?' Cardozo echoed.

'A case of mistaken identity. These things happen in the heat of the moment, in war, as you might expect.' Bannon then paused and stared at the lifeless forms.

'For Christ sake man, tell us what actually happened!' McIlroy raised his voice in exasperation.

'They came across a Falange unit. There was a misunderstanding and all hell was let loose. Apparently the Falange started it and we finished it. Lieutenant Hyde and Private Chute got caught. Both died on the spot.'

'And the other two?' Knickerbocker inquired.

'Oh...yes, our Spanish interpreters...Bove and...I'm not sure who the other one is.'

Bannon's omission of the Spaniards and then his admission of not knowing the identity of the interpreter struck Tom as callous in the extreme and undoubtedly racist. From the corpses there was no indication as to which was which as there was no identification on the sheets or tarpaulin wraps. In death there was absolute equality. It was then that 'Lieutenant Hyde' registered in Tom's consciousness, as did 'Bove'. Only the day before, both had been in his life. They had been very much alive and now both lay dead, in sacks, at his feet. For Tom, this was his introduction to the bloody reality of war, even more so than the extraordinary events on the train.

'But what happened?' Tom asked. 'We're miles from the front.'

'As I said, an accident. Apparently, our lads spotted the Falange on the other side of a gully and then they spotted our crowd. They went to greet each other and there was some sort of misunderstanding. We don't really know the ins and outs...but those who brought the bodies back say that the officer in charge of the Falange suddenly started shooting. He shot the interpreters on the spot. Captain O'Sullivan said that Bove had shouted '*Bandera Irlandesa del Tercio*' at the Spanish officer. He then, without saying a word, shot at both of them. The interpreters didn't make it. O'Sullivan and the other men dived for cover and returned fire. They continued firing at each other for some time and that was when Hyde and Chute were hit. The other side retreated when our machine-gun Company, D Company, arrived and we posted a number of hits. About thirteen Falange bodies have been found so far. They're from the Canaries apparently. Just a ghastly mistake all around it seems,' Bannon matter-of-factly reported.

'Some mistake!' Knickerbocker added. 'What's that the interpreter said again?'

'*Bandera Irlandesa del Tercio*', the Irish Brigade of the Foreign Legion. O'Sullivan thinks that they mistook it for the Reds...the Irish International Brigade or something? Whatever it was, it did for them. And the uniforms...'

'The uniforms?' Cardozo continued to parrot Bannon.

'The Falange may not have recognised our uniforms. They're not familiar with them...not being the same as the other Tercio. They may have mistaken them for the Reds. That may have been another factor. We just don't know…but I'm sure there will be some inquiry. Meanwhile, gentlemen, if you will excuse me, I need to arrange to get these men back to Cáceres. General O'Duffy is keen to give them the very best send-off. They are fallen heroes and we should glory in their sacrifice. No doubt you will report that in your dispatches? I'm not sure it will be necessary to mention the unfortunate circumstances, the *misunderstanding*? That would be a disservice to the deceased. Can I rely on your cooperation gentlemen?'

No one responded and it looked as though it was taken as said. Bannon then made for the ticket office and the correspondents stood around the miserable sacks of 'heroes' not quite knowing what to make of this first episode of the Irish mission. Two popular banderas were already dead, along with the two Spanish interpreters, and the enemy had not even been seen, let alone engaged. At best, it was a singularly unlucky start to the campaign. And, at worse, an augury of what was rapidly turning into a volume of chaotic and deadly misadventures.

14

GLASSILAUN

THE BEACH AT GLASSILAUN WAS DESERTED SAVE FOR THE
seagulls and a phalanx of jelly-fish that had been deposited
on the tide line. The white sand extended for a mile in each
direction and the perfectly formed bay with its high dunes
could, for all the world, be taken for the Caribbean, if were
not for the bitingly cold wind that provided a stark
reminder that this was Connemara. Suddenly, for the first
time in days, a hint of blue sky made an appearance
between what looked like a riotous herd of small, fluffy,
white and grey clouds.

Leaving her van at the head of the very narrow and pot-
holed boreen leading to the beach, Grace walked to the
shore and pondered the chances of the young Brother
appearing. He had not looked as if he had either the will or
the courage. Yet, she clung to the hope that his troubled
expression and general unease with himself were in her
favour. She waited a while before deciding to walk the
beach.

It was at times like this that she felt most alone in the
world. On this vast expanse of empty beach her physical

isolation also served up a sense of mental and emotional solitude. Up until now she had contained the notion of loneliness by having *things to do*. This seemed to allay any feeling of being cut-off or adrift from humanity. Whereas, on this beach, she felt an emptiness which magnified the distance between herself and the rest of the world. Her notion of time was all at sea; she was adrift and had no call for a clock or a watch. She had no attachment to the routines of others and the rhythm of her existence was now dictated by either the weather, her own sense of industriousness or a combination of both. Her daily life was now subject to whim and the winds.

'Miss Deben! Miss Deben!'

Grace had not heard the Brother as a result of walking into the head wind. The sand was being blown up by the strong breeze and she had covered her face and ears with her scarf.

'Miss Deben!'

Then she thought she heard a voice and stopped to look around. Brother Noel was making his way along the beach. He was running and at a distance he looked like a large child. Grace smiled at the image she conjured in her mind. As he got closer he slowed to a walk and within a few yards he stopped completely. He stood out of breath and looked at Grace.

'You've come,' she said.

'I have.' He had to shout to make himself heard above the wind.

She walked over to him, 'I'm glad.'

'Can we get out of the wind?'

Grace looked towards the end of the beach and indicated a cluster of rocks.

'Over there...'

They sat on some ready-made rock mantels that formed a natural wind break. She looked at the young man and could see that he was in his 'civvies'. For the first time he looked quite normal, although his untamed hair was more feral than usual and his acne appeared to have taken the day off. His raincoat was tied tightly at the waist and accentuated his narrowness. He didn't say anything as they looked out at the waves gliding in.

'I read the pieces,' he said. 'The letters...'

'You did? Good. Did you read them all?'

'Yes, I did.' He paused and appeared to be in thought, 'This Monsignor Flanagan is obviously out for the publicity. Typical Yank.'

'I don't think so,' Grace replied. 'He's famous enough as it is. He's no need to court more.'

'If it's true what they say, then the authorities, the Church itself, will see to it. I can't see any good in the likes of us getting involved.'

Grace was taken by his use of 'likes of us'. This was the first acknowledgement of a possible common mission.

'*If* it's true? And you know it is, then you're already involved.' She looked him in the eye and pursed her lips.

'Then they'll deal with it. The authorities will—'

'But they won't. They haven't...and they have every reason not to,' Grace's tone was adamant.

'So what can I - *we* - do about it?'

'We can tell the world.'

'Ha! Tell the world?' he shook his head and laughed mockingly.

'We can report what is really going on in the School.'

'We?'

'I can...with your help.'

'Will anyone listen?'

'Yes, if we tell the truth.'

'The truth? Who knows what that is? Will I be mentioned?'

'No...you don't have to be. Just provide me with some proof, some evidence and tell me what's happening inside that School.'

'I thought you said you already knew?'

'Only some...I need to hear it from you. I need more than local gossip and tittle-tattle. I need to know what you have seen and heard for yourself. I need you to be—' Grace stopped herself from saying 'eyes and ears'. That phrase had too many resonances.

Brother Noel stood and stretched his legs. He peered out at the sea and was clearly contemplating his position.

'Are you afraid?' Grace asked. 'About what might happen to you?'

'No...not really. I'm more worried about what I might do after. You see, I'm not sure about the life I've chosen. I don't know if I'm really cut out for it. I suppose I've always felt that...doubt that is. But now, after what I've seen myself, I'm having serious doubts alright.' He picked up a small pebble and threw it as hard as he could towards the waves.

'It's only natural, I should imagine. Doubting Tomas!' Grace tried to sound reassuring.

'Is it?'

'After what you have seen? What have you seen?'

'Terrible things. They're...all terrible things. No-one should witness.' He picked up another pebble and launched it out to sea. Grace could see the anger in him,

'Terrible things...done to the boys?'

'Every day. But it's not just the boys, it's the Brothers themselves. They are doing terrible things to themselves because of what they do to the boys.' Noel had a distant look and averted his eyes before continuing,

'I'm sure the School makes them that way. I don't think they go there like they are. I think it turns them into something else. And it's the same with the boys. They don't go there with all the troubles they now have. The School makes them bad. It damages them. And every day they're told how bad it is out here in this world! They have no view other than the blackest and cruellest that the School and the Brothers provide.' He turned and faced Grace.

'They run if they can. They'd rather be in the damnation of the outside world than the hell that is the School. That reminds me, Tighe is gone.'

'Tighe?'

'Yes, he ran away again. Only, he won't be back this time.'

'He got away?'

'No... no he didn't. There was an accident. They say he ran into a car trying to get away from the Guards, down in Clare somewhere. His leg got caught and they say he was lucky to keep it.'

Grace, clearly shocked, covered her face with her scarf.

'They've taken him to some new hospital in Ennis to see what can be done. They didn't seem to be that hopeful. He'll probably still lose it. He won't be running anywhere again that's for sure.'

Grace was obviously distraught at the news, 'Why did he run this time?'

Noel thought before divulging.

'Brother Vincent.'

'Brother Vincent?'

'Tighe told the Superior that Vincent had touched him.'

'What happened?'

'To Vincent? Nothing of course. He pleaded his innocence and the Superior believed him, no question. Tighe was a liar, everyone knew that. So he... so he let, Brother Matthew, the Disciplinarian, loose on him.'

'The Disciplin..? What's that?'

'The Disciplinarian. He oversees all the punishments. It's Brother Matthew and he takes wicked delight in his work. I know that for sure.'

'What happened to Tighe?'

'When I last saw him he was beaten black and blue. He was in a filthy bad state. I tried to help but was told to leave him be. It went on for a few days and then they put him out...in the yard...just to stand there. I'm told he got the hose down as well but I didn't witness it myself.' Noel paused and studied the pain on Grace's face.

'But somehow he still had the strength to run. He was powerful like that. Not physically, but you could see it in his eyes. There was something in him that was not going to stand for it. He'll not be doing any running now though.'

'Was that when you decided you had had enough?'

'Most likely, although I had had my doubts from my very first day. And meeting you on the mountain didn't help matters, I can tell you that!'

'What is going on isn't right. I think that you would have decided that for yourself someday, regardless of meeting me.'

Noel sat down and avoided looking at Grace by watching his heels digging into the sand. There was a long silence and then he spoke softly.

'I don't want become like them...the Brothers. And that might to happen to me if I stay and say nothing.'

'You could and will perhaps, if you don't do something to stop it.'

'How though? How can I stop it? It's been going on for

years and nobody has done anything. Why is that going to change?' he shouted and stood up again facing the sea.

Grace stood directly behind him and was unsure whether to place her hand on his shoulder. She wanted to comfort him.

'I can write about the School. I have contacts in the newspapers. They've taken my work before. I'll write what you tell me...what you know, what you've seen.'

'It's disgusting! They'll not publish it. Boys are being attacked...sexually and all. They are being interfered with on a daily basis. Young boys are being...raped. Yes, raped! It's more than a sin... it's...worse than anything...And it's not just one Brother. Everyone knows who they are. The Superior knows and the boys of course.'

'What exactly do they know?'

'I'd rather not say. It's too horrible.'

'Have you seen it?'

'Of course.'

'What did you see?'

'In the washroom...Vincent...playing with the boys. He was inspecting their parts ...and handling them. He pulled the skin back on their... It was a pretence. I asked him what he was doing and he said it for their hygiene! I could see he was excited. He was enjoying it.'

He paused and looked vacantly towards the breakers and could see the tide was changing.

'The nights are worse. The boys are taken from their beds. Any excuse will do now. Talking in bed, not being asleep. Anything is used to get them up. And then I've seen them, leaving the Brother's quarters sobbing and worse, especially the young ones.'

'Do they ever say anything?'

'The boys? No. Only sometimes the ones like Tighe

would let it be known.' He shook his head, bent down and with his finger drew a line in the sand.

'And the Brothers? Do they ever say anything to you?'

'No. They just look at you as if to say, '*It's normal. Why aren't you doing it?*' It makes me sick to my stomach,' he looked away again in the direction of the sea and followed the flight of a distant gull. 'I can't stand it anymore. I've prayed for it to stop...but He's not listening. No-one's listening. No-one wants to hear this sort of thing. No-one.'

'What about Flanagan's letter?'

'He's a Yank. He's not here. He can't do anything.'

'He's kicked up a fuss. You saw so yourself. That's why the authorities are trying to shut him up. We can stoke the same fire.'

'Do you really think that? Without being burned at the stake ourselves?'

'I do. I really do.'

'And what'll happen then, when it all kicks off?'

'They'll have to change their story. And some of those who are responsible may be punished. Then they'll have to start looking after those boys. That's what I'd like to happen.'

'The power of the press?' he said, shaking his head. 'I'm not sure.'

'Yes, the power of the press. It can work and I think it will in this case. We just need to have the proof. Are there any records?'

'Of the punishments? No, of course not. What do you think! It's all done in the dark.'

'But what about the work gangs? Is there any record-keeping about the payments?'

'Records, are you mad? The boys don't get paid!'

'I know...but payments to the School from McCready, Finnan and the others?'

'Father Boyle does all that.'

'Boyle? Father Boyle from Clifden?'

'Yes...he manages all the work for the School. The boys are sent out on his weekly instructions.'

'Boyle does it all? The farm, the workshops and the gangs?'

'As far as I know. He seems to have the run of the place. And he does very nicely for himself by the looks of things!'

'What do you mean?'

'Big swanky car that he doesn't drive himself. A fella from Clifden drives him. And his shoes! I've never seen a priest with such shoes. And he always carries the umbrella. It's tipped and I'm told it's solid silver. He's doing more than alright, by the looks of it.'

'And the Superior?'

'Number Two to Boyle himself I'd say. I think he gets the lists from Boyle and he just follows them. He does what he's told. Boyle must have something on him. It can't be just for the money.'

'It's a filthy dirty business.'

'It's a business. They work the boys alright. They must be making some money out of the lads. The boys never stop. They work them 'til they drop. You saw for yourself the legs of the boys on the hill. Those were from the farm work. I've seen that for myself. It's a workhouse. It's slavery; that's what it is.'

'And the shopkeepers in Letterfrack?'

'They get the boys for nothing.'

'For nothing? McCready said he donates to the School?'

'He might...but I doubt it. I've seen no sign of it. He's always up at the School...at the farm. I've seen him there with Finnan, Geoghan and all. I don't know what he does. He seems to be a great pal of ...'

'Who?'

'My God...Brother Matthew! I hadn't thought about it before now. Do you think they're interfering with...? Mary help us!'

'Are *you* going to help *me*?' Grace asked.

'I need time. I need time to think.'

'For the sake of the boys, please help?'

They began to walk towards the lane leading away from the beach and as they approached the road Noel turned and touched Grace's arm.

'Before I forget, I've been studying the local legends. I came across one which I think might interest you. Do you remember where you met me with the boys?'

'Diamond Hill?'

'It's Binn Ghuaire, in Irish. It's not one of the Twelve Pins by the way. No-one knows for sure what the twelve are. Twelve appears to be just a random number - like the disciples.' As they walked on Noel began to recount the legend,

'There's a place called Lemnaheltia just across from Doughraugh, the dark mountain, the one above Kylemore. It's the one you see when descending Binn Ghuaire. Well, the legend goes that Fionn Mac Cumhaill took his two dogs, Bran and Sceolán, hunting around Kylemore and he came across a herd of deer. The dogs chased the deer and managed to separate one of them. They drove it towards a cliff to the east of Doughraugh. The deer was a beautiful doe and she leapt from the cliff and Bran did likewise. Anyways, she made it across to Doughraugh and escaped. But Bran didn't and plunged to his death. The place has been called Lemnaheltia, 'the leap of the doe', ever since.'

Grace was not slow to understand the poignancy of the

legend: it was Tom, Noel and herself. She showed no sign of this recognition to Noel,

'What happened to the other dog?'

'Sceolán? I don't rightly know. I don't think anyone really knows.'

15
_____

PHILOMENA

GRACE DROVE TO GALWAY, A JOURNEY THAT SHE WAS NOW becoming accustomed to. Although on this occasion she nearly didn't make it. Just outside Moyard she met what may have been her old friend Titan, the veteran CIE bus, halfway across the road and heading in her direction. The snail was indeed flying. For once, the speed at which she was travelling was to be her saviour and it was only by reaching a berth in the road at precisely the same moment as they came together that she managed to steer her vehicle past the oncoming bus. Trembling and shaking, she stopped the van and tried to gather herself. Her delayed reaction was to hit the car horn as hard as she could, even though the offender had long since gone. She thought that this was far from being a good omen.

She made her way to the offices of the *Galway Observer* and an appointment with the Editor, Fearghal Nye. She had offered to write a column entitled '*A Connemara Diary*' in which she would recount the adventures of an English-woman who comes to stay in the 'Wilds of the West'. This was something she could produce without too much thought or effort, another piece of frippery. The fact that she was touting the work suggested to Nye that she would be cheap and it was largely on that basis he had invited her to come to his office and discuss terms. She didn't know whether he knew who she really was or indeed anything about her. He had only seen the quality of the sample article she had supplied. She had, however, consciously used her pen name, M.G.M. Deben, in all their correspondence.

Nye was a late middle-aged, stocky Galway man who looked more like a farmer than a newspaper editor. He was a very welcoming and friendly sort and, most important, keen to have a regular column by an 'outsider'. His terms turned out to be far from generous but they were nevertheless agreed over tea and a scone. Then, quite innocently, Grace took the opportunity to request some assistance with some local research whilst she was at the newspaper's offices. Nye was only too happy to accommodate her and summoned a young trainee to help.

The trainee's name was Philomena Devlin, an archetypal seventeen year old Galway girl. Short and rather round, she had long curling locks of bright red hair that were tied in a ponytail. She wore a pleated tartan skirt, a baggy white blouse, patent leather shoes and ankle socks that were the then standard for her age. Unusually for teenage girls, she also wore glasses that made her look like a student. Her official job title was 'Messenger' and she knew the newspaper better than her own bedroom. Grace was soon to be blessed by Philomena's knowledge and uncanny capacity to recall and link disparate articles, dates and persons contained in the enormous tomes of the bound back editions that the young girl could hardly carry. Grace helped her take the beasts down from the shelves.

They started the search with a general heading, 'Letterfrack Industrial School'. There was very little copy, apart from intermittent visits of Church or political dignitaries during the 1930s and later in the 'Emergency'. Grace noticed that in the articles concerning clerical patronage, the School was usually referred to as 'the Orphanage' at Letterfrack. There were far fewer entries under the heading St Joseph's Industrial School. The only story in recent times was a report on a minor success of the School at the Connemara Pony Show. There was a very poor photograph of the Superior receiving a trophy and Grace thought she recognised McCready in the background but she could not be sure. Despite Philomena's heroic efforts, their search was fruitless and they abandoned it after reaching March 1944. As they were preparing to give up the task, Philomena quite unexpectedly suggested, 'What about the Courts Miss?'

'The Courts?' Grace looked uncertain about the connection.

'Yes Miss. Everyone knows that the Schools are trouble. All sorts of bad things and all. It's not really surprising when you see who they put in them. Everyone knows they're bad places. My Ma used to say she'd put me in one if I didn't behave! So I behaved alright. But I think I've seen something about them in the Court reports before now. I'm sure I have.'

'Can we look? Have you got the time?'

'Do you really want to find out about them?'

'I do.'

'Then we should try. It's getting late but old Nye won't be after me now.'

They began the search again, only working backwards from the present. It was not long before Philomena pulled out a story and began to read it aloud:

'INDUSTRIAL SCHOOL ACCUSED OF RUSTLING'

'Today, in the lower sessions court, the Superior of St Joseph's

Industrial School in Letterfrack denied the claim that six Friesian cows that were found on the premises were 'rustled' from a Clifden man. Brother Marcel was successful in his counter-claim that 50 year old Timmy Donovan, of Muckneigh Clifden, was indebted to the School and that the cows had been legally signed over as an indemnity for the said debt. Father Boyle, also of Clifden parish, corroborated the Christian Brothers' counter-claim and the case was dismissed. Donovan may now face further charges of slander and wasting the Court's time.'

'When was that?' Grace asked.

'Two years past.' Philomena replied.

'Is there anything else?'

Philomena struggled with another giant tome and began to scan the pages.

'There's another Court Report here. It's about a boy... he...was found dead in the School. Three years ago.'

'Let me look,' Grace moved next to Philomena. 'Why was it in the court?'

'It's the Coroner's Court Miss. Look, *'Death by misadventure'*. Oh Jesus, God help us... He...he was found in the slurry pit! Just eight years of age.' Philomena turned and genuflected.

'What happened?' Grace said rhetorically as she read down the page. 'It says he fell in, accidentally, whilst unsupervised.'

'Brother Matthew, who was the superintendent of the Farm at the time of the accident, told the court that the boy was a 'wild one' who had previously disobeyed the very strict instructions not to be in the vicinity without the company of a senior.'

'The Court delivered a verdict of death by misadventure'.

'It praised the Congregation of Christian Brothers for their good works'.

'Are there any more?'

'Here's one...' Philomena turned the page of another tome.

'Another Coroner's...1942, September. *'Accidental death.'* Again...on the School Farm. *'Boy drowns in bog.'* He fell in... an unknown danger... while collecting the cows... eleven years of age!'

'Unsupervised?'

'Doesn't say. What'll you do with all these?'

'I don't know yet. I'll think of something.' Grace replied.

'I'd like to be writer. I'd love to be able to write stories. Do you think I could?' Philomena asked.

'Yes. Of course. You are very clever and from what I've seen, I'd say you could alright.'

'I'd love to do what *you* do.'

'I'm sure you will. Just one word, or two actually, of advice; you need to write every day and ...you might need to change your name!'

'Change my name?' The young girl looked genuinely shocked by the thought.

'Philomena is a lovely name...but not for English readers. You can change it to something they would recognise and not have to struggle with.'

'Why would they struggle with it? I don't know anyone who does.' She still looked alarmed at the notion of her name was a struggle.

'Just my advice my dear. It's just some advice.' Grace smiled and clasped the girl's hand. 'Now, I need to go to the Central Library. And you may need to go to Mr Nye and apologise on my behalf for keeping you.'

'He'll be long gone by now. You'll find him in the Salthouse public house. Can I come with you, to the Library? Please, I know how it works and I could carry on helping. I won't get in your way. I think this is fun. It's like a detective story. Is that what you're writing?'

'No...well, not exactly. Are you sure you won't be needed here?'

'It's past time already. I'll clock out and we can go.'

'But shouldn't you be getting home?'

'I live with an old dear. I'm her lodger and she won't be looking out for me. We need to go now, before the Library shuts.'

Grace couldn't resist her new assistant's enthusiasm and certainly needed her prodigious skills. They hurried off to the Library and began further investigations into the Industrial School system in general. Philomena had very little curiosity regarding the direction of Grace's inquiries; she mined the literature and uncovered all manner of background and current information that Grace might use. When all the notes were duly written up, they found the nearby Dinner Hall and Grace rewarded Philomena with a hearty supper. They talked about Galway, schooling, travel, England, becoming a writer and of course the weather.

In all her time together with Philomena, and indeed throughout the day as a whole, it had not occurred to Grace that many things were strangely familiar, or at least she had some recollection of the newspaper offices despite never having been there before. As they were about to leave the Dinner Hall, she remembered why: the *Galway Observer* was where Tom had worked as a young boy. It was where he had learned about newspapers. Yet Tom had hardly crossed her mind all day, which was a rare occurrence in itself, and she couldn't believe that she had not made the connection before now.

'I'd like to check something,' she hastily held Philomena's arm. 'One last thing.'

'But the Library will be closed.'

'No, it's not the Library. Back at the 'paper.'

'Mr Nye'll not be back.'

'It's not Nye I want to check. Is there a record of the employees?'

'Accounts and Records Office perhaps?'

'Anywhere else? It's from a long time ago...someone, a friend, I once knew. He worked for the 'paper.'

Philomena was thinking, 'The Archive. I've sometimes filed stuff about people who worked for us in there.'

'Can we go there, now?'

'Now?'

'It'll save me coming all the way back.'

'But it'll be shut.'

'I'm with you...we can say something about my research and how Nye wants us to get some information...or something like that,' Grace was almost imploring the young girl to accede.

'But...'

'I don't want to get you into trouble. Tell me if you'd rather we didn't.'

'No...I like helping...only...'

'I'll take the blame...' Grace held Philomena's hand tightly.

'It's not that. It's just that I'm not sure there'll be any record. It might all be for nothing.'

'Can we try, please?'

They set off for the newspaper office and arrived at the reception desk where the doorman was surprised but pleased to see Philomena even at that time of night. Her story about leaving some important notes in the Archive was accepted without any hesitation. They climbed the stairs to the second floor and entered the Archive, which turned out to be little more than a glorified storeroom. In a very dim light Philomena set about the search. It was not long before she pulled out a box which was concertinaed and inscribed with 'Curriculum Vitae'.

'When was it?' she asked.

'About '29. 1928-30 'ish I'd say.'

Philomena shuffled the box's content and lifted a wedge of paper, 'Here...my God that was easy!' She held the paper under the light. '1927-32. That's very organised don't you think, doing it by five years? Who am I looking for?'

'Tom Lees'

'Thomas?'

'No, Tomás. T.O.M.A.S... Lees. L.E.E.S'

'Irish?' Philomena was, by now, sifting the papers.

'Yes.'

'Yes! Here...' she whooped and held a sheet aloft.

'What's it say?' Grace could hardly wait to let her read and made for the sheet herself.

'18 years of age. Galway lodgings. 'Hand' He was just a hand, not even a Messenger!'

'What else?'

'Literate. School completed.' There was a pause and Philomena looked at Grace, 'St Joseph's Industrial School, Letterfrack.'

Grace nearly fell to the floor. Philomena caught her arm and steadied her.

'Is that what you were looking for?'

Grace could hardly answer, 'No...no...I had no idea. Oh Tom!'

'Who was he? What happened to him?'

'I knew him. Years ago...in Spain during the civil war.'

'Spain? Did they have a war? What was he doing there?'

'He wanted to become a writer.' She stopped herself

welling up with tears and wiped away a snuffle as she drew a deep breath.

'Philomena, I need to go now. I need to be getting back. Thank you, thank you so much for your help today. I would never have been able to do all this alone. You have been so helpful...so helpful...you'll never know. Can we just put these things away and I think we should go now?'

'I've enjoyed it. This has been one of the best days I've had at work, ever. Will you come again? Please. I'd like to help you again.'

'I'll try. If not, you should come and see me, out in Connemara.'

'My God...I don't want to be going all that way. There's nothing there at all. They say it's the desert.'

'I'm there!' Grace quickly corrected her.

'I might...I might come. Can I get a bus?'

'You can. To Letterfrack.'

Grace had no energy or inclination to drive back and after saying goodbye to Philomena booked herself into The Great Western Hotel in Eyre Square for the night. Tom being at the School was now all she could think about. She didn't sleep.

16

ETHEL CARNEY

AFTER THE TROOP TRAIN HAD LEFT THE STATION AND THE chaos subsided, Mary stood for a few minutes and collected her thoughts. The blown kiss had made her blush and she felt self-conscious and embarrassed that it had been seen by all. Suddenly, an arm went around her shoulder and she could see by the colour of the sleeve that it was Ethel Carney's.

'Heroes all!' she declared.

Mary did not answer.

'Don't be sad my dear, they are doing what they came to do.'

'I know,' Mary replied, all the while thinking of Tom rather than the Irish banderas.

'Coffee?'

Unbridling Mary, Carney grabbed her hand and gently pulled her in the direction of the station exit. They walked through the near-deserted streets of the town towards the main square. The rain was holding off for once and the little puddles in the pot-holed roads were glistening in what must have been the first glimmer of hazy sun they had seen in days. They found a small café and taking the rare opportunity to sit at a pavement table, ordered their coffee.

'I tried to get Bannon to reverse the order but he said it was not for him to do so. Only Bolín or Aguilera can change it. That man is impossible!'

'Which?'

'Bannon. He's...well, how should we say, *manipulative*. Always scheming and trying his luck. And he hangs on to Spanish Officers' coat-tails like no-one else. Do you know him?' Carney inquired behind her hand in case anyone should hear.

'Bannon? No, good God no! I think you're right, he is very *manipulative*,' Mary replied. 'He's O'Duffy's right-hand man though and a true believer as well.'

'That man couldn't be true about anything!'

'But he is a believer. They say he is probably the only real Fascist in the Irish ranks....always has been, apart from O'Duffy that is. He was in the Blueshirts from the beginning.'

'Then how does he make a living?' Carney seemed intrigued by the information Mary had just offered.

'I don't know. I ...' Mary hesitated and simply held up her hands.

'Do you know he has a young wife in Lisbon? She's staying at the *Condor*! How can they afford that? Have you been there my dear? It's quite swish by Portuguese standards. Nice views as well. The service is, well, too Portuguese for my taste.'

Mary was already in fear of having to listen to Carney's travelogue and immediately tried to redirect the conversation. 'Do you think they will ever let us go to front?'

'I doubt it my dear. I doubt it very much. Apparently, we are only allowed to go as far as the nurses go. For myself, I can't say I really want to go any further in any case. I was just teasing Bannon about the order. He suggested there were enough behind-the-scenes stories here in Cáceres for us. Can't say I fancy visiting the local hospital! Do you know he was once a journalist?'

'I think I'd heard. A Catholic weekly in Dublin they say.'

'Yes...the editor no less. Between you, me and the gatepost my dear, some say that he's doing some dabbling over here.'

'Who for?'

'I'd rather not say my dear...but it is close to my own neck of the woods.'

'The *Independent*?'

'I'd better not say any more. He suggested we girls write about Cáceres.' Carney lit a cigarette without any thought of offering Mary one. 'Have you heard about the executions... or 'summary justice' as he prefers to call it?'

Mary was taken aback by the suggestion. 'The executions?'

'Oh don't tell me you haven't heard my dear? The volleys at night...always around one o'clock? You must have heard? It's probably the only thing you can set your clock by...that and the Angelus.'

'Of course I have...but—' Mary's face was contorted by her own interpretation of those nightly sounds. It was not that she had no consciousness of the shootings that were occurring; they were already common knowledge amongst all the journalists. It was, however, that she had somehow partitioned the thought of the execution squads and refused to acknowledge the truth of what those deadly nightly sounds really represented. That and the fact that she had not seen for herself the consequences, meant that she could immunise herself against the deed. She now felt both guilt and shame about her singular ability to cut off those things that she did not wish or was too scared to confront. She knew it was a personal failing and one that she was determined to address.

'They are going to do some day shows,' Carney blithely announced.

Mary grasped immediately what she meant. 'Executions you mean?'

'Yes, Bannon told me...starting tomorrow he said. You need to go to the cemetery, early. He said it was absolutely necessary as the Reds have started to infiltrate the locals again. The night show was not really showing the town what they all need to see. So, they plan to have some daily...'

'Please, please...don't call them *shows*,' Mary intervened.

'But they will be my dear! Just like the Soviet show trials. And it's a tradition in any case, public executions were once all we had. I agree with Bannon, I think there is probably a good argument for bringing them back. If it stops the Reds, it might even save lives in the longer run.'

'How can you say that?' Mary was by now livid and very angry with Carney. Her whole manner was superficial and in many respects inhuman. She was repulsive when she was in this mode.

'As journalists, I think we need to be there,' Carney suggested.

'It's evil and it's disgusting!' Mary responded.

'But we are here to report such things my dear. Why else are you here?' Carney blew smoke directly into Mary's face as she spoke.

Mary was now in a state of acute professional and political conflict. The very thought of witnessing the deaths of what were, in all probability, people with whom she shared a common cause or, just as likely, complete innocents, made her feel sick to her stomach. On the other hand, she was there, as Carney had rightly stated, to report on what was happening. Running away from the reality would therefore be akin to condoning the crimes. She needed time to think through whether she could face up to situation.

'What time will they be?' Mary asked.

'Early, Bannon said...about 9. Sometime after Mass, I suppose. It'll give time for the priests to be there. Should I collect you?'

Mary still could not believe that she was arranging to watch people die at a prescribed time and place, and all in the manner of a lunch date.

'No...no... thank you. I'll make my own way, if you don't mind.'

'Very well. More coffee? It's wretched stuff I know.' There was another pause and then Carney reached across to touch Mary's hand, 'I do so much like you my dear. But you never talk about yourself. Have you a man? Is it Miss or Mrs Porteus? I detect a previous life somewhere?'

Mary was reluctant to go down this path or any other with Carney. She sat up stiffly and her whole manner indicated that she had no intention of answering.

'You seem to very much like the Irish boy? Did I see you blow him a kiss? And so young and sweet. He's a spy you know,' Carney half-whispered.

Mary pretended not to have heard correctly. 'A spy? Rubbish! That is a very poor joke and a sick one, if I may say so.'

'It's not my dear. I heard he's spying, for the 'Big Man',

De Valera, the Taoiseach himself. He's here to keep an eye on O'Duffy and his crowd.'

'How do you know this? Who told you that, Bannon?'

'Who else? Working for *The Press* and all that nonsense about being freelance. I must say, sending a complete unknown... a boy even...was either stroke of genius or complete desperation! Have you seen him write anything? I haven't. And he's always nosing around. I think Bannon has got his number. He's watching him very closely by all accounts.'

'His number?' Mary was now getting more than anxious about Carney's gossiping.

'Yes, his card...what he's up to? Oh please keep up my dear! The fact is, he's Dev's little spy.'

'That's complete and utter nonsense!' Mary could not help herself and smacked the table.

'Oh...you *do* like him! I thought so. Pity, I thought I might vie for your affection.' Carney looked genuinely disappointed, 'I still very much like you my dear. You can rely on that. Miss or Mrs...it makes little difference to me.'

This was not what Mary had been expecting and neither did she welcome the news regarding Bannon's suspicions. They sat sipping their coffee and not speaking for some time. Carney did however occasionally comment, harshly, on the lack of good looks of the Spanish women as they passed. She did not have a positive word for any of them. How little Carney understood their suffering, Mary thought. And to be judged on their 'looks' by this contemptible woman, sitting with her expensive cigarettes and coffee, was one of the most hideous things she could think of at that moment. Was this woman really a monster? She could not contain herself any longer.

'Are *you* a Fascist Ethel?'

'Me...? Certainly not my dear. I've been to Chancellor Hitler's Germany and I've seen what he *hasn't* done for women there. I've no time for their ideology when it comes to women. I don't believe women can or should be Fascists. That's for the men, it seems.'

'So, in your book, only men can be Fascists?'

'No...that would be silly, very silly. Women can try to be Fascist...but the men will not let them. Just like us trying to be war correspondents here I suppose?' She stopped and took some coffee and resumed, 'And those uniforms my dear...how dreadful we'd all look! All dressed the same. No, Fascism is certainly not for me...or you I'd say.' Carney's usual attempt to trivialise every subject had once more been kick-started.

'But do you believe in what the Fascists stand for?'

'I'm not a Fascist my dear...and I don't believe in anything. I'm not a political animal, not at all. I've no time for men and their politics, none at all.'

'But you support the Nationalists?'

'No, I'm against the Communists and that is quite a different position altogether. I think they already have all these unfortunate, terribly unattractive, Spanish women in exactly the same place as the Fascists would have them... wearing overalls. We will not see anything different, as women that is, if either side win this war. We are and always will be second best to men. As far as women are concerned, this whole war is quite, quite pointless. That is my considered view. That is what I believe, if anything.'

'But you don't write about that? Have you addressed the issue in your work here?'

'Of course not! That is not what my so-called editor or the readers want to hear.'

'But—'

'That is the way of the world my dear. We women just have to make the most of it. And, if I say so myself, I'm pretty damn good at doing just that.' She pulled herself back from the table and sat bolt upright. Her large frame appeared to symbolise her own sense achievement. It was a 'look at me, haven't I done well' pose.

She continued, 'And have you seen what they are doing back home, in Ireland I mean? Oh, of course not, it's not your home is it. Well, I shall tell you anyway. Apparently, our antediluvian President and his Neanderthals are tinkering, yes whilst we speak, with our sacred 1916 Proclamation of equal rights...and the '22 Constitution ...so that women like myself, working women, are to be made second-class citizens. Can you believe that? I'm sure De Valera hates women, either that or he is scared of us. If he has his way, we will be chained to the kitchen table in the morning and to the bed at night. That is all we are good for it seems. And if you are not married by thirty they think you are either a freak or mad...or both more likely, unless you are a nun of course. Even the Reds treat their women better!'

She reached into her bag.

'Can I just read you what the *Irish Times* is about to say regarding my objections to the proposed Constitutional changes? I was sent this by one of my dear friends on the *Times*. She was so outraged when she saw it that she telegraphed it to me this very morning. Can I read it to you?'

'Yes... read it if you must,' Mary replied.

'Am I boring you my dear?' Carney obviously sensed that Mary's mind was already elsewhere.

'No, not at all...it's just—'

'I'm so glad...but I *must* read this to someone...I think you will agree it can only have been written by a man. Listen up now.' She took the telegram and started to read:

'*On Miss Ethel Carney's competence to chronicle the movements, the vagaries, and the tittle tattle of what is called Society, or to deal with the nuances of fabrics, the fashion of garments, the models of hats, or the style and ensemble which constitute the last word in chic, we are not qualified to express an opinion, but at the risk of being unpolite we must tell her that she makes a sorry exhibition of herself when she ventures on an incursion into politics, of which she has yet to learn the rudiments.*'

'Unpolite!' Surely the word is *impolite*? These are your real Fascists my dear! Silence your critics by demeaning them. Keep women quiet by mocking them...that is the only politics *they* know. And this is the *Irish Times* we are talking about. What hope is there for us?'

Carney was now flush with an anger that Mary had not seen or experienced before. She was fascinated by Carney's ability to change intellectual gear when she engaged in women's issues. Yet Mary did not want to respond and reveal her own sentiments. Nevertheless, by now, she had had enough of listening to what was fast becoming a diatribe. She finished her coffee and insisted that they resume the conversation another time. She left Carney perusing the telegram, smoking her cigarettes and no doubt condemning not a few Irish politicians and every passing Spanish female. Just as Mary went to leave, the rain started again and she saw Carney move herself to a table under a small canopy. They exchanged a brief wave.

That night, Mary found the thought of trying to sleep before the imminent and murderous salvo quite impossible. She lay awake in anticipation, unable to read or write. It crossed her mind that holding the executions in the morning may at least postpone the night terrors. As the minutes slow-marched into the night, she held on to that small hope and attempted to doze as time elapsed towards the critical hour. Then, exactly on the stroke of one, the crack of the rifles was heard once more. It was obvious that, such was the production line of killing, the operation was simply being extended rather than being moved to broad daylight. She pulled the bed covers up over her head and committed herself to attend the macabre appointment the next day.

17

THE EXECUTIONS

THE ROAD LEADING TO THE CEMETERY WAS THRONGED WITH what seemed like the entire townsfolk. Civil Guards and some Falange militia were directing the human traffic and the atmosphere was more that of a carnival than a public execution. Coffee and churro stalls had been erected either side of road and these were acting as a funnel leading the townspeople to the site. Mary was shocked by the presence of whole families, including small children, and the fact that they all appeared to be dressed in their Sunday best clothes. She recognised Pedro Caravaca, the concierge from her hotel. He doffed his hat and came over to her.

'Good morning Señora Porteus. I did not expect to see you here,' he said most politely in perfect English.

'I was thinking the same thing Pedro.'

'This is not what you should be seeing.'

'The crowds you mean? The carnival?'

'No, Señora. No, I meant what is going to happen. It is not something you will want to see. You should go back now.'

'I know what is happening Pedro and that is why I had to

come. As you know, I'm a journalist and it's my duty to report what I see.'

'I understand...'

'And why are you here?'

'We have to be. Please, do not ask me such things.' He looked around anxiously.

'You were told to come?'

'Please...'

'It's alright Pedro. I understand. Can you stay with me? I'd like to know what is going on and I may need some help.'

'Yes, if you wish. Should we go to the front? We will not see anything from here. We will need to hurry.'

'A little distance perhaps...and only as near as we have to be, please.'

'Of course, I understand.'

They moved through the crowd and inched their way forward to a small raised vantage point directly to the side of the cemetery's exterior wall and just about twenty-five yards from the fulcrum. The firing squad were relaxing, sitting on the ground and nearly all were smoking. Civil Guard officers were in deep conversation with two clerics and there was no sign of the condemned. Mary could not help but notice that the wall to be used was already pitted with holes and smeared with blood stains. Looking around, the already cheerful atmosphere had descended into an even more disgustingly flamboyant holiday mood. People were laughing and acting as if this was just an ordinary, popular Sunday morning meeting spot. Nothing in their manner indicated that they had come to witness human slaughter. The fact that they were well-dressed, could afford coffee and in some cases carried trophy umbrellas all indicated that this was no ordinary mob. It was the relatively well-to-do of Cáceres, the bourgeoisie or what remained of it, as well as the largely conscripted working-class.

A lorry slowly made its way through the crowd with its horn blaring every few yards. Its roof was covered and only the militia outriders hanging on to some stanchions at the front and rear were visible. The lorry stopped in line with the Officers and clerics, its tailgate was lowered and the prisoners were dragged from the rear. Unbelievably, a ghoulish round of applause broke out in the crowd – just as it would on entertainers taking to a stage. The victims were now lined up against the cemetery wall and an officer with a list walked past each one checking their identity. The firing squad had assembled and constructed two lines of fire. The crowd was now more animated than ever, pointing and generally indicating their knowledge of the unfortunates and no doubt approval of their impending fate. From where she was standing, Mary could see that the doomed souls were an extraordinary cross-section of the population. It was as if they had been chosen scientifically to represent the locals. There were three women; two of whom were middle-aged and the third a lot younger. There were four elderly men, one of whom appeared to have wet himself and another who was bent and had trouble standing upright. The rest were all younger men and some who were thirty or so. One boy appeared to be in his teens and was visibly shaking. Twelve poor souls in all. They all stood gaping at the crowd in an entirely passive and controlled dignity. Each had their hands tied at their front.

The officer in charge stepped forward and began to read a proclamation.

'What's he saying?' Mary asked.

Pedro provided a simultaneous translation.

'They have all been tried and convicted of being Red

terrorists. The Tribunal...has found...them guilty as charged. They have all confessed. The sentence...is death by firing squad to be carried out this morning without delay. Everyone needs to note....that this is what we do with all those who support the Communist menace. God help them!'

The troops shouldered arms and then took up the ready. The crowd immediately hushed and made to move forward, to be closer to the action. The Civil Guards pushed them back. Taking a handful of ribbons from one of the priests, the lead officer offered the condemned blindfolds, which they all refused and turned their heads away as he passed down the line. He returned the ribbons to the priest and took out his pistol. Mary's heart was by now swollen and threatened to jump out of her breast. She still could not believe that this was actually taking place directly in front of her.

From a safe distance, the clerics began to offer the last rites and this was met with the only sign of resistance from the women prisoners; in unison they spat in the direction of God's envoys. A gasp of disbelief at their defiance came from the crowd, followed by some shouts which Mary could not understand. The priests soon stopped their prayers and moved away from the scene. Mary's heart went out to the condemned. The fact that the Church was sanctioning and thereby complicit in this murder only confirmed what she already knew, and that was their rank hypocrisy. The legitimacy of the Nationalist cause was undoubtedly enhanced by the men of God placing their imprimatur on the proceedings. Yet, for Mary, it had precisely the opposite effect. It revealed their true role lay in their functionality rather than their faith.

The firing squad took up two rows, one standing and

one on bended knee, and when their commander lifted his pistol they took aim. For what seemed like an eternity, the whole area went silent. Then, as if one, the three women who were now in the rifle sights lifted their skirts and shouted '¡*Viva La República!*' Revealing their complete womanhood, they fell as the shots rang out. Mary, like most others in the crowd, was stunned by the ghastly scene. The entire line lay crumpled in a tangled heap of bloodied torsos and limbs. Gaining the courage to look, Mary could see that two of the women were still writhing and one of them attempted to get to her knees. The nearest officer quickly went over and delivered the *coup-de-grace*. He continued to fire at all the bodies as he marched down the bloodied furrow that now separated the dead from the living. When he had finished, the crowd which had now become more hushed began to file away. One or two genuflected as they turned towards the deceased, others simply raised an eyebrow and some even smiled in perverse satisfaction at what they had just seen.

Mary was now trembling and felt her knees giving way under her. She reached out and Pedro managed to support her off the mound.

'You should drink some coffee,' he suggested. 'Quick, I will get you some. Please stay here.' He rushed away to the nearest stall that was already beginning to be packed up. Very soon he was back with what looked like a cup of black tar.

'Drink it...please.'

'Thank you.' Mary winced at the appalling taste of the concoction.

'Did you see those women?' Pedro asked.

'Yes, of course.' She was still staring at the motionless corpses. No-one else now appeared to be interested in them and they lay ignored and untouched. Their blood had seeped into the surrounding ground and was already drying into just a giant red stain.

Pedro was silent and looked around to see if there were any interlopers.

'They killed a priest. Father Andrade.'

'Is that true?' Mary could no longer bring herself to believe anything that might justify what she had just witnessed.

'Yes...It is known in the town. We all heard.'

'Why?'

'They were Reds. You heard them yourself....*Viva Republica!*' Pedro said softly.

'But why would they kill a priest here? In Barcelona perhaps...or even Madrid...but Cáceres?'

'Who knows?' Pedro looked and sounded ambivalent.

'You do,' Mary sensed.

'Perhaps...perhaps they did not like him?'

'Pedro! You don't kill a priest because you don't like him. How did they kill him in any case?'

'I don't like to say.'

'You must tell me—'

'I'd rather not...you being a lady and all.' He looked embarrassed.

'What did they do to him? Tell me please. I must know why they died.'

'They cut off his man part!'

'His man part?'

'His man part. His...what do you call it?' he looked down at his own lower body.

'His penis.'

'His penis, yes.' Pedro was now acutely red in the face as

he repeated the words. 'And then they cut his throat.' He made the slitting motion.

'Why? Why would they do that?'

'You saw why. You saw what they did. Showing themselves. They have no...how do you say, feeling of shame. They were prostitutes, all of them. Mother and daughter and mother's sister.'

'They were prostitutes? In Cáceres?'

'Yes, all of them.'

'And the priest? Did he...?'

'It was said he did. And there may have been a child.'

'Oh my God! They were shot because of a priest?'

'No...they killed him. A man. They were shot because they murdered him. And that was right. It was because he was a priest. No.'

'But why? Why would they have killed him? There must be other prostitutes and other priests?'

'I don't know about such things.'

'I don't believe you Pedro. You're a concierge!'

'I think they killed him because one was going to have a child...'

'By the priest?'

'Yes.'

'Which one? Which one was pregnant?'

'The young one, but she was not pregnant... now.'

'What happened? Where's the child?'

'There was no child. It was gone.'

'Aborted?'

'The priest made her have it. It's ...gone...'

'But that is against everything the Church believes in. It's an almighty sin.'

There was a silence and Pedro shifted from foot to foot. He kept glimpsing around nervously.

'It happens. Priests are men. I wish to go now. Are you okay to walk?'

'But why did they murder him?'

'I don't know. They were Reds *and* prostitutes. Perhaps it was political? They say the mother killed him first. We go now?'

'Yes...and thank you for this.' Mary held up the cup and poured the remainder of the contents onto the mound.

'I will take you back to the hotel. Take my arm please.'

'Thank you Pedro. I'm sorry I asked you so many questions.'

'I'm a concierge Señora Porteus. That's my job!'

Mary returned to her hotel room and cried. The full extent of the barbarity she had witnessed slowly overwhelmed her and images of the women and their bloodied bodies kept reoccurring whenever she closed her eyes. Even more vivid was their last defiant act. This was *the* moment of truth. Although it lasted barely a second, it captured a long history of struggle. It also revealed a spirit and courage that is seldom, if ever, seen in most people's everyday lives. It was the second before they died that would linger in her memory forever. She wanted to believe that, in that moment, the full truth of what it means to be a human being was somehow revealed. She knew that she would never have such courage, but she vowed nevertheless to try to live up to their example.

18

***

CIEMPOZEULOS

Nothing could have prepared the men of the Irish Brigade for what followed. Everything in Ciempozeulos was all but destroyed and most of the buildings were either rubble or on their way to becoming so. As they entered the ruins of the tiny casas, their domesticity looked as if it had been exploded from the inside and the vestiges of everyday life were scattered, fragmented, charred and strewn everywhere. And then they came upon the corpses. Each remnant of a house contained bodies that had inflated, congealed and sometimes combusted. Either that, or they had disintegrated, decomposed or had been half-eaten by the packs of wild dogs and flocks of crows that now scavenged on the carrion. These hellish sights made several of the young brigaders retch and others run out of the buildings. The carnage was uniform, house after house, and the relentless discovery of bodies, parts of bodies, and in some cases uncertainty as to whether the flesh was in fact human at all, began to take its toll on their instinctive tendency to genuflect over each and every gruesome discovery. Nothing had prepared them for this and perhaps nothing could? By the time they arrived at the railway station, one of the few structures that remained standing, they were now emotionally as well as physically exhausted and many were unable to say anything. Some of the younger recruits were clearly traumatised by their first real encounter with the bloody consequences of warfare.

At the railway station a group of Moroccan soldiers were packing up their equipment and leaving the ticket office. Dressed in their colourful galabias, turbans and rather ridiculous white plimsolls, it was their ebony skin which stood out above all else and the Irish couldn't help but just stand and stare at these exotic creatures. Few, if any, had encountered people of colour before and certainly not back home. Meanwhile, another small group of Moors approached the Brigade from the direction of the main square. They said nothing at all when they arrived and didn't even acknowledge their supposed Irish allies. They placed some sheets on the ground and immediately proceeded to populate them with an assortment of household and other personal items. It appeared that the contents of the homes of the locals had been thoroughly harvested. Both the necessities and the luxuries of ordinary life were now on the ground - shoes, clothing, belts, bags, cups, packets of tobacco, alcohol, mirrors, razors, children's dolls, paintings, jewellery, books, plates, hair brushes, icons and family photographs still in their ornate frames. All this was not just the spoils of war, it was Official loot. The Moors, it transpired, were sanctioned by Franco to spend up to two hours purloining the household contents of any population they 'liberated'. Their efficiency in this respect was matched only by their butchery and in Ciempozeulos this was clear for all to see.

Still struggling to come to terms with the horrors uncovered in the houses, one or two of the Irishmen sought to remonstrate at the gross indecency of the souk that was being set up before them. Some swore racist epithets at the Moors and others needed to be held back. For not a few of the men, the glaringly obvious contradiction of their plight was now brought home all too starkly: how could they, as Christian soldiers, be on the same side as these Muslims? What did they have in common? Many of the rotting cadavers must have been Catholic, albeit 'Red' Catholics, and as it was once said, '*even the atheists in Spain were Catholic*'. The children were certainly innocents, as were their mothers, sisters, grandmothers and aunts. Some of their menfolk had obviously died fighting, but their gratuitous dismemberment and ritual disembowelling was heinous and barbaric in the extreme. The tension between the two groups of soldiers was therefore palpable and even dangerous. It was difficult however to reconcile the atrocities committed by the Moors that had manufactured all these items for sale, with the Irish desire for the goods that were being laid before them. After a short while, the price of the packs of cigarettes and alcohol were being haggled over regardless of their origins. Business was brisk and the Moors soon left, but with most of the personal loot still wrapped in their blankets. As they did so, an incoming shell announced itself in the distance and the men were forced to take cover. The eventual explosion was more of a muted thud and came from the direction of the town centre. Some of the Irish cursed and secretly hoped it had found a Moroccan target. It was a salutary reminder that they were now at the front and in future they should not expect all incoming bombardments to be so polite as to give them advanced notice. Not long afterwards a whole volley of artillery shells rained down from the Republican guns just across the valley.

Tom arrived mid-afternoon with the Press convoy that, over the course of the journey, was now headed by the infamous yellow Mercedes of one Captain Gonzalo de Aguilera y Munro, the fourteenth Conde de Alba de Yeltes and a product of a Scottish mother and the English Public School system. Everyone had been told to expect the new Head of Press and Propaganda in Cáceres, but the fanciful way in which he announced his arrival at the head of the pack was entirely unexpected. Aguilera's car horn was blasted over and over again. No-one, it seemed, was to be left unaware of his existence. This was, after all, the man who had quite unashamedly boasted that on the first day of the coup he lined up six labourers on his estate and shot them. Tom and Mary had heard this account from a very reliable source and had no reason to doubt it. The public school educated aristocrat is reported to have said '*Pour encourager les autres, you understand.*' The man was more of a psychopath than a linguist.

Tom immediately sensed the desolation of Ciempozeulos in the eyes of some of the Irish Brigaders who were busy readying their quarters. This consisted, for the most part, of them emptying the few habitable structures of all human remains and lighting small fires to cover the sickening smell that permeated every dwelling where a pile of putrid flesh had been disturbed. As he stood and watched them reluctantly undertake this unholy task, he couldn't help but feel more sorry for the living than the dead.

After a brief stop at the railway station to take some propaganda photographs, Aguilera ordered the correspondents back into their cars and they were driven towards the town centre. On reaching the main square, Tom and the other journalists were able to comprehend the extent of the ruin that was now Ciempozeulos. Hardly anything was left standing and the devastation was almost complete. More bodies lay in the street and they looked as if they had done so for some time. Aguilera himself gave the impression of being surprised by the sheer scale and total nature of the destruction. The tall, stocky intimidating presence of the Spanish officer and his yellow Mercedes had all the trappings of a Hollywood lead actor in search of a film. Everything about him was for effect. He immediately summoned the Press Corps and proceeded to denounce this 'Red atrocity, the bestiality and barbarity of the atheistic hordes, which you can now witness for yourselves'. He did not mention the role of the Moors, who had by then completely disappeared, but not without a bloody trace.

In small groups, the Corps set about inspecting the remains of the town. The obvious draws were the two small churches adjoining the main square. Here they found what they were looking for - evidence of desecration and, more important, the corpses of a priest and two nuns. They had all been shot in the head and had their throats cut. They were also partially clothed. The priest was naked below the waist and had been dismembered. The habit of one of the nuns had been half-torn and this had exposed her breasts which had been engraved with bloody crosses. What looked like the remnants of a Rosary was left hanging out of the mouth of the other nun and a crucifix was engorged in the wound in her throat. Tom was fixated by the half-smile on what remained of the priest's face and what was directly above him, a perfect red hammer and sickle which had been graffitied on the wall. He thought that a great deal of care and attention to detail had been exerted on this scene of execution and that, altogether, it had a surreal as well as iconoclastic quality. It might well have been an exhibit in an art gallery. Or was this some sort of sadistic tableaux that had been put on especially for their benefit?

The sight of the mutilated bodies did not upset or even disturb Tom, contrary to what he had always expected and feared. Indeed, he was perturbed by his own lack of feelings. The anticipation and general expectation built up by any number of the atrocity stories that he had heard, especially in relation to the Red's treatment of the clergy and nuns, had been cathartic it seemed. The discovery of these bodies, proof of such 'Red sacrilege', was therefore unable to shock him. In fact he was left rather cold and in relation to the number of bodies he had already seen in the streets of Ciempozeulos, these three unfortunates did not seem to warrant any special privileges in death. Nevertheless, he did think that it must have been an especial hatred of who they were and, perhaps, more so what they represented that lay behind the ghastly manner of their deaths. Tom thought he knew or at least understood what such a level of hatred of the Church might be like. He was disturbed by his own confusion regarding the symbolism that now confronted him. These deaths had a meaning but it was not entirely clear to him what that might be. These particular bodies and what had happened to them, unlike the countless others that paved the roads outside the church, were obviously meant to demonstrate something very deep and powerful to all those who might come upon them. It was not just that their mortality was the same as everyone else's, it had to have something to do with the consecrated lives they were supposed to have led. Were they really sacred persons and were they now martyrs? Their decomposition had already started. Yet, in theory, and provided they had received the requisite sacraments, their purified souls should have prevented this. The fact that they were now beginning to putrefy in death might then be the measure of their corruption in life?

This was not how most of the other correspondents reacted to the find. The discovery of murdered clergy and perhaps even more so nuns who had been abused, was precisely what they had hoped for, especially McIlroy. They had had their beliefs confirmed. The Reds were inhuman and the Nationalist 'crusade' was a just cause, a legitimate 'Defence of the Faith'. They had their headline, their photographs and their copy had been written for them by the perpetrators, whoever they might be.

As soon as they left the church it started to rain and it was not just a shower. In fact it was to rain solidly for the next four weeks. This also made it even harder to pick out the incoming rounds of artillery, which might just as well have been thunder-claps that accompany a downpour were it not for their altogether more destructive effect. The rain did not deter the dogs picking on the human bones in the square and neither did it deter Captain Aguilera setting up a canteen for the Press Corps in an abandoned restaurant. He had commandeered a cook and various helpers to prepare an afternoon meal. All the Irish Brigade officers had been invited and Father Muldoon was the first to arrive, early of course, and ingratiated himself with Aguilera by conversing in Spanish. Tom watched as they shared what must have been a joke. The dull thud of yet another shell landing nearby made them all look up to the ceiling and Tom thought that Muldoon looked more concerned that the shelling would interrupt his meal than his time on earth. The other foreign correspondents were sitting at tables comparing notes or simply gossiping as usual. McIlroy looked completely absorbed in his work and Tom thought it best not to disturb him. And with his senses bombarded and his mind racing, he decided to go outside and explore further.

The deluge meant that he had to scurry from building to building in an attempt to keep dry. With an eye and an ear on the continuing but sporadic bombardment, he carefully negotiated a way out of the main plaza and down an inconsequential side alley. The town was completely deserted save the packs of emaciated dogs and cats who just stared at him rather than scuttle away as he approached. Then, as he exited the alleyway and entered another major square, he caught sight of a group of figures coming towards him. The greyness of the rain made it difficult to discern what or who they might be. He hid behind a shop front just in case they were combatants from the Republican side. He thought of beating a retreat whilst he still could and was just about to make his escape, when he saw the cast were coming ever nearer and ever clearer. There were half a dozen of the phantasms. Bare-footed, draped in soiled sheets and grinning and groaning uncontrollably they staggered towards him. Gurgling in Spanish, they held their arms out in some sort of exaltation. They appeared to be all female, although it was impossible to tell in some cases. Tom was scared and became rooted to the spot. It was then that he heard a second group advancing from the other end of the street. He was now trapped. When they arrived they surrounded him and began to try to touch him. He recoiled and held up his hands to fend them off. He could now recognise what they might be; they were inmates of some sort, probably from an asylum. Realising this, he didn't feel so endangered, only helpless to help them. He couldn't understand them and neither could he comprehend how they were here, in the midst of all this desolation, uncared for and quite forgotten it appeared. He wanted to run and just as he pondered his move, a shot rang out from the end of the street. The women shrieked and ran in all directions. A second shot was fired and then a third. Tom saw a Nationalist officer approaching. It was Lieutenant Ramires, one of the Spanish Liaison officers.

'What are you doing here?' he said.

'I got lost', Tom half-lied.

'These are dangerous...these people. You cannot go without an escort. Not even in these streets.'

'I didn't realise. I thought the town was liberated.' Tom replied.

'It is. But these people live here. They are very dangerous.'

'Who are they?' Tom asked.

'Mad people. Locos....they come from the clinic, the asylum. They are very dangerous. They have no guards. The nuns have all been killed by the Reds. They have to look after themselves. You could have been killed by them.'

'How many are there?' Tom sensed a story.

'I don't know. Many were killed. Many have run away. But there are many left up there,' and pointed to a citadel high above the town. 'Many. You must stay away from them,' the young Spanish officer insisted. 'We need to go now.'

Whilst Tom was most grateful to his saviour, the plight of the creatures from the asylum did not leave his thoughts on their way back to the main square. In fact he felt like they were following him and more than once he turned to check whether that was the case. By the time they had reached the restaurant where the correspondents were being hosted, he felt chastened by his experiences that afternoon. He certainly had no appetite and the thought of dining with Aguilera, Muldoon, McIlroy and the others made him feel quite nauseous. Instead he made his excuses to Ramires, thanked him again and went to the second small church for some solitude. As he did so, more rain and shells fell into the already flattened neighbourhood.

At dusk the car horns of the Press convoy were sounded as a reveille. Tom finished a diary entry and returned to the main square. The correspondents were lined up on parade and Aguilera was once more lecturing them on the depravity of the Republican forces and the righteousness of the Nationalist cause. He did however take a detour in his soliloquy and this began to grab Tom's attention:

'Sewers, gentlemen! Sewers are the root of all our troubles. The masses in this country are not like your Americans, nor even like the British. They are from slave stock. They are fit to be nothing but slaves and only when they are used as such are they content and happy with their lot. But we, the honest and decent people of my kind, made the grossest of mistakes by giving them housing, modern housing in the cities where we have our factories. We then put sewers in these cities... sewers in the workers' quarters! Not content with the work of God, we also interfered with His Will. And this is the result, the slave stock has increased beyond all measure.'

Aguilera paused and stood expectant of some form of affirmation. None was forthcoming. He continued, 'If we had let things be, if we had not provided them with sewers in Madrid, Barcelona, and Bilbao, all the Red leaders would have died before they were born or in their infancy. Instead, we have bred them strong enough to incite the rabble and cause Christian Spanish blood to flow. When this war is over, we should, we will, destroy all the sewers. The only birth control for Spain is the birth control God intended us to have. Sewers should necessarily be reserved for those who deserve and appreciate them, our leaders of Spain, not the degenerates of the slave stock.'

Aguilera stopped once more and looked around. His pose was pure Mussolini; puffed chest and unblinking eyes. He surveyed the assembled corps, many of whom appeared frozen in their disbelief at what they had just heard. Even those who were ardent supporters of the fascist cause had trouble digesting this incredulous account. Tom fumbled for his diary and made to look busy by noting down what was already apparent, these were the insentient ramblings of a man who was completely insane or worse.

Aguilera resumed his speech. 'With the introduction of modern sewage disposal and the like, they simply multiply too fast. They're like animals and you can't expect them not to be infected with the virus of Bolshevism. After all, rats and lice carry the plague. Now I hope you gentlemen can understand why we need to complete the regeneration of our dear Spain?'

Retaining the dictator's favourite pose, and determined not to be ignored, he raised his hands and clapped to draw full attention.

'It's our intention, you understand, to exterminate one third of the male population of Spain. That will cleanse the country and rid us of the Red proletariat. This is not just necessary for the health of the stock; it is necessary economically. Fewer proletarians will mean we will never have unemployment in Spain. And we need to make other important changes. For example, we'll reverse this Communist nonsense of equality for women. I am a breeder of horses and animals generally. Therefore I know about animals and I know all about women. There'll be no more of the ignominy of subjecting us men, gentleman, to the courts. If your woman's unfaithful, you should be free to shoot her like a dog. Interference of the law between a man and his wife is the work of the Bolshevist lesbians. Are there any questions, gentlemen?' Even the other correspondents showed some signs of embarrassment. They simply lowered their heads and avoided eye contact.

The rain had not stopped and all the assembled, with the exception of Aguilera, appeared to want to get out of what was now an incessant soaking. The occasional blast of the mortars and artillery shells did not appear to trouble the correspondents by comparison. Only McIlroy had the temerity to raise an umbrella. Suddenly, in mid-speech, a scream from the roof of a bell tower was heard above Aguilera. Tom could see one of the asylum inmates holding forth from a belfry that overlooked the plaza. She had a very strong voice but Tom was unable to translate what she was shouting. Aguilera turned and strode towards his car. He reached into the rear, passenger side of his yellow Mercedes and extracted a rifle from a special compartment he had built into the front seat. Everyone knew exactly what he intended to do. Taking aim through the telescopic sight, he squeezed the trigger. The crack of the rifle was met with silence. The shrouded figure was gone.

'She was warning the enemy. Guiding their bombs,' Aguilera claimed. He looked again through the scope at the tower. He seemed more than pleased with his accuracy. 'Gentlemen, we need to go.'

And with that they embarked the cars. No-one said anything. None of the other correspondents probably even knew about the asylum and its inmates. But they now all knew about the danger posed by Aguilera.

19

─────

ESCAPE

MEGAN DANZER CRASHED INTO MARY'S ROOM WITHOUT knocking.

'They've got Frances! They've taken her!' She screamed and grabbed Mary in a bear hug so tight that it drew out all her breath. It was the first time she had engaged the young American reporter and her first instinct was to try to release herself from the hold she was now in. However, the intensity of Megan's clutch and her sobbing made this impossible.

'Aguilera's men....they've arrested her,' the American screamed.

'Calm down, please. Please...calm down,' Mary replied. She was already grasping something of the gravity of the situation, whatever it entailed. 'When? Where is she?' she said, pulling the young woman off sufficient to continue.

'The garrison...the barracks. They came earlier this evening,' Megan spluttered and started sobbing uncontrollably.

'What did they say? Why have they arrested her? Did they say?'

'Spying, smuggling, taking copy out for Cardozo...and all

the others. Not going through the censor. They said she was spying!'

'Who said?'

'Lambarri, the Press Officer, the censor guy. He arrested her.'

'Lambarri? Why was he involved?' Mary asked.

'Oh my God, Aguilera and Bolín...they'll shoot her!' Megan sunk her head into Mary's chest.

'No. No, that's not going to happen. They wouldn't shoot a woman; especially a woman foreign journalist. That wouldn't do them any good. They won't shoot her,' she tried to reassure Megan.

There was a moment's silence and Mary looked into Megan's eyes. 'Why was it Lambarri that was arresting her? That's unusual, he's not their kind. That's not what he does,' she suggested, more to convince herself than the distraught youngster.

'Bolín ordered it. He's in Burgos with Aguilera and they found out. Somehow they found out. Someone must have told them. They're returning tomorrow, first thing.'

'How do you know this?' Mary asked.

'It's what Lambarri said.'

Mary disentangled herself and began to think aloud. She couldn't understand why she felt so calm given the circumstances. Her attempt to stave off emulating the near-hysterical Megan was perhaps the main reason. She could see what panic does to someone and it didn't appear to help.

'Have you tried to get hold of Cardozo?'

'He's at the front with the others,' Megan sobbed.

'Of course he is. We need to get Frances out, tonight. Where's Lambarri now, do you know?'

'He was at the garrison. He took her there. I followed,

but they wouldn't let me in to see her. He suggested I come to you,' Megan sobbed.

Lambarri's suggestion did not really register with Mary and she did not even question why her name had arisen. Instead she focussed on the imminent danger the young detainee was in. She knew it was impossible to predict the violence of Aguilera and Bolín and that, contrary to her earlier assertion, both could and would shoot people regardless, even a foreign woman journalist. Frances Davis was therefore in very real danger and Mary felt she had no choice but to try to help, even if she had no idea how exactly. Whatever she did, it probably meant that this was going to be her last night in Nationalist Spain. Surprised by her own perspicacity, she packed a small holdall and they headed for the garrison. Megan's and Frances' lodgings were enroute and they stopped to retrieve some papers and whatever belongings they could cram into a small overnight bag. By now, all Megan's tears were drained and she was leaving Mary to make all the decisions.

At the garrison they were met by two amiable Irish banderas who had been left to guard the various miscreants who failed to be either fit or sober enough to go to the front. Fortunately, they had no curiosity as to why two women journalists would want to see Lieutenant Lambarri at that time of night. Mary explained that it was an emergency and that Lambarri had asked them to attend. They were let through with directions to find him in the Officers' Mess.

The room was dark and Manuel Lambarri was slumped in an armchair with his head in his hands. A pile of cigarette ends had amassed in front of him, as well as a glass that was now empty. Mary thought he may even have been crying. He was nervous and disconsolate and, more than ever, looked most ill-suited to his role.

'Lieutenant? Lieutenant Lambarri, it's Mary Porteus. Can I speak to you, please?'

'Señora Porteus and Miss Danzer. I think I know why you are here. Miss Davis?' he looked up as they walked towards him.

'Is she OK?' Megan asked.

'Yes, she is,' he replied gently.

'Where is she? Mary inquired.

'In a cell. She's very frightened, scared and I'm afraid she cries—'

'Why have you arrested her?'

'But you know...you all know. She was taking information across the border. Uncensored information and without permissions.'

'Information? They were news stories, articles, copy. None of that 'information' was new or secret,' Mary said.

'But it is all information that has to be approved. You know that. Why did she smuggle it? Why? She could have got it approved, like all the others,' he said with a genuine air of despair and regret.

'It wasn't hers. There are many correspondents who used her. Everyone was using her.'

'Then they will all be punished,' Lambarri lit a cigarette without offering them.

'They sent it out that way to avoid your delays. That's all. Look at the articles. They always support your side. They are not criticising you. It is just that you take so long to approve anything. That's why they used her.'

'It is information that our enemy can use. It may be secretly coded. No matter, I have my orders. I was told to detain her. I had no choice,' he replied in an even more despondent voice.

Mary sensed that all was not well with the Lieutenant.

He was just following orders, albeit ones that clearly upset him. His moroseness and downbeat attitude suggested that he was also in the midst of a personal crisis of some sort. He was far from the usual bright self and the officer she thought she knew. She waited for him to look at her and then appealed to him,

'Do you want her to be shot?'

Megan gasped at the directness of the question and tears once again came to her eyes. There was a long silence and Lambarri drew on his cigarette and then stood looking away. Mary could see that he was struggling to respond and was trying to hold back his own feelings. Clearly something about this situation and his own part in it had unsettled him.

'Captain Bolín and Captain Aguilera will decide. It is not for me. Perhaps she will just be ...expelled?' he eventually offered.

'You don't believe that.' Mary responded quickly. 'You know them, they will shoot her if they want to and you know it.'

'No, that will not happen.'

'It could. Aguilera is capable. Bolín also. You cannot know what they will do. No one can,' Mary insisted. 'Do you want her to die at their hands? Are you afraid of them yourself?'

'Of course, who isn't?' he snapped back and stared into Mary's face.

Mary felt she needed to stop being so coy and go directly to the possible source of Lambarri's discomfort. 'Manuel, there will be no place for people like you in a fascist Spain. You know that don't you?'

'People like me?' and turned his face towards her.

'Creative, sensitive men—'

'I am a magazine designer. Spain will still need design-ers,' he tried to reassure himself.

'Male designers...in fashion magazines...under Franco? Manuel, they hate your kind.'

'My kind?' he gave a wry smile. 'What is my *kind*? What do you think I am?'

'You know what I mean. You too need to get out while you can,' Mary implored him.

He paused and looked away again. Without turning to face Mary he replied, 'And where will I go? With you, to London?'

'Yes, why not? Come back to London with us. To *Vogue*, or wherever.'

He turned to face her and replied sarcastically, 'And I suppose we take Miss Davis with us too?'

'Yes, tonight. Come with us. Save her...and save yourself. We can all go.'

'They will shoot all of us,' he choked and his eyes welled with what looked like tears.

'Not if we go now. We can make the border by morning, if we drive fast. Can you drive?'

'Do you have a car?'

'No, but Aguilera's is outside,' Mary replied.

Lambarri returned to his chair and flung his arms above his head at the incredulity of the suggestion.

'Ahh...you...you are completely mad! He will certainly shoot us if we take his car! If we just sit in it ...he will have us shot! Are you so mad? Loco!'

Mary knew she had to be more personal.

'Manuel, we have no choice. *You* have no choice. As a man who loves men, you cannot stay here. You are dead if you stay. There can be no future for you here. Come with us, now. Please I beg you. Save yourself and Frances Davis.'

'And in England? They will also put me a prison for being my kind?'

'Perhaps ...if you are unlucky or indiscrete ...but they won't shoot you!'

Lambarri smiled and, shaking his head, could not believe that this conversation was actually happening. He appeared to look at himself and the uniform and began to shake his head.

'How can we get her out? There are guards everywhere,' he shrugged.

Mary was stymied for a moment. And then, without any previous consideration of where the notion came from, suggested, 'There's a doctor, an Irish one, Freeman. He's still here. We can use him.'

'Freeman? Can you trust him?' Megan asked.

'No, but he won't know what's happening. We can use him to get out of here. We must do it now. Manuel? Please... please help us. And come with us.'

Lambarri didn't say anything and, after another silence and a long look at both women, simply nodded his assent.

Mary went back to the sentries and asked for the duty officer. A stiff Irishman appeared and gave her advice about not using Freeman, even in a medical emergency, and suggested instead a Dr Gates. Mary insisted on Freeman and indicated to the red-faced NCO that it was a 'feminine' problem and that Freeman was an eminent expert in that field back home in Ireland. The sergeant demurred and sent one of the sentries to rouse the doctor.

After what seemed like an interminable wait, Freeman arrived dishevelled and semi-conscious. As he was marshalled into the guardhouse it soon became obvious that he was in his reputational state of disrepair. It was common knowledge that this was due to his fondness for self-medication. He had little or no idea of his whereabouts, let alone the mission or indeed his part in it. Mary thought this was probably all for the best.

Lambarri escorted the party to the detention cells and smoothed a path past various guards. For once he looked the part of an officer. Most of the other inmates in the cells appeared to be Irish banderas who were sleeping off a tour of the local bars. Once in the cell with an unbelieving Frances Davis, Mary instructed Freeman to demand in his loudest that the prisoner be taken to hospital immediately. He couldn't see any reason to do this and simply shook his head in confusion. Lambarri stepped in and, in loud Spanish, stated that she must be taken to Cáceres' infirmary immediately. He also repeated the instruction in English for the benefit of any Irish guards who might be in earshot. They took the by now stupefied Frances Davis from her cell and out towards the parade ground where Aguilera's yellow Mercedes was parked. Mary had to constantly reassure Davis that Lambarri was indeed an ally and that she had nothing to fear. As soon as they had located the keys in the ignition and stowed their bags in the boot, the car was leaving the compound. The Irish sentries wished them well as they passed through the barriers which they had duly raised. Lambarri saluted them from the driver's side.

Lieutenant Lambarri was a terrible driver and only narrowly missed colliding with one of the 'meat lorries' that was heading for the execution walls by the local cemetery. By the time they had reached the town perimeter Freeman had also fallen fast asleep. They stopped the car and gently pushed him out and, for his own safety, laid him on an embankment at the side of the road. He was now in a self-induced near coma.

The journey to the border was remarkable in so far as

they were stopped just once. It appeared that as soon as the militia saw it was Aguilera's car they thought twice about stopping it. As a result, they were passed through checkpoints quicker than at any time they had chance to do so in the past. Even Mary had not reckoned on the bonus of this particular yellow Mercedes.

Just prior to the border they abandoned the car. Taking one of the two rifles from the compartment built into the back of the passenger seat, Lambarri shot out the tyres and put a bullet into the radiator, a symbolic gesture by the designer. Mary was unsure as to the wisdom of this but Lambarri said it was just something he had always wanted to do for the pure pleasure of it. They then threw both rifles into a nearby culvert and as they clattered into the gully below, Mary couldn't help but think about how many innocent lives had probably been taken with those particular weapons.

The dawn was breaking as they arrived at the very small and quiet border post. They walked to the sentry box and saw that the militiamen were still having their breakfast of coffee and cigarettes. Lambarri made them stand to attention and produced *salvoconductos* for the whole party. The border militia were nonplussed and waved them across, presumably so that they could continue their meal in peace. On the Portuguese side the action was more or less repeated. A cursory view and stamping of the passports was completed in no time and they simply marched off down the road. A horse and cart, posing as a taxi, was hailed and they headed towards the nearest town. They had escaped and it was to be the end of the war for all of them.

After the exhilaration came the shock and the pain. It took some time for Mary to realise what she had actually done. Saving the young American was a gallant act but one that she had had no time to think about. As such, she was pleased with her own selfless spontaneity. Only now, the unintended consequences were beginning to dawn on her. Unconsciously, she had deserted Tom. In such moments of reflection she felt like a mother who had abandoned her child. And this was complicated by the fact that she had not really established what her relationship to Tom was or even could be. She then tried to rationalise the situation and felt responsible for her 'secretary'. He was, after all, a grown man and aware of most if not all of the risks. At the next moment, she was his big sister. And then, something totally unexpected and not necessarily welcome overcame her; she felt the ache of what could even be called love. She instantly recoiled from the thought, but it obstinately refused to go away. She had long ago given up the sexual part of her existence and was adamant in her own mind that there was no such attraction to Tom. Much more important was the feeling of being her own true self and this had been awoken by his presence. Belatedly, she now realised that she had had such moments, despite his youth, their differences and his naiveté. She had felt alive in his company and it was that feeling she most wanted to continue.

Should she return to Spain? What would he think if she didn't? Would he understand? What might happen to him? The situation dictated that it would be almost impossible and suicidal to attempt to go back to Cáceres, if only for what Lambarri had done to Aguilera's car. Tom was at the front in any case and she would be unable to see him. She told herself that he would have done the same in the circumstances. Indeed, she hoped that most people would have done the same. If he was discovered to be her accomplice, the worst that might happen to him is that they would throw him out of the country. She consoled herself with such thoughts and since Lisbon was not safe from Aguilerra and Bolín's agents, she quickly left for London.

Manuel Lambarri had also not waited around. He knew that the Portuguese were likely to repatriate him as soon as they received notice of his desertion. He headed for Paris just as soon as he could purchase a train ticket. His last words to Mary were, 'Do NOT go back!' The American girls went to their embassy with hardly a word being exchanged. Mary later thought they were rather ungrateful but preferred to believe that this was due to the trauma of the whole experience.

20

T.O.M.A.S

GRACE COULD NOT WAIT TO SEEK OUT BROTHER NOEL AND more than once had waited in the village for an opportune moment to take him aside and inform him of her discovery. The fact that she had not told him anything about herself, Tom or Spain did not really matter. More than ever, she was confused as to where her emotions should lay, in the present or the past? Her knowledge of the current mistreatment of the boys made the thought of Tom's boyhood being spent in similar circumstances too painful to contemplate. That she once knew an 'inmate' was therefore sufficient warrant for her to use the Brother to gather more information about Tom's time in Letterfrack.

Rounding up his boys, Brother Noel stepped into the road and negotiated Grace's van which was poorly parked as usual. He recognised the vehicle and glanced into the driver's side window as he passed by. Grace nodded and opened her mouth and mimed, 'we must talk.' The Brother looked around, chose one of the older boys to take the gang to Geoghan's and instructed that they wait for him there. They looked happy enough to do so; no doubt as it meant they gained a few minutes of freedom from authority. Noel went back to the van and Grace wound down her window. He looked around anxiously. 'I don't think this is a good idea Miss Deben.'

'Grace please. Call me Grace.'

'If you wish.'

'I need you to do something for me, urgently,' she whispered.

'But I'm already doing what you asked, what we agreed.'

'This is something else. Something personal.'

'And what might that be?' he was now intrigued and leaned further into the van window.

'I want you to see if there are any records of a boy who was at the School in or around 1924.'

'1924!'

She was not put off by his tone of incredulity.

'It could be a year or so either way. The boy's name was Tomas Lees. That's T.O.M.A.S and Lees is L.E.E.S. He would have been about 12 years of age.'

'That's an awful long time ago. I don't know if there be anything I could get my hands on. Even if I could, why would you be wanting it? It's such a long time ago. Surely it can't be part of what we're doing already?'

'No...it's not. I knew the boy some time back. He was a young man then... and I was responsible for him. Ten years ago in Spain, in the civil war. And I've only just discovered he went to the School here. I want to know more.'

'You were there, in Spain?'

'Yes, but not with him when he disappeared. It's a long story and I'll tell you another time, I promise. Will you look for me, please? Anything will do. I really need to know why he was sent here. Anything. It's Tom Lees,' Grace paused and waited for a response. None was forthcoming. 'Shouldn't you be catching up with those boys?'

'You're right, I've got to take them back to the School right now. I won't promise anything. I'll look but it won't be easy. I'm not given access to that sort of thing.' He went to leave and then turned back, 'If I get anything, how will I find you?'

'Come to the cottage.'

'No...I'd rather not. How about Clifden, Saturday? Outside Dillon's Tea-Rooms, about 3 o'clock?'

'I'll be there,' she smiled and added, 'Brother Noel, please be careful.'

'It's Noel. I will. Now, I really must be going.'

She watched him move up the road and before long the troop of boys was following him back in the direction of the School. Not wishing to use the local shops, Grace decided to drive on into Clifden.

———

WHEN THEY MET in Dillon's Noel was dressed in his civvies and he looked just like any other young man. They ordered tea and sat in the corner furthest away from the Saturday afternoon shoppers. He reached into his inside coat pocket and produced a small brown notebook. Grace could see that he was more anxious than she was.

'It's all here. As much as I could get,' he said, looking around to see if they were being watched. They were of course and he looked away from the spectators.

'Should I look now?' Grace asked.

'I don't see why not.'

Grace opened the notebook. It was all hand-written and she had to put on her reading glasses.

'There's so many.'

'Just the ones I knew about and even some from this week,' Noel replied.

'Brother Avannel? Isn't he the Superior's clerk?'

'Secretary. He is.'

'And this one, Brother Daniel?'

'And Brother Michael.'

'Are they all abusing the boys? Are they all perverts?' Grace raised her voice and immediately looked around to see if the onlookers had heard.

'No, some of us are not. Please keep it down,' Noel insisted.

'Sorry, I meant—'

'What will you do with all this?' he asked.

'I don't really know yet. I need to send it to someone who can do something.'

'Who might that be? The Guards?'

'No, they'll not do anything, that's for sure. I'll go to the newspapers.'

'I'll not be mentioned? Please God I don't want to be in the headlines!'

'Of course not. Journalists don't reveal their sources. Not to anyone. I need to read this first. And I need to make another copy for myself. Thank you. I think I know how much courage this took. You've done the right thing.' Grace closed the book. 'And Tom? Did you manage to find anything out about Tom...Tomas Lees?

'Believe it or not, and by some miracle, I did.'

'And?' Grace was impatient.

'There wasn't a lot. He *was* an orphan. I couldn't get down all the record but I made some notes.' Noel again reached into his raincoat pocket and produced a sheet of paper. He started to read, *Tomas Lees, 10 years of age.*

Tydavnet, County Monaghan. Both parents deceased. Arrived St Joseph's on June 2nd 1921.'

'1921? Monaghan? I thought he was local. He told me he came from Connemara.'

'No, he was from Monaghan. And yes, 1921. I thought I would start in 1920.'

'He was 10 in 1921? That makes him older than I thought. He was 26 when...I thought he was younger, a lot younger. Was there anything else?'

'Yes, there was a note by the County Inspector in Monaghan about his mother's death. I copied most of it.' Noel began to read his notes again.

'Kathleen Lees, shot dead April 21. A police informer. Sign found on body at scene: 'Spies and informers beware. Tried, convicted and executed by IRA.' She was a known and convicted poteen-maker. Informed on the others in the trade.'

'Informer and poteen-maker. Informed for her own benefit it looks like, to cut out the competition.' Noel added.

'Informer? Poteen? The IRA shot her for that? Executed,' Grace was disbelieving.

'That and the fact that she was a Protestant and a spy perhaps?' Noel added.

'A Protestant? Who was she spying on?'

'The IRA. Why else would they kill her?'

'And Tom's father? Did it say anything about him? Did he die?'

'Nothing. Just deceased. Didn't give any reason or date. There was nothing at all about him.'

'His name?'

'No. Nothing. That's all I could find. Oh—' Noel started reading his notes again.

'...Tom left the School on his 15th birthday. He was put into the

temporary custody of Brendan and Bridget Callan of Moycullen, County Galway.'

'That's all. It's everything I could get,' Noel folded the paper and handed it to Grace.

'Thank you,' Grace reached across and touched his hand. Noel was surprised by the gesture and recoiled as if embarrassed by the possibility that others had seen it.

They finished their tea and agreed that they should leave separately. Grace sat in awe of Noel's bravery and at the same time in shock at the discovery of Tom's history.

21

TITULCIA

THE IRISH BRIGADE WERE NOW MAROONED IN CIEMPOZUELOS. Apart from trying to make their quarters habitable and occasionally sniping at the still scavenging dogs on the lookout for corpse meat, the only meaningful action for the Bandera was avoiding the daily incoming Republican shells. Bombardments were now accepted in much the same way as the weather. As these became more sporadic, a bingo blasé attitude or 'God's Will' outlook was soon adopted amongst the ranks regarding their number being on the next shell. The fact that so many of the Republican shells were faulty and failed to explode on impact only added to their increasing fatalism. Whilst some of the Banderas had set about restoring the churches, no doubt to win the acclaim of their mothers, the majority increasingly made for the few bars that remained open. Boredom, disillusionment, sickness and the persistent rain had become the main enemies, just as they had been for many back home in Ireland.

For Tom and the other correspondents, the choice was one of either staying in the inert atmosphere of Ciempozuelos or heading back to Cáceres, if Aguilera would allow them. Led by Cardozo, who was by now a bag of nerves, most pined for the latter. Whereas before Cardozo simply repeated the last phrase of whoever it was he was talking to, he was now unwittingly repeating almost everything that was said to him, not once but sometimes twice. It was as though he had become an echo chamber. Likewise McIlroy, when he was not half-drunk, he appeared exhausted and missing a comfortable bed. His growing contempt for O'Duffy and all his senior coterie also knew no bounds. He constantly referred to them as a 'fecking shambles' and memorably exclaimed that they were 'unfit to fight their mothers, let alone the Communists.' Only 'the famous' Red Knickerbocker was semi-intent on staying on and this was largely due to his unwillingness to board another train. Tom was also torn. He wanted to return to see Mary and report back on all that had happened. Her goodbye kiss was also still on his mind. On the other hand, he had come to see for himself what the Irish volunteers were confronting. He felt that the real story was always just about to happen and, if possible, he wanted to be around when it did. Contrary to all expectations, Lieutenant Lambarri had not objected to him staying with the Brigade, as long as he did not leave Ciempozuelos, 'under any circumstances'. However, the poor man appeared to be hugely distracted by the older journalists when he made this concession. Tom had quipped something about, 'What happens if the Reds take the town? Should I stay?' Lambarri, quite po-faced said he should, '...it was probably safer!' Tom took this as nothing less than a guarded reference to the censor's bosses, Bolín and Aguilera.

Locating himself in a small taverna opposite the bell tower in the main square, Tom's daily routine consisted of visiting the Bandera HQ and talking to those with inside knowledge, the junior officers and NCOs. They had come to accept Tom and freely engaged with him as a confidant. He therefore committed himself to recording their observations in his diary, off-the-record but on the record for his diary and Mary. The main talking point always turned out to be General O'Duffy and his senior, entourage. O'Duffy's often fleeting appearances at the front and his home-spun homilies were subject to particular complaint and more often than not, ridicule. What was once just a rumour about his heavy drinking had already been transformed into a hard, undeniable truth. Everybody could now see for themselves that the man had a severe drink problem. It was also said that he had homosexual tendencies, although no-one was willing or able to evidence this. Dalton, O'Duffy's Officer in Command (OC), was also no less a target of the junior officers' vitriol. It was generally felt that the man was well past his best and his rapidly deteriorating physical appearance only served to confirm these assertions. To no-one's surprise, it was not long before he was stricken with a mystery illness and had to be replaced by Captain Diarmuid O'Sullivan as OC. Most of the junior officers had countenanced against O'Sullivan's promotion and Tom had been reliably informed that his instatement had been a matter for O'Duffy alone. Once again close personal proximity to the General appeared to be the main qualification for an officer's elevation. As with Bannon and Fr. Muldoon, and the scabrous nature of both men, few were left in doubt that O'Duffy's ability to judge character was now severely and perhaps terminally compromised. Thankfully for all concerned, both Bannon and Muldoon were as infrequent visitors to the front as O'Duffy himself.

Apart from the occasional foot patrol that had developed into the sport of dodging the enemy snipers at the far end of the town, Tom could see that the ranks were getting increasingly restless and their morale, like the rain, was dropping steadily as each and every uneventful day passed. He also felt much the same way; the war was becoming something of an uncomfortable bore. Rumour abounded and none less so than the fact that the Republican snipers were actually members of the Irish International Brigade led by the famous Frank Ryan, the ex-IRA colleague of some of the Bandera. Ryan was said to have hailed his compatriots across the lines to the effect that 'What are you *Republicans* doing fighting for the fecking Spanish *Monarchists*?' No-one could actually confirm any of this and Tom thought it wise to put it down to the febrile Irish imagination or, as in some cases, a ghost from the past that had yet to be laid to rest.

More immediate relief from the monotony of inaction was however available for many of the Banderistas in the shape of the local cognac and astringent wine that had begun to appear whenever and wherever even a small number of them gathered. This was despite the Pledge badges most had dutifully pinned on their uniform in Cáceres. At first, it was just a case of an off-duty diversion but it soon became a regular and increasingly troublesome occurrence across the town. Whole groups of the Brigade began to descend into the bars and tavernas with the inevitable and often riotous result of explosive insults and large brawls being ignited all over Ciempozuelos. These incidents became the norm over the ensuing days and weeks of inactivity. Often, the excuse for the bar-room fights were petty regional or county hostilities, some of which harked back to their own civil war but others, if not most, were to do with hurling, football or the attractiveness of their respective mothers, sisters and daughters. The reputation of the women of Tralee was a particularly sensitive detonator of these by now daily eruptions. It was difficult for Tom to come to terms with the spectacle of the hard-drinking Irish male stereotype becoming a reality. More sinister still were the reports coming from the officers regarding the physical threats some were receiving from the ranks, especially if they tried to restore a semblance of order and discipline by returning some of the worst offenders to the garrison in Cáceres. Overall, the Brigade was fractured and splintered at all levels of the command. The initial enthusiasm, commitment and even excitement had dissipated with the atrophy which now defined their existence in the ruins of Ciempozuelos.

Everything was to change quite suddenly when an order to mobilise for action finally came. It was as though a bolt of electricity had shot through what was the near-corpse of the Brigade. They received orders to advance on the township of Titulcia which lay five miles further north on the Jarama River. A new offensive had begun and they were to have a key role; at least that was what they were told. No-one knew for sure what their mission would entail, but all ranks were just thankful to be on the move again. For Tom, the order to advance obviously threw him into a very real and difficult quandary with regard to Lambarri's explicit instruction to stay in Ciempozuelos *under all circumstances*. Yet, on the morning of the mobilisation, his chaperone, the jittery press censor, had gone missing. Tom searched the Brigade HQ and made enquiries at the Nationalist control point in town. Lambarri, it transpired, had been recalled to Cáceres by Bolín to deal with an 'emergency situation'. With little or no time to consider the consequences, Tom gathered his haversack and joined the convoy heading for the front. He was the only journalist to do so. So concentrated on their escape from Ciempozuelos were the Irish officers, no-one sought to question his presence and he simply blended into the throng.

When they arrived at the flooded banks of the Jarama they could see their objective, Titulcia, an unremarkable hamlet atop a steep cliff on the opposite side of the river. The engorged river was not the only barrier to their target however. A canal also intervened and between these two waterways lay a stretch of flat, grassy plain. It looked an impossible objective, especially to the untrained eyes of a young journalist. Tom could also see that the professional soldiers were also more than a little concerned about the intended path of any frontal assault. O'Sullivan kept looking through his binoculars and consulting a map. The junior officers surrounded him and started pointing to various features across the uninterrupted vista. Within a few minutes, the rat-a-tat-tat of machine-gun fire was heard. Momentarily, the pinging and tapping of the incoming fire was just a sound and then almost as suddenly the ground all around the officers' feet began to erupt. Tom fell prostrate onto the wet grass, as did all the men in the vicinity. This was a very warm welcome to the Brigade from the defenders across the river who, from their perch in the cliff, had obviously spotted their arrival and were signalling their intent. This was also the first real head-to-head engagement with the enemy for the Irish Bandera. When they thought the firing had stopped, they hastily retreated back to the safety of the trees that lined the road leading down to the river. For the next few hours they unloaded their munitions and equipment in preparation for what looked like what was going to be either a vainglorious chapter or just a deadly sentence in the Brigade's short history.

At midday O'Duffy arrived and assumed his usual pose

at the rear. Immaculately dressed in his full Field Commander uniform, he ordered the first assault and then immediately retired to the safety of the trees. Through binoculars he watched as the men fanned out and attempted to negotiate the bog that lay between road and the river. Tom had taken up a position at the rear of the main column and was more intent than ever on keeping his head down and staying safe. He was even amused by the thought that the conditions were so reminiscent of his Irish childhood, which meant that these troops were thoroughly prepared for the 'bog-trotting' they were now having to practise. Choosing the right tuft to stand on and then jumping to the next was always one of the greatest challenges of his youth. Without fail he chose unwisely and ended up to his knees in soggy, black peat. He could never have imagined that the same game would be played out in a foreign land, only with real bullets flying overhead and all around. To make matters worse, incoming artillery shells were now beginning to compete with the rain in showering the advancing party. The softness of the waterlogged terrain was however something of a godsend, as most of the republican ordnance landed with an uncharacteristic 'plop' and only exploded with a delay. The ensuing shower of mud and grass was far less threatening than the usual convulsions of hard ground or whatever else the shells impacted upon. The only exception to this was the occasional rock that penetrated the grass and whose shards and shrapnel took very few prisoners. Shells that happened to find one of these outcrops were the only real harbingers of death and destruction. For this reason the choice was stark, one either took cover from the machine-gun fire by going behind the rocks or, in case of the enemy artillery getting lucky, avoiding cover altogether. Tom decided to take his chance behind the rocks.

Crossing the canal was achieved by way of a number of small bridges that had been allowed to stand. The fact that what lay ahead was the unprotected, open plain made it more of a turkey-shoot for the enemy and this may have accounted for the bridges being left intact by the defenders. The sheer effort involved in trudging through the mud and the soft ground in general was taking its toll on the Irish banderas, especially those whose recent exercise had mostly consisted of lifting their drinking arm or fending off that of another. They were simply unfit, and Tom soon counted himself amongst their number. Despite the fact that he had no equipment to carry and was well shod, he still found himself panting and unable to muster the strength to advance at any great pace. His energy was being sapped as much by the concentration needed to keep alive as by the terrain. Furthermore, he had to remind himself what his role was in all this. His journalistic brain was repeatedly being stalled by his instinct to survive and he kept forgetting that his main task was to record the scene rather than simply experience it.

As they reached the open ground, all hell was let loose and what before had been a shower of artillery turned into a cloud burst. The bombardment was brutal and accurate. Tom was transfixed and lay prone. His raincoat was completely covered in mud and was already saturated. There was no way forward and the incoming explosives raining down made retreat just as dangerous. It was now Tom's turn to feel his whole body go cold and he started to shake quite violently. The noise of the shells whistling overhead just beneath the grey clouds, was followed by their landing with a damp thud, and this was followed in turn by muted explosions that were all the time intensifying. Just for a second Tom thought he had been turned upside down. Shells were now also flying over from the direction of the Nationalist side and were heading in the direction of Titulcia. Most appeared to by-pass the town on the cliff top and continue their journey beyond to who knows where. A full exchange of artillery between both sides was underway and Tom and the Brigade lay under it, unable to move and feeling alienated by what was taking place above and all around. Rather than active participants, they were spectators caught in a cross-fire and there was nothing they could do but look to the skies and watch the projectiles pass over in a shouting-match of deadly salvos.

By late afternoon the cloud had had enough of being pierced and began to drop to the plain. This cover enabled O'Sullivan to instruct his men to retreat back across the canal. In fact they did so without any real need to be ordered. Carrying on the assault was already widely recognised as being suicidal. What remained of the daylight was quickly extinguished and the gloom soon provided all the necessary protection for the men to file back to the relatively safe, firm ground of the road. They were very orderly and extraordinarily quiet in everything they did. Remarkably, there were only two fatal casualties and these were laid under blankets next to an ambulance that had accompanied O'Duffy's convoy. A further clutch of wounded, some on stretchers and others being manhandled, soon arrived and were taken into a makeshift field hospital.

Tom resumed his journalistic role and asked who the dead were. He was told that it was Sergeant Pat Hogan and young Mike Duggan. Hogan, the Drumshambo bigamist, had been hit in the back by some indiscriminate shrapnel. Some wit remarked that he now had the unique sobriquet of having not just one but two widows! Duggan had had his leg severed below the knee by heavy machine-gun fire and they thought the boy from Cork had died from a heart attack as a result of the shock of seeing the extent of his injury. Given the scale and nature of the engagement, it was a minor miracle that so many others had somehow survived relatively unscathed. For Tom, the randomness of war, the lottery of life and death, was never more glaring than at that moment.

Little did those men who returned blooded and wet suspect that a greater struggle was about to be conducted. Their weariness and disappointment were to be rewarded with the order to resume the assault at first light in the morning. Tom was informed by his coterie of young officers that the order from the Nationalist High Command had been received by O'Duffy with dismay but that he had nevertheless indicated his willingness to comply. No-one knew whether he was drunk at the time. The junior officers, on the other hand, had questioned his judgement and were continuing to do so. From the day's events, they knew that to renew the attack on Titulcia in broad daylight would result in their decimation. In effect, they were in a state of open mutiny. The main protagonist appeared to be Lieutenant Dermot Cahill, the otherwise competent and likeable leader of Company A. He was the most animated of the group of dissenters and his objections could be heard by all, including Tom, when within earshot of the mess tent where the Brigade commanders were in communion. At the end of the meeting, the mutineers had won the argument and this was signalled by the nods and winks that they imparted as they passed. Tom was relieved that for once the Irish had decided not to fight the impossible fight. After finding a passably dry stretch of the road that was half-protected by an overhanging branch, he laid out his blanket and fell into an exhausted sleep.

The sound of more in-coming artillery was his alarm call. The shells were however less accurate and more infrequent; a breakfast salvo. Now that the assault had been called off, it was a lot easier to relax and concentrate on keeping dry. For most of the Brigade the whole day was spent on cleaning their weapons and wringing out their ex-German uniforms, which had effectively become filthy, heavyweight green sponges. Eating had also become a priority. O'Duffy's car had once more disappeared and the rumour was that he had been summoned to explain his refusal to follow the Spanish orders to advance. Further counter-salvos passed over from the Nationalist side during the day, nearly all drifting over the crest of the imposing cliff-face and disappearing into the mist that yo-yoed around the town atop. Tom found a nook behind a cluster of rocks and began to write his diary.

22

———

'A GHASTLY MISTAKE'

THEY CAME VERY EARLY. HE HAD HAD ONE OF HIS RESTLESS nights and sleep had only arrived as the morning sun, which often appeared and then just as quickly disappeared at this time of the year, began to break through the clouds. The knock on the door was innocuous enough; it was certainly not as dramatic as one would expect when one is about to be arrested. Lieutenant Ramires was almost apologetic and he could see that Tom was in no condition to resist. He even offered to wait until Tom had a glass of coffee in his hand before accompanying him to the car waiting outside the taverna.

'Lieutenant, can you tell me what this is about? Why am I being asked to go with you? Where are we going?' Tom asked.

'Cáceres,' the officer replied.

'But why? Have I done something?'

'Yes, you have. You are not here with permission.'

'Permission? Who from? I've been here weeks.'

'Captain Aguilera...and Captain Bolín. You have to be taken to Cáceres.That is the order.'

'But Lieutenant Lambarri said it was okay for me to stay.'

'Lambarri has gone.'

'Gone? Gone where?'

'Disappeared.Gone.'

'Deserted?'

'Disappeared,' the Lieutenant replied.

The journey to Cáceres was broken by a few stops along the way. Troops moving to the front were in evidence and the amount of Italian and German hardware became more and more noticeable as they headed back towards the garrison town. The Lieutenant refused to comment on the contribution of his erstwhile allies.

Tom had time to reflect on the situation and decided that his stay in Spain may be drawing to a close. Bolín would probably threaten him and Aguilera was no doubt rehearsing his speech about all journalists being spies and that they should be shot. He imagined he would then be unceremoniously thrown out of the country. For Tom, this was now a prospect that he did not entirely object to. The Irish Brigade appeared to be finished and the story, such that it was, was nearly written. There seemed little more for him to report back on and he had had enough in any case. The whole experience had been 'interesting' but not one he wished to prolong or repeat. Even going back to London and having no job seemed to be something he could actually look forward to.

As they pulled into the barracks in Cáceres, Ramires was transformed. Suddenly he became more officious and insisted that Tom empty his pockets and hand over all his belongings. At first Tom objected and tried to resist the little Lieutenant who had begun to wrestle the haversack from his shoulder. The immediate response of the guards was to step forward and point their rifles at the prisoner.

Tom then had second thoughts about resistance and reluctantly handed his belongings to the Spanish officer. He was then marched into the building and down some stairs to the detention cells. Inside what was a roughly hewn tunnel with cells either side, he was bundled into a single berth.

'My things? Can I have my sack?' Tom asked, not expecting any response and he didn't get one. Ramires never answered. In fact, after entering the building, he never said another word.

Across from Tom there was a much larger, communal cell which appeared to be full with detainees. The men, all Spanish by appearance, were very quiet and only a few took any time to stare in his direction. Most of them were tending a man who lay stricken on the cell floor. The semi-darkness made it very difficult to see what was happening just a few feet away, so Tom gave up trying and sat on the stone bench in what was now fast becoming a dungeon.

'Cigarillo? Cigarillo?' The request came from the main cell across the passage.

'No, sorry. No cigarillo,' Tom held out his hands and pulled on his pockets.

'¿estás inglés'

'No...Irish. Soy irlandés.'

This was met with a sort of huff and snort and the men in the main cell turned away and resumed their watch over the man who was still prone. Tom felt a little annoyed that his being Irish had not sparked some interest or at least common sympathy. He wondered what their response would have been had he said he was English?

Tom thought it would only be a matter of time before he would be summoned and released. Meanwhile, he reminded himself of Mary's advice to look out for the small things, the details, and told himself to use this unsought insight into detention as an opportunity.

Nothing much happened for what seemed like an age. That is, until the men in the large cell opposite all began to shout and bang on the bars of their cage in unison. The din was vastly amplified by the tunnel structure and this made it sound as if there were twice their number if not more. In no time at all two guards appeared and they ordered the prisoners to be quiet, at least that was all that Tom could understand. It then became apparent that the man who was still on the floor had in fact died. His face was covered by a jacket and all the other detainees stood back from the body. The guards looked anxious and Tom could see that they were discussing their next move and that they did not believe the men in the cell. The jacket covering the head of the deceased was removed not just once but twice, and the dead man's hands and then his head were also lifted to convince the gaolers that he was indeed dead. Finally, reassured, they went back along the passage. One of the prisoners looked at Tom and crossed his throat with his hand to indicate death. Tom didn't quite know how to respond and merely shrugged his shoulders and tilted his head. He thought it was probably pointless to say he was 'sorry', not that he could in Spanish.

It seemed an eternity before another troop of guards arrived with what Tom took to be a doctor of some sort. After lining all the men up with their faces to the walls, they entered the main cell and examined the body. Loading it on to a stretcher, they quickly removed the corpse and locked the cage. There was more collective shouting from the inmates that again Tom could not comprehend, save the exception of '*Viva Republica!*' which completed every harangue. This was followed by complete silence.

It was very difficult to keep a sense of time. Tom tried to lie on the stone bench and catch up with his lost sleep, however it was so uncomfortable that he very soon gave up on the idea. He tried the floor, but again the cold and damp made this unbearable. The novelty of the arrest and his assuredness about his imminent release began to slowly drain away. It was therefore a relief to be summoned to stand back against his wall by two guards who suddenly appeared at his cell door. They stood either side of him and a little shove indicated his order to proceed along the tunnel. Tom nodded to the men in the collective cell and felt sure that he would probably never see them again.

Bolín was standing peering out of the office window. With his shiny riding boots and crop in hand, it looked for all the world as if he had just come from a local gymkhana. He did not look at Tom as he was led into the room and remained at the window. Then he turned, 'Buenos días Mr Lees.'

'Captain.'

'Have we been treating you well?'

'Yes, as well as one might expect, under the circumstances.'

'And what are the circumstances, as you understand them? Please sit down.' His English was class-perfect.

Tom pulled up the small wooden chair that was facing Bolín's desk.

'I'm not sure exactly. I think I was told that I did not have permission to be with the Irish Brigade.'

'At the front...permission to be at the front. Who you were with is neither here or there.'

'At the front?'

'There were explicit instructions, from your first day here and on all the cards you carry. You were not to go without authority.' He moved to the desk and picked up a piece of paper, 'Let me read you this – which you have no doubt heard before. It is from the Generalissimo himself:

Except for Italian journalists with safe-conducts issued by headquarters, only German and Spanish journalists who, as well as said document, also carry a special authorisation to visit the sector under your command may do so.

That, Mr Lees, is my command. I shall continue.

Those of other nationalities,

Such as yourself,' he looked directly at Tom and then resumed reading.

'..*must be accompanied by a press officer with a safe-conduct as a credential as a well as the previously mentioned requisites. No journalist will be allowed to remain in the sector without these requisites. General Franco 26th February 1937.*

Do you recall that order Mr Lees?'

'No. I can't say I do. Not specifically.'

'Not specifically?'

'I remember something like it. Lambarri—'

'Lieutenant Lambarri? He's gone,' Bolín interjected.

'Lambarri gave me permission.'

'And you have that?' Bolín reached down behind the desk and held up Tom's bag. 'I could not find it in your belongings.' He then tipped the contents onto the floor. There was no doubt that he was enjoying himself.

'I must have mislaid it.' Tom replied quickly.

'Mislaid it? I think not. I don't believe you ever had permission Mr Lees. I think you are lying.'

'Why would I do that?'

'You're a journalist. At least, that what it says you are here,' he held up Tom's accreditation card.

'Lambarri—'

'Mr Lees, please. Lambarri is not here to support your

story. You have no evidence, no proof. As a journalist, as I was myself once, when you have nothing to support your claims it is worthless to continue to argue otherwise. Why don't you just admit that you didn't have permission?'

The unintended irony of Bolín's defence of the ethics of journalism was not lost on Tom. He was going to have to be careful not to incriminate himself and he thought of Mary and her advice to 'watch his back' with Bolín.

'What were you doing at the front?' Bolín changed both his tone and tack.

'Reporting.'

'Just reporting?'

'Yes, that's what I do.'

'Who for?'

'You know who for, The *Irish Press.* I'm a freelance.'

'Then where are your reports, your dispatches?'

'They've been sent.'

'But they never appear it seems?'

'What do you mean?'

'There have been no dispatches in the *Irish Press* against your name. I've checked with my colleagues in the Irish embassy.'

'They don't always give me a by-line.'

'Never it seems. That is rather unusual in my experience.'

'I don't know. I'm fairly new to all this. In any case, there have only been three or so stories.'

'Just three in all the time you have been here?' Bolin tried to sound incredulous.

'Yes. Just three. On our arrival in Ciempozuelos, the massacres and the assault on Titulcia.'

'You have hardly earned your money then?'

'I was following the Irish Brigade and I've done that,'

Tom kept his response simple and tried not to show his growing discomfort with this line of questioning.

'And how would you summarise the contribution of your Irish to our cause?'

'That's difficult to say. Patchy perhaps?'

'Patchy? That is not what you say in here,' Bolín reached across the desk and produced Tom's diary.

'That's my diary!' Tom was shaken by the sight of his diary in Bolín's hands. He went to get up and immediately realised it would do him no good. He sat back in the chair.

'It is...and very thoughtful of you to have been so diligent in keeping this record. I found it very interesting, very interesting indeed. You write very well.' Bolín produced a false smile and turned the pages of the diary.

'Those are my *private* thoughts. They were not meant for anyone else. They're my personal thoughts.'

'As I can see.' Bolín's face hardened as he perused the pages.

'You don't think much of your countrymen?'

'Only some of them.'

'Most, I would say.'

'Most in this crowd, perhaps.'

Bolín continued to turn the pages and then looked directly at Tom. Only after an inordinate pause did he resume.

'And us Spanish? You appear to feel much the same? You do not think much of us either?'

'Only some.'

'Myself for example?'

Tom now knew that he was in deeper trouble than he had thought and he had to be doubly careful about what he said, if anything.

'You don't appear to have a very high estimation of me

Mr Lees? Your caricature is far from flattering I would say? A 'clown' indeed. And a 'dangerous one?' Is that how I appear to you?'

'Impressions. Just early impressions.'

'Oh, I think not. I believe you really think this about me, about Captain Aguilera and the others. Are you a spy Mr Lees?'

'A spy! No...who ...who would I be a spy for? That's insane.'

'I don't really know. And that's what I wish to find out. You write well ...but like a Red I suggest.'

'A Red? That's nonsense. I'm not a Red. There is no way—'

'I said you write like one.'

'I'm not a Red.'

Bolín stood and lit a cigarillo,

'Then why do you write like one? There is nothing in this that is at all in favour of the cause, our cause, on the Nationalist side of things? You have nothing to say in our favour. I would go so far as to say you are against our cause.'

'Perhaps I don't support your cause. And in the same way I don't support the Red one?'

'You are also highly critical of us trying save our Fatherland.'

Tom paused to think how best to answer.

'That's my impression, my personal view. It is not what appears in my despatches. I try to report the facts, as I see them.'

'As you see them?'

'Yes, I can't do anything else. These are my eyes and I try to keep them open. That's what I try to do.'

'Am I a 'clown' Mr Lees, dangerous or otherwise? Do I look like a clown? Is that what you see, with your eyes?'

Tom thought it best not answer.

'And my colleague, Captain Aguilera, you call him a 'psychopath' and a 'monster'? Is that your opinion or a fact, as you see it?'

'As I said, those...those are my impressions. I might well be wrong.'

'You *could* be wrong?'

'I might be.'

Bolin circled Tom and then stood directly behind him. Tom tried not to turn and continued to look directly ahead. He knew now that he was in a very difficult position.

'Are you a spy Mr Lees?'

'No, I've told you. That is a mad accusation.'

'But you do spy', Bolín returned to his desk and picked up the diary.

'This is full of your spying on everyone it seems?'

'Observations. I'm a journalist. It's just my private journal.'

'Spying, Mr Lees, is a very serious matter, especially in this zone. I would not make light of it if I was you.'

'I'm sure it is. And I was not making light of anything. I'm not a spy. What kind of spy would write down everything in a diary? That would be what we call plain daft.'

'A very clever spy perhaps?'

'I can't see that myself. It wouldn't be clever to keep all your spying in a book. And then to carry it around.'

'Perhaps you don't?'

'What do you mean?'

'A clever spy might carry this around to throw us off the scent? There may be other information elsewhere. Another book perhaps?'

'Now that would be clever. But it's not true in my case. That's all I have. Those are all my secrets.'

'Secrets?'

'My thoughts'

'But you do have some real secrets here. Captain Bannon for example? You accuse him of being a thief?'

'Have you read it all?'

'I have.'

'Bannon *is* a thief.'

'So you say. But have you any proof?'

Tom refused to answer.

'He steals from his own men you say. He has a wife in Lisbon who he needs to keep in luxury. Have you any evidence for all these accusations?'

'It's what I heard.'

'Gossip?'

'Reliably informed, I'd say.'

'And your source?'

'As a journalist, you know I cannot tell you.'

'As a Spanish Foreign Legion officer Mr Lees; you have to tell me.'

'In that case, I forget.'

There was a pause and Bolín went to the window, where he stood looking out for a good few seconds before announcing, 'Indeed, Bannon has deserted.'

'Really? So I was right? Or at least, my source was.'

'Perhaps. He took all their money and passports. And he is now in Lisbon, I'm told. And the large priest, Father Muldoon? You appear to have certain views about this man. A perverse bully? '

'He's also not to be trusted.'

'As I can see. A 'nancy' as you would say in your country? That is a big problem for a priest.'

'I didn't say that. I don't know. But he does behave inappropriately with some of the men.'

'Your evidence?'

'Reliable sources.'

Again there was a pause and Bolín returned to his desk.

'Muldoon has also flown. He left Cáceres, in a hurry, last week. We think he too has gone to Lisbon.'

'But not with Bannon?'

'No. I also gathered from your diary that they were not entirely amicable, as you might say?'

'They hated each other.'

'And why was that?'

'They knew each other's secrets. They also fought over O'Duffy's ear.'

'Ah yes, the General! Another of your favourite targets. You have a very low opinion of the Irish leader?'

'Doesn't everyone?'

Bolín did not answer immediately. Instead he took off his Sam Browne belt and laid it on the desk. He then took his pistol from its holster and began to examine it closely. He eventually looked up and replied, 'Perhaps. But you say here that O'Duffy is a drunkard.'

'Everyone knows that. Surely you've noticed?'

'According to you Mr Lees, I'm a clown. How could I possibly be as insightful as yourself?' Bolín's pistol was now pointing directly at Tom.

'The Irish are going home. We have had enough of them ...and you.'

'When will they go?'

'As soon as we can get rid of them, and you, I hope. O'Duffy and his men will not be going back the heroes they might have hoped or expected to be. More like dogs with their tails between their legs. I like that saying very much. The whole thing has been a big mistake and one that has cost us all dearly. You'll be pleased to hear that the Generalissimo agrees with you, when you say in your diary that they are *'completely useless. A joke.'* And that it has been a *'fiasco'*, as you call it.'

'Did I say that? You seem to know my diary better than I do.'

'You did. And I agree with you. It is an honest and correct assessment of your countrymen's contribution.'

There was another pause and Bolín replaced his pistol, picked up the diary and started to silently read a page. Finding what he was looking for, he asked, 'Miss Porteus? She features a lot in your thoughts?'

'Mrs Porteus?'

'Yes, you appear to have a lot of time for her. She appears on nearly every page.'

'We're colleagues, friends even. I met her in London. We work together.'

'She's a lot older than you?'

'Not a lot older but yes, older and wiser she would say.'

'Do you work *with* her or *for* her?'

Tom was immediately panicked by the question. How much did Bolín know about Mary?

'With her,' Tom replied. 'We're colleagues.'

He sensed that Bolín did not believe him.

'Are you in a relationship with *Señora* Porteus?

This question released his tension. Bolín obviously wanted to pry into their relationship rather than Mary's true identity and he felt more at ease with this line of questioning.

'No. We're not in a *relationship*. She's not my sort.'

'Do you know where she is?' Bolín asked.

'What do you mean? How could I? I was at the front and I've been locked up in here. So how would I know?'

'I didn't mean just today. You see, she too, has also gone missing.'

'Missing?' Tom was alarmed once more.

'Your Mrs Porteus has disappeared. She's missing.'

'What do you mean, disappeared? She was here in Cáceres.'

'She's gone.'

'When?'

'A week or five days ...or so.'

'But where? Where is she?' Tom was almost pleading.

'That's what I am asking you Mr Lees. From your diary, I suggest you have a more intimate knowledge of Mrs Porteus than you are telling me?'

'We were close but not intimate. I have feelings for her, but I don't know where she is. How could I? You need to find her. Something might have happened to her?'

'You are her friend and want to be more than a good one it appears from this,' Bolín said as he held up the diary. 'And you are telling me you don't know where she is? Perhaps you also know what she is? And what she really does? She doesn't appear to be a journalist and why would the *Rangoon Times* be interested in our internal affairs?'

'She is a journalist and she does write for the *Rangoon Times.* And I didn't know she had gone and I don't know where she is. Please, you must find her.'

For some reason, the smirk on his face perhaps, Tom suddenly sensed that Bolín was playing with him. 'But you *do*? You *know* where she is.'

'Yes, of course. Lisbon, with the others.'

Tom, couldn't think why Mary might have left Spain in such a hurry,

'Is that true? Why? I really don't understand. Why would she leave?'

Bolín got up from his chair and circled Tom.

'She took the Americans with her. The young American women...and Lambarri.'

'Lambarri?'

'Yes, Lambarri...the Nancy boy. I'm sure he has Basque blood. Of course, he'll be shot for desertion if he tries to return. In his case, I would do it myself, with pleasure.'

'Do you know *why* they went? This is crazy—'

'Lambarri? One does not have to guess, we know why he ran. As for the Americans, we know they were spies. We caught one sending messages to the enemy'.

Tom assumed this was the courier that all the correspondents had used. She was not a spy.

'And, as for your Señora Porteus, we believe she worked for the British Secret Intelligence Service. Yes, she was also a spy. They were all working together. There is no other explanation. Which leaves us with you. They have left you here to face the music perhaps? You said you were very close to Mrs Porteus, so you must have known her secret?'

'No, that's not the case. She is not a spy. It's not true. In fact it's ridiculous.'

'Which part is not true?'

'All of it. It's just not true. I would have known if she was a spy. She was definitely not a spy. That much I know.'

'But you were very close? Your diary suggests this.'

'Yes—'

'The Americans were definitely spies and very clever ones it seems. Being so young and pretty, who would suspect them?'

'You did?'

'I trust none of you. All journalists are spies as far as I am concerned. I used to be one of your number, remember?'

'I'm Irish. I'd hardly be working for British Intelligence!'

'It is not unknown Mr Lees for some of your countrymen to work for the British. If you are not spying for them, then an Internationalist? A Communist perhaps? Do you know a Mr Arthur Koestler?'

'No, but I've heard his name mentioned recently. Is he something to do with you? '

'Yes, I have finally caught Koestler. He's a Red spy and I finally caught him myself. He is working for the Russians. I caught up with him in Malaga. A great prize.'

'Is he here? Is he alive?'

'He is, for now. Are you sure you don't know him?'

'Yes, I'm sure.' Tom was now feeling exhausted both from a lack of sleep and now his concern for Mary. He had had enough of this spy business, 'Are we done here? Can I go now? I'm sorry if I broke any rules.'

Bolín had other ideas and continued the questioning,

'The Porteus woman, was she working for the British S.I.S.?'

Tom's flippancy resurfaced. 'The *Rangoon Times*.'

'The *Rangoon Times*? How convenient. Her reports were also seldom seen. Did she write anything?'

'You made her stay here and there was little for her to write about.'

'We made her stay in Cáceres so she couldn't spy.'

'I thought it was because she's a woman? And Ethel Carney? Is she also a spy?'

'Probably, but I just don't like her. She's a lesbian, a Nancy girl, would you say?' Bolín smirked and waited for Tom to respond. He didn't. So Bolín continued,

'Señora Porteus stole Captain Aguilera's car.'

'Really, I didn't know she could drive?'

'Lambarri drove it.'

'So you *do* know where they are?'

'Yes. As I said, they went to Lisbon and are probably in Paris or London by now. Captain Aguilera's car was badly damaged.'

'That's a pity, it looked a very good car. Very distinct as well, you couldn't miss it. Now, can I go please? I've nothing else to tell you. I don't think I can be of any further help. You appear to know more than I do.'

'You underestimate yourself Mr Lees. Captain Aguilera is not happy and he wishes to ask you about a number of things. I'm afraid you will have to be our guest until he arrives. Tomorrow perhaps or maybe the day after. Who knows?'

'What can I tell him? I wasn't there! I didn't know they had gone and taken his car! How can I help?'

'You can tell him yourself.'

'And then? Will I be free to go?'

'We'll see. You have broken an order from the Generalissimo. You have said some things that perhaps should not have been said. You have insulted Officers in the Spanish Army, myself included. You have consorted with known spies. You have spied on your countrymen. And you write like a Red.'

'Which of those is a crime?'

'If I were in your position Mr Lees, I would be taking this more seriously.'

'I'm not a spy Captain, and you know it.'

'Captain Aguilera will decide what to do with you. He is most upset I warn you. It was very special. He loved that vehicle. His chariot has been destroyed. If he has his way, I'm sure you will be shot. Unless that is, you confess? Good afternoon Mr Lees.' Bolín called for the guards.

Tom's whole body reverberated on hearing Bolín's threat. In that moment he realised the full extent of the danger he was now in. Despite his protestations and the seemingly trivial nature of his misdemeanours, it was the psychopathic Aguilera he was going to have to face. The ridiculous focus on the car was perhaps the most disturbing aspect of it all, as it highlighted how warped and irrational these people were. It was the complete unpredictability and sadistic nature of these men that Tom feared the most and it was a terrifying to think that *anything* could happen.

He was then taken back his cell. The collective in the opposite cell were as surprised to see him as he was them. The guards gave him a metal cup of water and a wedge of yesterday's bread and the door was locked behind him.

Much later that night, he couldn't be sure it was night or the hour, a company of soldiers and militia entered the tunnel and stood outside the main cell. They began calling out names and checking lists. The men in the large cell did not answer and turned their backs on the inquisitors. After a while, the counting of the prisoners was repeated a number of times. Something was clearly amiss.

'Once' the officer with the list said aloud. 'Once.' Tom knew this to be eleven.

'Doce..?' his lieutenant responded. They conversed loudly in Spanish and Tom could not understand a word, save 'once' and 'doce' kept on being exchanged. The counting off of the list was repeated once again.

Then, quite shockingly, they turned to Tom's cell and looked at each other.

'Doce!' which Tom also understood as 'twelve'.

They walked over to his cell and asked him something in Spanish. He didn't understand anything they said.

'Soy irlandés' Tom replied. 'I'm Press.'

The Nationalist officers did not respond and instead

spoke only to each other. They obviously then agreed as to what should happen next.

'Irlandés,' Tom repeated only this time more desperately.

They undid his cell door and two of the militia entered with a rope tie, which they quickly placed around Tom's hands. They pulled him into the tunnel corridor.

'Soy Irlandés! Irlanda!' Tom shouted.

'Rojo!' the officer shouted back.

'No, no. Press...soy Prensa! Prensa!' Tom remembered.

The main door of the large cell was opened and Tom was thrown in. The men were then ordered to come out one at a time and had their hands bound as they did so. Tom was the last to be taken. They were then tied together on to a rope like a string of beads and marched along the tunnel. Tom tried once again to protest the mistake but was hit from behind by a rifle in the back. For just a moment the pain was extraordinary but his increasing panic quickly subdued any thought of complaint. They were taken out into the night. The sky was clear and the stars provided a spectacular garland of light until the headlights of an awaiting lorry were switched on across the parade ground. As they were marched to the rear tail gate of the 'meat lorry', Tom thought he would try once more, 'Soy Irlandés Prensa! I'm a journalist! I'm Irish. I'm not Spanish! I'm not a Red! No Rojo!'

This time the rifle butt came down just above his back-side. He struggled to stay on his feet as he was pulled by the others onto the lorry via the common rope. He lay for a moment on the floor and finally resigned himself to his fate. There was nothing he could do. He gradually got onto his haunches and found a space on the bench-seat alongside the others. He was one of the condemned. The journey lasted no more than ten minutes, although to Tom it seemed even less.

His mind was swirling in the unreality of the situation. Nightmares are made of less. He was going to die, of that he was now sure. What do you do in the circumstances? He had no time or inclination for prayer. He had no last wishes. He found he had nothing he wanted to say. And in any case who to? He thought of Mary. The kiss. He hated her and he thought he loved her. Then he blamed himself. He had made the choices. He had chosen to come to Spain with her. He had made the mistakes. He had been stupid. It was all his own fault. Then it was Mary's fault again. She had cajoled him. She had fooled him. She had entrapped him. He loved her and he hated her. He wanted to live. He wanted to see her again. And so this dialogue went on until the lorry suddenly came to a halt.

Another car lit the way and the cemetery wall was ablaze with its headlights. The men were dragged from the lorry and the long rope was untied. They stood guarding their eyes against the bright spotlights of the car. Without any ceremony, the guns opened up and they all fell to the ground. The officers removed any last traces of life with their pistols. Tom did not have to think any more. It had all been a ghastly mistake.

23

THE PAST

Grace's attempts to garner recognition of the School scandal had come to nought. The editors of the major national newspapers had gone into hiding, or denial, and she had received not a single response to her many articles and letters. She had also tried the English newspapers but they were, it appeared, equally keen to avoid the subject or upset the Irish government. The Father Flanagan controversy had also subsided and there appeared to be no momentum behind any inquiry into his allegations. Letters to the Taoiseach, De Valera, the Minister of Justice and the local TD had all gone unacknowledged. She had little doubt that there was a conspiracy of silence.

It therefore came as a 'Eureka moment' when she began to read, quite benignly, an article advocating a Probation Service approach to dealing with juvenile delinquency. It suddenly screamed at her: '*...in opposition to the use of institutions such as the Industrial Schools*'. The article concerned the views of a certain District Justice, Henry McCarthy, of the Dublin Metropolitan Children's Court. Grace was elated to find such an enlightened perspective still existed and, what was more, actually being published. She had to rise from the table and raise her fists in the air. The Justice, it appeared, was a man of principle and this was evident from a quote attributed to him:

'It is always with the greatest reluctance that I commit any child to an Institution, because...they cannot supply to a child the loss of its natural home...Day after day, Courts are obliged to remove children from their homes only because their parents, who idolise them, and who are entitled to joy and solace of their companionship, are unable, through no fault of their own, to keep them from destitution. Surely this should not be tolerated in a State which has enshrined so eloquently its Christian principles in its Constitution.'

Grace immediately decided that Henry McCarthy was someone who could carry the torch regarding the abuse at St Joseph's. She set to work making a complete copy of her dossier and drove to Galway to dispatch it to the Dublin judge. It might as well have gone to Australia. Again, nothing was to be heard for days and Eamon, the postman, was always apologetic and empty-handed. She tried telephoning the Judge's office from Clifden but was told that, 'Yes, he had received her file' but 'No, the Judge was *very* busy'. It was over three weeks before her efforts received what was to be the type of attention she could never have anticipated.

In the *Times* it was reported that Judge Henry McCarthy, in a speech he had given to a group of TDs, had invoked Grace's evidence of abuse in the Industrial School. It was on the occasion of his calling for a committee to examine the Probation Service. Whilst not naming Grace, he had said that the evidence of the scandal was entirely the product of an English author, a woman, living in the Letterfrack area. Arguing that it had taken a 'stranger' to look at the facts of the case, he went on to suggest that independent scrutiny of such institutions was long overdue. His speech was reported by the National press and, without citing the detail of any of the Letterfrack cases, they focussed on the virtues of the 'outsider' against 'natural Irish introspection'. Of course, it was not long before the race was on to identify the intriguing source who was living in the Letterfrack area.

It took Ethel Carney less than half-an-hour in McCready's Bar to ascertain the address of the English-woman author. She also gathered her name, M.G.M Deben, from the bar-Post Office. The name meant nothing to Carney and there was no way she could do any research out here in 'the Wilds'. She also needed just a minimal incentive to coerce a local man to drive her to her prey, or at least the furthest he was willing to go on the basis that she had presented loose change as her entire budget. She had lied of course.

She was dropped off with just the two boreen gates leading to Grace's cottage to negotiate. By the time she arrived at the cottage, her inappropriate town shoes were already showing signs of wear, even tear. She felt most uncomfortable being outside of her orbit. There was a small sign of life emanating from the cottage, a thin whisper of smoke and the smell of burning turf. Ethel Carney was cursing and soon regretting ever chasing this story. The only saving grace she could think of was that, mercifully, it had not yet rained.

Arriving at the cottage porch, she rapped the door and attempted to wipe her shoes and tidy her hair. She had no idea what to expect but was determined that, now she was in this God forsaken place, she would accomplish her mission. She rapped the door harder and then heard a voice coming from behind.

'I'm coming!' Grace was emerging from the outside toilet. 'Just a moment.'

As she looked up and as Carney turned and saw Grace, both women held their hands to their mouths and audibly gasped.

'My God! It's you! Well...fuck, fuck fuck!' Carney was shaking her head in complete wonderment and disbelief,

'It is...Ethel. Yes, it's me. And I believe they say feck in these parts.'

'Mary...Port...Porteus! I don't believe this. You're now Dee-ben?'

'I always was. Actually it's Deb-en,' Grace volunteered.

'My God...what are you doing here? What are you doing in this shit-hole wilderness of a place?' Carney was still in shock at her discovery.

'Writing of course.'

'But why here?'

'Come in...you'd better.' Grace opened the front door and Carney only just managed to lower her towering self through it without knocking her head.

'Oh my dear...how horribly quaint! How on earth—' Carney was lost for words when she scrutinised the dimensions of the cottage. 'It's a cell! How can you live, let alone write here?'

'Very easily in fact.'

'Mary Deb-en? I can't say I've read anything of yours... recently,' Carney was still looking around the room rather than at Grace.

'It's M.G.M. Deben. That's my pen name.' Grace replied.

'I still haven't read anything...at least, that I remember.'

'Tea?' Grace asked.

'I think something stronger is probably called for don't you? We must celebrate our reunion.'

'I've only Brandy I'm afraid.' Grace felt quite embarrassed about the poverty of her bar.

'Let me look at you my dear,' Carney came over and placed both her hands on Grace's shoulders and then slowly ran them down her arms to hold her hands. Grace's rough and calloused fingers were inspected with more than a little disdain. 'You've filled out a bit...but you look just the same. How have you managed to do that after all these years? Is there a picture of Dorian or Doreen Gray hereabouts?'

'Fresh air and no journalists mostly.' Grace smiled and released herself from Ethel's grasp. She found the Brandy and two glasses. 'Please, sit down. You've not told me why you are here. But I think I can guess.'

'I was in Galway ...for the Races of course my dear. There's no other reason to go there! And my editor, an idiot of a man of course, sent a telegram to my hotel. And he asks that I try to find this 'Englishwoman author in Letterfrack' who has been wickedly stirring up the Church here in Ireland by making all manner of accusations. To tell the truth, I had absolutely no idea what he was on about! Where in God's name is Letterfrack I thought! So I telephoned him and after he tried to explain it all, it seemed a little adventure ...and possibly a scoop. You know me...' Taking the glass she lifted it and proposed a toast, 'Slaincha! I suppose one should say that out here!'

Grace raised her glass, 'Slaincha! And now that you've found me?'

'You've got to tell me all about yourself and the dreadful things you say are going on in this awful place. I'll write it up and hopefully we'll both get the things we want from it. You know how it works my dear. Remember?'

'Then you've not read my dossier?'

'What dossier my dear?'

'Of course not. How could you?'

'Have you a dossier? That sounds very organised. Very much like you were back then, in Spain.'

'Yes...I have a dossier and the evidence. It's all corroborated by my source inside the School.'

'I really don't know much about what all this fuss is about my dear. Can we start at the beginning? Tell me, what happened to you? Why did you disappear? We all missed you terribly. I did.'

'But that was a long time ago. Spain was a different life. A different me. I'd rather we talk about now and the Industrial School here.'

'Yes my dear...but we need to catch up whilst we are at it. I'm absolutely in shock at finding you here, of all places. Everyone thought...' Carney stopped herself.

'What did they think?'

'Everyone thought you were a spy. And the two girls that went with you, the Americans. They too were spies. A coven of spies!'

'I was a spy! Who was I supposed to be spying for?'

'The British of course. Who else? And the Irish boy with you...one of Dev's. It was a great pity about him...and so sad. Did you hear what happened? Ghastly business,' Carney raised her glass and made a gesture, a salute, in remembrance.

'Tom?'

'Was that his name? Yes, of course. Tom, the young man...he was from these parts wasn't he?'

'Yes, I believe so. Do you know what actually happened?'

'All I know was that it was all a frightful mistake as it turned out. But he actually was a spy, so I suppose it was always likely to happen, in the circumstances. Pity though.'

'I knew he had died.' Grace turned away and her breast

was palpitating. 'But not why or how? No-one would say,' she turned back to Carney.

'How? Shot, I'm sure. Executed I heard...by mistake apparently.'

'Why? Why was he shot?'

'An accident... They said the whole thing was a ghastly mistake.'

Grace faltered and took a large swig of Brandy, 'I don't understand.'

'Did you not hear my dear? Did no-one tell you? After all this time? They were holding him as a spy, which of course he was, and they took him... Anyway, after they realised what had happened, it was a fearful mess and all we journalists suffered as a result. We all had to keep quiet about it or face the consequences. So we did. Do you remember Bolín? He was livid...although he might have had the boy shot deliberately if you ask me! Then there was that psychopath...Aguilera...he could have ordered it quite easily as well. O'Duffy didn't seem too perturbed either...God Bless His Soul. You know he's dead of course? Died a drunk. Oh...do you remember...that proper Fascist...Bannon and his wife in Lisbon? He went completely off the rails. He deserted ... They say he went to the Nazis in Germany and worked for them! He was an assistant to the Joyce fellow, you know, Lord Haw Haw. Did you hear him during the war? An Irish man, can you believe that? He never sounded Irish.' She paused to finish her drink.

'Personally, I'd blame the Chaplain, Muldoon, for the boy's death. Do you remember Friar Tuck? Pervert of course. Just like the one's here! Oh my God...they're everywhere nowadays it seems! To be honest, I don't really mind...as it keeps the men together and out of the way of us women! Do you remember Muldoon? Constantly had his hand on his

crotch or that of one the boys. He might have had it in for
your boy as well? It was all in a diary they discovered apparently. Well, Philby found it. How, I don't know. Do you
remember Philby, of The London *Times*? The dapper
looking man, always chain-smoking. Now he definitely was
a British spy. One of your lot? So it appears that they all had
it in for poor little Tom. I think they probably organised the
whole business between them! Are you alright my dear?'
Carney helped herself to another glass of the Brandy.

'What happened to the diary?'

'I've no idea. Perhaps Philby still has it?'

'Tell me exactly what happened to Tom.'

'I can only tell you what I heard my dear. It was such a
long time ago and I've not given it much thought since then.'

'Please, I'd like to know.'

'But what about your dossier my dear?'

'We can discuss that after.'

'And you...you must tell me about yourself. Where did
you get to? Why did you run off like that? Cardozo was absolutely blazing that his American girls went as well. He was
also a spy...one of Franco's own. Horrible man. I can't think
why those beautiful girls...the Americans...I could never
really fathom why they would ever work with him...unless
of course they were spying on him...and spying on us. My
goodness, everyone it seems was a spy in those days! And
you and the British Secret Service!'

'I was never working for them Ethel. I was...I wasn't a
spy as such.'

'Oh...how disappointing. It makes it so much more
thrilling if you were. What do you mean...*as such*? You
weren't a spy...*as such*?'

'It's another long story. Will you stay for tea?'

Grace unburdened herself over the next few hours.

Carney was in a state of double-shock at the revelations but cognisant all the while that an 'exclusive' was taking shape.

'You're a Communist then? You were, all the while?'

'No...I was a writer. Yes, I had progressive views. A Socialist of sorts.'

'Same difference I'd say.'

'You never were politically discerning Ethel.'

'A Red?'

'Yes, a Red.'

'That makes you a spy. You were on the Franco side of the fighting and you were spying on the Irish boys. If they had known, it would have been you *and* the boy who were for it!'

'Yes, we knew that.'

'But you ran away, leaving him there?'

'I had to go. I had to help those girls. There was nothing else I could do. They were in danger and Bolín or Aguilera would have hurt them...or worse. I had to get them out.'

'But... the boy...Tom...you left him.'

'I had no choice. I never thought that he would be any danger, at least, not in the way it turned out. How could I? I suppose I am responsible for what happened. I admit it. It was my fault. The whole thing was my idea.'

'And you now regret it?'

'Every day.'

'Is that why you are here?'

'Yes, partly.'

'And this School scandal business? Is that also part of it?'

'In some way, I suppose it might be.'

'Atonement?'

'Yes, maybe.'

Grace had no intention of asking her visitor to stay in the cottage that night. Carney, in any case, would have baulked at the very idea of sleeping in the 'hovel'. They drove to Clifden and she secured the by now tipsy journalist a room in Brown's Hotel. Carney made a false promise to 'be in touch' and Grace reciprocated.

The journey back to the cottage was full of unremitting grief and regret for things said and unsaid, deeds done and undone. Her only comfort was the full moon and a sky that resembled a kaleidoscope of magnificent colours. She had to stop the van at her favourite spot, a small shrine with a Celtic cross that was silhouetted against the water overlooking Ballinakill bay. If there was a better place for solace and contemplation, she thought she had yet to find it.

24

EXCLUSIVE

GRACE WAS IN CLIFDEN, WHICH SEEMED EVEN DREARIER THAN ever. 'Is this the wettest and greyest place in the whole of Ireland?' she thought. Taking her time before returning to the cottage, she had secured the latest newspapers to read in Dillons Tea Room's. Apart from the horribly misplaced apostrophe, she could never understand why 'Rooms' was plural, as there was but one large room? However, that room was big enough for her to find a quiet spot, away from the Saturday afternoon crowd braving the monotony of Clifden and rewarding themselves with tea cakes and scones. Their cosy conversations had steamed up the entire shop front and the condensation of their red-hot gossip was creating little rivulets down all the windows. The smokers were only adding to the already dense atmosphere inside the tearoom. Grace had to fend off inquirers after her spare chair, and as she did so the waitress gave her 'the eye'. She seemed intent on moving Grace on before she had even settled. Single women, especially those with national newspapers, were naturally suspect it seemed.

There was nothing about anything in particular that

took Grace's interest in either the *Irish Press* or the *Irish Times*. The *Irish Independent* was the only newspaper that she was really interested in and she had put it aside like a tea-cake to be savoured after bread and margarine. And there it was, '*AUTHOR EXPOSED...EXCLUSIVE...By our Special Correspondent ETHEL CARNEY*'

Grace knew immediately what the piece was about; herself. She looked around the tearoom and thought that everyone else had also discovered her identity at that very same moment. She imagined that they were all looking at her. She lowered her head, adjusted her glasses and began to read. What followed was both shocking and painful. How could anyone doubt the power of words?

Carney had exposed Grace as an 'English spy'. The whole story centred on the war in Spain and her part in bringing about Tom's death. She was named as '*the English Communist and woman author ...who spied on the Irish Brigade and ... now admits she caused the death of an innocent young Irish reporter.*' She could hardly believe her eyes. '*English Communist...?*' The '*woman author*' was perhaps the only accuracy in the entire article. It went on,

'*Now she accuses the Church...with her atheistic inclinations...Her record of duplicity and lying to authority... and now ..her unfounded accusations...Her intentions must be questioned...given her guilt about the death of the promising young, Connemara writer Thomas Lee. ...and she is now taking liberties with Irish hospitality...*'

Carney had lost none of the skills of distortion she had honed in Spain. She had even got Tom's name wrong! Grace sat near-paralysed by her emotions. Every muscle had stiffened and she was hardly able to breathe. This was her worst nightmare and physical pain rolled into one excruciating mental and bodily monster. She felt as if she had just died.

It was what she most wanted to do. Carney's cruelty knew no bounds it seemed.

Her despair was quickly replaced by anger at Carney's betrayal of trust. Grace knew that it was her own fault for considering, even for one second, that Carney had had her feelings or interests in mind. She had been unbelievably stupid in thinking that the monster had changed after all these years. Carney was, after all, a seasoned professional journalist who, since the first time they had met, always put her story and her career ahead of the truth. She had done her job in the only way she knew how. It was a very good story for her, an 'Exclusive', despite containing not one word of truth. With perfect hindsight, Grace now realised that this was always going to be the case. Yes, she had forgotten or neglected to remind herself about the mercenary qualities of most journalists. Spain had taught her to be on her guard, but she had forgotten that lesson and trusted Carney to tell the truth for once. It was as if the full horror of the Press Corps in Spain was being disinterred and Carney was the spectre chosen to come back and haunt her.

Looking around, the Tea Room now conjured up the memory of her first meeting with Tom, in the Lyon's Coffee House in the Strand, in London. Suddenly, it was too much to bear and she had to leave. She gathered her newspapers and quickly paid the bill. As she made for door the accusatory eyes of the 'Rooms' appeared to be following her every step. The waitress, in particular, seemed to congratulate herself on having identified Grace as a potential troublemaker.

Whilst she could still think, Grace collected all the provisions necessary for the week, thereby avoiding any immediate need to venture into Letterfrack. She needed to keep her distance from the village for the time being and think through her next move in the isolation of the cottage. She knew that the content of Carney's piece would only be read by a small number of the locals and that it would then, in Chinese whisper fashion, find its way out into the wider population. No doubt she would be a serial killer by the end of the month. She also decided not to contest Carney's version and let it all blow over, as it surely must.

Contrary to all expectations, over the course of the next few days she was as productive in her writing as at any time since her arrival. The weather was slowly changing for the better and her walks on the beach had once more become a pleasure; a small reward she gave herself on completion of a day's work. The fact that she could not continue the campaign against the School was the most difficult aspect of the whole situation and one which she had still to come to terms with. She felt the need to contact Noel somehow and let him know what had happened, but that would mean going into Letterfrack at some point. However, she managed to postpone this mission for over a week by eking out her larder.

Driving into the village proved to be every bit as difficult as she had imagined it would be. Although prepared for the dark looks and even the odd remark that might be directed towards her, Grace tried to rehearse her own defence. She would have no time to tell her side of the story; the context and background would always be missing and the real course of events would be impossible to recount in any brief encounter. What could she say, apart from the fact that 'one should not always believe what one reads in the newspapers'? The problem here was that most people would not have actually read the story but would have been told by someone and retold, suitably embellished, by others.

Furthermore, they tended to believe only people like themselves or the priest.

She sat and waited to catch sight of Noel and all the while felt that her conspicuous van was now a liability. Fortunately, the wait only produced the odd passer-by nodding in her direction and little else. She saw no-one she knew or knew her. A few boys from the School were in evidence and she thought she recognised the little ones from McCready's but they did not see her. Then, just as she was about to give up, around the corner came a whole troop of boys. They always looked happy to have completed their day's labour; the only time they looked like normal youngsters in fact. As they passed the van, Grace saw that it was a different Brother who was shepherding them. It definitely wasn't Noel. Her disappointment was palpable and, without even thinking, her reaction was to throw open the van door and chase after whoever it was.

'Brother Noel?' she said, as she managed to grab the new Brother's arm.

'Excuse me!' He was shocked by the assault of this unknown woman.

'Sorry...I'm sorry,' Grace apologised and wiped some imaginary dirt from his sleeve. 'I'm looking for Brother Noel. Where is he? I need to see him.'

The Brother, a very tall, thin man with bulging eyes, looked at Grace and then told the boys to continue up the road.

'Is it Brother Noel you're after? And who might be asking after him?'

'My name is Grace Deben. I've met Brother Noel and I wanted to...recommend a book to him,' Grace struggled with an excuse.

'Brother Noel is no longer with us at the School.' The Brother turned and began to walk away.

Grace caught up and grabbed his arm again. 'No longer with you? Where's he gone?' She undid her grip when he stared at her.

'That I can't say. The Superior may be able to assist you if it is necessary. Now, I have to attend to the boys.' Once more he attempted to walk away and Grace kept up with him as he tried to put on a pace.

'When...when did he go?'

'I can't rightly say. A week or so ago I believe. It was all of a sudden. If you give me the name of the book I'll try to get it passed on to him.'

'Do you know why? Was he sent away?'

'It's normal. Brothers come and go all the time. We have to go where we are needed and where the Good Lord's work needs to be done. Are you to give me the name of the book or not?' By now the Brother was almost running to escape this mad woman. Grace relented and watched him go.

'Animal Farm...it's by George Orwell. Thank you,' she shouted after him and turned and walked slowly back to her van. She felt she needed a drink and headed towards McCready's bar.

For once there was no-one in the bar. The tables were shining in the dust filled rays of the sun that had begun to cascade through the window. She sat at the bar and waited to be served. No-one came. After a while she got up and walked to the Post Office door and asked, 'Is there anyone there?' There was no response. She repeated a little louder, 'Hello, is there anyone in?'

Returning to her bar stool she looked into the large mirror behind the counter. It was not long before she began to think that she was not alone and was being watched. She thought she saw some movement in the reflection and looked around. There was no-one there and so she waited. She kept looking into the mirror in an attempt to catch a glimpse of her observer. Then she thought she heard something or someone in the Post Office and went to the door again.

'Is there anyone in?'

Again, no reply. She went into the Post Office, which was also deserted. Everything appeared as it should be, only there was no sign of life. Again, she felt that she was under scrutiny.

'Hello?' Grace shouted. No-one and nothing could be heard and she returned to the bar. She about to help herself to a drink but quickly thought better of it given the circumstances. Being accused of stealing would not be the best course of action at that moment. She went up to the large mirror, straightened her hair and, looking closely at her reflection, thought she could discern a shape, a body, behind the counter. By the time she turned around it had gone. This was a game she had no time for. There was no point waiting any longer, so she returned to her vehicle and the journey home. The streets were empty and not a sound could be heard from any of the shops. Letterfrack was now a ghost town.

It was not until she was half way back to the cottage that it occurred to Grace that her failure to get served might not have been entirely accidental. She quickly dismissed the idea as a product of some emerging paranoia. Similarly, the sudden 'disappearance' of Noel was rationalised as '...*just what happens. It's normal...*', rather than some sort of conspiracy. But, by the time she arrived at the second gate in the boreen, she was no longer so sure and her initial doubt had returned, only stronger. It now seemed all too coincidental.

Over the course of the next few days her paranoia seemed to grow in proportion to her isolation. Things around the cottage started to disappear, tools and even some potted plants went missing. The gates to the boreen were often to be found open, something almost unheard of in these parts; the locals closed gates as naturally as they breathed. A water pale that she had left by the wall leading to the spring was holed by what looked like a fork. If it were the Tinkers or Travellers they would have surely taken the bucket? There were also branches strewn across the lane at a time of the year when the wind and storms had hardly visited. A rotting sheep's carcass even appeared outside the turf shed. The animal had obviously been long dead before it had miraculously made its way to her door. She had also not seen Kitty at the well and in fact had not seen her neighbour for over a week now. John Fahey had not paid her a visit, whereas in the past he would drop by at least once a week using any pretext. Grace's isolation was becoming orchestrated and total.

And finally, one morning the ultimate disaster struck: her motor-van failed to start. She could not get to Clifden or anywhere else. She tried looking under the bonnet for any obvious sign of trouble. She might as well have been looking at the inside of an Atomic bomb; it was scary and made no sense to her whatsoever. She was afraid to tinker with anything in case she exacerbated the problem. She knew it had fuel. She knew it had oil and water. She just did not have any spark in the engine. Using the starter-handle, she tried to turn the engine over. Nothing. She was relieved to find that there were no obvious signs that the vehicle had been interfered with. The van, it appeared, had died in the night.

Solitude and isolation were no longer her friends. She

thought she might try to find Kitty, or go to John Fahey if she could hitch a lift. She needed, in any case, to get some more food and toilet paper. Perhaps she could catch the bus in Letterfrack? But would it stop for her?

Grace waited by her cottage and then wandered down to the spring. Kitty was nowhere to be seen. The farm was deserted and even the dogs were in hiding. There was nothing left for her to do, she had to walk to Letterfrack. Her decision was met by one of those showers of fine rain that sometimes feel as if they penetrate one's clothes far more effortlessly than the heavy sort. By the time she reached the end of the boreen, where it joined the main road to the village, she was already sodden.

As she walked down the road Grace heard an unusual sound coming up behind her, a far off but closing 'whooshing' noise. She turned and saw a boy on a very large bicycle speeding towards her. He didn't look at her as he passed but she knew, by the look of him, that he was certainly from the School. Her first thought was that he had stolen the bicycle and was running away. If so, she wanted to warn him that he was heading in the completely wrong direction. He carried on riding ahead of her for some distance and then appeared to suddenly stop and look around. Grace thought to look around at the same time and noticed that a second boy on a bicycle was following her. She was sandwiched between them. She continued walking and the boys remained some fifty feet to the front and rear. After a minute or so she shouted, 'Hey, what do you think you are you doing? What do you boys want?'

They either couldn't hear her or, more likely, they didn't want to. She walked on and they maintained their equidistance.

She shouted at them again, 'Boys, can I have a word, please? Speak to me, please?'

They kept to their patrol. It was no use Grace thought, they were obviously under sort of instructions or plan. She made up her mind not let them intimidate her.

Coming into Letterfrack, and about a mile from the village itself, the lead boy disappeared from view. The boy at the rear kept up the surveillance and diligently saved the interval between himself and his quarry. He too vanished by the time they reached the main Clifden road. When Grace arrived at the stores, none were open. There were no notices or explanations and their 'CLOSED' signs had simply been turned to face front. There was not a living soul to be seen. Grace began to feel threatened, even endangered. She thought about courage and, at that very moment, a vision of the women she had seen executed in Spain came into her mind. So many of these memories of Spain had surfaced in the last few days. 'This, by comparison, was nothing', she told herself. She was in no immediate danger and it was just 'sticks and stones'. She walked to the bus stop and waited.

It was not long before a van pulled up alongside the bus shelter. On its side read: '*D. Tooley Livery Merchant*', it was not a name that Grace was familiar with. Opening the passenger door and reaching across, the driver, a rather plump, wild-haired, middle-aged man, spoke. 'A lift is it?'

Grace was unsure how to respond and looked him straight in the face. 'Where you heading?'

'Clifden, where else? Get in now, before I leaves yer.'

She wanted to get out of Letterfrack as soon as possible and had little alternative but to take up the offer, 'Are you sure?' The question was almost rhetorical.

The van smelt heavily of new leather, brass polish, B.O. and stale cigarette smoke.

'Mr Tooley?'

'Denis Tooley. Best Livery merchant to these parts and the whole of Connemara, Galway and the Free State and all.' He whistled his delight at his acclaimed status.

'Thank you for the lift.'

'My pleasure entirely. It's good to have company. And you might be?'

'Grace. Grace Deben.'

'Pretty name that, Grace. You're English by the sound of it?'

'Half-Irish.'

'From these parts?'

'No, Clare.'

'Oh Pretty County Clare! I've left my heart there a few times.'

Not wishing to inquire any further about his Clare affairs, Grace spotted a leaflet on the dashboard and picked it up to read:

'*Orders Received in Tailoring, Bootmaking, Carpentry, Bakery, Cartmaking, Smithwork. Also Wire Mattress, Hosiery, Hearth Rugs, Motors Repaired, Petrol & Oils Supplied.*'

The heading was *St Joseph's Industrial School Letterfrack*.

'You know the School then?' she asked.

'I do. Indeed I do. Great business with them. Great business all round.'

Grace was perturbed by the response and knew that she had to proceed carefully.

'Great business?'

'Oh aye, great business! Doing very nicely with them I am. They make those saddles and boots. Good little workers. I go there once a month, today it is, to pick them up. That's where I've been now. And then I'm off to the fairs. All round the county and the country now that I have the van here. You can't just be doing Connemara or Galway itself. That's where I've been for the last few weeks, around the country and the fairs. Good business.' Again he whistled tunelessly his delight at his accomplishments.

It didn't take long for Grace to realise that that is why he had probably not heard of the English woman author story. He was entirely ignorant of the boycott and she could relax.

'You have to watch out for the Tinkers with a van like this. The Roma don't drive but he knows the parts that sell. He'll have them off you before you know it. You need someone to ride shotgun in some parts of the country. Bad it is. Very bad. Wexford now is the worst.'

There was a pause and he resumed his tuneless whistle. Then he struck up again.

'We should have got rid of 'em all, in the Emergency, we should. We could have sent them all packing, once and for all. And what happened? They all disappeared for a while. Now they're all back. More in fact. The country's swarming with them, especially around Wexford way. Hundreds and thousands I'd say. I had to sleep here in the van. Can you believe that now?'

Grace was getting annoyed with his comments, his racism, and the smell in the van, but felt it best not to engage with him. She knew he spoke for many around here and she tried to change the subject.

'Do you know Father Boyle?'

'Great man. Great, great man! I owe him everything. Have you met him yourself?'

'No, but I heard about him.'

'Great man. Business has been grand with him. Never better. That's how I got the motor. He helped me buy it. Do you know Fahey's garage in Clifden?'

'I do. I know John Fahey.'

'Well, the Father did the deal with your man Fahey there. Fahey sells me the motor, I have the van, and they get the School saddles sold. We're a team alright.'

'Do you know the Brothers?'

'A few of them. Nice crowd. Very committed. Very, very committed. Good souls.'

'And a Brother Noel? He's very young, a fresh-faced one.'

'Brother Noel? Can't say I do. They all look young to me!'

Grace dropped the subject so as not to alert him. His tuneless whistle was however immediately encored and she realised that conversation was the only effective antidote. After the weather had been exhausted, he unilaterally moved to another subject.

'I was in Leenane last night.'

'That's nice. I like Leenane. It's very pretty.'

'There's a German on the run they're saying. In Hamilton's Bar I was when I heard it.'

'In Leenane?'

'Yes, so they said. A strange fish. Some even say it's Hitler himself. He's taken a cottage up by the Little Killary Harbour and he doesn't eat any meat. Just tinned stuff they say. Some think he's mad. He must be, living up there I'd say and not eating meat! And he only talks to the birds! Why would anyone want to come and live hereabouts and like that? And not eating the meat!'

Grace gathered the impression that Tooley would have forgiven Hitler for the concentration camps, if only he had not been a vegetarian. She also considered a good number of reasons for educating Mr Denis Tooley as to why people would choose to live hereabouts, but she thought better of it. He need only look out of the window. The remainder of the journey was taken up with his inquiries about the many dangers and pitfalls of living in London; the crowds, the dirt and the pigeons, which were a real curse, he'd heard them say. He never thought to ask why Grace was living in Connemara, for which she was grateful. He took her all the way to Fahey's garage. Whilst the lift had been stressful, it had also been useful and she was more than relieved to see him on his way. She had no idea what the tune he had been whistling was supposed to be and she doubted whether he was any wiser.

John Fahey was not in when Grace arrived at his garage. Eoin, the young fitter, obviously not wanting to tell an untruth, said that he didn't know where his boss had gone. There was nothing she could do but wait, which she did. John eventually appeared at the entrance to the workshop and Grace followed him in from the pavement outside.

'John...John.'

'Miss Grace. I wasn't expecting to see you here. I didn't see the van,' he said attending to some tools lying on the bench.

'That's why I'm here.' Grace replied.' It's packed up. I can't get a spark. It won't turn over or anything.'

'Where is it? At the cottage?'

'Yes.'

'Ah, that's a pity. I can't help you I'm afraid. I'm up to my eyes at the minute. The Pony Show and all. I'll not be out for a few days, if then. I'm just too busy to be doing house calls,' he carried on sorting the tools and tidying the bench. Grace thought that this housekeeping was not entirely necessary, given that he was so busy.

'But you will come?'

'As I said, I'm fully booked for the next few days and so. The Show brings lots of work and I need to be in town.'

'And Eoin? Could you not send him out? I'm sure it's

nothing major or complicated. He should be able to manage it.'

'No, I need him here.'

'John you know how dependent I am on the van. I'd appreciate it, I really would, if you could—'

'I'm sorry but it's impossible Miss Grace. The work is already piling up and we need to be here. I'm sorry, but I'll get out just as soon as I can.'

She realised that John's reluctance to come to the cottage was not just because of the Pony Show. His whole manner was distant and quite unlike his usual self. This man would have gone out of his way to help her just weeks ago and he would not have let her down in this way. She sensed that something was terribly wrong. She felt like she had in Letterfrack earlier in the day.

'Have you heard something?' Grace asked.

'Heard something?'

'About me?' Grace looked him square in the face. He turned away.

'I really can't get out to you at the mo—'

'Have you heard something John?'

'I'm sorry. I'm up to my neck at the minute. I haven't time to stand and talk.' With that, he went to what passed as his office, a small cupboard at the end of the workshop. Grace followed him.

'John, what have you heard?'

'About you? Nothing, I've not heard a thing.'

She knew he was not telling the truth.

'It's not true John. I promise you. Whatever you have heard is not true. If it's the newspaper thing, that's a pack of lies. I knew the reporter from way back and she had it in for me.'

'It's not about that.'

'It's not?"

'No. Look Miss Grace, I think you should leave. For your own sake.'

'What's it about John? Why are you being like this? I thought we were friends? I thought you liked me?'

He paused and then looked into her eyes, 'You should leave. The School, we all need the School. I need the work. Everyone needs the work. You're messing it all up with your accusations and all. You're going to hurt a lot of people if you carry on with that business. You need to go. Let it be.'

'Let it be? John, those boys!'

'Leave 'em be. They'll survive. They have in the past. They'll grow out of it.'

'John, they're being abused!'

'That's discipline. They need some discipline. We had it ourselves when we were that age. It won't do them any harm. Not at all.'

'No harm? John, do you know what is happening to them up there?'

'I do.'

'And you say that'll do them no harm?'

'In the long run, it won't harm them.'

'Do you really believe that?'

'I do.'

'And the Brothers, the ones who hurt the boys and worse. You know it's not just beating don't you?'

'I do. I'd heard. But they'll get over that as well.'

'They're being sexually violated John. Young boys...the very young ones...by these men...these *Brothers*.'

'That's not our business. The Church will see into that. There's nothing we can do.'

'Your business John? That's what it is all about for you?'

'I have to make a living!' John raised his voice for the first time and immediately looked towards Eoin in the workshop to see if he was attending their discussion. He lowered his voice again.

'I have to make a living. You see that boy there? His whole family depends on me keeping him on. I need to work. He needs the work. Everyone needs the work around here. It's survival. Yes, it's business. I can't be looking after all the boys in the School as well.'

'Has anyone told you to treat me like this John?'

'Told me? Who would be telling me that now?'

'Father Boyle perhaps? The Superior?'

'You'd best be going.'

'It is. It's Father Boyle. He's in charge isn't he?'

'I don't know what you're talking about.'

'Do you work for him John? Father Boyle?'

'I do some odd bits here and there. I drive him sometimes.'

'You drive him. You're his chauffeur? That big car's his isn't it?'

'I'm not his chauffeur. I wouldn't call it that. I drive him sometimes and I get to look after his car. That's all.'

'And has he told you to steer clear of me?'

'You'd best be going. I'm awful stretched here and I need to get on.'

'He has. He's told you to boycott me, like the rest.'

'Like the rest?'

'The whole of Letterfrack. No-one's talking to me. No-one will serve me. The shops shut when I go to the village. I'm being followed everywhere by boys from the School. Things have gone missing from the cottage and it's getting worse. I thought my van had been tampered with. John, they're boycotting me.'

'No-one would do that. They'll not tamper with the van.'

'The other things?'

'I don't know anything about that. Perhaps you should leave?'

'Run away you mean? Go?'

'Yes, leave. Let us be.'

'So you can all carry on abusing the boys in the School?'

'I've not done that!' Once more he turned towards his young fitter to see whether he had heard.

'I didn't mean that John. Not you, of course not. But if you don't stop it, you're part of it.'

'I'm not. I've no say in it and I can't do anything. It's not my problem. I'm just trying to make a living. I'm doing the best I can. That's all.'

'You'll not help me then?'

'I can't Miss Grace. I can't.'

'If you did?'

'I can't. No-one can. You'd best leave altogether...for everyone's sake.'

'I'll not do that John. I'll not run away from what's happening. Those boys need our help and the Brothers need to be brought to book. They're evil and they should be punished, not the boys.'

'It'll not happen. It'll carry on. You'll be wasting your time. They're too powerful.'

'Boyle?'

'All of them. The whole crowd.'

'McCready...Geoghan?'

'All of them. There's too much at stake for them all.'

'And you John?'

'Oh aye, and me,' and looking around at Eoin, '...and him. I'll get out to you as soon as I can. It'll not be for a few days now.'

'John, you're a good man. I understand what you're

saying but I think you're wrong. Stopping what's happening to those boys should come before your business. That's the way I see it.'

'That's because you're not from around here. It's easy for you, being a stranger and all. We have to live here. We're not going anywhere. I'll be here tomorrow and the day after. I need to fit in. I can't be upsetting people.'

'As I said, I understand, but that doesn't make it right.'

'I never said it was right!'

'True, but knowing it's wrong should mean you do something about it?"

'We can't. There's too much to lose. Everyone would suffer if we did.'

'That may be a price worth paying?'

'No, not in these parts.'

Grace felt that the conversation had reached its natural conclusion. John was adamant and unlikely to change his mind. His position was assailable but she had no inclination to destroy the respect she had for him as a person.

'Perhaps I'll see you in a few days then?' Grace walked towards the workshop exit and back out onto the now ever wet streets of dismal Clifden.

25

———

BOYCOTT

It was Sunday morning and Grace awoke to a view across the bay from the cottage that was breathtakingly beautiful. She went to the window and stood drinking the best cup of tea of the day. The Twelve Pins were beckoning and the sun sprinkled the water with iridescent flakes of light. The colours were pure Connemara; the greens, browns, purples and greys, mingling and transforming with the light and shade. Whispers of clouds jigged around the peaks and the blueness of the sky radiated the whole scene. The air felt so clean one could have drank it. There are not many days or even hours like this and every minute needed to be savoured.

As she stood transfixed by the view, a cluster of dark objects began to appear out in the bay. Vaguely, as they came into view, she could see that it was a gathering of small boats headed by a larger curragh. She thought at first that they were taking advantage of the weather and preparing for a regatta. She would have very much have liked to have been out there herself. Then she noticed that they were heading towards the bay and the cottage. Taking her ancient binoculars, she could see the form of a priest standing on the bow of the curragh and that there were half-a-dozen oarsmen and even a few passengers in the main boat. The tide was still out and the nearest they could come without beaching was about fifty yards from the shoreline. The other four boats in the flotilla were rowing-boats with two oarsmen and one or two other passengers. Grace watched as they congregated directly in front of the cottage. And then she heard a muffled voice.

'The Lord is not slow in keeping his promise. Instead he is patient with you, not wanting anyone to perish, but everyone to come to repentance. Let the wicked forsake their ways and the unrighteous their thoughts. Let them turn to the Lord, and he will have mercy on them, and to our God, for he will freely pardon.'

Grace looked out again through her binoculars and could see the priest was holding a loudhailer.

'Seek the Lord while he may be found; call on him while he is near.'

She could hardly believe what was happening. This was an armada that had come to invade and there could be little doubt that she was the intended target.

'I will judge each of you according to your own ways, sayeth the Sovereign Lord. Repent! Turn away from all your offences; then sin will not be your downfall.'

Looking again at the priest she saw that he was quite short, grey-haired and rather podgy. Over his arm he carried an umbrella. At once, she knew this was Boyle.

'And Peter said, but let not one of you suffer as a murderer or a thief or an evil-doer, or as a spy upon other people's business.'

The 'service' went on for some fifteen minutes. Hymns were sung and the fusillade of epithets continued. Grace decided that she could listen no more and, gathering a bucket of turf from the lighted fire and some kindling by the hearth, she went to the beach. Using some seaweed, it did not take her long to create enough smoke to camouflage the cottage. There was one last bombardment.

'For in a short time the evil-doer will be gone: you will go searching for his place, and it will not be there.'

With that the boats drifted way. If they were to return the following Sunday or any Sunday thereafter, Grace vowed to be prepared and have the fire on the beach primed.

26

THE STRANGER

'Do words have a home?' Grace pondered. There was now little doubt that she was being 'boycotted' and the origins of that term were to be found not a few miles from where she was standing. Let loose on the world and employed as a tactic in many struggles, the idea that it would come to be applied to herself, in this of all places, had been as distant as the moon. Yet, considering its local parentage, boycott was no doubt in the folk memory and perhaps even in the blood of those who now visited it upon her.

In some respects the boycott and her physical isolation were proving to be something of a mixed blessing. Even when she was not being shunned, the state of the weather ('rain'), the cost of eggs ('*so expensive for what they are*'), the state of roads ('*deathly*') and 'the emigration' ('*worse than the Famine*') were subjects that lend themselves to a very limited dialogue with the locals. And Grace had recently all but exhausted her stock of responses. As a result, she had managed to write more of the novel over the course of the boycott than at any time since coming to Connemara.

However the price she was now paying for this enhanced productivity was increasing isolation, even loneliness. Never a gregarious person, she did nevertheless crave human company after what had now been nearly three weeks of solitude.

Sitting admiring the view from the kitchen window, for no good reason she suddenly remembered Tooley, the livery merchant and what he had said about the mysterious visitor to Leenane. Without really thinking it through, she resolved to see if she could find the stranger who was reputed to be even stranger than herself. It was in any case a 'fine' day, which in these parts was one where it didn't rain heavily all day, and a long walk to Killary harbour would do her good. More important, what she really yearned for above all else was a challenge. Life sometimes has a way of exceeding even our most fanciful expectations and the deliverance of this stranger to her doorstep was an opportunity that she was not about to readily pass up. She was both intrigued by the gossip and in need of a mission.

The 'Hun-on-the-run', 'the Gestapo fellow', even 'Hitler himself' was supposed to hiding up at Little Killary harbour and she was intent on finding him. From her now sole communicant, Eamon the postman, she sought to discover whether 'Talk of Leenane' was in fact any of these things. Eamon was legally obliged to deliver the post and if she didn't meet him, he left deliveries under a bucket. This morning Grace, to catch a word, laid in wait at the first gate to the boreen. It was not in Eamon's character to enforce the no-speaking rule of the boycott; it was impossible for him to send anyone to 'Coventry'. It was however entirely in his nature to pass the time of day with whoever he met on his round and he couldn't deny this instinct whenever he happened to meet Grace. Talk of the 'mad German' in the vicinity was, in any case, irrepressible.

'Has he got a name Eamon?'

'He has, but I can't say it.'

'You won't tell me?'

'No, I can't say it. Look for yourself,' he found a bundle of letters in his bag and lifted them out to show her.

In her current predicament just the name was enough for her to let out a half-swallowed yelp of delight, 'Oh my God!'

'Are you 'right there?' Eamon asked quite innocently. 'D'you know him?'

'Yes, yes…I'm fine. Thank you. This is astonishing. I can't believe it. I can't believe it's really *him*.'

'You do know him then?'

'No, no I've just heard of him. I read something, somewhere.'

'Is he famous then?' Eamon was by now completely confused and not a little exasperated by her reaction.

'Sort of. Yes, he's sort of famous, I suppose. He's a professor in England.'

'Is that it? A professor?' Eamon was singularly unimpressed by this denouement.

'Thank you Eamon. And not just for this. I do appreciate what you are doing. I hope all this nonsense comes to an end soon and we can get back to how things were.'

'So do I Miss Deben. So do I.'

With that, Eamon left Grace at the gate and she watched him slowly disappear around the corner of the boreen. On most days this was now the sum total of her interaction with others.

Grace wandered back very slowly to the cottage and kept repeating to herself the name that had now entered her diminishing universe, 'Professor Ludwig *Wittgenstein*'. As with a great number of people, she was aware of his renown but almost completely ignorant of his ideas. He had been the subject of one of her progressive London circles, but she had not really understood his philosophy and even less his importance. What really intrigued her now was that he had taken on the mantle of being 'the mad one' in this distant and largely deserted landscape. That, and the fact that what she longed for above all else was a conversation, especially with an outsider, was simply too inviting. However, Wittgenstein was obviously no ordinary outsider; by reputation he was an intellectual Mount Everest, yet he was here amongst the relatively diminutive Twelve Pins. Grace thought it was as bizarre as it was irresistible not to set herself the challenge of seeking him out. Little did she know the man, his manner, his state of mind and even less the nature of his philosophy. No matter, they were both here and this was perhaps her one and only chance to engage him. She told herself that it had to be more than serendipitous that their paths should cross in this place and under these circumstances.

After walking to the end of Loch Fee and on a small raised bank at the foot of *Binn Choona*, Grace surveyed the whole valley. Everything appeared magnificent, pure, unblemished, crisp and clear. The glassy, still blue water of the loch was stark and in contrast to the verdant mountains that were mirrored in pin-sharp focus on its surface. She threw a pebble and disturbed the stillness. Walking back along the road to the junction, she took the high road towards Little Killary harbour. This was also a pleasant walk, up until the point that she turned towards the sea and a very fine, incoming mist became more noticeable. Its small droplets amassed and had begun to penetrate her clothes by the time she had reached The Coach House at Salrock.

As she arrived at the small harbour and the cottage at Rosroe, Grace spotted a man in the backyard of the small dwelling. He was quite small, gaunt, dishevelled and Wellington-booted. In his hand was a bird. She stopped and feared to disturb him as he appeared to be dressing the poor creature's wing. His sensitivity was apparent and he muttered inaudibly to the bird as he tended it. For Grace, this vision of the 'madman' was entirely unexpected. Slowly, and as quietly as she could, she stepped up to the gate, yet Wittgenstein, for it was surely he, did not once acknowledge her presence. After a short while, he released the bird and it limped across the yard with its poor wing trussed. Taking up a walking stick, Wittgenstein gently poked his patient along. He carried on his ministrations; a modern day St Kevin, she thought. It was the same St Kevin who, allegedly, whipped a young woman with nettles as she undressed before him. Grace stood and thought for a moment before trying to get his attention and introducing herself.

'He'll not thank you for it'.

Wittgenstein turned suddenly and as if in a half-panic shouted, 'Who are *you*?' It was a semi-bark that sent the invalid bird scuttling and tumbling across the yard.

'Grace Deben'.

'Do you know *me*?' This reversal of common courtesy took her by surprise.

'Professor Wittgenstein, I presume?' she tried to lighten the situation using the apocryphal greeting.

'I'm busy. Can't you see I'm busy? What do you want?' he snapped and began to wave his stick.

'To get out of this rain? Some tea? And some conversation would also be welcome, if it's not too much bother that is?'

He didn't respond at first and made to follow the injured bird across the yard.

'Would one out of three suffice?'

She hadn't expected that answer and which one had he in mind? 'I'm used to the rain and I'm already wet through. So, yes, the tea will do nicely,' she smiled and was pleased with her quick-wittedness.

'If you have tea, I would presume you would already be out of the rain? And I don't do *conversation*, polite or otherwise,' he barked.

'Tea it is then' said Grace. This man had no time for pleasantries or small talk it seemed, even in his obvious isolation. She already knew that this would be more like an examination than a conversation.

'Put the kettle on then,' again this sounded as if it was an order rather than a request. 'I'll be in in a while.'

He turned and walked past her and out of the gate. He didn't just walk, he marched quite stiffly, military style and Grace was left standing, just watching him make his way up the path.

The cottage was typically small, dingy and smelled much like Keely's cottage had on her arrival. Despite being daylight outside, the kitchen-living room was very dark and she struggled to see where things were. A peat fire was dying in the grate and in an attempt to revive it she instinctively fed it a turf. She found the kettle already filled and placed it on the hotplate next to the fire. But she could only find one cup and a tea pot which looked as if it had been seriously under-employed in recent times. Tinned food of all varieties was arrayed along the remaining two shelves of the cupboard. She opened a small underlying cabinet in search of a tea caddy and found there was nothing but more tinned food, all regimentally aligned. There was also writing paper everywhere she looked. Notes and handwritten jottings, mostly in German with crossings-out a-plenty, lay amongst a scattering of books and journals. Being a writer, she knew not to disturb this universe of creative disorder. The whole place reeked of damp and very much of a man who was living alone.

The walking stick came through the door before he did and was tossed into the nearest corner. His most noticeable feature was his forehead. The great philosopher's cranial cupboard was disproportionate to the rest of his face and was topped with a bush of uncontrolled, corrugated and beginning-to-grey hair. It had obviously not seen a comb in an age, if at all. His face was incredibly lined and the eyes were piercing, much like Grace's own in fact, only as cobalt blue as the water in the loch had been that morning.

'Did you make tea? *Can* you make tea? Is it ready?' The mixture of denigration and impatience in his voice was not lost on Grace.

'Where is your tea? I couldn't find any,' she indicated by opening the cupboard doors.

He reached for a tin amongst the many. 'Here, where it always is.'

'And a cup? And do you have any milk?'

Wittgenstein merely pointed towards the sink in the corner where a milk bottle lay in a bowl of water alongside two or three well-soiled tea mugs, plates and various pieces of used cutlery. Grace carefully disentangled an unwashed cup, rinsed it and took the milk over to the fireplace. She returned for a teaspoon but could find no strainer. Wittgenstein, still in his wet tweed jacket and Wellington boots, sat by the fire in a small armchair. As he did so he took a piece of paper from the floor and inspected it closely. He then started a discussion with himself.

'Sugar?' Grace inquired.

'Sugar!' he snorted. 'This is Connemara! Whatever next? Cake? Cucumber?' She interpreted that as a definitive 'no'.

Whilst the tea brewed, Grace watched as his debate with the piece of paper was developing. She took over his cup of tea. There wasn't a second armchair so she moved one of the kitchen chairs nearer to the hearth and Wittgenstein appeared to be more than a little discomforted by her proximity. She, in turn, also felt quite uncomfortable now that she was at the feet of the Oracle - or ogre? He had a presence that made it difficult to feel anything other than uneasy and disconcerted, and that was just in anticipation of what he might say next. Yet, she was already being drawn to his strange aura. She could feel that something important was about to be said and that she must listen, regardless of what that might be. Inexplicably, she found herself attracted to him, as the mountaineer is to a dangerous mountain, with a mixture of awe and predictable pain, coupled with the promise of future reward for the effort. She had never felt like this about anyone before and tried to rationalise it as the consequence of her situation, the boycott, her loneliness and desperation to talk to someone, anyone.

'What do you want? Why are you *really* here? Can't you respect a man's privacy? I didn't ask for you to come. You arrive without any invitation. Who are you? What do you want with me?' There was no civility in his manner.

'I heard that you were here and I needed to talk. To have a conversation.'

'Con-ver-sation? Why? Why don't you just talk to your neighbours? The Irish always have plenty to say. I have nothing to say to you. I've no time for conversation. I'm very busy.'

'We all need to talk sometimes, especially when you live alone and especially out here. Solitude has its limits, even if one chooses it. I presume that is why you are here? For the solitude, to get away?'

'I'm here to think, not to converse,' he said as he poked the fire. 'Are you English? You sound very English. What are you doing here? Are you on holiday?'

'No, I'm a writer. I'm here to work. I'm trying to write. I thought we may have that much in common?'

Wittgenstein raised himself from the chair and stood with his back to Grace. The only sound was the spitting of the turf as it momentarily produced a tiny flame. He appeared to be transfixed by the fire and Grace thought for a moment that he had actually forgotten that she was in the room.

He suddenly turned. 'I'm *not* a writer! First, you have to have something to write *about*. That is my task: to discover what to write about. Writing is only the after-thought. It is secondary. What do you write in any case? What is it you're supposed to be writing?'

'A novel. I'm writing a novel.'

'Ah, fiction. So, what are your books, any books, apart from words?' Wittgenstein looked directly into her eyes. Grace thought she had never before experienced such a cold, violent stare. It penetrated her and she now knew she was in the presence of someone who was quite extraordinary. She had not imagined that anything like this could happen to her. She felt as though she was being slowly peeled and all the complexity, chaos and emotion of her life was in danger of being laid bare by the surgical precision of this examination. It was as though she was about to discover the meaning of her life, a prospect which was both extraordinary and immensely threatening at the same time.

Wittgenstein returned to his chair and started stirring the top of his tea with his finger. After what seemed like a long silence he eventually spoke.

'I've come here to wipe my pages clean, to start anew. To cleanse myself. I'm contaminated! I'm infected with other people's ideas! I need to cut them out, amputate them. But I need isolation and I need to think for myself.'

'To cleanse yourself?' Grace replied, knowing only too well what that meant. It was her sole purpose in writing her novel.

'Yes, that's why I'm here. I need the darkness of this place. There are no distractions in this dark pool and I work better in the dark. I have always worked best in such places. Here I can think, if I don't get any unnecessary distractions that is!' He said pointedly.

'Is that what I am, a distraction? There are always distractions. I've found that it's impossible to isolate yourself, even here. The world has a way of invading one's life, even if you try to hide from it.'

'We shall see,' he said and reproduced the frozen stare. Grace thought better of saying anything.

'Many people should stay silent and we, the whole world, would be all the better for it. I sometimes think that the world would be a better place if so many things had remained unsaid, if people had simply remained silent. Half of all books in existence should never have been written. And there are things that just cannot be written, no matter what words you have. Have *they*...have *you* considered that? There are things about which you can say absolutely nothing.'

Grace found herself gently nodding in agreement. Words had certainly failed to capture the grief and the guilt that had accompanied her coming to Connemara. She had been unable, even frightened, to express how she was responsible for what had happened to Tom.

Wittgenstein stood, as if on an imaginary podium, and continued to look directly at Grace as if waiting for a reaction.

'You must have found that, as a writer? There are things that escape words, not just yours but anyone's words. Things that just cannot be said and therefore cannot written.' Wittgenstein drank his tea and emptied some remaining dregs directly on to the cottage floor. Grace could not believe what he had just done and nodded her head in obvious disapproval.

There was another long pause and both stared at a tiny flame in the grate that had once more begun to flicker into life. Wittgenstein threw himself back into the chair.

'Do you think history repeats itself? Are we destined to commit the same errors over and over again?' Grace asked.

'Almost certainly, but not always exactly. History tries to plagiarise itself and it is always and everywhere usually a very poor form of plagiarism. Parts of it are missing or changed by default.'

'As tragedy and as farce, as Marx famously said?' Grace asked.

'As anything you care to make it. Farce and farce, tragedy and tragedy, what does it matter? It's just a story we invent, play and write - another form of words. Change the words and you can change history, as we all now know. Daresay you can change one of your stories by just adding or omitting a word or two? In some cases, even if it is historical, you can still change the ending!'

With that Wittgenstein stood up and collected his rain-coat and trilby hat from the hook on the door. Without another word he simply walked out leaving the front door open. More bemused than anything else at the way the discussion had ended, Grace quickly gathered her own coat and followed him.

She watched as he made his way, marching at pace down the yard towards the small jetty at the foot of the property. There she saw him board a small rowing boat that had been waiting. The boat was occupied and as soon as Wittgenstein had safely boarded it set off. The oarsman was facing Grace and the Philosopher had his back towards her. After a short while they were well clear of the shore and a shaft of light broke through the clouds. The light appeared as a spotlight searching the sea below. It never fully illuminated the great man and he was to remain always on the borders of the light and shade. Where he was heading she had no idea.

Making her way back to Leenane, Grace had plenty of time to ponder the things that she wished and should have said to Wittgenstein. The conversation in her head was quite unlike that which had actually taken place. Although she was far more coherent in her imaginary discussion, somehow his arguments became more and more convincing the further she walked. In particular it was the idea that history does indeed repeat itself and in her case as tragedy rather than farce. By the time Grace arrived at the second gate in the boreen, she knew how she could finish her Spanish novel. Somehow, Wittgenstein had woven his spell.

27

———

LEAVING

GRACE REALISED THERE WAS A DISTINCT POSSIBILITY THAT SHE could end up living a hermit-like existence, like that of Wittgenstein, if she stayed in Keely's cottage and the boycott continued. Whilst there were differences between his and her situation, there were nevertheless dangers of becoming as isolated and withdrawn from people as he seemed to be, albeit in his case out of choice. One result was that his cottage had become a chaotic, self-made hovel and he gave the impression of being devoid of any sense of inhabiting a world that existed outside of his head. The only control he seemed to have was over the orderly lines of tins in his cupboards. Similarly, Grace only had real control over her writing. She could, for instance, be evicted from Keely's cottage at any moment if the powers that be ordered John Fahey to do so. Therefore they differed only in that she had no wish be as detached from the world and its wrongs as Wittgenstein appeared to be. Grace even thought that while his caring for injured birds was admirable, ultimately it made little or no difference to the root cause of their suffer-ing, nature itself. Whereas there would always be causes and struggles that would find a way of inviting themselves into her life and that she could still contribute in some small way to changing the world. However, she also knew that if she stayed in her cottage, broken-winged boys from the School would continue to find their way to her door and there was little or nothing she could do to help them. She had tried her best but the forces of opposition had proven to be too powerful. Therefore she came to the conclusion that she had to finish her Spanish novel and leave Connemara as soon as possible.

As she reached the door of the cottage, Grace had already decided that her Tom character would not die in Spain. He was to disappear at the front and later mysteriously reappear in Cáceres. His time spent missing would become the subject of all manner of speculation amongst the foreign correspondents and especially Aguilera's office, where of course he would be suspected of being a spy. Where he went and what he did was unknown and this becomes the central question of the novel. The answer would slowly unfold in tandem with the account of the Irish Brigade's disastrous misadventures. The story was to end with Tom falling in love with one of the young American reporters and having to dramatically escape from the psychopathic clutches of Aguilera and Bolín with the help of Lambarri. It was now to be Tom's mentor, her Mary character, who was to get arrested, imprisoned for months and later deported after the war. There was to be no mention of unrequited love.

Based on some known facts and mostly on her imagination, Grace had also charted the destiny of her other main characters. Captain Thomas Bannon was to be exposed as a German spy by Ethel Carney. Moreover, it would be revealed that he had also been systematically robbing the

Irish Brigade in order to support a needy young mistress in Lisbon. Carney's vengeance was to be spawned as a result of her advances on Bannon's young mistress being rebuffed. Bannon would try to flee but would be caught by the Republicans just as he is about to cross the border into France. The driver he had hired was a 'Red' who would drive him to the doorstep of his captors. Later he is exchanged in Berlin for Frank Ryan, the Irish International Brigade leader. He then goes to work producing propaganda for the Nazis during the war and was to die in a British air-raid in 1943.

At the end of the Spanish civil war, the Brigade Chaplain, the gross Father Muldoon, was to join the Francoist regime in Madrid. He was to become the Head of an 'adoption' agency that stole Irish babies, those born to unwed girls in convents and Industrial Schools, and delivered them to fascist families in Spain. On returning to Ireland many years later, he would be arrested on charges of indecent assault on young boys in an Industrial School in Limerick. Having made a full confession, he was to die of heart failure before coming to trial. Finally, the good Lieutenant Lambarri was to go to Paris and start a hugely successful fashion magazine empire.

———

A WEEK AFTER MEETING WITTGENSTEIN, M.G.M. Deben had a complete draft of her Spanish novel. Despite being on the 'losing side' in both Spain and Connemara, she was leaving Ireland with a renewed sense of optimism and a confirmed belief that she was on the right side of history. That is, her own efforts, as insignificant as they might appear, will not have been in vain and perhaps one day will be seen as a contribution to making the world a better place. A sense of being at peace with the past had also descended upon her as a result of living amid the Twelve Pins.

Pat Duguid of Leenane Motors succeeded in resurrecting Grace's van and she was able to quite comfortably pack all her belongings into its capacious box. She left the key to Keely's cottage as she had found it, in the door. Closing the first gate to the boreen for the last time, she thought she spotted Kitty in the distance and for one moment she wanted to stop and say her farewells. The figure stood motionless and watched from afar. Grace took this as a sign that some things are indeed best left unsaid.

Just as she met the main Clifden road the rain began to fall heavily. The Twelve Pins were hiding behind the low, dark clouds which seemed intent on denying her one last glimpse of their splendour. A curtain of mist and rain fell on the landscape and nothing of the colour and texture of her beloved Connemara could be seen. The landscape reverted to a bleak and foreboding surface, one which belied the beauty that she knew lay below. Tears welled and a deep sense of loss came over her. This was not the ending she had either imagined or wished for and it was, perhaps, to be the last time she would come to Connemara.

The remainder of her journey to Galway was entirely uneventful; even the overtaking of Titan just outside of Oughterard passed off without incident. As Grace left Connemara she thought about the legend of Lemnaheltia, the leap of the doe and Sceolán. All the while, what she longed for above all else was a last sighting of Noel, who had now taken Tom's place in her heart and conscience.

After Mary and Grace, perhaps it was time for M.G.M Deben to become Maude?

POSTSCRIPT

• Captain Luis Bolín was to become the first Head of the Spanish Tourist Authority under Franco and conducted guided tours of the civil war battlefields in a yellow Mercedes. He went on to write books on Eugenics and left Spain to live in Chile.

• On 26 August 1964 Captain Gonzalo Aguilera shot both his sons and wounded his daughter-in-law with a high-powered hunting rifle in the family mansion near Salamanca. He was committed to a mental asylum and died one year later incarcerated amongst what he had once called the 'atavists'.

• In 2009 the Commission on Child Abuse in Ireland, the Ryan Report, was published and the extent of the abuse in the Letterfrack Industrial School was documented in detail. It found evidence of the widespread abuse that had taken place over decades by the Christian Brothers Congregation, much of which had been covered up.

'The School was run on the harshest of lines because it was

deemed appropriate for the kind of children sent there, yet the Congregation concede that Letterfrack was particularly harsh in the 1940s when the children were mostly orphans, abandoned or neglected.'

The Industrial School at Letterfrack was closed on 30th June 1974.

ABOUT THE AUTHOR

Peter Hodgkinson lives in Norfolk in the UK.
You can contact him here:

peancobooks@gmail.com
facebook.com search **PeancoBooks Peter**
twitter.com **@peancobooks**

Also by Peter Hodgkinson:
Orwell Calling